JAMES TWINING
THE BLACK SUN

"There's something for thriller fans of all types in
The Black Sun . . . Twining weaves history, legend and lore
with his keen imagination to tell his story . . . A thrill-
a-page story . . . From London to St. Petersburg and on to
Munich, Zurich and Westphalia in Germany, *The Black Sun*
never loses speed—all the way to the story's culmination."
USA Today

"Gripping and suspenseful . . . This is a can't-
put-down thriller."
Seattle Post-Intelligencer

"Tom Kirk . . . [is] heir to the throne of the twisty
international thriller, a seat that has belonged to
Tom Clancy's Jack Ryan for more than two decades."
Cleveland Plain Dealer

"Twining plunges into the story on page one and rarely
slows down until the finale. Fast-paced and exciting, with
a bigger-than-life villain, a conflicted hero, and a solid
payoff. What more does a thriller need?"
Booklist

"The perfect read for anyone . . . who mourns the passing
of Robert Ludlum. A whirlwind plot . . . The sheer breathless pace of the thing will carry you along to the end."
Birmingham Post (UK)

"If you enjoyed James Twining's action-packed art-theft
thriller *The Double Eagle* you're sure to get a similar
charge from its sequel, *The Black Sun*."
Chicago Tribune

By James Twining

THE BLACK SUN
THE DOUBLE EAGLE

THE
BLACK
SUN

James Twining

HARPER

An Imprint of HarperCollins*Publishers*

This is a work of fiction. The characters, incidents, and dialogue are drawn from the author's imagination and are not to be construed as real. Any resemblance to actual events or persons, living or dead, is entirely coincidental.

HARPER

An Imprint of HarperCollins*Publishers*
10 East 53rd Street
New York, New York 10022-5299

First Harper paperback printing: December 2007
First HarperCollins special printing: December 2006
First HarperCollins hardcover printing: December 2006

If I have seen further,
it is by standing on the shoulders of giants.
—SIR ISAAC NEWTON, LETTER TO HOOKE, 1675

ACKNOWLEDGMENTS

As ever my thanks to my agents, Jonathan Lloyd and Euan Thorneycroft at Curtis Brown in London, and George Lucas at Inkwell Management in New York, for their hard work and insight.

Thank you also to my editors, Wayne Brookes and Alison Callahan, who, along with the whole sales, editorial, marketing, and creative team at HarperCollins in both the UK and the US, have continued to work wonders for me. This novel is a real testament to your combined skill and enthusiasm, and I feel incredibly privileged and fortunate to work with you all.

In researching this novel I owe a huge debt of gratitude to three excellent books: *The Spoils of World War II*, by Kenneth D. Alford; *The Order of the Death's Head*, by Heinz Höhne; and *Berlin: The Downfall, 1945*, by Antony Beevor. I would also like to acknowledge the Hermitage Museum, St. Petersburg; the Kreismuseum Wewelsburg, Germany; the National Cryptologic Museum, Fort Meade, Maryland; and the Pinkas Synagogue in Prague.

Many people helped in the editing of this novel and in supporting me through the lonely months it took to write it, but special thanks go to Ann, Bob, and Joanna Twining; Roy, Claire, and Sarah Toft; Kate Gilmore; Jeremy Green; Anne O'Brien; Florian Reinaud; Nico Schwartz; Jeremy

Walton; Tom Weston; and, as ever, Rod Gillett. I am also indebted to the suggestions made by Adrian Loudermilk only a few days before he was tragically killed.

Victoria and Amelia, thank you for putting up with me. I love you. You make it all worthwhile.

LONDON, OCTOBER 2005

Historical Background

This novel is inspired by the incredible true story of the Hungarian Gold Train and its desperate journey across a ravaged continent in the dying days of the Second World War. When it was eventually discovered by U.S. troops in a remote Austrian tunnel, it was found to contain several billion dollars' worth of stolen gold, art, and other treasures.

All descriptions and background information provided on works of art, artists, thefts, architecture, and Nazi uniforms and rituals are similarly accurate. Descriptions of the workings of the Enigma machine have been simplified.

THE
BLACK
SUN

**EXTRACT FROM
THE *VÖLKISCHER BEOBACHTER*,
OFFICIAL JOURNAL OF THE NAZI PARTY
(EDITION A, NO. 270, SEPTEMBER 27,
1934), FROM *WEWELSBURG 1933–1945:
A CULT AND TERROR CENTRE OF THE SS*,
BY KARL HÜSER;
TRANSLATED BY ROBIN BENSON**

Today the old defiant Wewelsburg Castle, situated in a historical location in the old land of the Saxons, has passed into the care of the SS of the NSDAP and is to serve, in future, as the Reich Leaders' School of the SS.

As a result, Wewelsburg Castle, which can look back on a long and glorious role in German history, has also been assigned a place of historical importance in the Third Reich.

For it is here that the men are to be instructed in a worldview and beliefs as well as to receive physical instruction, whose calling it is to assume the office of leaders in the SS, and who are to march forward as examples and leaders before the nucleus of our healthy German youth.

**EXTRACT FROM *THE SPOILS OF WORLD WAR II*,
BY KENNETH D. ALFORD**

On May 16, 1945, the 3rd Infantry Division, 15th Regiment, A Company, commanded by Lieutenant Joseph A. Mercer, entered the Tauern Tunnel 60 miles south of Salzburg. To their astonishment, they discovered a partially concealed train crammed with gold and other valuables . . . . The 1945 estimated value of the contents of the train was $206 million—which would translate into several billion dollars today.

PROLOGUE

*The broad mass of a nation . . .
will more easily fall victim to a big lie
than to a small one.*

ADOLF HITLER
Mein Kampf

CHAPTER ONE

ST. THOMAS' HOSPITAL, LONDON

December 27—2:59 A.M.

A sh cash.

That's what medical students call it. Every crema-
tion or burial release form requires a doctor's signature, and
every signature earns its donor a small fee. Death could be
good business for a doctor who happened to be in the right
place at the wrong time.

To Dr. John Bennett, however, shouldering the icy rain as
he walked briskly over to the main hospital building from
the ugly hulk of the accommodation block, the prospect of
a few extra quid was small compensation for being paged at
three A.M. Very small. As if to emphasize the hour, Big Ben,
its face suspended in the air like a small moon on the other
side of the river, chose that moment to chime, each heavy,
deadened strike shaking Bennett a little further awake.

He stepped out of the cold into the warm blast of the heat-
ers positioned in the entrance vestibule, the sudden change
in temperature making his glasses fog. He took them off and
wiped them clean on his shirt, the moisture streaking across
the lens.

A red LED display glowed into life overhead as the elevator
made its way down to him, the declining numbers scrolling

rhythmically across the panel. Eventually, there was a muffled sound of machinery as it slowed and the door opened. He stepped inside, noting as the elevator lurched upward that the bronzed mirrors made him look healthier than he felt.

A few moments later, he walked out onto the ward, the wet soles of his shoes faintly marking the scarlet linoleum. The corridor ahead of him was dark, the lights dimmed apart from the emergency exit signs that glared green above the doors at either end.

"Doctor?" A woman's voice rang out through the gloom. He slipped his glasses back on to identify the approaching figure.

"Morning, Laura," Bennett greeted her with a warm smile. "Don't tell me you've killed another one of my patients?"

She shrugged helplessly. "I've had a bad week."

"Who was it this time?"

"Mr. Hammon."

"Hammon? Well, I can't say I'm surprised. He was in a pretty bad way."

"He was fine when I came on duty. But when I looked in . . ."

"People get old," Bennett said gently, sensing she was upset. "There's nothing you could have done." She smiled at him gratefully. "Anyway, I'd better take a look. Have you got the paperwork ready?"

"It's in the office."

The windowless room was positioned about halfway down the ward, the only light coming from the glow of two surveillance monitors and the LED display of the video recorder beneath them. One monitor showed the corridor where they had just been standing; the other flicked between the patients' rooms, pausing a few seconds in each. The rooms were identical, a single narrow bed dominating the space with a few chairs drawn up under the window and a TV set fixed high up on the facing wall. The only variation was in the quantity of flowers and get-well cards on one side of the bed and monitoring and resuscitation equipment on the other. Unsurprisingly, there seemed to be a direct correlation between the two.

Laura rummaged around on the desk for the file, the blue glow from the monitors staining her red nails purple.

"Do you want the light on?"

"Please," she replied, without looking up.

Bennett reached for the switch, when suddenly something caught his eye. The roving camera had settled momentarily in one of the patients' rooms. Two dark figures were silhouetted against the open doorway, one slight, the other improbably tall.

"Who's that?" Bennett said with a frown. The picture jumped to the next room. "Quick, get it back."

Laura switched the system to manual and scanned the rooms one by one until she found the men.

"It's Mr. Weissman's room," she said in a low, uncertain voice.

The two figures were now standing on either side of the bed looking down at the sleeping patient. Even on the monitor he looked thin and frail, his skin pinched, his cheeks hollowed by age. Various wires and tubes emerged from under the bedclothes and led to a heart-rate monitor and some sort of drip.

"What the hell are they playing at?" Bennett's surprise had given way to irritation. "You can't just come in here whenever you feel like it. What do people think we have visiting hours for? I'm calling security."

As Bennett reached for the phone, the tall man on the left snatched a pillow out from under the sleeping man's head. He awoke immediately, his eyes wide with surprise and then, as he blinked at the two men looming above him, fear. His mouth moved to speak, but whatever sound he might have been trying to make was smothered as the pillow was roughly pushed down onto his face. Helplessly, his arms and legs flapped, like a goldfish that had leapt out if its bowl.

"Jesus Christ!" Bennett gasped, his voice now a whisper. He jammed the phone to his ear, the white plastic slippery against his sweaty skin. Hearing nothing, he tapped the hook switch a few times before locking eyes with Laura. "It's dead."

On-screen, the tall man nodded to his companion, who lifted a black bag onto the bed and reached in. The teeth of

what Bennett instantly recognized as a surgical bone-saw
sparkled in the light. Deftly, the figure slid back the man's
left pajama sleeve and placed the blade on his arm, just below the elbow. The man jerked his arm but to no avail, what
little strength he had left clearly ebbing away in his attack-
er's strong grasp.

Bennett glanced at Laura. She was standing with her back
to the door, her hand over her mouth, her eyes glued to the
monitor.

"Don't make a sound." His voice was thin and choked.
"We'll be fine as long as they don't know we're here. Just
stay calm."

The saw sliced through the skin and muscle in a few easy
strokes before it struck bone, the main artery gushing darkly
as it was severed and the blood pressure released. In a few
minutes the arm had come free, the limb expertly amputated across the joint. The stump oozed blood. Abruptly, the
struggling stopped.

Working quickly, the figure wiped the saw on the bedclothes, then returned it to his bag. The arm, meticulously
wrapped in a towel snatched from the foot of the bed, soon
joined it. The victim's face was still masked by the pillow,
the bedclothes knotted around his legs like rope where he'd
kicked out and got himself tangled up. The heart-rate monitor showed only a flat line, an alarm sounding belatedly in
the empty nurse's station down the corridor.

The two men moved away from the bed, across the room,
careful not to touch anything. But as he was about to shut the
door, the tall man suddenly looked up into the far corner, into
the camera lens, straight into Bennett's eyes, and smiled.

"Oh my God," Bennett whispered in slow realization.
"They're coming for the tapes."

He jerked his head toward the other monitor. The thin
man was walking slowly up the corridor toward them, the
blade of the knife in his hand glinting like a scythe.

Laura began to scream, a low, desperate, strangled call
that grew louder and louder as the image on the screen drew
closer.

PART I

*All that is necessary for the triumph of evil
is that good men do nothing.*

EDMUND BURKE

CHAPTER TWO

PINKAS SYNAGOGUE, PRAGUE, CZECH REPUBLIC

January 2—10:04 A.M.

The shattered glass crunched under the leather soles of Tom Kirk's Lobb shoes like fresh snow. Instinctively, he glanced up to see where it had come from. High in the wall above him white sheeting had been taped across a window frame's jagged carcass, the plastic bulging every so often like a sail as it trapped the biting winter wind. He lowered his gaze to the man opposite him.

"Is that how they got in?"

"No."

Rabbi Spiegel shook his head, his side locks bumping against his cheeks. Although smartly dressed in a dark suit and white shirt, he was thin and frail, and the material seemed to hang off him like loose skin. A faded black silk yarmulke covered the top of his head, firmly clipped to a fierce growth of wiry gray hair. His face was hiding behind a wide spade of a beard, his watery eyes peering through small gold-framed glasses. Eyes that burned, Tom could see now, with anger.

"They came in through the back. Broke the lock. The window . . . that was just for fun."

Tom's face set into a grim frown. In his midthirties and

about six feet tall, he had the lithe, sinewy physique of a squash player or a cross-country runner—supple yet strong. He was clean shaven and wearing a dark blue cashmere overcoat with a black velvet collar over a single-breasted gray woolen Huntsman suit; his short, normally scruffy brown hair had been combed into place. His coral blue eyes were set into a handsome, angular face.

"And then they did this?" he asked, indicating the devastation around them. Rabbi Spiegel nodded and a single tear ran down his right cheek.

There were eighty thousand names in all—Holocaust victims from Bohemia and Moravia—each painstakingly painted on the synagogue's walls in the 1950s, with family names and capital letters picked out in blood red. It was a moving sight, an unrelenting tapestry of death recording the annihilation of a whole people.

The bright yellow graffiti that had been sprayed over the walls served only to deepen the unspoken weight of individual suffering that each name represented. On the left-hand wall, a large Star of David had been painted, obscuring the names underneath it. It was pierced by a crudely rendered dagger from which several large drops of yellow blood trickled toward the floor.

Tom walked toward it, his footsteps echoing in the synagogue's icy stillness. Up close he could see the ghostly imprint of the names that had been concealed under the paint, fighting to remain visible lest they be forgotten. He lifted a small digital camera to his face and took a picture, a loud electronic shutter-click echoing across the room's ashen stillness.

"They are evil, the people who did this. Evil." Rabbi Spiegel's voice came from over his left shoulder, and Tom turned to see him pointing at another piece of graffiti on the opposite wall. Tom recognized it as the deceivingly optimistic motto set above the gates of all Nazi concentration camps: *Arbeit macht frei*—work sets you free.

"Why have you asked me here, Rabbi?" Tom asked gently, not wanting to appear unfeeling but conscious that anything useful that the rabbi might have to tell him could soon be lost in the emotion of the moment.

"I understand that you recover stolen artifacts?"

"We try to help where we can, yes."

"Paintings?"

"Amongst other things."

Tom sensed that his voice still had an edge of uncertainty to it. Not enough for the rabbi to pick up on, perhaps, but there all the same. He wasn't surprised. It was only just over six months since he had gone into business with Archie Connolly. The idea was simple: they helped museums, collectors, governments even, recover stolen or lost art. What made their partnership unusual was that, after turning his back on the CIA, Tom had spent ten years as a high-end art thief—the best in the business, many said. Archie had been his long-term fence and front man, finding the buyers, identifying the targets, researching the security setup. For both of them, therefore, this new venture represented a fresh start on the right side of the law that they were still coming to terms with, Archie especially.

"Then come upstairs. Please." The rabbi pointed toward a narrow staircase in the far corner of the room. "I have something to show you."

The staircase emerged into a vaulted room, the pale morning light filtering in from windows set high in the white walls. Here there was no graffiti, just a series of shattered wooden display cases and a tiled floor strewn with drawings and watercolors, some torn into pieces, others screwed up into loose balls, still more covered in dirty black boot prints.

"This was a permanent exhibition of children's drawings from Terezin, a transit camp not far from here. Whole families were held there before being shipped east," the rabbi explained in a half whisper. "You see, there is a certain awful innocence about war when seen through the eyes of a child."

Tom shifted his weight onto his other foot but said nothing, knowing that anything he might mumble in response would be inadequate.

Rabbi Spiegel gave a sad smile. "Still, we will recover from this as we have recovered from much worse before. Come," he said, crossing to the far wall, "here's what I wanted to show you."

A gilt frame, perhaps two feet across and a foot wide, hung empty on the wall, only whitewashed stonework visible where the painting should have been. Tom edged toward it.

"What was there?"

"An oil painting of this synagogue completed in the early thirties."

"It's been cut out," Tom said thoughtfully, running his finger along the rippled canvas edge where the painting had been sliced from the frame.

"That's why I asked you to come," the rabbi said excitedly. "They could have left it in its frame if all they wanted to do was damage or destroy it. Do you think maybe they took it with them?"

"I doubt it," Tom said with a frown. "The people who did this don't strike me as art lovers."

"Especially not a painting by this artist," the rabbi agreed grudgingly.

"Why, who was it by?"

"A Jewish artist. Not well known, but dear to us because he lived here in Prague—until the Nazis murdered him. He was called Karel Bellak."

"Bellak?" Tom drilled him with a questioning look.

"You've heard of him?" the rabbi asked, clearly surprised.

"I've heard the name," Tom said slowly. "I'm just not sure where. I'll need to speak to my colleague back in London to be sure I'm thinking of the same person. Do you have a photo of the painting?"

"Of course." Rabbi Spiegel produced a photograph from his pocket and handed it to Tom. "We made a few copies of this one a few years ago for the insurance company. They told us the painting wasn't worth much, but to us it was priceless."

"May I?" Tom asked.

"Keep it. Please."

Tom slipped the photograph into his overcoat.

"From what I remember of Bellak . . ." Tom began, pausing as two Czech policemen stepped into the room and peered around at the damage.

"Go on."

"Is there anywhere a little more private we can go?"

"Why?"

Tom tilted his head toward the policemen.

"Oh." The rabbi sounded disappointed. "Very well. Come with me."

He led Tom back down the stairs and across the main body of the synagogue to a thick wooden door that he unbolted. It gave onto a small open space, the oppressive cinder gray walls of the surrounding apartment blocks looming down on all sides. A few trees reached into the small window of gray sky overhead, their leafless branches creaking in the wind and occasionally scraping their skeletal fingers against the stifling walls. Ahead of them, the ground undulated in a series of unexpected mounds and dips and was peppered with dark shapes.

"What is this place?" Tom asked in a whisper.

"The old Jewish cemetery," the rabbi answered.

It suddenly dawned on Tom that the dark shapes in front of him were in fact gravestones, thousands of them in all shapes and sizes, some leaning against others for support, some lying prostrate as if they had been sprinkled like seeds from a great height. They were jammed so close to each other that the ground, muddy and wet where the morning's frost had melted, was barely visible between them. Tom was certain that if he were to topple one, the rest would fall like a field of overgrown dominoes.

"For hundreds of years this was the only place the city allowed us to bury our dead. So each time it filled up we had no choice but to put down a layer of earth and start again. Some say there are eleven levels in all."

Tom knelt down at the stone nearest to him. A swastika had been etched on the stone's peeling surface. He looked up at the rabbi, who gave a resigned shrug.

"The war may have ended long ago, but for some of us the struggle continues," the rabbi said, shaking his head. "Now, Mr. Kirk, tell me—what do you know about Karel Bellak?"

CHAPTER THREE

It was a little game he played, something to pass the time on his rounds. As he came upon each exhibit he would test himself against the display's information cards to see how much he could remember. After twenty years he was pretty much word-perfect.

First there was the Myer flag system, a line-of-sight communication tool devised in the Civil War by an army doctor who went on to form the Signal Corps. The glass cases held the original flags, battle-torn and stained with age.

Satisfied, he walked on, his rubber soles squeaking rhythmically on the floor like a metronome marking time, the polished toe caps of his boots glowing with a white sheen from the dimmed overhead lights.

Al Travis had been a guard at the National Cryptologic Museum since it had first opened. He liked it there. He'd finally found a place where he felt he was part of something special, something important. After all, technically he worked for the NSA, the agency responsible for protecting Uncle Sam's information systems and breaking the bad guys' codes.

Hell, the NSA was right in the thick of things with this whole War on Terror.

He came upon the next exhibit—the Cipher Wheel. A series of rotating wooden discs, the wheel had been used by European governments for hundreds of years to encrypt sensitive communications. According to the card, it was designed to be used with French, the international language of diplomacy until the end of the First World War.

The Cipher Wheel's cylindrical shape nestled snugly in its display case, the wood polished by generations of anxious fingers. He paused, looked at it, and checked with the information card that he was right in believing this to be the oldest such device in the world.

And then of course there was his favorite exhibit—the big one, as he liked to say—the Enigma machine. The museum had several versions on display in two large glass-fronted cases, and Travis never failed to pause when he walked past, running his eyes appreciatively over them. He found it incredible that, in breaking the code generated by this oversized typewriter, Polish and then British mathematicians had helped win the war for the Allies in Europe. But that's what the card said, and who was he to argue?

A sudden noise made Travis stop. He checked over his shoulder and then peered into the semidarkness ahead of him.

"Anyone there?" he called out, wondering if someone had come to relieve him early. As he paused, waiting for an answer, a steel wire shaped into a noose was lowered from above him until it was hovering just over his head, glinting in the lights like a silver halo. Then, just as Travis was about to move on again, it snapped past his face, the wire tightening around his neck and pulling him three feet off the ground.

Travis's hands leapt to his throat as he scrabbled at the wire, his legs thrashing beneath him, his throat making an inhuman gurgling noise. Two dark shapes materialized out of the shadows as he struggled, and a third man dropped down noiselessly from where he had hidden himself in the roof space above the ceiling tiles.

One of the men pulled a chair over from the wall and positioned it under Travis's flailing legs. Travis located the top of the chair with his feet and, wavering unsteadily, found that he was just about able to perch on tiptoe and relieve the choking pressure on his throat, his lungs gasping for air, blood on his collar where the noose had bitten into the soft folds of his neck.

Teetering there, his mouth dry with fear, he watched as the three figures, each masked and dressed in black, approached the left-hand display cabinet. Working with well-drilled efficiency, they unscrewed the frame, levered the glass out, and leaned it against the wall. Then the man in the middle reached in, took out one of the Enigma machines, and placed it in his accomplice's backpack.

Travis tried to speak, tried to ask them what the hell they thought they were doing, to point out that there was no way they were ever going to make it off the base, but all that came was a series of choked grunts and whispered moans.

The noise, though, made the men turn. One broke away from the others and approached Travis.

"Did you say something, nigger?"

The voice was thin and mocking, the last word said slowly and deliberately. Travis shook his head, knowing that these were not people to be reasoned with, although his eyes burned with anger at the insult.

The man didn't seem to be expecting an answer. Instead he kicked out and knocked the chair from under Travis, who plunged toward the floor, the steel wire twanging under tension and snapping his neck.

For a few seconds Travis's feet drummed furiously, then twitched a few times, then were still.

CHAPTER FOUR

CLERKENWELL, LONDON

January 3—5:02 P.M.

Tom was sitting at his desk with a copy of *The Times* in front of him, folded into four so that only the cryptic crossword was visible. He had a ballpoint pen in his mouth, the end chipped and split where he had chewed it, his forehead creased in concentration. Much to his frustration, he hadn't filled in a single word yet.

The desk itself was French, circa 1890, solid mahogany carved with fruit, foliage, and various mythological creatures. It had four drawers on the left and a cabinet on the right, each opened by a lion-mask handle. Caryatids and atlantes flanked the corners, supporting the overhang of the polished top.

Tom and Archie had bought the desk not for its rather obvious beauty but because it was identical on both sides, a subtly symbolic statement of equality that had resonated with the two of them. And despite his occasionally feeling like one-half of some odd Dickensian legal couple, for Tom, at least, the desk had come to encapsulate his new life—a solid partnership on the right side of the law.

There was a knock at the door.

"Yeah?" Tom called, grateful for the interruption. He had

been staring at the paper so long that the clues had started to swim across the page.

The door opened and a woman wearing jeans, a pale pink camisole, and a tight black jacket walked in, her right arm looped through the open visor of a black motorcycle helmet.

"Catch," she called.

Tom looked up just in time to see a tennis ball flashing toward his head. Without thinking, he shot a hand out and snatched it from the air, his fingers stinging as they closed around it.

"How was your game?" Tom asked with a smile as Dominique de Lecourt stripped off her jacket, hitched herself up onto the side of his desk, and placed her helmet down next to her. She had a pale, oval face that had something of the cold, sculpted, and remote beauty of a silent-movie star, although her blue eyes, in contrast, shone with an immediately inviting blend of impulsive energy and infectious confidence. Her right shoulder was covered with an elaborate tattoo of a rearing horse that was only partially masked by her curling mass of blond hair. Her left arm, meanwhile, was sheathed in a glittering armor of silver bangles that clinked like a hundred tiny bells every time she moved. Just about visible, under her top, was the bump of her stomach piercing.

"Didn't play. Decided to go to that auction instead."

"I knew you wouldn't be able to resist." Tom laughed. "See anything good?"

"A pair of Louis XV porphyry and gilt-bronze two-handled vases." Her English was excellent, with just a hint of a Swiss-French accent.

"Made by Ennemond-Alexandre Petitot in 1760." Tom nodded. "Yeah, I saw those in the catalog. What did you think?"

"I think two million is a lot to pay for a couple of nineteenth-century reproductions made for the Paris tourist market of the day. They're worth twenty thousand at most. It's a lawsuit waiting to happen."

Tom smiled. Sometimes he found it hard to believe that Dominique was still only twenty-three. She had an instinct for a deal, coupled with an almost unnatural ability to retain even the most incidental detail, that rivaled all but the most seasoned pros. Then again, Tom reminded himself, she'd had a good teacher. Until he died last year, she'd spent four years working for Tom's father in Geneva. When Tom had relocated the antiques dealership to London, she'd readily accepted his offer to move with it and help run the business.

The antiques store itself was a wide, double-fronted space with large arched windows, vital for attracting passing trade, although most visitors to Kirk Duval Fine Art & Antiques called ahead for an appointment. At the rear were two doors and a staircase. The staircase led to the upstairs floors, the first floor currently empty, the second floor Dominique's apartment, the top floor Tom's. It was supposed to have been a short-term arrangement, but the weeks had turned into months. Tom hadn't pressed the point, sensing that she would move out when the time was right for her. Besides, he valued her company and, given his pathological inability to form new friendships, that gave him his own selfish reasons for keeping her around.

The left-hand door opened onto a warehouse accessed via an old spiral staircase, while the right-hand door gave onto the office. The office was not a big room, perhaps fifteen feet square, the space dominated by the partners' desk. There was a single large window, which looked out over the warehouse below, a low bookcase running underneath it. Two comfortable armchairs were positioned on the left-hand side of the room as you went in, the brown leather faded and soft with age. Most striking, though, was the wall space behind the desk, which was taken up with Tom's glittering collection of safe plates—an assortment of brass and iron plaques in various shapes and sizes, some dating back to the late eighteenth century, each ornately engraved with the safe manufacturer's name and crest.

"How are you getting on with the crossword?" she asked with a smile, peering down at the unfilled grid in front of him. "Any easier?"

"Not really," he admitted. "I mean, take this: 'Soldier got

into cover for a spell.' Five letters." He shook his head. "I just don't see it."

"Magic," she answered after a few seconds' thought.

"Magic," Tom repeated slowly. "Why magic?"

"A soldier is a GI," she explained. "A cover is a mac. Put *GI* into *mac* to get a spell. Magic."

She tapped her long, graceful finger playfully on the tip of Tom's nose as if it was a wand.

"I give up." Tom, defeated, threw his pen down onto the desk.

"You just need to keep at it." She laughed. "One day it'll all just click into place."

"So you keep saying." Frustrated, he changed the subject: "When's Archie back?"

"Tomorrow, I think." She picked at a frayed piece of cotton where her jeans were ripped across her left thigh.

"That's twice he's been to the States in the last few weeks." Tom frowned. "For someone who claims to hate going abroad, he's certainly putting himself about a bit."

"What's he doing there?"

"God knows. Sometimes he just seems to get an idea into his head and then he's off."

"That reminds me—where did you put those newspapers that were on his desk?"

"Where do you think? I threw them away along with all his other rubbish."

"You did what?" she exclaimed. "They were mine. I'd been keeping them for a reason."

"Well, try the bottom left-hand drawer then," Tom suggested sheepishly. "I stuffed a bunch of old papers in there."

She slipped off the desk and opened the drawer.

"Luckily for you, they're here," she said with relief, pulling out a large pile of newspapers and placing them down in front of him.

"What do you want with all these anyway?" Tom asked. "Are you collecting coupons or something?"

"Do I look like I collect coupons?" She grinned. "No, I wanted to show you something. Only you might not like it . . ."

"What are you talking about?" Tom frowned. "You can tell me anything, you know that."

"Even if it's about Harry?" she asked.

"Harry?"

Harry Renwick. The mere mention of his name was enough to make Tom's heart rise into his throat. Harry Renwick had been his father's best friend, a man Tom had known and loved since . . . well, since almost as long as he could remember.

That was until it transpired that dear old Uncle Harry had been living a double life. Operating under the name of Cassius, he had masterminded a ruthless art-crime syndicate that had robbed and murdered and extorted its way around the globe for decades. Only last year, Renwick had tried first to frame Tom for murder and then to kill him. The betrayal still stung.

"You told me he'd disappeared after what happened in Paris. After the—"

"Yeah," Tom cut her off, not wanting to relive the details. "He just vanished."

"Well, wherever he's gone, someone's looking for him." Dominique unfolded the top newspaper, the previous day's *Herald Tribune*. She turned to the Personals section and pointed at an ad she'd circled. Tom began to read the first paragraph.

"*Lions may awake any second. If this takes place alert me via existing number.*" He flashed her an amused glance. She indicated that he should read on. "*If chimps stop their spelling test within one or so hours, reward through gift of eighty bananas.*" He laughed. "It's nonsense."

"That's what I thought when I first saw it, but you know how I like a challenge."

"Sure." Tom smiled. Among her many attributes, Dominique had an amazing aptitude for word games and other types of puzzles. It was partly this which had driven Tom, never one to be outdone, to attempt the crossword. Not that he was making much progress.

"It only took me a few minutes. It's a jump code."

"A what?"

"A jump code. Jewish scholars have been finding them for years in the Torah. Did you know that if you take the first *T* in the Book of Genesis, then jump forty-nine places to the fiftieth letter, then another forty-nine places to the fiftieth letter after that, and so on, it spells a word?"

"What?"

"*Torah.* The book's name is embedded in the text. The next three books do the same. Some say that the whole of the Old Testament is an encoded message that predicts the future."

"And this works in the same way?"

"It's a question of identifying the jump interval. In this case, it's every eighth letter."

"Starting with the first letter?"

She nodded.

"So that makes this *L*"—Tom counted seven spaces—"then *A . . .*" He grabbed a pen and began to write down each eighth letter: "Then *S . . .* then *T. Last!*" he exclaimed triumphantly.

"*Last seen Copenhagen. Await next contact.* I decoded it earlier."

"And there are others like this?"

"After I found this, I looked back through earlier editions. There have been coded messages using the same methodology every few weeks for the last six months or so. I've written them out here—" She handed Tom a piece of paper.

"*HK cold, try Tokyo,*" he read. "*Focus search in Europe . . . DNA sample en route . . . Reported sighting in Vienna . . .*" He looked up at Dominique. "Okay, I agree that someone seems to be looking for someone or something. But there's nothing to say it's Harry."

Dominique handed him a newspaper from the bottom of the pile and opened it at the Personals page.

"This was the first and longest message." She pointed at a lengthy ad she'd circled in red.

"What does it say?"

"*Ten million dollar reward. Henry Julius Renwick, a.k.a. Cassius, dead or alive. Publish interest next Tuesday.*"

Tom was silent as he tried to digest this news. "Did anyone reply?" he asked eventually.

"I counted twenty-five replies in all."

"Twenty-five!"

"Whoever's behind this has got a small private army out there trying to track Harry down. The question is why."

"No," Tom reflected, "the question is who."

CHAPTER FIVE

Where had it all gone wrong?

When had he passed from being a high achiever to an average Joe, a stand-up guy, but one who, according to his superiors, didn't quite have what it took to go all the way? How was it that people almost half his age were accelerating past him so fast that he barely had time to spit their dust from his mouth before they were a speck on the horizon? When had hanging on long enough to max out his pension become his only reason for getting up in the morning?

Special Agent Paul Viggiano, forty-one, slipped a bullet into each of the five empty chambers of his shiny silver Air-Lite Ti Model 342 .38 Smith & Wesson as each question registered in his mind.

The gun loaded, he snapped it shut and stood contemplating it for a few seconds before raising it to eye level. Again he paused and took a deep breath.

Then, breathing out slowly, he emptied the gun into the target at the far end of the indoor shooting range as fast and as loudly as he could, each successive bang magnifying the noise of the one before it, until it seemed that the whole room was echoing in sympathy with his plight.

"Sounds like you really needed that," the woman in the booth next to him said with a smile. He managed a tight grimace in response as she turned to take aim. And how was it, her intervention reminded him, that in some misplaced drive for gender equality, the bureau was falling over itself to promote *women*? Women like that bitch Jennifer Browne, who'd got moved upstairs while he'd been posted here. Wherever here was.

One small oversight, that's all it had been. One little slip in an otherwise spotless career. And here he was, drowning in mediocrity.

He shook his head and hit the button to retrieve the target from the other end of the gallery. It whirred toward him, the black silhouette ghosting through the air like a vengeful spirit, before jerking to a halt just in front of him. He examined it for holes.

To his disbelief there were none. Not a single one.

"Nice shootin', Tex." The FBI armorer smirked, sneaking a look over his shoulder. "Hell, you're as liable to blow your own balls off as hit the bad guy."

"Screw you, McCoy."

Viggiano's distinctive New Jersey drawl somehow suited the Italian ancestry suggested by his thick black eyebrows and hair and permanent five o'clock shadow. His dark looks were complemented by a firm, unyielding jaw that jutted out like a car bumper, giving the impression that, if you threw something at him, it would bounce off like a rock hitting a trampoline.

The woman next to him squeezed off her shots one by one with a plodding, rhythmic monotony, confirming Viggiano's impression that she probably ironed her husband's socks. She then carefully placed her gun down in front of her and retrieved her target. Viggiano couldn't help but peer over.

Eleven holes. She had eleven holes in her target. How was that possible unless . . . unless it was her six and his five? He'd been so worked up he'd fired at the wrong target.

The woman had obviously come to the same conclusion. She looked up at him, her eyes dancing, her laughter only seconds behind. He threw his ear protectors down on the bench and stalked out of the room before she could show anyone else.

"Oh, sir, I was kinda hopin' I'd find you down here."

Byron Bailey was an African American from South Central L.A., a bright kid who'd made it the hard way, winning a scholarship to Caltech on the back of good grades and an evening job packing shelves in his local 7-Eleven.

He had bad acne, which had left his ebony skin pitted like coral, while his nose was broad and flat and his eyes wide and eager. What struck Viggiano most, though, was his tail-wagging enthusiasm, a sickening trait that he shared with most rookies and one that only served to make Viggiano feel even older than he already did.

"So, you found me." Viggiano marked his indifference by fastidiously picking invisible pieces of lint off the lapels of his immaculately pressed suit.

"Er, yessir." Bailey seemed momentarily unsettled by Viggiano's irritable tone. "We got a tip-off about that heist from the NSA complex in Fort Meade. You know, the one the boys back in DC are all choked up about. It sounds like it might be for real."

"Slow down and you might start making sense." Viggiano caught his reflection in a glass door as he spoke and adjusted his tie so it was centered precisely under his chin.

"You ever heard of the Sons of American Liberty?"

"Who?"

"The Sons of American Liberty."

"Nope."

"They're a fringe group of white supremacists. Our mystery caller fingered them as the people behind the theft."

"Did you get a trace?"

"No. The call was made right here in Salt Lake, but that's all we know. Whoever he was, he had the sense to hang up before we could get a fix on his location."

"Any intel on the caller's ID from the tape?"

"Forensics are still working on it. They don't think they'll get much. Only thing they're saying at the moment is that he doesn't sound like he's from these parts."

"That's it?" Viggiano sighed heavily. "Jesus, it hardly narrows it down."

"No, sir," Bailey agreed.

"Where are these jokers based?"

"Malta, Idaho."

"Malta, Idaho!" Viggiano exclaimed in mock celebration. "Just when I think I've run out of two-bit shithole towns to visit, another one shoves its head right up my ass."

"If it's any consolation, sir, Carter said that he wanted you to head up the investigation at our end."

"Regional Director Carter?" A flicker of interest in Viggiano's voice now.

"That's right. Apparently you dealt with a similar situation a couple of years back. He said that you were the only one available with the right level of experience for this. He suggested I help you out too, if that's okay, sir."

Viggiano clipped his gun back into its holster. "Well, for once Carter's right," he said, running a hand through his hair to check that the part was still right. "Saddle up, Bailey. You're coming along for the ride. Paul Viggiano's gonna show you a shortcut to the big time."

CHAPTER SIX

BOROUGH MARKET, SOUTHWARK, LONDON
January 5—12:34 P.M.

The market stalls were tightly packed under the rusting cast-iron railway arches, their shelves groaning with freshly imported produce: Camemberts from Normandy as big as cartwheels, pink Guijelo hams, and bottles of olive oil from Apuglia that glowed like small suns.

Shoals of eager shoppers, wrapped up against the cold, battled their way along the aisles, their movements seemingly governed by whatever enticing smell, be it fried ostrich burger or warm bread, the wind happened to bring their way. Overhead, trains screeched and scraped their way along the elevated track, an intermittent rolling thunder that grew and faded as quickly as a summer storm.

"What are we doing here?" Archie snapped irritably as he dodged between two strollers and then squeezed past a long queue in front of one of the many flower stalls.

In his midforties and only of average height, Archie had the stocky no-nonsense build of a bare-knuckle boxing champion, his cauliflower ears and slightly crumpled unshaven face reinforcing the image. So there was a certain incongruity about his choice of a tailored beige overcoat over an elegant dark blue pinstripe suit, and his neatly clipped hair.

It was a contradiction reinforced by an accent that Tom had never quite been able to place, although he was the first to admit that his own—a transatlantic hodgepodge of American and British pronunciation and idioms—was hardly easy to nail down. In Archie's case, the street-speak of the market stall where he had first learned his trade mingled with the rounded vowels and clipped *T*s of a more middle-class background.

Tom suspected that Archie, ever the opportunist, had developed his own unique patois to enable him to move unchallenged between two worlds. It was a neat trick, but one that left him, like Tom, fully accepted by neither.

"You're meant to be coming to dinner tonight, remember? I thought I'd splash out."

"Oh shit." Archie slapped his forehead with the palm of his hand. "I'm sorry, mate, but I'd completely forgotten."

"Archie!" Tom remonstrated. What made Archie's unreliability especially annoying was its very predictability. "We spoke about it last week. You promised."

"I know, I know," Archie said sheepishly. "I just plain forgot and now . . . well, Apples has got a game round at his place tonight. Big money. Invitation only. I can't get out of it."

"More like you don't want to get out of it." Tom's voice was laced with disappointment. "This whole gambling thing's getting a bit out of control, isn't it?"

"No, it's just a laugh." Archie spoke a little too emphatically, as if it wasn't just Tom he was trying to convince.

Looking back, Tom sometimes found it hard to remember that throughout the ten years Archie had been his fence, he had known him only as a voice at the end of a phone line. Archie had always insisted it was safer that way. For both of them.

Tom still remembered his anger when Archie had broken his own rule the previous year, back when they were both still in the game, tracking him down to convince him to follow through on a job. And yet from that first difficult meeting, a friendship had developed. A friendship that was still finding its way, perhaps, as they both struggled to overcome a life built around suspicion and fear, but a friendship nonetheless, and one that Tom increasingly valued.

"Besides, I need a bit of excitement now and then," Archie continued. "The art recovery game, well, it's not exactly got the buzz of the old days, has it?"

"I thought you got out because you'd had enough of the old days."

"I did, I did," Archie conceded. "It's just, well, you know . . . sometimes I miss it."

"I know what you mean," Tom mused. "Sometimes, I miss it too."

"Dom told me about those ads in the paper, by the way."

Tom nodded grimly. "Seems the FBI aren't the only people looking for Renwick."

"You all right with that?"

"Why wouldn't I be? He deserves everything that's coming to him."

They had left the market now and were making their way down Park Street toward Archie's car. Although the pub on the corner was busy, the crowds soon thinned out away from the main market, and Tom was relieved that it was easier to make himself heard now. They walked past a succession of small warehouses, the faded names of earlier, now forgotten enterprises still just about visible under the accumulated grime.

Archie reached for his packet of cigarettes and lit one. Smoking was a relatively new vice of his. Tom put it down to his missing the buzz of the underworld. Archie put it down to the stress of being honest.

"Did you find what you were after in the States?"

"More or less," Archie replied. From the way his eyes flashed to the ground, Tom sensed that he didn't really want to talk about it. "How was Prague? Worth following up?"

"Maybe. You ever heard of a painter called Bellak?"

"Bellak? Karel Bellak?"

"That's him." Tom had long since ceased to be amazed by Archie's encyclopedic knowledge of the art market, painting especially.

"Yeah, course I've heard of him. What do you want to know?"

"Is this one of his?"

Tom reached into his pocket and withdrew the photograph the rabbi had given him. Archie studied it for a few seconds.

"Could be." He handed it back. "Bleak palette, heavy brushstrokes, slightly dodgy perspective. Of course, I've never actually seen one in the flesh. As far as I'm aware, they were all destroyed."

"That's what I told the rabbi," Tom said, "that the Nazis are said to have burnt them all. I just couldn't remember why."

Archie took a long drag before answering.

"Bellak was a journeyman artist. Competent but, as you can see, no great talent. A portrait here, a landscape there, basically whatever paid that month's bar bill. Then in 1937 an ambitious SS officer commissioned him to paint Himmler's daughter Gudrun as a gift for his master."

"But wasn't Bellak Jewish?"

"As it turned out, yes. But by then a grateful Himmler had hung the portrait in his office on Prinz-Albrecht-Strasse in Berlin and even commissioned a second painting. When he discovered the truth, he had the SS officer shot and Bellak arrested and sent to Auschwitz. Then he ordered that every last one of Bellak's works was to be tracked down and disposed of."

"Clearly, some survived," Tom said. "This one was stolen a few days ago."

"Why bother pinching that? The frame they had it in was probably worth more than the painting."

"I don't know. Maybe because he was Jewish," Tom said.

"What do you mean?"

"You should have seen the place." Tom was surprised at the instinctive anger in his voice. "Someone had done a real number on it. Swastikas and graffiti sprayed all over the walls. Children's drawings from a local death camp torn to shreds, as if they were trying to make confetti."

"Bastards," Archie muttered, flicking his cigarette butt into the gutter. "And the painting?"

"Sliced out of its frame and taken with them."

"But what would they want with it?"

"That's what I've been wondering."

"Unless . . ."

"Unless what?"

Overhead, a train crashed its way toward London Bridge, and Archie waited until the raucous clanking had subsided before answering.

"Unless the painting was what this was all about. Unless they were trying to be clever by disguising an old-fashioned robbery as some sort of anti-Semitic attack."

"Exactly," Tom said, reassured that Archie had come to the same conclusion as him. "So I made some calls. And from what I can work out, it seems that over the last year or so there have been six thefts of alleged Bellak paintings from various private homes and collections across Europe."

"Six? I'd no idea that many had survived."

"Well, they're not exactly the sort of thing anyone would bother cataloging, are they? Even now, no one's managed to join the dots. The cases have just stuck with the local police in each area. The insurance companies haven't got involved because the pictures aren't worth anything. I only found out because I knew who to ask."

"Someone's going to a hell of a lot of trouble to steal a bunch of supposedly worthless paintings." A pause. "Tom? You listening?" Archie looked up at him questioningly.

"Don't turn round," Tom said in a low voice, "but I think we're being followed."

CHAPTER SEVEN

BLACK PINE MOUNTAINS, NEAR MALTA, IDAHO

January 5—5:34 A.M.

W hat's the latest from inside the compound?" Special
Agent Paul Viggiano spoke over the background
noise of technicians and ringing telephones, a trim, muscular figure in his blue windbreaker, *FBI* stamped in large
yellow letters across the back.

Bailey, sitting at the kitchen table of the cabin they had
commandeered the previous evening as their operational
HQ, was the first to speak.

"No movement, nothing. Not a single phone call. Even
the generator shut down this morning. I figure it ran out of
gas. No one's come out to fix it."

"What about the dogs?" Silvio Vasquez this time, the leader
of the fourteen-man FBI Hostage Rescue Team that had been
assigned to the investigation, sitting to Bailey's right.

"What?" Viggiano frowned. "What the hell's that got to
do with anything?"

"Didn't someone say they had dogs? Have you seen them?"

"No." Bailey shook his head. "Nothing."

"So that's weird, right?" Vasquez concluded. "A dog's gotta
take a leak."

"When did it last snow?" Viggiano asked. Bailey noticed

that he had found some loose matches and was arranging them into neat parallel lines as he spoke.

"Two days ago," Vasquez answered.

"And there are no footprints? You're seriously saying no one has stepped outside that farmhouse for two days?" Peering over, Bailey could see that he had rearranged the matches into a square.

"Not unless they can fly," Bailey confirmed. "And that includes the dogs."

"I still say you boys have screwed up big-time."

It was the local sheriff's turn to speak. A tubby man with ginger hair and a closely trimmed mustache, Sheriff Hennessy seemed to be in a permanent sweat, the perspiration beading on his pink forehead and cheeks like condensation on glass.

"I know these people," he continued, the top of his clip-on tie losing itself in the fleshy folds of his neck. "They're law-abiding, God-fearing folk. Patriots."

"So you say," Bailey began, a small knot of resentment forming in his chest. "But they also happen to be on a federal blacklist for suspected links to the Aryan Nations and the Klan."

Bailey saw Viggiano give a slight shake of the head, warning him to back off. "Now, Sheriff, it's true we don't know for sure that these people have done anything wrong," Viggiano resumed in a conciliatory tone, "but we do know that three days ago an exhibit was stolen from the National Cryptologic Museum in Maryland. We know that whoever took it left no physical evidence that we've been able to find."

"Apart from the security guard they strung up like a hunk of meat in cold storage," Bailey couldn't help himself from adding.

"We also know," Viggiano continued as if he hadn't heard him, "that our Salt Lake office got a call yesterday suggesting these law-abiding patriots of yours were involved."

"I know all that," Hennessy said, dabbing his brow with a paper napkin taken from the dispenser at the side of the table. "But any crackhead could have made that call. It don't prove nothing."

"It proves that the caller knew about the theft. With the press blackout the NSA have imposed, the only people outside of law enforcement agencies who could know about that are the people who did it. So this is a lead, Sheriff, that we're going to follow up whether you agree with it or not."

Hennessy slumped back into his chair, muttering under his breath. Bailey smiled, feeling somewhat the better for his capitulation.

"So what's the plan?" he asked.

"Well, I'm not sitting on my ass till these jokers run out of water and crackers," Viggiano declared. "We're going in. Today."

There was a murmur of approval from around the table, Hennessy excepted. "But I want to keep this simple," Viggiano continued. "We've got no reason to assume things will get ugly, so we keep the Humvees under cover and the choppers on the ground. Hopefully we won't need them. Vasquez?"

Vasquez got to his feet and leaned over the table. His face was dark and pockmarked, his lank black hair tucked under an FBI baseball cap, which he wore back to front, his dark eyes glowing with excitement.

"The sheriff's men have put roadblocks here and here"— he indicated two roads on the map spread out in front of them—"blocking all routes in and out of the compound. I want SWAT teams here, here, and here, in the trees on the high ground to cover the windows. First sign of any hostile activity once my guys are inside the compound, they put down covering fire while we fall back to the RV point here."

"You got it," said Viggiano.

"The two HRT teams will come in from the front and the rear. Based on the blueprints, we estimate we'll have the main building secured in about three minutes. Then it's over to you."

"Good," said Viggiano as Vasquez sat down. "Now remember, when this thing goes down, I want it done by the numbers. No exceptions. There are families in there— women, kids." He pointed at the pile of manila folders containing photos and profiles of all the people the FBI had identified as living in the building. "So we knock on the door nice and easy. We ask to come inside. Any sign that this is more than a plain vanilla secure-and-search operation, we pull back. The last thing I—the bureau can afford right now is another high-profile hostage situation. Besides, if it gets hot, the DC brass will want to handle it themselves. They always do."

Vasquez nodded his agreement. "You got it."

"Okay then." Viggiano slapped the table. "Let's move out. There's a shitload to do, and I want to hit this place after lunch."

CHAPTER EIGHT

Followed? You sure?" Archie asked.

"Tracksuit, bomber jacket, and white sneakers. Noticed him glancing over at us five minutes ago. Just saw his reflection in that van's rear window about thirty yards back."

"We're nearly at the motor. We could make a run for it."

Tom followed Archie's gaze to his DB9 about thirty yards down the road. It was a recent purchase, and for Archie—who had always said that the cardinal rule of being a criminal was not to attract undue attention by living beyond your means—an uncharacteristic indulgence. When he had handed over the check, twenty years of pent-up spending frustration had been released with one cathartic swish of his pen.

"Oh shit!" Archie swore. A wheel clamp glowed bright yellow against the gunmetal gray bodywork. "They've only gone and bloody clamped me."

He quickened his pace, but Tom laid a restraining hand on his arm. Something felt wrong. Behind them a man who had followed them from the market; ahead, a street sweeper whose shoes looked a little too new; parked next to Archie's car, a van with its windows blacked out; and the car itself conveniently immobilized. It was textbook.

"This isn't right," he breathed.

"I see them too," hissed Archie. "What do you want to do?"

"Get out of here. Now!"

As Tom shouted, the rear doors of the van flew open and three men jumped to the ground. At the same time the street sweeper threw his broom away and swung a semi-automatic out from under his coat. Tom heard the heavy thud of fast-approaching feet from behind.

Before the sweeper could get a shot off, Archie peeled away to the left, while Tom darted right, down a small alleyway that emerged onto a narrow lane bordered by a wire fence. Grabbing the galvanized mesh, he hauled himself up its shuddering face, the metal clanging noisily. He was on the point of vaulting over to the other side when he felt a hand close around his left ankle.

The man who had followed them from the market had somehow managed to catch up with him and was now hanging off his leg, to drag him to the ground. Instead of trying to shake him off, Tom lowered himself slightly until his feet were level with the man's head and then kicked out, freeing his foot from the man's grasp and striking him across the chin. With a strangled gasp, the man fell to the ground.

Tom swung himself over the fence into a strip of wasteland that had been turned into a temporary parking lot for the market. He heard the clang of metal behind him and saw that two of the men from the van had arrived at the fence and were clambering up it.

At least they hadn't shot him, Tom thought as he sprinted out of the lot, narrowly avoiding a car that was turning in, and headed back toward the market. If they'd wanted him dead, whoever they were, they could have taken him right there, through the fence. Clearly they had other plans.

At that moment a forklift loaded with market produce swung out of a hidden turning ahead of him. Tom jinked around it, the driver slamming on his brakes just in time to avoid hitting him.

"Watch it, moron!" the driver yelled, leaning on the horn to emphasize his point.

Tom ignored him, leaping over the spilled vegetable crates and then plunging back into the market. As soon as he was inside, he slowed to a walk, snaking in and out of the lines of shoppers. He knew that he would be safer in a busy place and hoped that Archie had had the good sense to come to the same conclusion. When he judged he was far enough inside, he stopped next to a wine stall and glanced back over his shoulder. His pursuers had reached the market entrance and were scanning the crowd for him. Both had their right hands tucked inside their coats, where each was presumably concealing a gun.

Tom turned abruptly and slammed into a man carrying a case of red wine, knocking it out of his hands. The box landed with a crash, the bottles shattering noisily. Tom glanced back toward the entrance and saw that the men, alerted by the noise, were already fighting their way over to him.

"I'm sorry," Tom said, pushing past.

"Hey!" the man shouted after him. "Get back here!"

But Tom didn't stop. Dropping to his knees, he crawled under a stall, then ducked under two more until he was a couple of aisles away from the site of the collision. From the cover of a pyramid of olive oil drums, he checked the progress of the two men. They were standing by the box of shattered wine bottles, gesturing frantically. They'd lost him.

He cautiously made his way toward the north exit, attaching himself to a group of tourists who were chattering excitedly about the whole deer they'd seen strung up on one of the stalls. As they left the market, he broke away, heading for the main road and the river.

With a screech of brakes, a large black Range Rover pulled up alongside him. Tom turned on his heel but slipped, the road surface rendered treacherous by the wet cardboard boxes, lettuce leaves, and plastic bags generated by the morning's trading. Before he could scramble back to his feet, the rear passenger door flew open and he caught a glimpse of who was sitting in the backseat.

Archie.

The front passenger window retracted a few inches, and a pale hand appeared in the crack clutching a government identity badge.

"Enough fun and games, Kirk. Get in."

CHAPTER NINE

January 5—12:56 P.M.

The driver's square, close-shaved head emerged from a thick gray woolen turtleneck. He flicked his eyes up to the mirror and then back to the road, a smile playing around the corner of his mouth as the car accelerated away.

The man in the passenger seat peered back over his shoulder and nodded at them both.

"I'm William Turnbull."

He extended his hand back over his shoulder toward them as he spoke, but they both ignored it, staring at him in stony silence. From what he could see of Turnbull, Tom estimated that he must weigh about two hundred fifty pounds, little of it muscle. He appeared to be quite young, though, about thirty-five, give or take a few years, and was dressed in an urban camouflage of jeans and an open-necked shirt that barely contained the roll of fat around the base of his neck.

"Sorry about . . . that." He waved vaguely in the direction of the market. "I guessed that you probably wouldn't come if I just asked, so I brought some help. I didn't quite expect you to make us—"

"Let me guess," Tom interrupted angrily. "Somebody's got knocked off and you think we might know something about it? Am I right? How many times have I got to tell you people, we don't know anything and, even if we did, we wouldn't say."

"This has nothing to do with any job," was Turnbull's unsmiling response. "And I'm not the police."

"Special Branch, Interpol, Flying Squad, PC bloody Plod . . ." Archie shrugged. "Whatever you want to call yourselves, the answer's still the same. And this is harassment. We're clean and you know it."

"I work for the Foreign Office." Turnbull flashed his identity card at them again.

"The Foreign Office?" Archie said incredulously. "Well, that's a new one."

"Not really," said Tom quietly. "He's a spook."

Turnbull smiled. "We prefer 'intelligence services.' In my case, Six."

Six, Tom knew, was how insiders referred to MI6, the agency that dealt with overseas threats to national security. It wasn't the sort of organization Tom wanted to get caught up in. Not again. He'd done five years in the CIA, seen how they worked, and had only just lived to regret it.

"So what do you want?"

"Your help," came the toneless reply as the car slowed to a halt at a set of lights.

Archie gave a short, dismissive laugh.

"What sort of help?" Tom asked quietly. Until he knew exactly what he was up against, he was forcing himself to play along.

"As much as you want to give."

"Oh, that's easy," Tom said. "None." Archie nodded his agreement. "Not unless you know something I don't . . ." People like Turnbull never made a move unless they had an edge, some sort of leverage. The key was to flush it out.

"No reason." Turnbull smiled. "No threats. No phony deals. No 'I'll scratch your back if you scratch mine.' If you help us it will be because, by the time I've finished telling you what I've got, you're going to want to."

"Come on, Tom, we don't have to listen to this shit. They've got nothing on us. Let's get out of here," Archie pleaded. But Tom hesitated. Something in Turnbull's voice had piqued his curiosity, even though he knew Archie was probably right.

"I want to hear him out."

The lights changed to green and the car drew away again.

"Good." Turnbull released his seat belt and turned to face them. He had a flat, featureless face, his cheeks rounded and fleshy, his chin almost disappearing into his neck. His brown eyes were small and set close together, while his long hair was parted in two wild cowlicks in the middle of his head and fell like curtains that he had draped behind his ears.

In many ways, Tom thought, he was a most unlikely-looking spy. The best ones always were. Certainly he had an easygoing confidence that Tom had observed in other field agents in the past, and good agents at that.

"Have you ever heard of a group called Kristall Blade?" Turnbull asked.

"No," said Tom.

"No reason you should have, I suppose. They're a small band of extremists with loose ties to the Nationalde-mokratische Partei Deutschlands, or the NPD, the most active neo-Nazi political group in Germany. They're supposedly run by a former German Army captain called Dmitri Müller, although no one's ever seen him to confirm it. To be honest, we don't know a huge amount about them."

Tom shrugged. "And?"

"And from the little we do know, these aren't your regular skinheads cruising around the suburbs looking for immigrants to beat up. They're a sophisticated paramilitary organization who are still fighting a war that the rest of us think ended in 1945."

"Hence the name?" It was more a statement than a question. Tom knew his history well enough to guess that Kristall Blade must have drawn their inspiration from Kristallnacht—the fateful night in late 1938 when Nazi-inspired attacks on Jewish businesses had left the streets of Germany's cities littered with broken glass.

"Exactly," Turnbull said eagerly. "They used to fund their activities by hiring themselves out as freelance hit men behind the Iron Curtain, but these days they're into small-scale drug and protection rackets. They're suspected of involvement in a range of guerrilla-style terrorist atrocities aimed primarily at Jewish communities in Germany and Austria. There are no more than ten or twenty active members, with a wider group of supporters and sympathizers perhaps a hundred strong. But that's what makes them so dangerous. They slip under the radar of most law-enforcement agencies and are almost impossible to pin down."

"Like I said, I've never heard of them."

Turnbull continued, undeterred. "Nine days ago, two men broke into St. Thomas' Hospital and murdered three people. Two of them were medical staff—witnesses, most likely. The third was an eighty-one-year-old patient by the name of Andreas Weissman. He was an Auschwitz survivor who moved here after the war." Tom was silent, still uncertain where this was leading and what it had to do with him. "They amputated Weissman's left arm below the elbow while he was still alive. He died of a heart attack."

"They did what?" Archie sat forward at this latest piece of information.

"Cut his arm off. His left forearm."

"What the hell for?" Tom this time.

"That's where we want your help." Turnbull smiled, revealing a disconcerting set of overlapping and crooked teeth.

"My help?" Tom frowned. "It's nothing to do with me."

"I thought you'd say that," said Turnbull, bracing himself against the window as the car turned a corner. "The killers stole the surveillance tapes from the ward, but one of them was caught on CCTV as they left the building." He produced another photo and passed it back. Tom and Archie took it in turn to examine the image, but both shook their heads.

"No idea," said Archie.

"Never seen him before," Tom agreed.

"No, but we have," Turnbull continued. "Which is how we were able to make the link to Kristall Blade. He's Dmitri's number two, Colonel Johann Hecht. Last time we caught up with him was in Vienna about three months ago when one of our agents snapped him in a restaurant." He handed Tom a third photograph. "He's about six foot seven and has a scar down his right cheek and across his lip, so you can't exactly miss him."

"I'm still waiting for the punch line here." Tom's frustration was mounting, and he passed the photo to Archie without even glancing at it. "What's this man got to do with me?"

"Christ!" Archie grabbed Tom's arm. "Look at who he's sitting opposite."

The color drained from Tom's face as he recognized the man that Archie was pointing at.

"It's Harry," he stammered, the smiling, carefree face in the photo instantly sweeping away the fragile barricades he had sought to erect around that part of his life over the last six months. "It's Renwick."

CHAPTER TEN

TIVOLI GARDENS, COPENHAGEN, DENMARK

January 5—2:03 P.M.

Harry Renwick paid his admission at the Glyptotek entrance on the corner of Tietgensgade and H. C. Andersens Boulevard and walked inside. It was still quiet at this hour, most people, he knew, preferring to visit after dark when the Tivoli turned into a light-filled oasis of over 115,000 incandescent bulbs amid the city's dark winter nights.

Despite the time, though, most of the rides were already open. The oldest, a large wooden roller coaster known to locals as Bjergrutschebanen, or the Mountain Roller Coaster, roared in the distance, the screams of its few passengers evaporating into the thin winter air in clouds of warm steam.

Renwick was certainly dressed for the weather, a blue velvet trilby pulled down low over his ears, a yellow silk scarf wound several times around his neck before disappearing into the folds of his dark blue overcoat. With his chin buried in the warmth of his upturned collar, only his nose and eyes could be seen, intelligent, alert, and as cold and unfeeling as the snow that coated the trees and rooftops around him.

He paused in front of a souvenir stall, icicles dangling menacingly from the overhanging roof. As he scanned its contents he shifted his right arm in his pocket, wincing slightly. No matter how well he wrapped it up, the cold penetrated the stump where his hand had once been and made it ache. Eventually he found what he was looking for and pointed it out to the sales assistant, handing over a hundred-kroner note. Slipping his purchase into a red bag, she counted out his change and smiled as he tipped his hat in thanks.

He walked on, past the skating rink, and then the lake, the only part of Copenhagen's original fortifications to have survived the city's growth as it swallowed up land that, like Tivoli, had once stood outside its moat and ramparts. Reaching the Chinese pagoda, he stepped into the warmth of the Kinesiske Tårn restaurant housed within, stamping his feet in the entrance vestibule to shake the snow off his shoes. A welcoming cloakroom attendant relieved him of his hat and coat, revealing a charcoal gray double-breasted suit.

In his midfifties, Renwick was tall and still obviously strong, his shoulders and head held high and stiff as if on parade. He had a full head of white hair, usually immaculately parted down one side, but the removal of his hat had left it sticking up in places. Nestled under a pair of thick, craggy eyebrows, his large green eyes looked younger than his face, which was etched with wrinkles and sagged a little across the cheeks.

"Two, please. In the back," he demanded.

"Of course, sir. This way, please."

The maître d'hôtel steered him to a table. Renwick opted for the seat that left him with a clear view of the entrance and the windows overlooking the lake. He ordered some wine and checked his watch, a rare gold 1922 Patek Philippe chronograph that he kept in his top pocket on a thin gold chain fixed to his buttonhole. Hecht was late, but then Renwick was early. Experience had taught him to take no chances.

He surveyed the dining room. It was the usual lunchtime crowd. Young couples, hands clasped, gazing into each other's eyes with looks that spoke volumes. Older couples, having long since run out of words, silently gazing in opposite directions. Parents, struggling to control their children, trying desperately to keep an eye on everything at once. Little people with little lives.

Hecht arrived five minutes later, towering over the waiter who ushered him over. He was wearing lace-up boots, jeans, and a cheap brown leather jacket decorated with zipper and press-stud pockets that looked stiff and plastic.

"You are late," Renwick admonished him as he sat down, awkwardly folding his long legs under the table. Hecht had a cruel, lumbering face, a white scar down his right cheek pulling his mouth into a permanent grin, his gray eyes bulging and moist from the cold. His dyed black hair had been plastered to his scalp with some sort of oil.

"We watched you all the way from the main gate," Hecht corrected him. "I thought I'd give you a few minutes to get settled in. I know you like to choose the wine."

Renwick smiled and indicated for the waiter to fill Hecht's glass. "So? Did you get it?"

Renwick's tone had been casual, but Hecht wasn't fooled. "Don't insult me. You wouldn't be here if you didn't think I had."

"Where is it then?"

Hecht unzipped his jacket and withdrew a short cardboard tube. Renwick snatched it from him, popped the plastic cover off one end, and emptied the canvas scroll into his lap.

"Is it the one?"

"Patience, Johann," Renwick chided, although he was having difficulty disguising the excitement in his own voice.

Holding the painting out of sight below the table with his left hand, he unscrolled it across his lap and inspected its battered surface. Seeing nothing there, he flipped it over to examine the reverse. His face fell. Nothing. "Damn."

"I don't know where else to look." Hecht's voice was laced with disappointment. "That's six we have taken, and none of them the right one—or so you say."

"What are you implying?" Renwick snapped.

"That perhaps if we knew what you were looking for, it would help us find the right painting."

"That is not our arrangement. I am paying you to steal the paintings, nothing more."

"Then perhaps it's time the deal changed."

"What do you mean?" Renwick asked sharply, not liking the mischievous sparkle in Hecht's eyes.

"That Jew you asked us to keep an eye on . . ."

"What about him?"

"He's dead."

"Dead?" Renwick's eyes widened. "How?"

"We killed him."

"You killed . . . You idiot," Renwick spluttered. "You have no idea what you are meddling in. How dare you—"

"Don't worry." Hecht interrupted him with a wink. "We got it."

Renwick nodded slowly, as if trying to calm himself, although in truth Hecht's revelation was no surprise; he had known for several days now about Kristall Blade's thoughtless attack on Weissman. If things had been different, he might even have been in a position to prevent it. No matter. For now, the important thing was for them to think they had gained an advantage. If they felt they were in control, it would make them complacent. And their complacency would eventually present him with the opportunity to make his move. Until then, he was happy to grant them their small victory and pretend to have been outsmarted.

"And now I suppose you think that little bit of cleverness entitles you to a seat at the top table?"

"This is bigger than an old painting. We can sense it. We want a share in whatever it is you are after."

"And what do I get in return?"

"You get the arm and whatever it can tell you."

There was a pause as Renwick pretended to consider Hecht's offer. His wineglass sounded like a deadened bell as he rhythmically tapped the squat gold signet ring on his little finger against the rim.

"Where is the arm now?"

"Still in London. One phone call from me and it will be flown out here—or destroyed. You choose."

Renwick shrugged. "Very well. Eighty-twenty split." He had no intention of splitting anything but knew it would arouse suspicion if he didn't try to negotiate.

"Fifty-fifty."

"Do not push your luck, Johann," Renwick warned him.

"Sixty-forty then."

"Seventy-thirty. That's my final offer," Renwick said firmly.

"Done." Hecht took out his phone. "Where do you want it delivered?"

"I will go to London," Renwick said with a wry smile. "Things are already in motion there. Maybe we can use this to our advantage."

"You still haven't told me what this is all about."

Renwick shook his head. "I will talk to Dmitri. What I have to say, he should hear first."

Hecht leaned into the table and raised his voice ever so slightly. "He will only speak to you once I have verified your story. If we are to be partners, he needs more than promises."

"Very well." Renwick sighed. "I will tell you what you need to know, but no more. The full story will have to wait for Dmitri. Agreed?"

"Agreed."

Renwick reached into the red bag by his chair. Hecht's hand flashed across his chest as he felt for his gun.

"Careful, Renwick. No tricks."

"No tricks," Renwick agreed. His hand emerged from the bag clutching a small model steam train. He placed it on the table and pushed it over to Hecht. The miniature pistons pumped merrily as it rolled over the tablecloth until it bumped into Hecht's plate with a resonant *ping* and came to a stop.

"What is this? Some sort of joke?" Hecht's tone was suspicious.

"No joke."

"But it's a train," he said dismissively.

"Not just any train. A gold train."

CHAPTER ELEVEN

"What's he got to do with this?"

Tom's voice was at once angry and uncertain. He couldn't talk, couldn't even think about Harry without remembering how much of himself he had lost the day he finally uncovered the truth. It was as if half his life had been revealed as one long lie.

"That's what we'd like to find out."

"What do you know?"

"Not as much as you"—Turnbull snorted—"given that you and dear old Uncle Harry were almost family."

"You'd be surprised," Tom said bitterly. "The Harry Renwick I knew was intelligent, funny, kind, and caring." Tom couldn't stop his voice from softening at the memory of Renwick in his tatty old white linen suit. Renwick, who'd never forgotten his birthday, not once. His own father had never managed that. "The Harry Renwick I knew was my friend."

"You were taken in then, just like everybody else? You never suspected the truth?" Turnbull sounded skeptical.

"Why are you asking me, if you already know the answers?" Tom snapped. "I don't want to talk about Harry Renwick."

"Talk to me about Cassius then," Turnbull pressed. "Tell me what you knew about him."

Tom took a deep breath and tried to calm himself.

"Everyone in the business knew Cassius. Knew *of* him, that is, because nobody had ever seen him. Or rather, not seen him and lived."

"He was a ruthless, murdering bastard, that's who he was," said Archie. "His crew had a crooked finger in every crooked scam going. Thefts, forgeries, grave robbing, smuggling—you name it. And if you didn't play along, well . . . I heard he once put a man's eyes out with a fountain pen for not authenticating a forged Pisanello drawing he was trying to shift."

"No one realized that all along Cassius was Uncle—was Renwick."

"Have you spoken to him since?"

Tom gave a short laugh. "Last time I saw him, he was trying to shoot me—right up until I severed his hand in a vault door. We're not exactly on speaking terms anymore."

"Yeah, I've read the FBI case file on what happened in Paris." Tom met his eye, surprised. "Believe it or not, we do occasionally share information with our American colleagues," Turnbull explained with a wry smile. "Especially now he's made their Most Wanted list."

"And what did the file say?"

"That, although a known thief, you cooperated with the U.S. government to help recover five priceless gold coins stolen from Fort Knox. And that during the course of that investigation, you helped unmask Renwick as Cassius and apprehend a rogue FBI agent."

"And Renwick? What did it say about him?"

"Not much more than what you've just told us. That's the problem. We've picked up on some rumors, but that's it. That his syndicate has disintegrated. That he's lost everything. That he's on the run."

"From you?"

"Us, Interpol, the Yanks—the usual suspects. But we're not the only ones."

"What do you mean?"

"We've intercepted messages from a group of people who seem to be trying to hunt Renwick down."

"The coded Personals ads in the *Tribune*?"

"You know about those?" Turnbull's surprise was evident.

"Only since yesterday. Any ideas on who's running them?"

"They're sent by post. Typed. Standard HP laser printer. Different country of origin each time. Could be anyone."

"Well, I don't care either way." Tom shrugged. "Whoever gets him first will be doing us all a favor. Good luck to them."

"Except that this isn't just about Renwick. Despite what the media might say, not all terrorists wave a Kalashnikov in one hand and a Koran in the other. Kristall Blade is a violent, fanatical sect bent on restoring the Third Reich, whatever the cost. Up till now they've remained in the shadows, carrying out deadly but mainly small-scale operations within a limited geographical area. Our sources tell us that this is about to change. They are looking to fund a massive expansion of their activities, in terms of personnel, size of target, and geographic reach. If Renwick's helping them to achieve their goal, we'll all pay the price."

"And what do you expect me to do about it?"

"We'd like your help. You know Renwick better than anyone, understand him and his methods and the world he operates in. We need to find out what he's working on with Hecht before it's too late. I suggest you start by looking at these hospital murders."

Tom laughed and shook his head. "Look, I'm sorry, but I investigate stolen art, not stolen arms. No one wants to see Renwick stopped more than I do, but I'm not getting involved. That life's behind me."

"Behind us both," Archie chimed in, thumping the seat next to him for emphasis.

"And how long before Renwick decides to come looking for you? How long before he decides it's time to settle old scores?"

"That's my problem, not yours," Tom said with finality. "And it's certainly not a good enough reason to do anything other than walk away from your mess without making it any worse. I don't trust you people. Never have. Never will."

There was a long pause, during which Turnbull stared at him stonily before turning to face the front again and letting out a long sigh.

"Take this, then." Turnbull held out a piece of paper, his arm bending back over his shoulder. It had a number scrawled on it. "In case you change your mind."

The car slowed to a halt and the door flashed open. Tom and Archie stepped blinking out onto the street. It took them a few seconds to realize that they were back at Archie's car. The clamp had been removed.

"So, what do you want to do?" asked Archie as he beeped the car open and slipped behind the wheel.

"Nothing, until we've checked him out," Tom said, settling back into the soft black leather passenger seat just as the engine snarled into life. "I want to know what he's really after."

CHAPTER TWELVE

January 5—1:22 P.M.

The room hadn't changed. It only seemed a little emptier without him, as if all the energy had been sucked out of it. The faded brown curtain that he'd refused to open fully, even in the summer, remained drawn. The dark green carpet still bristled with dog hair and ash. The awful 1950s writing desk had not moved from the bay window, while on the mantelpiece the three volcanic rocks that he'd picked up from the slopes of Mount Etna when on honeymoon with her mother many years before, radiated their usual warm glow.

As she crossed the room, Elena Weissman caught a glimpse of herself in the mirror and flinched. Although only forty-five, and a young forty-five at that, she knew the last week had aged her ten years. Her green eyes were puffy and red, her face flushed and tired; the lines across her forehead and around her eyes and mouth had deepened from shallow indentations to small valleys. Her black hair, usually well groomed, was a mess. For the first time since her teens she was wearing no makeup. She hated being this way.

"Here you go, my love." Sarah, her best friend, came back into the room with two mugs of tea.

"Thanks." Elena took a sip.

"These all need to be boxed up, do they?" Sarah asked, trying to sound cheerful, though her face betrayed her disgust at the state of the room.

Stacked up against the walls and fireplace and armchairs, and every other surface that would support them, were precarious towers of books and magazines—hardbacks and paperbacks and periodicals and pamphlets of various shapes and sizes and colors, some old with smooth leather spines stamped with faded gold letters, others new and bright with shiny dust jackets.

She remembered with a sad smile how the piles used to topple over, to an accompaniment of florid German curses. How her father would then try to stuff them into the overflowing bookcase that ran the length of the right-hand wall, only to admit defeat and arrange them into a fresh tower in a new location. A tower that would itself, in time, tumble to the floor as surely as if it had been built on sand.

Her grief took hold once again and she felt an arm placed around her shoulders.

"It's okay," Sarah said gently.

"I just can't believe he's dead. That he's really gone." Elena's shoulders shook as she sobbed.

"I know how hard it must be," came the comforting reply.

"No one deserves to die like that. After everything he'd been through, all that suffering." She looked into Sarah's eyes for support and found it.

"The world's gone mad," Sarah agreed. "To kill an innocent man in his bed and then . . ."

Her voice trailed off and Elena knew that she couldn't bring herself to repeat what she herself had told Sarah only a few days before, although it seemed a lifetime ago now. That her father, a frail old man, had been murdered. That his body had been butchered like a piece of meat. She still couldn't quite believe it herself.

"It's like a terrible nightmare," she murmured, more to herself than anyone.

"Maybe we should finish this another day," Sarah suggested gently.

"No." Elena took a deep breath and fought to bring herself under control. "It's got to be done at some stage. Besides, I need to keep busy. It keeps my mind off . . . things."

"I'll go and grab some boxes then, shall I? Why don't you start with the bookcase?"

Sarah went off in search of boxes as Elena, clearing a space in the middle of the room, began to empty the shelves onto the floor, sorting the books as she went along. Her father's taste had been eclectic, but the bulk of his library seemed to be devoted to his twin hobbies of ornithology and trains. There was a vast array of books on each subject, many of them in French or German, and she found herself wishing that she'd kept her languages up so that she would know what was the French for *bird* and the German for *railway*.

Together, they emptied the first set of shelves and were about halfway down the middle set when Elena noticed something strange. One of the books, a leather-bound volume with an indecipherable title in faded black letters, refused to move when she tried to grab it. At first she assumed that it must be glued there, no doubt the result of some careless accident years before. But once she had removed all the other books from the shelf, she could see that there was no sign of anything sticking it down.

She gave it a firm tug with both hands, but still it wouldn't come free. Exasperated now, she reached around behind the book and, to her surprise, felt a thin metal rod emerging from it and disappearing into the wall. Further inspection revealed that the pages, if any had ever existed, had been replaced by a solid block of what felt like wood.

She stepped back and stared at the book pensively. After a few seconds' hesitation, she stepped forward and with a deep breath, pressed gently against the book's spine. The book edged forward easily as if on some sort of track, and at the same time there was a click as the right-hand edge of the central bookcase shifted about half an inch. Hearing the scrape of wood, Sarah looked up from where she was kneeling on the floor.

"Found something, dear?"

Elena didn't reply. Grasping one of the shelves, she pulled

the bookcase toward her. It swung open noiselessly, skating just above the carpet, until it had folded back on itself.

"Oh my!" Sarah exclaimed breathlessly, struggling to her feet.

The bookcase had revealed a section of wall still covered in what looked like the original Victorian wallpaper, an ornate floral pattern painted over with thick brown varnish. In a few places the paper had fallen off, revealing the cracked and crumbling plaster beneath.

But Elena's eyes were fixed not on the wall but on the narrow green door set into it. On the hinges glistening with oil. Recently applied oil.

CHAPTER THIRTEEN

Large damp patches had formed around his armpits and across his back as he leaned forward on the long table and stared at the jet black conference phone that lay in the middle of it, a small red light on one side flashing steadily.

"What is it?" The voice that floated up from the phone was calm and cold.

"We've found him."

"Where? In Denmark, like we thought?"

"No, not Cassius."

"Who, then?"

"Him. The last one."

A pause.

"Are you sure?"

"Yes."

"Where."

"London. But we were too late. He's dead."

"How do you know?"

"I've seen the police report."

"And the body? Did you see the body?"

"No. But I've seen the photos taken at the autopsy and a copy of the dental records. They match."

A long silence.

"So," the voice eventually sighed, "it is over. He was the last."

"No, I'm afraid it's just the beginning." As he spoke, he spun the gold signet ring on his little finger. The ring's flat upper surface was engraved with a small grid of twelve squares, one of which had been set with a lone diamond.

"The beginning?" the voice laughed. "What are you talking about? Everything is safe now. He was the only one left who knew."

"He was murdered. Killed in his hospital bed."

"He deserved a far worse death for what he had done" was the unfeeling response.

"His arm was cut off."

"Cut off?" The question was spat into the room. "Who by?"

"Someone who knows."

"Impossible."

"Why else would they have taken it?"

Silence.

"I will have to call the others together."

"That's not all. British Intelligence is involved."

"I'll call the others. We must meet and discuss this."

"They're working with someone."

"Who? Cassius? We'll have caught up with him before he gets any further. He's been sniffing around this for years. He knows nothing. The same goes for all the others who've tried."

"No, not Cassius. Tom Kirk."

"Charles Kirk's son? The art thief?"

"Yes."

"Following in his father's footsteps? How touching."

"What do you want me to do?"

"Watch him. See where he goes, who he talks to."

"Do you think he could—"

"Never!" the voice cut him off. "Too much time has gone by. The trail is too cold. Even for him."

CHAPTER FOURTEEN

CLERKENWELL, LONDON

January 5—8:35 P.M.

Tom had never really been one for possessions before now. There had been no need, no point even, in owning anything: until recently he had rarely spent more than two weeks in the same place. He had accepted that this was the price for always having to stay one step ahead of the law.

It was not, in truth, a price that had cost him too dear, for he had never been a natural hoarder or acquirer of belongings. He had gotten into the game because he loved the thrill and because he was good at it, not so he could one day enjoy a comfortable retirement sipping cocktails in the Cayman Islands. He'd have done the job for free if money hadn't been the only way of keeping score.

He was, therefore, well aware of the significance of the few pieces he'd recently bought at auction and scattered throughout his apartment. He recognized them as a tangible sign that he had changed. That he was no longer just a packed suitcase away from skipping town at the slightest sign of trouble, a mercenary wandering wherever the winds of fortune blew him. He had a home now. Roots. Responsibilities even. To him, at least, the accumulation of "stuff" was a proxy for the first stirrings of the normality he had craved for so long.

The sitting room—a huge open-plan space with cast-iron struts holding up the partially glazed roof—had been simply furnished with sleek modern furniture crafted from brushed aluminum. The polished concrete floor was covered in a vibrant patchwork of multicolored nineteenth-century Turkish kilims, while the walls were sparsely hung with late Renaissance paintings, most of them Italian, each individually lit. Most striking was the gleaming steel thirteenth-century Mongol helmet that stood on a chest in the middle of the room, leering menacingly at anyone who stepped into its line of sight.

"Sorry I'm late," Dominique panted as she came through the door, hitching her embroidered skirt up with one hand and clutching her shoes in the other. "Went for a run and sort of forgot the time."

"Well, at least you're here," Tom said, turning away from the stove to face her, his face glowing from the heat.

"Oh no, Tom, he hasn't canceled again, has he?" she said. "Let me guess. He had a card game, or greyhound racing, or he got tickets to a fight?"

"Right first time," Tom said with a sigh. "At least he's consistent."

"I can't believe that you used to place your life in the hands of someone so unreliable," she said as she sat down at the breakfast bar that separated the kitchen area from the main sitting room and slipped her shoes on.

"Yeah, well, that's the thing. Archie never got the job wrong, not once. He might forget his own birthday, but he'd still be able to tell you the make and location of every alarm system in every museum from here to Hong Kong."

"You don't think it's all getting a bit out of control?"

Tom rinsed his hands under the tap as she finished rearranging her top.

"He's always been a gambler of one sort or another. It's in his nature. Besides, in many ways this is an improvement. At least now he's just playing for money. The stakes were much higher when we were both still in the game."

"If you ask me, the gambling's all an excuse anyway," she said, her eyes twinkling. "I think he just doesn't like your cooking."

Tom grinned and flicked water at her.

"Stop it." She laughed. "You'll ruin my mascara."

"You never wear makeup."

"I thought I might jump on the bike and go to a club after dinner. Lucas and some of his friends said they would be going out. Do you want to come?"

"No, thanks." He shrugged. "Not really in the mood."

"Are you okay?" she asked.

"Me? Fine. Why do you ask?"

"You just seem a bit down, that's all."

Tom hadn't mentioned the afternoon's detour with Turnbull. There was no reason to, and besides, he didn't really want to relive the whole Renwick discussion again. The wounds were still too fresh. Wounds that he clearly wasn't concealing particularly well.

"It's nothing."

"I just wondered whether it was because . . . well, you know, because it's today?"

Tom gave her a blank look. "What's today?"

"You know, his birthday."

"Whose birthday?"

"Your father's, Tom."

It took a few seconds for the words to register in Tom's brain.

"I'd forgotten." He could barely believe it himself, although part of him wondered whether, subconsciously, he'd deliberately blocked it out, like all those other things he'd blocked out from his childhood. It was easier that way. It made him feel less angry with the world.

There was a pause.

"You know, it might help if you sometimes spoke about him with me. With anyone."

"And say what?"

"I don't know. What you felt about him. What you liked. What annoyed you. Anything other than the big hole you're always trying to step around."

"You know what he did to me." Tom could feel the instinctive resentment building in his voice. "He blamed me for my mother's death. Blamed me, as if it was my fault she let me drive the car. I was thirteen, for God's sake. Everyone else accepted it was an accident, but not him. I got sent to America because he couldn't bear to see me around. He abandoned me when I needed him the most."

"And you hated him for it."

"That's not the point. The important thing is that I was prepared to try and start over. I really was. And you know what? It was working. We were just beginning to get to know each other again, to find our way back, to build something new. Then he died. I almost hate him more for that."

A long pause.

"You know he never forgave himself for what he did to you?" Dominique sounded awkward and her eyes flicked to the floor.

"What do you mean?"

"He talked about it a lot. It never left him. I think that's partly why he took me in. To try and make things right."

"Took you in? What are you talking about?" Tom said, frowning.

"The thing is, he never wanted to tell you, because he thought you might be jealous. And it was never like that. He was just trying to help me."

"Dom, what are you talking about? You're making no sense."

She took a deep breath before answering.

"I never knew either of my parents," she began, her normally confident voice strangely small and muted, her words rushed as if she was worried that if she paused, even for a second, she wouldn't be able to begin again. "All I remember is being passed from foster home to foster home as quickly as it took me to set fire to something or get into a fight. When I was seventeen I ran away. Spent a year living on the streets in Geneva. I was this close to the edge . . ."

Tom had always known that Dominique had a darker side. That she was a little wild. This, however, was totally unexpected.

"But those stories about your family, about studying fine art, about going to finishing school in Lausanne—you made that stuff up?"

"We all have our secrets," she said softly, her eyes locking with his. "Our own ways of blocking out the things we're trying to forget."

"Did my father know?" He picked up a knife and began to slice some vegetables distractedly.

"I first saw him at a taxi stand one night. I think he'd just been to the cinema. A re-release of *Citizen Kane* or something. I never expected him to see me. Normally the mark would be halfway home before they'd notice their wallet was gone. But not your father. He was so quick."

"You stole his wallet?" Tom hoped that his voice didn't betray the fact that he was not so much shocked as impressed.

"Tried to. But he caught me with my hand still inside his jacket. And the amazing thing was that, rather than call the police, he just told me to keep it."

"He did what?" Tom couldn't help smiling as he pictured the scene.

"He told me I could keep it. But if I wanted a fresh start in life, I should bring it back to him at his shop and he would help me. I stared at that damned wallet for four days, desperately wanting to open it and take the money, but knowing that, if I did, I might lose my one chance to get out. And then on the fifth day I went to see him. Just as he'd promised, he took me in. Gave me a job working in his shop, taught me everything I know. He never asked for anything in return. I wouldn't be here today without him."

For a few seconds Tom was silent. Dominique's confession certainly explained some of the contradictions in her character that he had never quite been able to put his finger on before. Less clear was his father's motivation in taking her in, or indeed his reasons for keeping it a secret. Every time Tom thought he was beginning to understand him, a new revelation seemed to draw yet another veil between them.

"He should have told me," Tom said, unconsciously gripping the knife he had been slicing the vegetables with until the tips of his fingers were white. "You both should."

"You're probably right," she said. "But he was worried about what you might say. I think we both were. I'm only telling you now because I think that today, of all days, you should know that, all the time he was with me, he was trying to make up for not being with you. He knew that he would never be able to forgive himself for what he had done. But he always hoped that, one day, you'd understand and not hate him so much."

There was a long silence, broken only by the hum of the refrigerator and the throb of the oven fan. Abruptly, Tom threw the knife down with a clatter.

"I think we should have a drink. A toast. To him. What do you think? There's a bottle of Grey Goose in the freezer."

"Good idea." She gave him a brave smile and swiped a finger across the corners of her eyes. Then, standing up, she crossed to the refrigerator. The door to the freezer compartment came open with a wet, smacking noise.

She gave a short, sharp scream.

Tom was across the room in an instant. She pointed into the freezer, the cold air swirling inside it like fog on a wet winter's morning. Tom could just about make out what she was pointing at.

An arm. A human arm. And it was holding a rolled-up canvas.

CHAPTER FIFTEEN

BLACK PINE MOUNTAINS, NEAR MALTA, IDAHO

January 5—2:09 P.M.

The large H-shaped farmhouse and its rambling assortment of outbuildings nestled in a wide clearing in the middle of the forest. A single dirt track, wide enough for one car, snaked its way over three miles back to the nearest blacktop. Here and there animal tracks materialized and then faded away again, hinting at life without ever fully confirming it, the forest's muffled silence broken only by the call of an occasional eagle knifing through the air far overhead before vanishing into the sun.

Bailey lay in the snow, hidden among the trees, the crisp blue vault of the sky just about visible through their dark, oily branches. He was already cold, and now he could feel the moisture seeping in through the knees of his supposedly waterproof trousers. Viggiano was lying on one side of him, a pair of binoculars glued to his face, with Sheriff Hennessy on the other.

"How many people did you say were in there?" asked Viggiano.

"Twenty to twenty-five," Bailey replied, shifting position to relieve the stiffness in his arms. "Each family's got their own bedroom in the side extensions. They all eat and hang out together in the main building."

"Goddamned cousin-fuckers," Viggiano muttered. Bailey sensed Hennessy shifting uneasily beside him.

Viggiano picked up his radio. "Okay, Vasquez—move in."

Two teams of seven men rose from their hiding places along Phase Line Yellow, their final position for cover and concealment, and emerged running in single file from the trees at opposite ends of the outer perimeter. Still in formation, they vaulted over the low wooden fence and passed Phase Line Green, the point of no return, rapidly moving in on the front and rear entrances to the main building. Once there, they crouched along the side walls to the left of each door.

Using his own set of binoculars, Bailey checked the farmhouse for signs of life from inside—a shadow or a twitching curtain or a hurriedly extinguished light—but detected nothing apart from a few flakes of white paint peeling from the window frames and fluttering in the wind.

Then he ran his binoculars along the two SWAT teams in their helmets, gas masks, and bulletproof vests. Against the whiteness of the snow they looked like large black beetles, the visors on their helmets winking in the afternoon sun. In addition to submachine guns and pistols, one man in each unit was also equipped with a large metal battering ram.

"Okay," came Vasquez's voice over the radio. "Still no sign of activity inside. Alpha team, stand by."

A voice amplified through a bullhorn rang out. "This is the FBI. You are surrounded. Come out with your hands up."

"I said to keep it low-key, Vasquez, you macho idiot," Viggiano muttered under his breath.

Silence from the farmstead.

Again the amplified voice blared out. "I repeat, this is the FBI. You have ten seconds to show yourselves."

Still nothing.

Viggiano's radio crackled. "Nothing doing, sir. It's your call."

"Make the breach," Viggiano ordered. "Now."

At each entrance the man with the battering ram stepped forward and slammed it into the lock. Both doors splintered on impact and flew open. A second man then lobbed a tear-gas canister through each open doorway. A few seconds later, the canisters exploded, sending dense, choking clouds of gas billowing out of the front and rear of the building.

"GO, GO, GO!" yelled Vasquez as the men disappeared into the house.

From their vantage point, Bailey could hear muffled shouting and the regular pop and fizz of further tear-gas grenades being let off, but nothing else. No screams. No crying children. Certainly not a gunshot. The seconds ticked by, then turned into minutes. This was going better than any of them had expected.

The radio crackled into life. "Sir, this is Vasquez . . . There's nobody here."

Viggiano pulled himself up into a crouching position and grabbed the radio. "Say again?"

"I said there's nobody here. The place is empty. We searched every room, including the attic. It's deserted and it looks like they left in a hurry. There's half-eaten food on the table. The whole fucking place stinks."

Bailey swapped a confused look with Viggiano and then with Hennessy, who looked genuinely concerned.

"There must be someone there, Vasquez. I'm coming down," Viggiano said.

"Negative, sir. Not until we've secured the whole area."

"I said, I'm coming down. You and your men stay put till I arrive. I want to see this for myself."

CHAPTER SIXTEEN

BLOOMSBURY, LONDON
January 5—9:29 P.M.

C offee?"
"I need a drink." Tom went to the decanter on the side table and poured himself a large glass of cognac. He took a mouthful, swilling it around before swallowing it, and then sat down heavily in one of the armchairs and glanced around him.

This was only the second time he'd been to Archie's place. It was a realization that brought home to Tom how little he knew about his partner—who he was, what his passions were, where his secrets lay—although he now saw that, after the evening's revelations, he could say the same of Dominique. Perhaps that said more about him than either of them.

Despite this, he was able to detect in the room itself some hints of Archie's character. Immediately apparent, for example, was his love of Art Deco, as evidenced by the Emile-Jacques Ruhlmann furniture and the various pieces of Marinot glassware that adorned the mantelpiece. And a collection of Edwardian gaming chips displayed in two framed cases on either side of the door betrayed his fascination with gambling.

More intriguing was the teak coffee table, which Tom immediately identified as a late nineteenth-century Chinese opium bed. The brass fittings around its edge would once have housed bamboo poles to support a silk canopy that preserved its occupant's anonymity.

"Sorry about your game," Tom said, his gaze returning to Archie as he settled into the chair opposite him.

"Don't worry." Archie dismissed the apology with a wave of his hand. "I was losing anyway. Is she all right?" He tilted his head in the direction of the closed bathroom door in the hallway.

"She'll be fine," Tom said. If what he had learned about Dominique's past had confirmed anything, it was her ability to tough it out.

"What the hell happened?"

Tom handed him the rolled-up canvas.

"What's this?"

"Take a look."

Archie unscrolled the painting on the coffee table. He looked up in surprise. "It's the Bellak from Prague." Tom nodded. "Where did you find it?" Archie ran his hands gently over the painting's cracked surface, his fingers brushing against the ridges in the oil paint, pausing over a series of small holes that punctured its surface.

"It was a gift. Somebody kindly left it in my freezer."

"In your what?" Archie wrinkled his forehead as if he hadn't heard properly.

"In my freezer. And it wasn't the only thing they left."

Archie shook his head. "I'm not sure I even want to know."

"There was a human arm in there too. In fact, come to think of it, it's still in there."

For once, Archie was speechless, his eyes bulging in disbelief. When he did manage to get a word out, it was in a strangled, almost angry voice.

"Turnbull."

"What?"

"It's that two-faced bastard Turnbull."

Tom laughed. "Come on, Archie. You said he checked out."

"He did. At least according to my contact. MI6, originally

on the Russian desk at GCHQ. But that doesn't mean he didn't do it. Think about it. He shows up wanting our help. We refuse, and a few hours later the missing forearm miraculously shows up amongst your frozen peas. It's a bloody setup. I expect he's round there now, waiting for you to get home so he can nick you."

"You're assuming the arm belongs to Turnbull's Auschwitz survivor."

"Too right. How many severed arms do you think there are floating around London?"

"Not many," Tom conceded.

"Well, there you are then."

Tom stood up and moved over to the window. Below, a couple of taxis rattled past, their gleaming black roofs flickering with pale orange flames each time they passed under a streetlight. On the other side of the street, sheltering behind thick iron railings, the somber façade of the British Museum peered through the night with patrician indifference, the granite lions flanking the main entrance standing permanent guard.

"I'm just saying that you shouldn't jump to conclusions," Tom continued. "Besides, there is another option . . ."

"Here we go," Archie muttered.

". . . whoever is behind the murder of that old man is also behind the theft of the painting."

"You think it's Renwick, don't you?"

"Why not? We know he's working with Kristall Blade, and we know they killed that man. Given that, thanks to me, he only has one hand, he of all people probably appreciated the irony of dropping off someone else's limb as his calling card."

"And the Bellak paintings?"

"Stolen by them at his request," Tom said with a shrug.

"Bellak?" Unnoticed by either of them, Dominique had emerged from the bathroom and slipped into the room. Her earlier shock had been replaced by a calm resolve, and there was something almost ethereal about her as she stood there, a slim silhouette framed by the open doorway. "The painter?"

Tom and Archie exchanged uncertain glances.

"You've heard of him?" Even Tom was impressed by this latest example of Dominique's ever-expanding mental database of the art market.

"Only by name."

"How come?"

"Because your father spent the last three years of his life looking for Bellak paintings."

"What?" Tom said disbelievingly.

"Don't you remember? It became quite a big thing for him. He had me scanning databases and newspaper files and auction listings to see if I could find anything. I never did. By the end, I think he had almost given up."

"That's where I'd heard the name before," Tom said, snapping his fingers in frustration at not having remembered this. "Now you mention it, I think he even asked me to see if I could come up with anything."

"But why on earth would he want to collect them?" Archie asked, disdainfully holding up the painting of the synagogue to prove his point.

"He wasn't collecting them," Dominique corrected him, sitting down cross-legged on the hearth rug. "He was looking for one in particular—a portrait of a girl. He said it was probably in a private collection somewhere. He said that it was the key."

"The key to what?" Archie asked.

"He never told me." Dominique sighed. "Remember what he was like with his secrets."

"Well, whatever it is, clearly Renwick knows," Tom said bitterly. "That's why he's put this here—to show me how close he is to finding it."

"Which is precisely why you shouldn't let him get to you," Archie said firmly. "He wants to get a reaction. We'll just dump the arm and pretend none of this ever happened."

"Never happened?" Dominique countered, her eyes shining defiantly. "You can't just ignore something like this, Archie. They killed someone—I heard you say so. They killed someone and we might be able to do something about it."

"That's not what I mean," Archie protested. "Look, I know Cassius. This is just another one of his sick games. It's too late to help the old man that arm belonged to, but we can still help ourselves. Tom? What are you doing?"

"Calling Turnbull," answered Tom, picking up the phone and extracting the slip of paper with Turnbull's number from his wallet.

"Didn't you hear what I just said?" pleaded Archie.

"I heard what you both said, and Dominique's right—we can't ignore this."

"He's playing with you. Let it go."

"I can't let it go, Archie," Tom snapped, before taking a deep breath and continuing in a gentler tone. "If you want to stay out of this, fine. But I can't. This involves my father. And if Renwick's after something my father spent years looking for, then I'm not just going to stand by and watch him get it first. I'm not having him make a fool of me. Not again."

CHAPTER SEVENTEEN

BLACK PINE MOUNTAINS, NEAR MALTA, IDAHO

January 5—2:19 P.M.

Viggiano and Bailey set off downhill through the trees as fast as they could, stumbling awkwardly as their legs disappeared into snowdrifts or their feet snagged on camouflaged undergrowth. Eventually they emerged, breathless, on the far right-hand side of the compound. Leaving fresh tracks in the snow, they both clambered over the wooden fence and made their way to the front entrance, where they were met by one of Vasquez's men, his mask and helmet discarded, his face blank.

"This way, sir."

He led them through an entrance hall piled high with sneakers and boots and old newspapers. Several pairs of antlers had been nailed to the wall, grimy baseball caps and odd socks hanging off them like makeshift Christmas decorations. Vasquez was waiting for them in the large kitchen. The long oak table was set for dinner, roaches scuttling across the worktops and over a joint of beef that had been left out, its sides bristling with fungus. The air was thick with flies and a heady smell that Bailey recognized only too well. The smell of rotting flesh.

Vasquez nodded toward a door. "We haven't checked the basement yet."

"The basement?" Viggiano frowned as he scrabbled to retrieve the plan of the compound from his jacket. He smoothed it out, borrowing tacks from an out-of-date NRA calendar to pin it to the wall. "Look—there is no basement."

"Then what do you call that?" Vasquez threw open the door to reveal a narrow staircase leading down into the darkness below, a blast of warm, noxious air rushing up to meet them.

Guided by Vasquez's flashlight, they negotiated the stairs. At the bottom was a narrow, unlit corridor. Vasquez lit their way with a series of green chemical flares that he cracked into life and threw to the ground at regular intervals.

Bailey felt himself beginning to sweat as they approached the end of the passage. The temperature was noticeably higher here than upstairs, the smell making his stomach turn. Vasquez signaled for them to wait as he entered a doorway. He reemerged, grim-faced, a few seconds later.

"I hope you guys skipped lunch."

Viggiano and Bailey stepped inside. A massive oil-fired boiler hugged the far wall, the heat radiating off its sides. The stench was unbearable, the buzzing of the flies so loud it sounded like the revving of a small engine. The center of the room was taken up by a large German shepherd, its tongue lolling out of the side of its mouth, its brown fur matted with blood and rippling with maggots. Next to it were two blood-soaked pit bulls and a scraggy-looking mongrel whose head had been almost blown off.

"Guess now we know why no one had seen the dogs," commented Vasquez drily.

He pointed his flashlight down at the floor near where they were standing. The gray concrete was peppered with brass shell casings, their shiny hides glinting like small eyes.

"M16 casings. Couple of mags' worth. They weren't taking any chances."

"But where is everyone?" Bailey asked. "Where have they gone?"

"Sir?" Another of Vasquez's men appeared in the doorway behind them. "We got something else."

They followed him back along the green flare-lit corridor into another, smaller room that was empty apart from a desk pushed up against one wall. Here the floor was covered not with dog carcasses and shell casings but with small heaps of discarded paper. Bailey knelt to pick up a printout. It was a list of flight times to Washington, DC.

He stood and made his way over to the far side of the room. Here, a large architectural drawing had been pinned to the wall, with various parts of the building circled in red. In the bottom left-hand corner was an inscription: *National Cryptologic Museum—Plans*; *Structural Drawings*; *Heating/Ventilation System—1993*. He pointed it out to the others.

"Looks like these were our guys."

"What's through there?" Viggiano pointed to a rusty metal door set into the facing wall.

Vasquez approached and shone his flashlight through a small glass inspection panel set into the door.

"We got 'em!" he exclaimed. "They're in here. This opens onto a second door, which opens into another room. Jesus, they're squashed in tight."

"Let me see." Viggiano peered in.

"Are they still alive?" Bailey asked.

"Yeah. One of them has just seen me."

He stepped back and Bailey took his turn at the window. "She's waving her arms," he said with a frown. "Like she wants us to leave."

"Let's get these doors open," Viggiano urged.

"Are you sure?" Bailey asked cautiously. "She sure doesn't look like she wants it opened."

"Screw what she wants," Viggiano fired back.

"Sir, I really think we should check it out first," Bailey insisted, sensing from the woman's desperate expression that she was trying to warn him of something. "There must be a reason they're signaling. Don't you think we should at least make contact and see what the hell they're doing in there?"

"It's pretty goddamned obvious what they're doing in there, Bailey. Some fucker locked them in. And the sooner we get them out, the sooner we all get a hot shower. Vasquez?"

With a shrug, Vasquez unbolted the first door and pulled

it open. But as he reached the door on the other side, a shout stopped him in his tracks.

"Look!" Bailey pointed his flashlight at the inspection window of the second door. It was almost entirely taken up by a scrap of white material on which a message had been hastily scrawled in what appeared to be black eyeliner.

You'll kill us all.

"What the hell . . . ?" Viggiano began, but he was interrupted as Vasquez began to cough loudly, his body doubling over with the effort.

"Gas," he gasped. "Get out . . . gas."

Bailey grabbed him by the shoulders and dragged him toward the exit, his last sight the woman's face pressed to the inspection panel, her eyes large and round and red. As he watched, she collapsed out of sight.

"Get everyone out of here," Bailey shouted, shoving a convulsing Viggiano back up the stairs, into the kitchen, out through the hall, and back outside. The rest of the SWAT team spilled out onto the snow ahead of them.

"What happened?" Sheriff Hennessy came running up as they emerged, his sweaty face creased with alarm.

"The place has been booby-trapped," Bailey said, panting, releasing Vasquez into the care of a team of paramedics, then bending to rest his hands on his knees as he caught his breath.

"Booby-trapped?" Hennessy looked in bewilderment at the farmhouse entrance. "How?"

"Some sort of gas. It must have been rigged to the door. They're all still inside. They're dying."

"They can't be," Hennessy cried out in an anguished voice, his desperate eyes wide with fear and confusion. "That was never the deal."

Bailey looked up, his exhaustion and revulsion momentarily forgotten. "That was never *what* deal, Sheriff?"

CHAPTER EIGHTEEN

The stump was bloody and raw, with strips of muscle, nerve fiber, and severed blood vessels hanging loose like wires, and the tip of the ulna peeking out from under the loose skin with a white smile.

"Well, the wounds are certainly consistent with the manner in which the victim's arm was removed . . ." Dr. Derrick O'Neal rotated the limb, examining it under a high-powered magnifying lens, the glare of the overhead halogen lamps making it appear waxy and fake, like something wrenched from a shop mannequin. "But the DNA tests will confirm whether it's his. We should have the results in a few hours."

He yawned, clearly still missing the warmth of the bed from which Turnbull had summoned him.

"It's remarkably well preserved. Where did you find it?" O'Neal asked, looking up. He had a large, misshapen nose speckled with odd hairs. A thick, wiry beard covered the lower half of his face, and his small green eyes sheltered behind a large pair of black-framed glasses that he kept balanced on his forehead, only to have them slip to the bridge of his nose whenever he leaned forward.

"In someone's freezer."

"That makes sense." He yawned again. "Strange thing to hang on to, though. Who did you say you worked for again?"

"I didn't, and it's better you don't know," Turnbull replied. "What can you tell me about this?" He pointed at the loose, pale flesh of the inner arm. A livid red rectangle showed where a patch of skin had been cut out.

O'Neal's glasses slid down his face again as he bent for a closer look. "What was there?"

"A tattoo."

"Strange shape. What sort of tattoo?"

"The sort you get in a concentration camp."

"Oh!"

Turnbull could see that this last piece of information had finally jolted O'Neal awake. "I need to know what it said."

O'Neal sucked air through his teeth. "Oh, that could be tricky. Very tricky. You see, it depends on the depth of the incision."

"In what way?"

"The skin is made up of several layers . . ." O'Neal reached for pen and paper to illustrate his point. "The epidermis, dermis, and hypodermis. Typically, the ink on a tattoo is injected under the epidermis into the top layer of the dermis. It's actually quite a delicate and skillful operation. It has to be deep enough to be permanent, but not too deep to scar the sensitive layers below."

"You think this was done delicately?" Turnbull asked with a hollow laugh.

"No," O'Neal conceded. "As far as I know, the Nazis employed two methods for tattooing. The first involved a metal plate with interchangeable needles attached to it. The plate was impressed into the flesh on the left side of the prisoners' chests and then dye was rubbed into the wound."

"And the second . . . ?"

"The second was even more crude. The tattoo was just carved into the flesh with pen and ink."

"So, hardly skillful?"

"Right," said O'Neal. "Which means that it will be deeper than usual. And, over time, the ink will have penetrated the deep dermis, maybe even the lymph cells, which could also assist us with recovery. But even so, if the people who have done this have cut right down into the hypodermis, it's unlikely we'll find anything."

"And have they?"

O'Neal examined the wound more closely.

"We might be lucky. Whoever's done this has used some sort of scalpel, and he's sliced the top layer clean off."

"So you might be able to get something back?"

"It's possible, yes. If the scarring is deep enough it will show up. But it's going to take time."

"Time is one thing you haven't got, Doctor. I was told you were the best forensic dermatologist in the country. I need you to work some magic on this one. Here's my number—call me as soon as you get something."

PART II

In war, truth is the first casualty.

AESCHYLUS

CHAPTER NINETEEN

A passing storm had left the sky bruised and the pavements slick and shiny. Turnbull was waiting for them outside number 52, a handsome Victorian redbrick house identical to all the others on the terrace. Standing up, he looked even larger than he had the previous day, a situation not helped by a cavernous dark blue overcoat whose heavy folds hung off his stomach like the awning of a Berber tent.

"Thanks for meeting me here," Turnbull said, holding out his hand. This time, Tom and Archie shook it, though Archie made no attempt to disguise his reluctance. Turnbull didn't seem to mind. "And for helping."

"We're not helping yet," said Tom firmly.

"Well, for turning in the arm, at least. You could have just got rid of it. Others would." Tom noted that he glanced at Archie as he said this.

"What are we doing here?" Archie demanded impatiently.

"Meeting Elena Weissman. The victim's daughter."

Turnbull opened the gate and they made their way up the path under the watchful gaze of the bearded face that had been carved into the keystone over the front door. There was no bell, just a solid brass knocker in the shape of a lion's head. Turnbull gave it a loud rap, and they waited patiently until they heard the sound of approaching footsteps and saw a shadow through the rippled glass panels.

The door opened to reveal a striking woman with jet-black hair, secured in a chignon by two lacquered red chopsticks, which matched her lipstick and nail polish. Tom put her age at forty, or thereabouts. She was wearing foundation that gave her skin a bronzed, healthy glow, although it couldn't fully disguise the dark circles under her sad green eyes that betrayed a lack of sleep. She was dressed very sharply though, a black cashmere cardigan worn over a white blouse and black silk trousers, her feet clad in what looked like a very expensive pair of Italian shoes.

"Yes?" She had an immediately arresting, even formidable presence, her voice strong, her manner ever so slightly superior. Tom found himself wondering what she did for a living.

"Miss Weissman? My name is Detective Inspector Turnbull. I'm with the Metropolitan Police." Turnbull flashed a badge which, Tom noticed, was different from the one he had shown them yesterday. No doubt he had a drawer full of badges to choose from, depending on the situation. "It's about your father . . ."

"Oh?" She looked surprised. "But I've already spoken to—"

"These are two colleagues of mine, Mr. Kirk and Mr. Connolly," Turnbull continued, speaking over her. "Can we come in?"

She hesitated for a moment, then stepped aside.

"Yes, of course."

The house smelled of wood polish and lemon-scented floor cleaner. Faint squares on the walls showed where pictures had hung until recently, their outlines preserved where they had shielded the aging wallpaper from forty-odd years of London pollution.

She showed them into what Tom assumed had once been the sitting room. It had been stripped, brass rings clinging forlornly to the curtain rail, a single naked lightbulb drooping from the yellowing ceiling. A sofa and two armchairs were covered in large white dustsheets, and several cardboard boxes stood in the far left-hand corner, their lids taped down.

"I apologize for the mess," she said, flicking the dustsheets onto the floor and indicating that they should sit. "But I've got to go back down to Bath. I run a property business down there, you see. I'm going to have to leave the place empty until all the legal and tax issues are sorted. I'm told it could be weeks before you even release the body." She flashed an accusing stare at Turnbull.

"These matters are always very difficult," he said gently, settling onto the sofa beside her while Tom and Archie sat on the two armchairs opposite. "I understand how very painful this must be, but we must balance the needs of the family with the need to find those responsible."

"Yes, yes of course." She nodded and swallowed hard.

Tom, with the benefit of a childhood spent in a country where the open display of human emotion was applauded, marveled at her uniquely English struggle to balance grief with the need to maintain dignity and self-control in front of strangers. Just for a second, he thought she would succumb and cry, but she was clearly a proud woman and the moment passed. She looked up again, her eyes glistening and defiant.

"What did you want to ask me?"

Turnbull took a deep breath. "Did your father ever talk about his time in Poland? In Auschwitz?"

She shook her head. "No. I tried to talk to him about it many times, to find out what happened, what it was like there. But he said he couldn't, that he had locked it away in a dark corner of his mind that he couldn't look into again. In a way, that told me all I needed to know."

"And the tattoo on his arm—his prisoner number—did he ever show you that?"

Again she shook her head. "I saw it, of course, now and again. But he seemed to be embarrassed by it and usually wore a long-sleeved shirt or pullover to cover it up. I've known other survivors who regarded their tattoos as a badge of suffering, something they were proud of showing, but my father wasn't like that. He was a very private man. He lost his entire family in that place. I think he just wanted to forget."

"I see," said Turnbull. "Was he religious?"

She shook her head. "No. People tried to bring him back into the Jewish community here, but he had no time for God. The war destroyed his faith in any force for good. Mine too, for that matter."

"And politics? Was he involved in any way? Jewish rights, for example?"

"No, absolutely not. All he was ever interested in was railways and birds."

There was a brief pause before Turnbull spoke again. "Miss Weissman, what I'm about to tell you may be difficult for you to hear."

"Oh?"

Turnbull, looking uncomfortable for the first time since Tom and Archie had met him, hesitated before speaking. "We have recovered your father's arm." He snatched a glance at Tom as he said this.

"Oh." Her reaction was one of relief, as if she'd been dreading a more traumatic revelation. "But that's a good thing, isn't it?"

"Yes . . . Except that his tattoo, his concentration camp number, had been . . . removed."

"Removed?" Now she did look shocked.

"Sliced off."

Her hand flew to her mouth in horror. Now that he was closer to her, Tom saw that her carefully painted nails were chipped and worn where she'd clearly been biting them.

"Oh, my God."

"However, by analyzing the scar tissue and pigment discoloration in some of the deeper skin layers," Turnbull continued quickly, as if the technical language would help lessen the impact of what he was saying, "our forensic experts were able to reconstitute his camp number."

He paused and she looked from him to Tom and Archie, then back at Turnbull.

"And . . . ?"

"Are you familiar with the coding system employed at

Auschwitz?" She shook her head silently. He gave a weak smile. "Neither was I, until this morning. It seems Auschwitz was the only camp to tattoo its prisoners systematically. This was made necessary by the sheer size of the place. The numbering system was divided into the regular series, where simple consecutive numbers were employed, and the AU, Z, EH, A and B series, which used a combination of letters and sequential numbers. The letters indicated where the prisoners were from, or ethnic groupings. *AU*, for example, signified Soviet prisoners of war—the original inmates of Auschwitz. *Z* stood for *Zigeuner*, the German word for gypsies. The numbers on Jewish prisoners mostly followed the regular unlettered series, although in many cases this was preceded by a triangle, until the A and B series took over from May 1944."

"Why are you telling me all this?" There was a slightly hysterical edge to her voice now. Tom sensed that this time she really was on the verge of breaking down.

"Because the number on your father's arm didn't follow any of the known Auschwitz numbering series."

"What?" Even her makeup couldn't disguise how white she had gone.

"It was a ten-digit number with no alphabetical or geometric prefix. Auschwitz numbers never rose to ten digits . . ." He paused. "You see, Miss Weissman, it is possible that your father was never actually in a concentration camp."

CHAPTER TWENTY

3:16 P.M.

They sat there in embarrassed silence as she rocked gently in her seat, hands covering her face, shoulders shaking. Tom gently laid his hand on her arm.

"Miss Weissman, I'm sorry."

"It's okay," she said, her voice muffled by her fingers. "I've almost been expecting something like this."

"What do you mean?" Turnbull leaned forward, his brow creased in curiosity.

She lowered her hands and they could see now that, far from the tears they'd been expecting, her face shone with a dark and terrifying anger. With rage.

"There's something I have to show you . . ."

She got up and led them out into the hall, her heels clip-clipping on the tiles.

"I haven't touched anything in here since I found it." Her voice was strangled as she paused outside the next door down. "I think part of me was hoping that one day I would come in and it would all just be gone as if it had never been here."

She opened the door and led them inside. Compared to the rest of the house, it was dark and smelled of pipe smoke and dust and dogs. Boxes of books were stacked in one corner of the room, their sides compressing and collapsing under the weight. At the other end, in front of the window, stood a desk, its empty drawers half-open and forming a small wooden staircase up to its stained and scratched surface.

She walked over to the window and pulled the curtain open. A thick cloud of dust billowed out from the heavy material and danced through the beams of sunlight that were struggling to get through the filthy panes.

"Miss Weissman . . ." Turnbull began. She ignored him.

"I found it by accident."

As she approached the bookcase, Tom saw that it was empty apart from one book. She pushed against the book's spine. With a click, the middle section of the bookcase edged forward slightly.

Tom sensed Archie stiffen next to him.

She tugged on the bookcase and it swung open to reveal a flaking green door set into the wall. She stepped forward and then paused, her hand on the door handle, flashing them a weak smile over her shoulder.

"It's funny, isn't it? You love someone all your life. You think you know them. And then you find out it's all been a lie." Her voice was flat and unfeeling. "You never knew them at all. And it makes you wonder about yourself. About who you really are. About whether all this"—she waved her arm around her—"is just some big joke."

Tom had to stop himself from nodding in agreement, for she had described, far more coherently than he'd ever managed, the way he'd felt when he unmasked Renwick. It wasn't just that he'd lost a friend and a mentor that day. He'd lost a good part of himself.

The door swung open and Tom gave a start as a featureless white face suddenly loomed out of the darkness. It took a moment for him to realize that it was a mannequin in full SS dress uniform. Behind it, on the far wall of what appeared to be a small chamber, a vast swastika flag had been pinned, the excess material fanning out across the floor like a sinister bridal train. The right-hand wall, meanwhile, was lined with metal shelving that groaned under the weight of a vast collection of guns, photographs, daggers, swords, identity cards, books, badges, leaflets, and armbands.

Turnbull gave a low whistle and Tom immediately wished he hadn't. The sound seemed strangely inappropriate.

"You never knew about this?" Tom asked.

She shook her head. "He would lock himself in his office for hours. I thought he was reading. But all the time he must have been in here."

"It's possible this was some sort of post-traumatic reaction," Tom suggested. "A morbid fascination brought about by what happened to him. Stress, shock . . . they make people do strange things."

"That's what I hoped and prayed too," she said. "Until I saw this—"

She reached past them and removed a photograph from the top shelf, then took it across to the window. Tom and Turnbull followed her. As she angled it to the light, the photo revealed three young men in SS uniform standing stiffly in front of a bookcase. They looked rather serious, even a little aloof.

"I've no idea who the other two are, but the man in the middle . . . the man in the middle is . . . is my father." Her voice was completely expressionless now.

"Your father? But he's wearing . . ." Tom trailed off at the pained expression on her face. "When was this taken?"

"In 1944, I think. There's something else written on the back, but I can't read it. I think it's Cyrillic."

"*December*—that's Russian for December," said Turnbull, peering over Tom's shoulder.

"Tom, we should take this . . ." Archie's voice came, slightly muffled, from inside the chamber. He appeared a moment later, carrying the mannequin's jacket and peaked hat.

"Why?" Turnbull asked.

"You ever seen anything like this before?" He pointed at the circular cap badge, which appeared to show a swastika with twelve arms rather than the usual four, each shaped like an SS lightning flash. "I know I haven't."

"You think Lasche can help?" Tom asked.

"If he'll see us," said Archie, sounding unhopeful.

"Who?" Turnbull butted in.

"Wolfgang Lasche," Tom explained. "He used to be one

of the biggest dealers in military memorabilia. Uniforms, guns, swords, flags, medals, planes, even whole ships."

"Used to be?"

"He's been a semi-recluse for years. Lives on the top floor of the Hotel Drei Könige in Zurich. He trained as a lawyer originally. Eventually made a name for himself pursuing German, Swiss, and even American companies for alleged involvement in war crimes."

"What sort of war crimes?"

"The usual—facilitating the Holocaust; helping finance the Nazi war effort; taking advantage of slave labor to turn a profit."

"And he was successful?"

"Very. He won hundreds of millions of dollars in compensation payments for Holocaust survivors. Then, rumor has it, he hit the jackpot. He uncovered a scam by one of the big Swiss banks to slowly appropriate unclaimed funds deposited by Holocaust victims and shred the evidence. It ran to tens of billions of dollars and went all the way to the top. So they bought him off. The Hotel Drei Könige belongs to the bank he investigated. He gets to live on the top floor and they pay him just to keep quiet."

"So his antiques dealership . . . ?"

"Part of the deal was that he got out of the Nazi blame game. With his contacts and backing, it was an easy switch. He's a major collector in his own right now. Nobody knows that market better than him."

"And he never goes out?"

"He's sick. Confined to a wheelchair with twenty-four-seven nursing care."

"And you think he might be able to identify that?" Turnbull indicated the jacket and cap.

"If anyone can, he can," said Tom.

"I could have forgiven him, you know . . ." While they had been talking, Elena Weissman had disappeared into the chamber. "I loved him so much. I could have forgiven him anything if he'd told me . . ." she sobbed as she reemerged.

Tom saw that she was clutching a Luger pistol in her right hand.

"Even this," she continued, her strained voice rising to a hysterical scream as she raised her eyes to the heavens. "You could have told me."

She lifted the gun to her mouth, the black barrel slipping between her lips, bright red lipstick smearing along it.

"No!" Tom leapt to knock the gun out of her hand before she could pull the trigger.

But he was too late. The back of her head exploded across the room, a fine mist of blood spraying in short bursts from the severed blood vessels as her body slumped to the floor.

CHAPTER TWENTY-ONE

Paul Viggiano fetched himself another cup of filter coffee from the machine. There was a tidemark in the glass jug where the coffee had evaporated since the last fresh pot had been made that morning. The remaining liquid looked dark and thick, like molasses. With scientific precision, he poured in one and a half servings of creamer, added one level teaspoon of sugar, then stirred it three times.

Satisfied with his handiwork, he turned to face Sheriff Hennessy and his attorney, Jeremiah Walton. A wiry, aggressive man with a thin face, hornbill nose, and sunken cheeks, Walton seemed unable to sit still on the molded plastic seats, forever shifting his weight from one bony buttock to the other. Bailey was sitting on the opposite side of a flimsy-looking table that had been screwed to the floor, staring at Hennessy with hostile intensity, his pen suspended motionlessly over a notepad. A tape recorder hummed gently to his right.

"Face it, Hennessy, it's over," Viggiano said, trying to sound calm but struggling to contain the excitement in his voice. Less than forty-eight hours ago he'd been wondering what he was doing with his life. Now here he was running a multiple homicide investigation. Funny how someone else's bad luck could be just the break you've been praying for. "Whatever little scam you've been running up there is finished now. So you might as well tell us what you know and make this a whole lot easier on yourself."

Hennessy stared at Viggiano stonily, dabbing himself every so often with a handkerchief that his sweat had turned from pale red to deep vermilion.

"My client wants to talk about immunity," Walton said in a high-pitched, nasal whine, pinching his right earlobe between finger and thumb as he spoke.

"Your client can go to hell," Viggiano snapped. "I got twenty-six corpses out there." He waved in what he assumed to be the direction of Malta, Idaho, although in the small windowless room it was difficult to be sure. "Women. Kids. Whole families. That's twenty-six people—dead. Immunity isn't even in the dictionary as far as your client is concerned." His fingers made quote marks in the air.

"You got nothing. Just one man's word against another." Walton glanced at Bailey. "A throwaway comment made in the heat of the moment that has been taken completely out of context. A pillar of the local community has seen his integrity questioned and his reputation dragged—"

"For an innocent man, he sure got you down here pretty damn quick," Viggiano interrupted.

"My client has a right—"

"Hell, maybe you're right," said Viggiano. "Maybe we don't have much. But we'll find it." He leaned across the table toward Hennessy. "You see, we're going to go through your bank records and high school reports and college files. We're gonna turn your life upside down and shake it real hard and have a good long look at everything that drops out. We're gonna go through that farmhouse that you claim you've never been to before with a ten-man forensic team that'll find out if you even so much as farted in its general direction in the last six months. Whatever we need, we'll find it."

Walton flashed a questioning glance at Hennessy, who raised his eyebrows in response and then gave a brief shrug, suggesting that they had planned for this outcome.

"Very well, then," Walton conceded, pinching his left earlobe now. "We want a deal."

"This is the biggest homicide investigation in Idaho since the Bear River Massacre in 1863," Bailey reminded him in a cold voice, his eyes never leaving Hennessy.

"The best deal he'll get is avoiding the Row," Viggiano added. "Accessory to multiple homicides before and after the fact. Criminal conspiracy. Armed robbery. Hell, by the time you get out, *if* you ever get out, the Jets might have won the Super Bowl again."

"And if he cooperates?" Walton whined, licking the corners of his mouth.

"If he cooperates, we won't push for the death sentence. And there may be the chance of parole down the line."

"A minimum-security facility?"

"We can do that," said Viggiano. "But we want everything— names, dates, locations."

"I want this in writing."

"You tell me what you got, then I'll tell you if it's enough. You know how it works."

Hennessy glanced at Walton, who bent toward him and whispered a few words in his ear. Hennessy straightened and nodded slowly. "Okay, I'll talk."

"Good." Viggiano pulled a chair away from the table and sat on it back to front. "Let's start with some names."

"I don't know his name," Hennessy began. "Not his real one, at least. Everyone just called him Blondi."

"This is the guy who you think did this?"

"Uh-huh."

"Where was he from?"

"Not sure. He approached us."

"Who's us?"

"The Sons of American Liberty."

"Now, Bill," Walton cautioned him, with a nervous twitch of his wrist, "let's not get into details."

"Why? I'm not ashamed," Hennessy said defiantly, before turning back to face Viggiano. "Yeah, I was one of them. Why the hell not? It's like I said before, they're patriots." He locked eyes with Bailey. "True Americans. Not a bunch of lazy, drug-dealing immigrants."

"Oh, they're patriots, all right," Bailey snapped angrily, his pen digging into the notebook and blotting the paper with a rapidly growing ink spot. "They're patriots who more or less executed a security guard up in Maryland."

"I didn't know anything about that," Hennessy said sullenly.

"Where was this Blondi from?" Viggiano continued.

"Europe."

"That's two hundred and fifty million people," Bailey observed drily.

"I'm telling you what I know," Hennessy hissed. "It's not my fault you don't like it."

"What did he want?" Viggiano again.

"He said that he wanted an Enigma machine. That he would pay us to get him one."

"How much?"

"Fifty thousand. Half up front, half on delivery."

"And you agreed?"

"Who wouldn't? That sort of money was big news for us. Besides, it wasn't the first time."

"Now, Bill," Walton cautioned.

"Blondi worked for someone else," Hennessy continued, ignoring the warning. "We never knew who and, to be honest, we didn't care. When he needed to get hold of something, we'd get it for him. He never asked how we'd got it or where it had come from, and he always paid in full and on time."

"Then what?" Viggiano pressed.

"He had all the plans and blueprints and everything. Three guys volunteered and they hit the museum. From what I hear, the whole thing went pretty smooth."

"Apart from the guard they lynched."

"I guess he got in the way." Hennessy shrugged. "Besides, one more or one less . . . Who gives a shit?"

"One more or one less what?" Bailey was on his feet, his pen spinning to the floor. "Go on, say it. One more or one less nigger, is that what you mean?" He clenched his fists so hard the tips of his fingernails went white. "Say the word. I dare you."

Hennessy smirked but seemingly had the good sense to say nothing.

"And then what happened?" Viggiano intervened again, laying a hand on Bailey's trembling shoulder and pressing him back down into his chair. "After they got the machine?"

"I don't know. I wasn't there."

"Yeah, let's talk about that for a second."

"Talk about what?"

"Talk about how come he managed to get everyone else into that room apart from you. Did you know what he was planning? Is that why you weren't there? Did you cut a deal to help lure them there? Did you help kill them?"

"Back off, Agent Viggiano." Walton sprang to Hennessy's defense, his long, bony finger wagging at him angrily. "There is no way that my client knew—"

"No," Hennessy's vehement denial interrupted him. "I was meant to be there, but there was a snowstorm that night and I couldn't get through." Viggiano glanced at Bailey, who confirmed this piece of information with a reluctant nod. Three inches of snow had fallen in town, so it would easily have been double that up in the mountains. "All I knew was that it was meant to be a straight swap. The cash for the machine. The first I heard about there being a problem was when you guys showed up saying that you were going to raid the place."

"So you're saying it's just dumb luck you're the only person who's met him who's still alive?" Bailey's tone was disbelieving.

"Hey, I never said I met him."

"But you said—"

"We never met. I only ever saw him twice, and each time I was on the other side of the compound. The boys were careful to keep me away from outsiders in case word got out that I was part of the group."

"You're lying," Bailey snapped.

"I'm not. These people were my friends. Some of them were just kids, for Chrissake. If I knew the son-of-a-bitch who'd done this, I'd tell you. I want you to find him."

"And how do you suggest we do that if everyone who has met him is dead?"

CHAPTER TWENTY-TWO

THE CAPTAIN KIDD, WAPPING HIGH STREET, LONDON

January 6—4:42 P.M.

Tom gazed through the window, his finger tapping absentmindedly against the table's pitted and cigarette-charred surface. Outside, the Thames slid past, slate gray and viscous from the cold.

"How are you feeling?" Archie sat down opposite him and handed him a pint of Guinness. Tom went to take a mouthful but pushed it away, untouched.

"That poor woman," he said, shaking his head.

"I know," Archie agreed. "Jesus, I can still see—"

"It was our fault, Archie. We should have broken it to her more gently. We should have known she might do something like that."

"No, it wasn't," Archie reassured him. "We didn't tell her anything she hadn't guessed already from seeing that photo. We had no way of knowing she'd do that."

"At least Turnbull dealt with the cops."

Turnbull had told them both to leave him to handle the police, perhaps not wanting to field too many awkward questions about why he'd brought two ex-criminals to a murder victim's house. To be honest, they'd been more than happy to accept his offer—anything to escape the Met's suspicious embrace.

"What do you make of him—Turnbull?"

Tom shrugged.

"Well, he clearly knows more than he's telling us. No surprise there. Spooks love their secrets. But, given that he's in their antiterrorist unit, it's clearly these Kristall Blade people he's really after. Renwick . . . that was just the bait to get us on board."

"Do you buy his story?" Archie reached for his cigarettes and lit one.

"About Weissman?" Tom pushed the ashtray across the table as a signal to Archie to keep the smoke away from him. "I guess so. A lot of people had secrets to hide at the end of the war. About things they'd done. About things they'd seen or heard. Posing as a concentration camp survivor would have been one way to escape and start a new life."

"Bit extreme, isn't it?"

"Depends what or whom he was escaping from. I'd say it was even more extreme to have to live the rest of your life as a lie. To fabricate an entire family history to back up your story. And all the while concealing the truth in that little room."

"And the tattoo?"

"Who knows? Maybe it's just a botched attempt to fake a concentration camp serial code. Maybe there's more to it than that. Somebody obviously thinks it was worth having. Hopefully Lasche will be able to explain some of this."

"Oh yeah, that reminds me," Archie said with a smile. "Hand me the uniform, will you?"

"What for?" asked Tom, reaching down and opening the bag at his side, hoping that no one would notice.

"I found something else in that room. Something I thought you'd want to keep Turnbull well away from." Archie took the jacket from Tom and reached into the inside pocket. His hand emerged clutching a faded brown envelope, from which he removed a dog-eared photograph. "Recognize this?"

He handed the photograph to Tom, who looked up, eyes wide with surprise.

"It's the Bellak from Prague—the synagogue. How . . . ?"

"That's not all," Archie continued triumphantly. "There are two more." He flicked the faded black-and-white photographs down on the table one on top of the other, as if he was dealing a hand of poker. "A castle somewhere . . . and look at this one—"

"It's the portrait." Tom breathed heavily, taking it from him. "The one my father was looking for. It must be."

"No oil painting, was she?" Archie grinned at his own joke.

"Is anything written on the back of them?" Tom asked, turning over the photograph he was holding.

"No, I already looked. But there is this . . ." On the reverse side of the envelope someone had written a return name and address in cramped italic script, the black ink now a dark brown, the white paper yellowed and frail. "Kitzbühel, Austria."

"Until we know exactly what Renwick wants with these paintings, let's keep this to ourselves. It's got nothing to do with Turnbull."

"Too bloody right," Archie agreed, then paused as if he had been on the point of saying something else and had thought better of it.

"What is it?" Tom inquired.

"It's just that, the more we find out, the uglier this gets. We should leave the whole mess for Turnbull to sort out. Stay out of it."

There was a long pause as Tom returned the items to the bag. Then he took his key ring from his pocket and placed it on the table between them.

"Do you know what that is?" he asked.

"Looks like a chess piece," Archie said with a shrug. "A rook. Made from ivory."

"It was a gift from my father, a few weeks before he died. It's one of the only things he ever gave me. I know it sounds strange, but I think of him every time my fingers rub against it in my pocket. It's like it's a tiny piece of him." He looked up and locked eyes with Archie. "Whatever Renwick's doing, it involves something my father was working on. Something that mattered to him. Another small piece of him. So I'm not going to just stand by and watch Renwick steal it like he's taken everything else from me. As far as I'm concerned, I'm already involved. I've always been involved."

CHAPTER TWENTY-THREE

HOTEL VIER JAHRESZEITEN KEMPINSKI, MUNICH,
GERMANY

January 7—3:07 P.M.

Harry Renwick walked into the hotel and up to the main reception desk. The concierge, steel-rimmed pince-nez teetering on his nose, looked up with tired eyes. Renwick noticed that the golden crossed keys he wore pinned to the lapel of his black suit coat had twisted around, suggesting he was approaching the end of a long shift.

"*Guten Abend, mein herr.*"

"*Guten Abend.* I am here for Herr Hecht."

"Ah, yes." He switched seamlessly to English. "I believe he is expecting you, Herr . . . ?"

"Smith."

"Smith, yes." He gave a distracted smile as he searched through the entries on the screen in front of him. "He is in the Bellevue Suite on the seventh floor. You'll find the lifts on the other side of the lounge. I'll ring ahead and let Herr Hecht know you are here."

"Thank you."

The concierge, his hand shaking a little from what Renwick guessed was tiredness, reached for the phone as

Renwick turned on his heel and walked toward the bank of elevators at the far end of the lobby.

Places like this disquieted him. Not because of any increased security risk; if anything, hotels offered a multiplicity of escape routes and the comfort of civilian cover. Rather, the hotel offended him aesthetically. It was, in his view, a Frankenstein creation, the bastard child of a monstrous marriage between an idealized vision of a British colonial club and the uncompromising functionality and ugliness of an airport executive lounge.

Although the lobby was luxurious, it was in an impersonal, mass-market sort of way. The dark wooden paneling was laminate, millimeters thin. The carpet was bland and soulless and industrial. Reproduction antiques had been "casually" scattered. The mahogany-effect furniture was squat and square, lacking any delicacy or subtlety, the chairs upholstered with a coordinated palette of indifferent reds and golds and browns. Its very inoffensiveness offended him. Even the elevator music, it seemed, had been sanitized, with complex orchestral pieces reduced to a syrupy flute solo.

A sign on the seventh floor pointed him toward the Bellevue Suite. Renwick knocked, and a few moments later Hecht opened the door. Renwick stared at him, unable to tell whether his toothy grimace was a genuine smile or a byproduct of his scar. Hecht held out his right hand, but Renwick offered his left instead, still not able to bring himself to let others feel his prosthetic hand's unnatural hardness. Hecht swapped sides with an apologetic nod.

The suite, although large, replicated most of the lobby's failings. The ceiling was low and oppressive, the furniture thick and ungainly, the curtains and cushions and carpets all in varying shades of brown, the walls red. Hecht led Renwick through to the sitting room and waved him to a beige sofa, then sat down heavily on the one opposite. This time he smiled, Renwick was sure of it.

"Drink?"

Renwick shook his head. "Where is Dmitri?"

"He is here."

Renwick got to his feet and looked around him. The room was empty. "We agreed—no games, Johann."

"Calm yourself, Cassius."

The voice came from a speakerphone that Renwick had not noticed until now. It had been placed in the middle of the white marble-effect table between the sofas. The accent was a mixture of American vowels and clipped German consonants, no doubt the product of some expensive East Coast postgrad program.

"Dmitri?" he asked uncertainly.

"I apologize for the rather melodramatic circumstances. Please do not blame Colonel Hecht. He was adamant that we should meet in person, but unfortunately it is very difficult for me to travel unobserved."

"What is this? How do I even know it is you?" Renwick, suspicious, had remained standing.

"We are partners now. You must trust me."

"Trusting people do not live long in my business."

"You have my word of honor, then."

"The difference being . . . ?"

"The difference being nothing to a businessman like yourself, but everything to soldiers like Johann and me. To a soldier, honor and loyalty count above all else."

"A soldier?" Renwick gave a half-smile. "In whose army?"

"An army fighting a war that has never ended. A war to protect our Fatherland from the hordes of Jews and immigrants who daily defile our soil and desecrate the purity of our blood." As Dmitri's voice grew in intensity, Hecht nodded fervently. "A war to remove the shackles of Zionist propaganda, which for too long has choked the silent majority of the German nation with guilt, when it is *we*, the true Germans, who suffered and died for our country. When it is we who continue to suffer, and yet are condemned to silence by the lies of the Jewish-controlled press and the undeserved power of their financial and political institutions." Dmitri paused as if to compose himself, then continued. "But the tide is turning in our favor. Our supporters are no longer ashamed to show where their loyalties lie. In the cities and the towns and the villages they march for us once more. They fight for us. They vote for us. We are everywhere."

Renwick shrugged. The speech sounded rehearsed and left him unmoved. "Your beliefs are no concern of mine."

There was a pause and when Dmitri next spoke his voice was almost gentle. "Tell me, what do you believe in, Cassius?"

"I believe in me."

Dmitri laughed. "An idealist, then?"

Renwick sat down again. "A realist, certainly. I think I will have that drink now." He turned to Hecht. "Scotch."

"Excellent," the speakerphone chuckled as Hecht raised himself to his feet and shuffled over to the liquor cabinet. "Let's get down to business."

Hecht returned with Renwick's drink and then sat down again.

"Your war is no concern of mine," said Renwick. "But what I have to tell you will give you the means to win it."

"I have here in front of me the little toy that you gave to Colonel Hecht in Copenhagen. Most amusing. He mentioned a train. A gold train?"

"There is more to this than gold," said Renwick. "Much more."

CHAPTER TWENTY-FOUR

HOTEL DREI KÖNIGE, ZURICH, SWITZERLAND
January 7—3:07 P.M.

The hotel, lovingly crafted from the careful blending of four or five separate medieval town houses, had a timeless, almost rustic quality that gave it a feeling of permanence and history that even the incongruously fresh mortar couldn't erode.

The interior, however, could not have been more of a contrast. Here, only the faintest traces of the original building survived in a few rough stone walls and oak beams that had been left exposed. The rest was uncompromisingly modern: the floor a shiny gray marble, the walls white, the furniture black, recessed halogen lights washing everything with a bleaching glare. Most impressively, a huge glass-and-steel staircase and elevator had been inserted through the center of the building like some shiny medical implant.

Tom, gripping a large brown leather carryall, walked up to the semicircular walnut reception desk. The attractively fresh-faced girl behind it smiled a welcome.

"I'd like to see Herr Lasche, please."

Her smile vanished as quickly as it had materialized. "We have no guest here by that name."

"I have something for him." He deposited the bag on the desk.

"I'm sorry, but—"

"Believe me, he'll want to see this. And give him my card."

He slipped one of his business cards across the desk. Tom had to admit that after years of striving never to alert the authorities to his existence, there was something rather therapeutic about advertising himself in such a public way. The design was simple: just his name across the center together with his contact details. His one extravagance had been to have the reverse printed in a deep vermilion, with the firm's name, Kirk Duval, in white. It was only later, when Dominique commented on the similarity to his father's business cards, that he realized he had chosen exactly the same color scheme. The receptionist shook her head. Then, still holding his gaze, she reached under the counter and pressed a button. Almost immediately a burly man wearing a black turtleneck and jeans appeared from the room behind her.

"Ja?"

Tom repeated what he had just said to the girl. The man's face remained impassive as he opened the bag and unzipped it, feeling gingerly around inside. Satisfied that it contained nothing dangerous, he jerked his head toward an opening in the wall.

"Wait in there."

Tom stepped into what turned out to be the bar. It was empty apart from the barman, who stood in front of a wall of bottles, polishing glasses. The remaining walls were covered with a soft reddish leather to match the stool and bench upholstery and, together with the dimmed lighting, combined to give the room a relaxed, almost soporific feel. No sooner had Tom sat down than two men entered and seated themselves opposite him. Neither said a word as they both fixed him with a disconcertingly steady gaze, as if it were a blinking contest. A few minutes later, the receptionist beckoned him back through to the lobby. The two men followed close behind.

"Herr Lasche will see you now, Mr. Kirk. If you don't mind, Karl will search you before you go up."

Tom nodded, knowing he had little choice.

The first guard approached Tom with a black handheld scanner that he passed over his body, pausing only when it bleeped as it went over his wrist. Tom lifted his sleeve to reveal his watch, a stainless steel Rolex Prince that he wore whenever he traveled abroad. The guard insisted that he hand it over for closer inspection. Tom winced as the man grasped its fragile winder in his thick hands and roughly turned it a few times to check that it worked. Satisfied, he returned it to Tom and escorted him to the elevator.

Tom stepped inside but, rather than follow him, the guard simply leaned in, waved a card across a white panel, and then stepped back. Tom's last sight before the doors closed and the elevator started up, was of the three men standing in the lobby staring at him, arms folded with menacing intent.

The door opened into a large room where the décor left Lasche's interests in little doubt. Three windows ran along the left-hand wall, but their shutters were closed, narrow fingers of light seeping through the slats. In between, ornate arrangements of antique swords, pistols, and rifles radiated like steel flowers, the polished metal glinting fiercely.

Looking up, Tom saw that the ceiling had been removed, allowing the room to extend right up into the attic space. Overhead, naked joists were exposed like the ribs of a wrecked ship. And from each joist a regimental flag had been suspended, the once bright colors now sun-bleached and battle-worn, even bloodstained in a few places. Along the right-hand wall, brass helmets were displayed in glass cases, their polished domes adorned with a mixture of eagle feathers, bear fur, and horsehair. Beneath them, a second tier of cabinets was crammed with artifacts—guns, bullets, medals, cap badges, ceremonial daggers, bayonets. Even the desk had been assembled from an uncompromising slab of black granite supported by four huge brass shell casings.

But Tom's attention was immediately grabbed by a massive bronze cannon that sat parallel to the desk on two thick oak plinths. He stepped closer to study the strange characters that encircled its girth. In the room's dimmed light, the cannon's tarnished hulk glowed with a dark menace that was at once terrifying and utterly compelling. He found himself unable to resist stroking its smooth flanks, the metal tight and warm like a racehorse who had just come off the track.

"Beautiful, isn't she?"

The sound of Lasche's voice made Tom jump. A door had opened to the right of the desk to admit a man in a wheelchair, closely followed by what appeared to be a male nurse, his white coat worn open over a shiny gray suit, his blond hair clipped short. He was eyeing Tom sourly, gripping the brown bag in one hand.

Lasche himself was almost bald, the few remaining wispy hairs scraped back across his scalp, which was pink and covered with liver spots. The skin hung off his face like an oversized glove and seemed thin and papery, the red capillaries beneath the surface lending a faint thread of color to his unhealthy yellow sheen. His gray, misty eyes peered at Tom through thick steel-framed glasses. Tom thought he detected a few crumbs from an interrupted snack on his lapel.

"It's a sister to the cannons the British melted down in order to provide the metal for the Victoria Cross," Lasche continued in a German accent that seemed almost comically thick, although frail and weak compared to the robust whirring of the wheelchair's electric motor as he drew near. Strapped to the undercarriage and back of the wheelchair were a variety of gas bottles and small black boxes from which ran wires and tubes that disappeared into the front of his pajamas and the sleeves of his brown silk dressing gown.

"I was hoping to sell this one to the British government when they ran out of metal . . ." He spoke haltingly, drawing breath with a deep, rasping, asthmatic rattle between sentences. "Unfortunately for me, however, their stock at the Central Ordnance Depot in Donnington remains unexhausted. It seems that British heroism has been in short supply recently."

The wheelchair jerked to a halt a few feet from Tom, and Lasche smiled at his own joke. His lips were blue and veiny, his teeth yellow and worn. An oxygen mask hung limply around his neck like a loose scarf.

"So it's Chinese?" Tom asked.

Lasche nodded laboriously. "You know your history, Mr. Kirk," he said, obviously impressed. "Most people think the metal used to make the Victoria Cross came from Russian cannons captured at the battle of Sebastopol in the Crimean War. But, yes, in fact it came from Chinese weapons. Apparently, the man sent to retrieve them confused Cyrillic with Mandarin. The sort of clerical error that is all too common in the military. Unusually, though, this one did not cost any lives. Still, I don't suppose that's why you're here . . . ?"

"No, Herr Lasche."

"I don't normally receive visitors. But, given your reputation, I thought I would make an exception."

"My reputation?"

"I know who you are. Difficult to be in my business and not to know of you. Not to have heard of Felix, at least." Felix was the name that Tom had been given when he first got into the art-theft game. Once a shield to hide behind, it sat uneasily with him now, reminding him of a past life and a past self that he was trying to escape. "I'd heard you'd retired."

Lasche began to cough, and the nurse, who had been following the exchange with mounting concern, leapt forward and slipped the oxygen mask over his face. Slowly, the coughing subsided and he signaled at Tom to continue.

"I have retired. But I'm looking into something that I wanted your help with."

Lasche shook his head. When he spoke, his voice was muffled by the mask. "You're referring to the bag you sent up? I haven't opened it. Like you, I'm also retired."

"Please, Herr Lasche."

"Herr Lasche is unable to help," the nurse intoned protectively.

"Just take a look," Tom appealed, ignoring the nurse. "It will interest you."

Lasche's large gray eyes considered Tom for a few moments, and then he summoned the nurse forward, his raised arm shaking with the effort. The nurse handed the bag to Tom, fixing him with an accusing stare. Tom drew back the zipper and removed the jacket. The jet-black material was rough against his hands and seemed to radiate a sinister, malevolent presence.

Lasche put the wheelchair in reverse and navigated his way to the far side of his desk, then indicated that Tom should hand the jacket to him. He pulled the oxygen mask away from his face and looked up. For a second, Tom saw in his eyes the man he had once been, strong and determined and healthy, not the shriveled shell he had become.

"The light, please, Heinrich," he muttered to the nurse, who turned on the desk lamp. The lamp shade consisted of six leather panels sewn together with thick black thread and decorated with flowers, small animals, and even a large dragon. It cast a sickly yellow glow across the granite surface. Tom shuddered as it dawned on him that the "leather" was in fact human skin.

"A lone survivor from the extensive private collection of Ilse Koch, wife of the former camp commandant at Buchenwald," Lasche said softly, noticing Tom's reaction. "I'm told she had a handbag made from the same material."

"But why keep it? It's . . . grotesque," said Tom, struggling for a word equal to the horror of the lamp, his eyes transfixed by it as the light revealed a spider's web of red capillaries still trapped within the skin.

"War produces great beauty and great ugliness." Lasche pointed first at the cannon, then the lamp shade as he said this. "And people pay handsomely for both. I keep this here to remind me of that."

He turned his attention to the jacket, his hands shaking as he held it, although it was hard to know if this was from anticipation or old age.

"It's obviously an SS uniform," he said between strained breaths, pointing at the distinctive silver double lightning bolts on the right-hand collar badge. "And its owner was probably German, since in theory only Germans were allowed to wear the Siegrunen. And you see the national eagle and swastika worn high on the left sleeve? Only the SS did this. Every other fighting service wore it on the left breast. The uniform is based on the M1943 design, but from the

fabric and quality I'd say it was tailor-made rather than produced by the SS-Bekleidungswerke, which is strange . . ."

Tom tilted his head at the unfamiliar word.

"The SS clothing works," Lasche explained. "Tailoring
was common for senior officers, but not for an *Unterschar-
führer*." He pointed at the left-hand collar badge, a single
silver pip on a black background.

"A what?"

"It's the owner's rank. I suppose it would translate as corporal. So either this particular officer was very rich or . . ."

Lasche had just caught sight of the cuff title, a thin strip
of black material embroidered with gold that had been sewn
to the left-hand sleeve just below the elbow. The sight seemed
to trigger a hacking cough and a frenzied gasping for breath
that had the nurse behind him pressing the oxygen mask to
his face and feverishly adjusting taps on the gas bottles until
he was able to speak again.

"Where did you get this?" he croaked, waving the nurse
away.

"London. Why?"

"Why? Why? Because, Mr. Kirk, this jacket belonged to a
member of Der Totenkopfsorden. The Order of the Death's
Head."

CHAPTER TWENTY-FIVE

"The Order of the Death's Head?" The voice from the speakerphone sounded skeptical. "Never heard of it."

"Not many people have." Renwick got up and began to pace back and forth behind the sofa as he spoke. Hecht observed him with a detached leer. "It has taken me years to piece together the little that I know. But it existed, I promise you that."

"I know every regiment, every division, every company that the Third Reich ever formed. And I have never heard of this so-called Order," Hecht said dismissively.

"Let him speak, Colonel," Dmitri snapped. Hecht shrugged, heaving his booted feet up on the coffee table and settling back into his seat.

"As you know, Heinrich Himmler turned the SS into the most powerful force within the Reich, a state within a state, its tentacles reaching into almost every facet of German life and influencing agricultural, racial, scientific, and health policies."

"It was a marvel," Dmitri agreed. "The pride of the Fatherland. In charge of the police, the secret service, and the death camps, as well as running its own businesses and factories."

"Not to mention controlling an army of nine hundred thousand men at its peak," Hecht added enthusiastically.

"Right from the start, Himmler realized that loyalty could more easily be bought by ensuring that people felt they were part of something special. So everything about the SS, from the black uniforms to the runic symbols and badges, was designed to enhance their mystique and elite status. And it worked. Almost too well . . ."

"How can it have worked too well?" asked Hecht, frowning.

"Because with increasing power came the need for the SS to expand. It was forced to recruit in such numbers that there was no choice but to draw from a wider and less exclusive pool of applicants than had originally been the case."

"Which threatened its integrity and exclusivity," Dmitri said thoughtfully.

"Exactly. So Himmler began to look to romanticized history and pagan ritual to unite the disparate groups that made up the SS. He longed for a return to a more feudal age, a time of myth and legend and chivalric ideals. He was particularly obsessed with King Arthur and the story of how he gathered his twelve bravest and most noble knights at a round table to defend the Celtic way of life. Inspired by this story, he chose twelve men, all of Obergruppenführer rank, to be his knights. These twelve were to stand for everything that was best about the Aryan nation and the SS brotherhood."

"How is it I have never heard of this?" The voice from the speakerphone was laced with skepticism.

"The existence of the Order was unknown even to the Führer himself. They wore no outward badge or sign that they belonged to the SS's most exclusive club—except when they were together. For their secret meetings, they swapped their normal uniforms for ones that declared their status."

"In what way?"

"Standard SS uniforms display the regimental title on their cuff."

"Of course"—Hecht dropped his feet to the floor and sat

forward—"*Liebstandarte Adolf Hitler; Das Reich, Theodor Eicke.* These are names that have gone down in history."

"The Order was no different, except they used gold rather than silver thread."

"Why has this never come out before?" Hecht asked, his impatience clear.

"Because every single member of the Order vanished in early 1945, and with them their secret. Some say that they escaped abroad. Others that they died defending Berlin. But I believe that they lived . . . Or, at least, they lived long enough to carry out one last order."

"Which was?"

"To protect a train."

CHAPTER TWENTY-SIX

The season was in full swing and Kitzbühel's snow-laden streets were buzzing with people. The skiers were beginning to make their way off the slopes, squeezing themselves onto sweaty buses or clomping noisily along the treacherously icy roads in their unfastened boots, skis precariously balanced on one shoulder. The nonskiers were emerging from long, late lunches and steeling themselves for the heavy dinner that lay ahead, the women, especially, dressed in billowing curtains of fur. A few dogs danced through the legs of the café chairs lining the pavements, or in between the expensive SUVs that purred effortlessly along the narrow streets, their owners fruitlessly calling them to heel.

Archie picked his way through the traffic, one eye on his map and the other making sure he didn't knock anyone over. Luckily, the house he was searching for was conveniently located on a large plot only a short way from the town center, and he pulled into the drive with relief.

The house looked better cared for than its overgrown garden; the walls had been painted a bright yellow, and the wooden cladding that surrounded the upper story looked to have been recently replaced and treated. To the left, a makeshift carport constructed of rough timber and plastic sheeting was sagging under a fresh blanket of snow.

The front door was to the right of the main building, up some steps and under a separate covered porch. Archie rang the bell. There was no reply.

He stepped back from the porch and looked up at the house with a pained sigh. It was bad enough being abroad, he thought, but it would be worse still if this turned out to be a wasted trip.

He stepped forward and rang again. This time the door opened almost immediately, taking him by surprise.

"*Ja?*" It was a woman, about thirty years old, her hair tied up in a blue polka-dot scarf, her hands sheathed in bright yellow rubber gloves. She was wearing tennis shoes and a baggy tracksuit. In the hall behind her he could just about make out the shape of a kid's tricycle and a football.

"*Guten Tag,*" Archie said haltingly.

Unlike Tom and Dominique, Archie had a vocabulary extending little beyond hello and good-bye in any language other than French, and the latter only because he had mastered the principal phrases used in Baccarat.

"I'm looking for Mr. Lammers—Herr Manfred Lammers," he said, reading from the back of the envelope he had found at Weissman's house. Fearing that his pronunciation might be more hindrance than help, he held out the envelope so she could read the name for herself. She studied the handwritten name and address, then looked up at him with a sad expression on her face.

"I'm sorry," she replied with a thick accent, "but Herr Lammers is dead. Three years ago."

"Oh." His face fell. Back to square one.

"Can I help? I am his niece, Maria Lammers."

"I don't think so," Archie said with a resigned shrug. "Not unless you recognize these." He handed her the three photographs. "Your uncle sent them to someone in England. I was hoping to find out where the original paintings were."

She took the photographs and leafed through them, shaking her head. "*Nein* . . . no, sorry. I have never . . ." As she came to the last picture, she paused midsentence.

"What?"

"This one"—she held up the photograph showing a painting of a castle—"this I have seen before."

"Where?" Archie stepped forward eagerly. "Do you have it here?"

"No."

"Can you show it to me?"

A pause as she weighed her answer. "You have come from England to see this?"

"Yes, yes, from England."

She slowly peeled off her rubber gloves and then pulled the scarf off her head. Her hair, dyed a vivid henna, fell around her face in a scruffy bob.

"Come."

She grabbed a coat off the back of the door, tugged it on, and led him down the drive and back out onto the street. Turning left, she cut through a small park where children were hurling snowballs at each other. Quickly leaving their laughter and screams behind, they passed under a large arch and down a hill, Archie treading carefully to avoid patches of ice that remained unsanded. Along the way, Maria passed several people she knew, greeting them with a wave as they looked Archie up and down, obviously curious as to who he was.

Eventually they came to a steep staircase cut into a buttressed wall that led up to the main parish church, its snow-covered gothic steeple towering above the surrounding roofs.

Despite the church's rather drab external appearance, its interior had clearly benefited from a Baroque renovation at some stage in the eighteen hundreds and was, as a consequence, surprisingly ornate and bright. Everything of value appeared to have been gilded, from the picture frames that lined both walls, to the icons benevolently peering down from their elevated vantage points on each of the four central pillars, and the intricately decorated altarpieces that flanked each side of the chancel. The apse, meanwhile, was dominated by an enormous black and gold-leaf reredos, that reached almost to the top of the high, ribbed ceiling.

"Kommen Sie."

She led him down the nave to the marble-floored chancel and then turned right into the side chapel.

"You see?"

The light outside was fading fast, and Archie peered into the gloom in confusion. Although the ceiling had been decorated attractively enough with painted plaster moldings, there was nothing else there apart from a rather gaudy icon of the Virgin and Child mounted high up on the left wall, and a massive marble font.

But then, instinctively almost, he looked up to the stained-glass window overhead.

CHAPTER TWENTY-SEVEN

S o there were twelve members of the Order?" Tom asked.
"Yes. Like the Knights of the Round Table. Himmler
himself selected them, not only for their Aryan looks and
racially pure bloodlines, but also for their total loyalty to
him. They were his own Praetorian Guard."

"But you said that the twelve knights were all Obergruppenführer rank and above. Yet that uniform belonged to a
corporal. How can that be?"

"I'm not sure." Lasche shook his head. "As far as I know,
no one outside the Order has ever seen one of these uniforms before. It's possible that in some act of ritual humility
they all assumed lowly rank to emphasize their brotherhood
and unity."

"Or maybe, if they were knights, they had retainers?
Someone to assist them in the performance of their duties,"
Tom speculated.

"Yes. Yes, that is also a possibility."

"It would certainly explain why someone so young got to
wear such a coveted uniform."

"Who?"

"The man this uniform belonged to. He died ten days ago.

He was in his eighties. There was a photo, taken in 1944, of him wearing the uniform. That would have made him about twenty at the time."

"What was his name?"

"Weissman. Andreas Weissman." Tom saw the surprised look on Lasche's face. "It's a Jewish name, I know. He adopted an alias in order to escape after the war. Passed himself off as a concentration camp survivor—even tattooed a fake camp number on his arm. We don't know his real name."

"You know, many members of the SS had their blood type tattooed on their left underarm, twenty centimeters up from the elbow. It was done so that field medics might quickly determine a wounded man's blood type. After the war, Allied investigators used the blood group tattoo to identify potential war criminals. Many SS members burned or disfigured their underarm to avoid capture."

"Or perhaps tattooed another number over the top to disguise it . . . ?" Tom mused, recalling the difficulty Turnbull's forensic people had had in deciphering some of the numbers recovered from Weissman's arm.

"Possibly."

"Did the Order have any specific symbols or images that they used, apart from the regular SS ones?"

"Just one. A black disc surrounded by two concentric circles with twelve spokes radiating from its center in the form of SS lightning bolts. One for each member of the Order. They called it the Schwarze Sonne—the Black Sun."

"Like this?" Tom asked, handing Lasche the cap recovered from Weissman's house and pointing at its badge. Lasche grasped it unsteadily, a glimmer of recognition flickering across his face.

"Yes, yes. It is as I thought!" He looked up at Tom excitedly, straining to get the words out between breaths. "This is the symbol of the Order, a corruption of an Alamannian sun-wheel from the third century AD. It was intended as a reference to a time when the SS would shine down on the world as their racial masters."

There was a pause as Tom let this new piece of information sink in.

"What happened to the Order in the end?"

"Ah," said Lasche, "the, how you say, six-million-dollar question. The answer is simple: nobody knows."

"Nobody?"

Lasche gave a smile, more gums than teeth. "Not for certain. Although . . . Well, let's just say I have my own ideas."

"Go on," Tom urged him with a nod.

"Himmler, for all his failings, had a clearer view of the way the war was going than Hitler did. He even tried to negotiate a separate peace with the Allies in the final days of the war. And with the specter of defeat looming, he would never have been able to contemplate his precious knights being captured or imprisoned or otherwise humiliated by their enemies."

"So what do you think he did?"

Lasche paused, as if to collect his strength. "Are you aware what happened to King Arthur when he lay dying?" he wheezed.

"He asked one of his knights to throw Excalibur into the lake."

"Yes. Sir Bedivere—who refused three times, like Peter denying Christ. And then, when eventually he did comply, a ship with black sails appeared and carried Arthur to Avalon, from where it is said he will rise one day to save his people when they are next in mortal peril."

Tom frowned. "I don't follow."

"Many cultures have a similar legend. In Denmark, it is believed that Holger the Dane sleeps beneath Kronborg Castle, from where he will emerge when the fatherland is in need. In Germany, Emperor Frederick II—Barbarossa— is said to sleep beneath the Kyffhäuser mountain, from where he will return at the end of time. In my opinion, Himmler wanted a fittingly epic end for his own knights. In December 1944 he summoned the Order for one last meeting. It's not known what instructions he gave them, but not long afterwards they disappeared and were never seen again."

"You think they escaped?"

"Who knows? Maybe they were killed by the advancing

Soviet army. Maybe they lived out their days on a banana plantation somewhere in Paraguay. Or maybe, as we speak, they are waiting beneath some mountain or castle for the time when they will be called upon to restore the German Reich."

CHAPTER TWENTY-EIGHT

"Finally, we get to the train." Hecht sighed sarcastically.

"It's what was on the train that I want to know about!" came the voice from the speakerphone.

"And you would be right," said Renwick. "Because that is where the story gets really interesting. You see—"

Before he could continue, the door burst open and three uniformed men with shaved heads sprang into the room, machine guns slung around their necks. Renwick snapped his eyes to Hecht, but he seemed unperturbed.

"What is it, Konrad?" Hecht asked the first man, a square-set blond with a flat, stupid face.

"Fünf Männer," Konrad panted. *"Mehr draussen. Stellen unten fragen."*

"Problem?" Renwick asked Hecht, setting aside his annoyance at Hecht's breaking his promise that they would not be interrupted. The tension in Konrad's voice suggested this was not the moment to raise it.

"We've got company."

"Police?"

Hecht looked questioningly at Konrad, who responded, *"Ja. Ut Bundesnachrichtendienst."*

"The secret service?" It was Dmitri's turn to speak. "How the hell did they get on to us so fast?"

"The concierge," said Renwick slowly, recalling the man's fingernails tapping nervously on the counter and the anxious look in his eyes. "I thought he was just tired, but he knew something. He was expecting me."

"We'll deal with him later," Dmitri snarled. "Have you got a way out, Colonel?"

"Of course, sir."

"Gut. Use it. We'll continue this later." He hung up and the line hummed noisily until Hecht leaned forward and punched the off button.

"How are we going to get past them?" Renwick asked casually, masking his concern. Normally he wouldn't have been too worried. He had been in worse situations, much worse, and still slipped away unnoticed. But on those occasions he had been operating alone, able to think for himself, to react as he saw fit, to take whatever steps he deemed necessary. For the first time in as long as he could remember, he was relying on others for his safe passage, people he didn't know or trust. He didn't like it.

"With these—" Konrad reappeared carrying several uniforms identical to the ones he and the other two men were wearing. He threw them to the floor and then indicated that Renwick should put one on. *"Schnell."*

Renwick picked up a thick blue jacket and examined it skeptically. "What is it?"

"Fireman's uniform," said Hecht, grabbing one and pulling it on.

"Where is the fire?" Renwick asked as he buttoned up the jacket, then stepped into a pair of trousers, pulling them up over his suit.

"Right where you're standing. Karl, Florian—"

The two men disappeared into what Renwick assumed to be the bedroom, returning with a couple of large jerry cans. Rapidly and methodically they made their way around the room, sloshing gasoline over the carpet, sofa, and curtains. The smell, sweet and metallic, hit the back of Renwick's throat.

Meanwhile Hecht and Konrad were busy wiping the door handles, table, whiskey bottle, and anything else that any of them might have touched or used, even smashing Renwick's glass against the wall. It was slick and professional, and within thirty seconds the room was clean. Renwick felt his concern easing.

"Take this." Konrad handed him a pale yellow helmet, its surface chipped and covered in soot in a way that suggested its owner was a veteran of many years' hard-fought firefighting experience. When on, the built-in respirator and goggles almost completely obscured the wearer's face.

"Ready?" Hecht asked. They all nodded, put their helmets on, and followed him out into the hall. Hecht walked up to the fire alarm between the twin elevator shafts and smashed it with a jab of his right elbow.

The corridor was immediately filled with a piercing shriek as the alarm sounded, followed a few seconds later by the sound of doors opening and faces peeking out of rooms farther down the corridor. The sight of Renwick and the others standing there in full firefighting gear turned their expressions from concern, and in some cases annoyance, to undisguised fear and panic. Within seconds, guests in various states of undress were stampeding toward the fire escape and the safety of the ground floor.

"The alarm automatically shuts off all the lifts, making it impossible for our friends downstairs to get up here that way . . ."

". . . And the crowd heading down the fire escapes should delay their progress if they try to use the stairs." Renwick completed his sentence for him, admiring the simplicity of the tactic. "But how do we get out?"

"There's a lift at the rear of the building that remains operational even in a fire, provided you have a key." Hecht dangled a small key in front of Renwick's face. "The fire brigade will be here within three minutes. As soon as they arrive, we'll take the lift down to the basement and then go through the car park. In the confusion, no one will notice five more men in uniform."

Hecht slipped a box of matches out of his pocket and shook to check it was full. He turned to face the suite's open doorway.

"May I?" Renwick inquired.

"Of course." Hecht handed over the matches with a small bow and an amused grin. "You look like you're going to enjoy this."

Renwick took one last, disdainful look at the clumsy furniture, beige carpet, gold cushions, and brown curtains before striking the match and holding it in front of him.

"More than you could possibly know."

CHAPTER TWENTY-NINE

Given that it was the only stained-glass window in the entire church, Archie felt rather foolish for not having noticed it sooner. What made it special, though, was not its uniqueness but the fact that it was an identical copy of the painting of the castle in Weissman's photograph.

"How long has this been here?" was his slightly bemused question.

"It was gift from my uncle. In memory of my aunt."

"When did she die?"

Maria shook her head. "Before I was born. In fifty-five, fifty-six. Cancer. He used to come here to pray for her . . ."

"Do you mind if I take a picture?"

She looked nervously over her shoulder, saw that the church was empty, and shrugged her consent.

"*Ja*, okay. No problem."

Archie slipped the digital camera Tom had loaned him out of his pocket and took several shots of the window and the plaque underneath it, the flash spitting its incongruous white light into the church's gloom.

The window was unmistakably modern, the glass smooth, the lead fittings crisp, with none of the rippled imperfections or sagging geometry typical of older church windows. Yet, for all that, it had been classically executed, depicting a castle on a hill, a couple of birds wheeling overhead and, in the foreground, a few trees clustered around a bubbling spring.

When he was satisfied that he had enough shots, he turned to face Maria again.

"What did he do, your uncle? You know, for a job."

"He was professor at Universität Wien," she said proudly. "The oldest German-speaking university in the world."

"Teaching . . . ?"

"Physics."

"And before that? In the war?"

She snorted, half in frustration, half in amusement. "Pah. Always the war with you English. It is obsession for you, *ja*?"

"No, it's just that—"

"Uncle Manfred didn't fight," she said. "He told me. He was too young."

They had begun to walk back toward the entrance as they were speaking and were now standing by the door. Archie pulled his collar up in anticipation of the sharp slap of cold air when they stepped outside.

"Just one last thing"—Archie had almost forgotten to mention it—"Would you take a look at this for me? Tell me if you recognize anyone."

He handed over a copy of the photograph of three men in SS uniform that they had found at Weissman's house. She took it from him and studied it carefully. When she looked up her eyes were angry and her voice hard.

"Is this English sense of humor?"

"No, why?"

"You have made this as a joke, yes? To make fun of me?"

"No, of course not."

"I not believe you. This picture is a lie." She was almost shouting now, her voice resonating off the whitewashed stone walls. "Why you come here? To trick me?"

"Is one of those men your uncle?" Archie guessed.

"You know this. Why else are you here?"

"We found this picture yesterday in London, together

with the envelope I showed you," Archie explained. "I swear, until just now I had no idea your uncle was in it. Which one is he?"

She looked down at the photo again, gripping it tightly. "The man on the left. That was Uncle Manfred."

"I'm sorry." Archie sighed.

"Sorry? Why?" Her tone switched from anger to indifference. "This is mistake. Simple mistake. He was too young to fight. He told me."

"I'd love to believe you," said Archie. "But you see the man in the middle? His daughter didn't think he had fought either. She was wrong. He'd lied to her. He'd lied to everyone."

"He had a daughter?" She sounded less sure of herself now.

"Older than you, but not by much. She was the one who discovered this photo, not me."

"And she thinks . . . she thinks this is real?" Maria seemed to have shrunk before his eyes, her voice fading to a whisper, her eyes brimming with tears.

"Oh yeah," Archie said gently, trying to erase the image of Elena Weissman's bloody corpse that had been burned into his mind. "You see, she discovered a room, a secret room where her father had kept all his wartime mementos hidden from her. Uniforms, flags, guns, medals."

"Medals?" She looked up, wiping the palm of her hand across her cheek. "War medals?"

"Yes." Archie frowned. "Why?"

"Folgen Sie mir." She drew herself up straight once again. "I must show you. *Kommen Sie*."

She threw the door open and hurried out through the churchyard. As she reached the top of the steps leading down to the road, she hesitated for a second, her head swiveling to the left, then back again, muttering under her breath all the while.

Archie turned his head to see what she'd been looking at. It was a black marble gravestone, newer than those that flanked it. Although he couldn't read the epitaph, the name, picked out in large gold letters, was clearly visible.

DR. MANFRED LAMMERS.

They retraced their steps in silence. Maria's shock seemed to have been replaced by an unsmiling resolve. Once inside the house, she directed him to the sitting room and disappeared into one of the rooms at the back.

Archie stepped into the room, removed his coat and gloves, and sat down on the cream sofa. The self-assembly furniture looked new and cheap. A gaudy brass and crystal-effect chandelier hung from the middle of the ceiling, casting a yellow wash over the clip-frames that adorned the white walls, each containing a shiny Picasso print.

Maria came back into the room carrying a small wooden box made from an attractive polished walnut that glowed like the dash of an old sports car. Archie's eyes lit up at the sight of something old and well made. It was about eight inches across and five inches wide, with a small brass key protruding from the lock. The lid was flat and sat slightly raised above the sides, which rose four inches above a flared base.

But it was the symbol inlaid into the lid that grabbed his attention. Two concentric circles with a black disc at their center and runic lightning bolts radiating out from the middle, twelve of them in all. It was identical to the symbol he had seen on the cap badge of Weissman's uniform.

"He died in a fire." She placed the box on the white plastic coffee table in front of him. "The house had to be almost completely rebuilt. This was the only thing that survived. I found it in his car. I thought he had bought it at a fair somewhere, that it wasn't his. Now . . ." Her voice faded and she sat down opposite him, staring at the box with an expression halfway between fear and suspicion. "Please take it with you. I don't want it in the house anymore."

Archie turned the key and gingerly opened the lid. Inside, on a red velvet lining, lay a medal, its black, red, and white ribbon folded underneath it. The shape was unmistakable.

A Nazi Iron Cross.

CHAPTER THIRTY

As he approached Viggiano's office door, Bailey heard raised voices, then the sound of something being thrown or kicked across the room. Whatever it was, he guessed that it must have made a rather large dent in the wall.

Before he had a chance to knock, the door flew open and Viggiano marched out, his face red with rage. He paused midstride and looked Bailey up and down with disdain, his left eye twitching furiously, both his hands clenched. Then, with an angry snort, he shouldered roughly past him toward the exit.

Bailey watched his retreating back until he disappeared from view, then turned to face the open doorway. Regional Director Carter was sitting at Viggiano's desk. In front of him, neatly arranged on the blotter, were a service revolver and an FBI badge. An upended wastepaper basket lay beneath a deep scar in the wall.

"Bailey"—Carter's voice was cold and businesslike—"get in here. And shut the door."

Bailey closed the door behind him and sat down nervously at the chair indicated by Carter. The story was that the director had joined the FBI after a car accident and a collapsed lung had ended his professional football career before it had even begun. It was a story that the director's appearance did little to dispel; tall, broad-chested, with a tanned, square face, deep-set brown eyes, and an aggressive manner that seemed more suited to calling plays than running an investigation. The irony was that he was often mistaken for a realtor, having a seemingly endless supply of striped polyester ties and button-down white cotton shirts.

He fixed Bailey with a silent, slightly questioning gaze, his hands steepled pensively under his chin. Bailey's eyes flicked nervously to the floor, the silence increasingly awkward as he waited for Carter to speak. Finally, unable to bear it any longer, Bailey coughed and mumbled an apology.

"I didn't mean to disturb you, sir."

"You weren't disturbing anything. As you can see, Agent Viggiano and I were just clearing up a few . . . administrative details." His eyes drifted to the gun and badge. "After what went down in Idaho, it's best for him and for us that he sits out the next few months until we get a clear picture of exactly what happened up there. Anyway, it's out of my hands now."

Bailey felt his heart sink. He'd been around long enough to see where this was heading. With twenty-six civilians confirmed dead, the suits in DC were looking for scapegoats. Everyone who'd been up in the mountains that day was going to get sucked in. By the time it was over, he'd be lucky if they gave him a job in the car pool.

"Vasquez tells me you cautioned against opening that door. Is this true?" asked Carter.

"Eh . . ." Bailey hesitated, the question catching him off-guard. "Yes, sir. I thought I saw someone signaling at us not to come in."

"But Viggiano overruled you?"

"Well . . ." Bailey wavered. The last thing he wanted was a reputation as a snitch.

"Don't worry, Vasquez gave me the full rundown." Carter smiled, his earlier, rather distant manner melting away. "Said you saved his life. Way I see it, you did a great job up there. A great job. If Viggiano had listened to you instead of . . . Well, let's just say you did a great job."

Bailey's smile quickly faded at the memory of the body bags arranged on the fresh snow outside the farmhouse like the spokes on a wheel.

"It would have been a great job if we'd saved those people, sir."

"You did the best you could. I can't ask anyone to do any more than that."

"No, sir."

"So where are you taking this next?"

"I'm not sure what you mean, sir." Bailey frowned.

"Viggiano's off the case, but you don't get off so easy. What leads have you got?"

"We've got a composite sketch of our Unsub, based on Hennessy's description."

"Any use?"

"European male. Five ten. Cropped blond hair. Unshaven. About a hundred and ninety pounds."

"That's it?"

"'Fraid so. And now Hennessy's attorney is arguing that, until he sees a written offer, that's all we'll get."

"A written offer for what in return?" Carter demanded. "I mean, he's not given us much, has he? No ID, no distinguishing marks, just some bullshit story and a name that's probably an alias."

"Blondi?"

"Yeah."

"You know that was the name of Hitler's dog."

"What?" Carter looked nonplussed.

"Hitler's favorite dog was called Blondi."

"You think that might be relevant?"

"Well, so far we've got someone using the name of Hitler's dog, the theft of a Nazi Enigma machine, and the involvement of a neo-Nazi group. It sure doesn't sound like a coincidence."

"You could be right," Carter said. "Let's get everything we can on the Sons of American Liberty and any other extremist groups they might have links to. See if this Blondi surfaces anywhere else. Let's check out the Enigma machine too—see if we can come up with a list of likely buyers."

"Actually, sir, I've already done some work on that." Bailey laid the file he'd been clutching on the desk.

"You have?"

"An Enigma machine is a pretty unusual item to steal. I figured that Blondi might be working for a collector or dealer. So I ran down all the major military memorabilia auctions over the last five years and cross-referenced the lists of buyers."

"And?" Carter asked expectantly.

"There are about twenty dealers who account for about eighty percent of the volume."

"I hate to sound negative, but it could take us years to link one of them back to our guy."

"I've narrowed the list down to European dealers, since that's where Hennessy said Blondi was from. That cuts it down to seven."

"Still too many."

"That's why I asked Salt Lake City International to supply security footage for all flights to the cities where those seven dealers are based. I figured Blondi would want to be out within forty-eight hours of picking up the Enigma machine from Malta, so it was worth taking a look through the tapes in case any of the passengers matched our sketch."

"When did you last get some sleep?" Carter asked.

"It's been a long day," Bailey conceded.

"And?"

"One man. Boarded the American flight to Zurich under the name Arno Volker." Bailey opened the file and pointed at a fuzzy still taken from a surveillance tape, then laid the sketch next to it. There was a definite resemblance.

"That could be him," said Carter. "That could be him, all right. Good work."

"Thank you, sir," Bailey said proudly.

"What's your next move?"

"Track down the dealer in Zurich and put him under surveillance," Bailey said confidently. "If Blondi is working for him, the chances are he'll surface there, given that he doesn't know we're on to him yet."

Carter sat back in his chair, as if weighing the merits of Bailey's plan.

"Okay," he said eventually. "I want you to run with this."

"Sir?"

"It's unusual, given your inexperience, but I'm a big believer in giving responsibility to those who show they can handle it. I'm going to hook you up with an Agency buddy of mine in Zurich. Ben Cody."

"You want *me* to fly to Zurich?" Bailey couldn't believe what he was hearing. A few minutes ago he'd thought Carter was going to ask for his badge.

"Let's be clear—I'm not cutting you loose out there. I just want you to observe and report back to me on anything you learn or see, you got that? Nothing happens without the green light from me."

"Yessir. Thank you, sir." Bailey hoped that the slight tremor in his voice was not as obvious as it sounded to him.

Carter leaned across the desk and shook his hand. "By the way," he said as he turned to leave, "what did you say this dealer's name was?"

Bailey consulted his notes before answering. "Lasche. Wolfgang Lasche."

CHAPTER THIRTY-ONE

January 7—7:12 P.M.

It was a Friday night and the station was busy. A large group of teenage snowboarders were waiting in the middle of the concourse for their train to appear on the overhead monitors. They were huddled around a boom box as if it was a campfire, the continuous thump of its bass drowning out the occasional shrill whine from the PA system.

The café that Tom had chosen afforded him a good view of the platforms as commuters spilled off the trains on their way home. Settling into a chair strategically positioned under a heat lamp, he ordered a strong black coffee from the bored-looking waiter. This was as good a place as any to kill time. But no sooner had his coffee arrived than his phone rang. It was Turnbull.

"Any news?" said Turnbull, clearly in no mood for small talk. That suited Tom just fine. Theirs was a working relationship, a transaction based around a shared need and simple convenience that would end as soon as they both had what they wanted.

"Yeah. But none of it makes any sense."

Tom summarized Lasche's account of the Order of the

Death's Head and its disappearance in the dying days of the war.

"How does that help us?" Turnbull's response echoed the conclusion Tom himself had reached. "What's a Nazi secret society got to do with all this?"

"Beats me. I feel I know less now than when I started. And I still don't see what Renwick or Kristall Blade's angle on all this is."

"Didn't Lasche come up with anything else?"

"Not much. Just that the badge we found on Weissman's cap was the symbol of the Order. And that some SS officers had their blood group tattooed on their inner arms. If Weissman had tried to disguise his so he could pass it off as a prison tattoo, it would explain why your forensics people had a problem reading some of the numbers."

"That ties in." Turnbull's tone was more positive now.

"What about your end? Any further intel on Weissman?"

"Well, as you can imagine, the records from back then are pretty thin. First sighting we have is in northern Germany. One of the war crimes investigators reports Weissman being picked up, half-starved, near the Polish border by a patrol looking for Nazi officials. He claimed he'd been liberated from Auschwitz and had given the Russians the slip so he could find what was left of his family. Our boys wanted to check that he didn't match the description of anyone they were looking for. He didn't, and the tattoo sort of clinched it for him. Eventually he was offered the choice of asylum in the U.S., Israel, or Britain. He chose us. He'd trained as a chemist before the war and got a job working for a pharmaceutical company. After that, nothing. Not even a parking ticket. He paid his taxes. Lived a quiet life. The model citizen."

"Did he ever travel abroad?"

"He renewed his passport three years ago. Went to Geneva, according to his daughter's statement, to attend some bird-watching conference. Apart from that, he stayed put."

"Clearly he had, or knew, something. Something Renwick and your Kristall Blade people wanted enough to kill him for."

"Seems that way." A pause. Then, "Did Connolly find anything in Austria?"

Tom drained his coffee. "I'll tell you in a couple of hours. I'm meeting him for dinner as soon as he gets in."

CHAPTER THIRTY-TWO

RESTAURANT ZUNFTHAUS ZUR ZIMMERLEUTEN,

NIEDERDORF, ZURICH

January 7—9:02 P.M.

Tom had arranged to meet Archie in a restaurant a short walk from the station in the old town. The building, originally a carpenters' guildhall, dated back to 1336. From the outside it resembled a small castle perched on the banks of the river, complete with turret and flagpole.

Inside, a baroque staircase led up to a baronial dining room, oak paneling covered the walls, thick stone mullions separated stained-glass windows emblazoned with various coats of arms. It was a favorite with local banking grandees and tourists alike, but at this hour it was relatively quiet.

"Whiskey," Archie called out as he approached the table where Tom sat waiting for him. "No ice."

The waiter looked to Tom in confusion.

"*Ein Whiskey*," Tom confirmed. "*Ohne Eis. Danke.*" Archie dropped his bag to the floor and sat down with a sigh as the waiter disappeared. "Good trip?"

"Delayed, and the stewardess had a mustache. Apart from that, perfect."

Tom laughed. "And what did Lammers have to say?"

"Not much. I think the six feet of earth and the gravestone may have been muffling the sound of his voice."

"He's dead?" Tom exclaimed.

"Three years ago. House fire."

"Shit!" Tom shook his head ruefully. "So we're right back where we started."

"Not quite." Archie smiled. "It turns out that his niece now lives in his old house. I showed her the photos of the paintings and she took me to see this . . ." He took Tom's digital camera from his pocket and handed it over.

"It's the same castle as in the painting," said Tom, scrolling through the images.

"You mean it's an exact bloody copy. Lammers donated the window in the fifties after his wife died of cancer."

"Meaning that he must have had access to the original."

"Exactly. Question is, where is it now? Assuming it survived the fire, of course." Archie sniffed. "Do you mind?" He held out a box of Marlboro Reds questioningly. Tom shook his head. He lit up.

"What I'd like to know is what was so important about the painting that he had the window made in the first place?"

"Presuming that it wasn't just because he liked it," said Archie, wrinkling his nose to suggest how unlikely he thought that was.

"What about the niece? Did she know anything?"

"This was all news to her. You should have seen her face when I showed her the photo of Weissman and the two other men in uniform. Guess who she recognized?"

"Uncle Manfred?"

Archie nodded. "She didn't take it very well. But she did give me this." He reached into his bag and pulled out the walnut veneer box. "Said she didn't want it in the house anymore. Open it." Tom turned the small key in the lock and eased back the lid. "It's an Iron Cross," said Archie, drawing heavily on his cigarette.

"Not quite . . ." Tom had taken the medal out of the box and was studying it intently. In his palm, the forbidding black shape pulsed malevolently under the candle's bluish glow. He rubbed his thumb across it, feeling the raised swastika and the date, 1939, beneath it.

"It's a Knight's Cross," he said. "I've come across them before. Looks the same, but there's a different finish. The ribbon clasp is much more ornate, the edge is ribbed rather than smooth, and the frame is made from silver rather than just lacquered to look like silver."

"So it's a higher award?"

"It's one of the highest the Third Reich could give. I think only about seven thousand were ever awarded, compared to millions of Iron Crosses. They're very rare."

"Meaning that either Lammers was a collector, or . . ."

"Or it was his and he'd done something that merited special recognition." Tom turned it over and then looked up with a frown. "That's weird."

"What?"

"These normally had an embossed date on the back—1813, from when they were first issued in the Napoleonic wars."

"What's that one got? I didn't really look."

"You tell me." Tom held it out, reverse side up. It was engraved with a series of seemingly random lines and curves and circles that looked for all the world like the mindless doodling of a young child.

"You know, there was a medal like this round the neck of that mannequin at Weissman's house. I had to unclip it before I could get the jacket off."

"Worth checking out," Tom said. "Anything else in here?" He picked up the box and shook it.

"I don't think so," Archie said with a half smile. "Take a look for yourself."

Tom opened the box again, carefully studying its interior. Finding nothing, he put his index finger into the main compartment to measure its depth. It came up only to his second knuckle.

"That's strange," he muttered, frowning.

He pressed his finger against the side of the box. This time, it came right up to his knuckle. The inside was an inch shallower than it should have been.

"There's a false bottom," Tom exclaimed.

"I think so," said Archie. "Christ knows how to open it, though. I thought you might have seen something like it before, so I didn't muck about too much. Didn't want to break it."

"It's like one of those Russian trick boxes. Normally you have to slide one of the pieces of wood to get inside."

Given the lack of dents or telltale ridges in the box's glossy, unbroken veneer, it was not immediately apparent which section might move. So Tom tried each side in turn, pressing his thumb against the wood, just above the bottom edge, and pushing it away from him.

Nothing.

He repeated the exercise in reverse, tugging each side toward him. Again nothing moved initially, but his persistence was finally rewarded by the bottom section of the right side moving maybe a quarter of an inch to reveal a tiny hairline crack. But there his progress stalled, for no matter how hard he pulled the lip of wood that sat raised above the front of the box, nothing would come free.

"Try the opposite side," Archie suggested. "Maybe there's some sort of locking mechanism. It might have released a panel on the other side."

Tom tried to slide the opposite panel sideways, then down, then up. On his last attempt it moved easily, rising about two inches and exposing a small drawer with an ivory handle. His eyes wide with anticipation, Tom slid the drawer out.

"What is it?" Archie asked, straining to see.

Tom looked up, his eyes shining. "A key, I think."

The drawer, like the main compartment, was lined in red velvet. Under the restaurant's dimmed lighting the object it contained glinted like tarnished silver. Archie reached in and grasped it, the metal fat and solid in his square fingers.

"Funny sort of key."

About two inches long, the key was square rather than flat, and it had no teeth. Instead, each of its gleaming surfaces was engraved with a series of small hexagonal marks.

"I think it's for a digital lock. You know, like the one in that private bank in Monte Carlo."

"And what do you make of this . . . ?"

The key's sleek steel shaft was housed in an ugly triangular handle made of molded rubber. On one side of the handle was a small button, but nothing happened when Archie pressed it. The other side had been stamped with a series of interlocking calligraphic letters. Tom thought he could make out a *V* and a *C*, but it was hard to tell. "Owner's initials? Maker's logo? Could be anything."

"How are we going to find out?" Archie asked, returning the key to the secret drawer and shutting it again.

"We're in Zurich—how do you think I'm going to find out?" Tom asked with a smile.

"You're not serious."

"Why not?"

"Raj?" Archie sounded deeply suspicious.

"Who else?"

"Can we trust him?"

"I guess there's only one way to find out," Tom said with a shrug.

CHAPTER THIRTY-THREE

WIPKINGEN, ZURICH

January 7—10:40 P.M.

Away from the town center, the river Limmat flexes its way northwest into Zurich's industrial zone, an uninspiring agglomeration of low-level warehouses and soaring concrete factories, black slate tiles slung over oppressive cinder grey walls, chimneys and heating vents coughing smoke.

Tom and Archie made their way across the Wipkingen bridge, along Breitensteinstrasse and finally left down Amperestrasse, then negotiated the steep steps leading down to a poorly lit path that ran parallel to the river.

"Are you sure it's down here?" Archie asked, his tone suggesting that he found it highly unlikely. An embankment loomed nearly thirty feet above their heads, its brickwork obscured at ground level by decades of graffiti and flyer posting. On the opposite bank a few dull and greasy windows punctuated the blank gaze of a factory's rear elevation like embrasures in a castle wall.

"It was, last time I came," Tom answered.

"You've been here before? When?"

"Three, four years ago. When we did that job in Venice, remember?"

"Oh yeah." Archie chuckled. "If only they were all like that."

"If it hadn't been for Raj, I'd have had to drill my way into that safe."

"All right, all right," Archie conceded. "So he's a good locksmith."

"He's the best in the business and you know it."

"Mmm . . ." Archie shrugged noncommittally.

Tom sighed. Six months out of the game had done little to dull Archie's natural wariness toward almost every other living being he came across—especially when money was involved. Dhutta still owed them a couple thousand bucks for some information they had supplied him a few years before, and he had proven remarkably elusive ever since, hence Archie's misgivings. To Archie, debtors—especially anyone in debt to him—were to be treated with the utmost caution.

Tom stopped beside a steel door set into the embankment, its original black paint barely visible under a thick collage of posters advertising raves, DJ nights, and various other local events. Above the door was a bright yellow sign showing a lightning bolt within a black triangle.

"You must be joking!" Archie gave an impatient laugh. "Here?"

"You know what he's like about personal security. This helps keep most people at a safe distance."

Tom ran his hand over the brickwork to the right of the door at about waist height. Eventually he found what he was looking for, a single brick that protruded a little beyond those around it. It sank slightly under his touch, then sprang back to its original position. From somewhere deep within the embankment, they heard a bell ring.

"I want you on your best behavior, Archie. Don't get started. Raj is jumpy enough without you stirring things up."

Archie growled a response that was interrupted by the hum of an invisible intercom.

"Yes, hello?" A high-pitched, almost feminine voice.

"Raj? It's Tom Kirk and Archie Connolly."

There was a long silence, then: "What do you want?"

"To talk."

"Look, I haven't got the money, if that's what this is about. I can get it. Tomorrow. I can get it tomorrow. Today's no good. I'm busy. I've been very, very busy. Tomorrow, okay?" Dhutta spoke quickly with a strong Indian accent, barely pausing between sentences.

"Forget the money, Raj," Tom said, earning himself an angry look from Archie. "We need your help. Let's just call it quits on what you owe us."

There was another, even longer pause, then the door buzzed open.

"Half that money's mine, don't forget," Archie reminded Tom as they stepped inside. "Next time, you might want to ask me before just giving it away."

"You drop more than that every time you pick up a hand of cards," Tom said quietly. "I don't think you'll miss it."

They found themselves in a steel cage, half blinded by the powerful lights trained on them from the far side of the room. Several dark shapes loomed on either side of them, none of them moving, while the smell of decay rose from the damp concrete floor.

"Raj?" Tom called, holding his hand up to his face and peering through his fingers in an attempt to see beyond the glare. A silhouette appeared in front of the lights.

"Quits?" came the voice again.

"That's right," said Tom. "We're not here to make any trouble, Raj. Just to get some advice."

The lights snapped off and Tom made out a slight figure approaching the cage, fumbling with a huge bunch of keys. Raj Dhutta was a willowy five foot four, with slender arms and skinny wrists. He had wavy black hair with a knife-edge part on the left-hand side, and a narrow, feline face, his eyes furtively skipping between them, his black mustache quivering nervously.

He selected a key and inserted it into a lock. Then he repeated the action with a second and then a third lock, pausing before the final turn of the key.

"We have a gentleman's agreement?" said Dhutta, his tone still disbelieving.

"Yes, we've got an agreement," Tom confirmed.

"Excellent!" Dhutta's face broke into a broad smile. "Excellent." The cage door finally swung open and Tom and Archie were able to step into the room, Dhutta immediately slamming the cage shut behind them and sliding the deadbolts into place.

"Let's shake on it." He grabbed Tom's hand and pumped it up and down vigorously, his grip surprisingly fierce.

"This is the first time you two have actually met, isn't it?" asked Tom, retrieving his hand.

"Yes, indeed." Dhutta turned his smile on Archie. "It is a pleasure to meet you finally, Mr. Connolly."

They shook hands awkwardly, as if renewing a dimly remembered acquaintance.

"Is there somewhere we can talk?" Tom asked.

"My apologies." Dhutta gave a half bow. "I am indeed a poor host. Come, come."

He scampered across to the far side of the room, Tom and Archie now able to see that the dark shapes they had noticed previously were large pieces of rusting industrial equipment, long since decommissioned.

"What is this place?" Archie asked, watching where he was stepping. "Or rather, what was it?"

"An old electricity substation." Dhutta led them up a short flight of stairs to another steel door, which he unlocked with a second set of keys.

"You live here?" Archie again.

"No, no, no. This is merely my workshop. I reside on the street overhead. There's access through the cellar so I never have to go outside. Come, come," he urged, stepping through the doorway.

On his previous visit, Tom had not been invited into this part of the complex, Dhutta having insisted that he wait within the gloomy confines of the anteroom they had just come from. Now he saw that the door opened onto a vast hall, the arched brick ceiling rising twenty feet above their heads. A series of lights hung down at regular intervals, their steel shades as big as umbrellas. The concrete floor had been whitewashed and covered in an uneven quilt of overlapping rugs that felt soft and warm beneath their feet.

"Tea?" asked Dhutta. "I have many different varieties from my uncle in Calcutta—Earl Grey, Darjeeling, Assam, Nilgiri . . . Whatever tickles your fancy. I have just boiled the kettle."

"Earl Grey," Archie replied distractedly, still taking the room in.

"Coffee. Black," said Tom, to Dhutta's obvious disapproval.

"As you wish. Please make yourselves at home."

Dhutta waved them to two battered and threadbare sofas arranged around an old tea chest on the left-hand side of the room as he darted to the sink and busied himself with mugs and milk. Tom and Archie both dropped their small overnight bags by the door and sat down.

"I must admit, I am surprised to see you, Mr. Tom. I had heard that you would no longer have need of my services."

"It's true. Archie and I have moved on."

"The business is losing all its gentlemen." Dhutta sighed. "The young people coming through have no respect."

"Things change, Raj," Tom replied.

"In the Hindu religion, we would say that you have moved on to *Vanaprastha*, or retirement, when you will delegate responsibility to the younger generation and perform selfless social services yourself," Dhutta said solemnly.

"And after that?" Tom asked in mock seriousness.

"*Sanyas*. The complete renunciation of the world for union with God."

Tom laughed. "I think I'm a few years from either of those."

Dhutta handed them their drinks and sat down opposite.

"You not having anything?" Archie asked.

"Just this." Dhutta reached behind him for a bottle of brightly colored cough mixture. Tom and Archie watched in disbelief as he unscrewed the white cap and took a long swig, emptying almost a quarter of the bottle.

"That can't be good for you," Archie observed with a frown.

"Prevention is better than cure, Mr. Archie." Dhutta nodded toward a shelf above the sink that was stacked with medicine bottles full of pills and vitamins and other unidentifiable supplements, not to mention a rainbow of neon-colored syrups and liquids. "Would you like to try something?" he suggested eagerly. "Maybe for hay fever or malaria?"

"We're just here for some information," said Tom.

"Information?" Dhutta's gaze flicked regretfully from the shelf, back to Tom. "What sort of information?"

"There's something I want to show you," said Tom. "Obviously, what we're about to discuss doesn't leave this room."

"Of course."

Tom placed the walnut box on the tea chest's rough surface.

CHAPTER THIRTY-FOUR

January 7—11:31 P.M.

Dhutta pulled the box toward him, then hesitated before opening it, his fingers rubbing across the twelve-armed swastika on the lid.

"This?"

"No. Something inside it."

Dhutta flicked the box open, frowning when he saw it was empty. He picked it up and shook it, then examined it again. Tom eyed him with amusement, wondering how long it would take him to work out that the box had a false bottom, let alone how to get into it. But in four quick movements, Dhutta slid the various interlocking pieces of the box aside and exposed the secret drawer.

"I see you've not lost your touch," Tom said with a smile.

But Dhutta had already slid the drawer out and snatched up the key and didn't seem to be listening. He looked at them, his mustache quivering as he turned the key over between his fingers.

"Well, well!" he exclaimed. "Interesting. Very interesting. May I ask where you obtained this, Mr. Tom?" Tom arched his eyebrows and pressed his lips together, unwilling to divulge any more than he had to at this stage. Dhutta shrugged. "Not everything has changed, I see," he observed wryly.

"What do you think it's for?"

"A safe? A deposit box? Something like that. Somewhere with tip-top security."

"What about the initials? Do they mean anything to you?"

Dhutta squinted at the italic script etched into the key's rubber grip. "It looks like a *V* and a *C*," he said, shaking his head. "But that's impossible."

"Why impossible?"

"It's the logo for Völz et Compagnie, the private bank. But they do not offer safe-deposit boxes. Not anymore."

"I've never heard of them," said Tom.

"You wouldn't have, unless you had an account there." Dhutta twirled the key between his fingers. "They're based here in Zurich. Very prestigious. Very secretive. They don't advertise, don't even have a sign on their building. If they think you are suitable, they find you."

"Well, if their logo's on it, the key must have some connection with the bank," Tom insisted.

"Come, gentlemen"—Dhutta jumped up, tossing the key in the air and deftly catching it again—"I want to try something."

The hall was divided into three main areas. The smallest was the one they had just come from, a sort of makeshift sitting room on the left. Steel shelving formed a ten-foot-tall metal barricade separating this area from the rest. Dhutta led them through a gap in the shelving to his workshop area.

Several industrial metalworking machines—grinders, drills, saws, and the like—were bolted to the low workbench or freestanding, and small piles of metal shavings crunched under their feet. The shelves were full of baskets that contained further pieces of cutting and shaping and welding equipment. At the far end of the workshop area, thousands of keys dangled from huge black boards that had been screwed to the shelves. House keys, car keys, safe keys, shop keys: every possible combination of size, shape, and color glinted in the overhead light like the individual links in some enormous chain-mail shirt.

Without pausing, Dhutta led them to a gap in the next

bank of shelving and through to the far end of the hall. As he walked into the third area, Tom's eyes widened. Where the workshop had been primitive and grimy, reeking of oil, this final area was a sleek, symbiotic amalgam of stainless steel and silicon.

Along the far wall were half a dozen LCD panels, each plugged into a different piece of hardware, their screens small puddles of light. In the left corner two large racks groaned and hummed under the combined weight of the computer and telecom equipment loaded on them. Scanners, printers, CD burners, and other unidentifiable pieces of electronic hardware jostled for space along the right-hand wall, their displays flashing like a Times Square billboard. Three plasma screens dominated the left-hand wall, each tuned to a different news channel; one, Tom noticed, was showing a cricket match. Dhutta caught sight of Tom's surprised expression.

"The steady march of progress," Dhutta explained with an excited sweep of his arm. "Nowadays people are preferring to place their trust in passwords and firewalls rather than springs and tumblers. But a lock is a lock, and I have to keep ahead of the game, whether the key is made from metal or from binary code."

He pulled a chair out from under the worktop and, switching on a desk lamp, examined the key carefully.

"It is as I thought," he exclaimed after a few seconds. "A three-dimensional laser-tooled varying matrix." He sounded impressed.

"Which means what, exactly?" Archie asked.

Dhutta turned to him with a smile. "The key has no teeth, Mr. Archie, as you can see. Instead, when you insert it into a lock, four separate electronic eyes examine these laser-burned markings to ensure that they are correctly sized and positioned. It's almost impossible to duplicate."

Tom's eyes met Archie's.

"And if I'm not mistaken . . ." Dhutta pointed the key at a black box screwed to the wall and pressed the small button in the key's rubber grip. Almost immediately a long series of numbers flashed on the screen beside him.

"What's that?" Tom asked.

"When the key has been inserted into the lock and successfully read by the laser, you press this button to trigger an infrared data exchange with the locking mechanism. Based on this"—he indicated the display on the screen—"it seems to be an algorithm, probably a 128-bit key. Very hard to break. A complex mathematical formula changes the code at regular intervals—once a day, once a week, depending on how it has been programmed. Unless the codes match, the lock won't open."

"You ever see anything like this before?"

"Only once, on a system developed for the Israeli military for access to their missile silos. Except that they insisted on one extra level of security."

"Which was?"

"A key can be lost, stolen even." He flashed his teeth at Tom and gave him a knowing wink. "Biometric analysis was therefore deemed a necessary additional precaution to ensure that the person inserting the key was indeed meant to have it."

"Analysis of what?"

"In the Israeli case, palm prints."

"So we've no way of getting in without—"

"Raj," Archie interrupted, "how many numbers are there in a typical Swiss bank account?"

"Between eight and sixteen. It depends on how many accounts they have and the security setup."

"So ten digits, for example, could make up an account number?"

"Oh, certainly," said Dhutta.

"What are you thinking?" Tom took a step toward Archie, curiosity in his voice.

"I'm just wondering whether that's why Cassius wanted Weissman's arm. Maybe the tattoo was an account number, not a camp number."

"But why would Weissman have had the account number and not the key?" asked Tom.

"Just because we didn't find a key, doesn't mean he didn't have one."

"And we don't know for sure that Lammers had the key but no account number," Tom said, picking up on Archie's logic. "They probably both had access."

"It would make sense," Archie agreed. "Especially if what they were hiding was valuable. The only problem is, they're both dead. Even if we're right about the key and the account number, there's no way we can get into that box."

Tom smiled. "Isn't there?"

CHAPTER THIRTY-FIVE

AU-HAIDHAUSEN DISTRICT, MUNICH

January 7—11:55 P.M.

The garage was small but well equipped, with tools hanging neatly along the far wall and oil sumps and inspection hatches set into the concrete floor. Toward the rear stood two large hydraulic car lifts, squat as tanks, their stainless-steel pistons gleaming in the muted light.

"Could we not have met here rather than the hotel?" Renwick asked angrily. "Then we could have avoided tonight's little circus."

Although, in the end, their escape from the hotel had gone well enough, he had since had time to reflect on the evening's events. It had been a mistake, he realized now, to place himself in the hands of people he did not know or trust. He had made himself vulnerable.

"Because the staff would still have been here then," Hecht explained patiently. "The owner is a sympathizer. He lets us use his premises after hours if we need to, but that's it." There was a pause. "Besides, Dmitri is cautious . . ." Hecht spoke with an apologetic tone now. "He prefers not to let outsiders get too close to our operation."

"His caution very nearly got us all caught," Renwick snapped, gingerly rubbing the place where the prosthetic hand joined his arm. "Next time, I will choose the venue and you can leave the fancy dress at home." He flipped a hand at the fireman's uniform he had just discarded.

"Next time, there will be no need," Hecht reassured him. "You're with us, now."

"I am with nobody," Renwick corrected him. "We have an arrangement. Nothing more."

"As you wish," Hecht conceded. "And your plan . . . You're still confident?"

"If I'm right that the painting's sitting in some private collection somewhere, then he's the one to find it."

"How can you be so sure?"

"Because he is the best. And because he has every incentive to succeed."

"What incentive is that?"

"Stopping me. All we need to do is watch him and make our move at the right time." Renwick pulled his gold watch from his top pocket and glanced at it. "Talking of which, what is keeping them?"

"I don't know." Hecht frowned. "They should have been back . . . Ah."

A car had pulled up outside, its yellow headlights flooding in through the cracks around the sides of the steel roller shutter, before being extinguished. The sound of doors opening and closing was followed by the murmur of voices, then footsteps and something heavy being dragged. A minute or two later the shutter rattled as someone knocked heavily on the narrow door cut into it.

Hecht opened the door. Konrad stepped in first, followed by the two men from the hotel, Karl and Florian, heaving a large sack, which left a smeared trail of oil and dust in its wake. All three were still wearing their fireman's trousers but had stripped down to T-shirts, the tapestry of angry, twisting tattoos that adorned their arms and torsos slick with sweat.

"Any problems?" Hecht asked.

"*Nein*," Konrad answered. "Except he cries like a girl." Karl and Florian both laughed as they heaved the sack upright. Konrad produced a heavy-duty hunting knife from inside his left boot and slit the rope that secured the top of the bag. The material concertinaed to the floor like a thick curtain to reveal the concierge, his mouth covered by packing tape, his face addled by fear. Konrad pushed him into a wooden chair, swiftly taping his ankles to the chair legs and his wrists to the wide, flat armrests.

Hecht approached the man. Without a word, he punched him—a heavy blow across the cheek that jerked his head sideways as if it were on a spring. The concierge slowly turned his head back to face them, his eyes wide, his lip split open, blood pouring from the wound. Hecht punched him again, so hard this time that the chair toppled over and sent the concierge crashing to the cold concrete floor. The sharp tang of urine rose into the air.

"He's wet himself," Karl laughed. "The dirty pig."

"Pick him up," Hecht barked. The smile vanished from Karl's face and he heaved the chair upright.

"Now that you're listening"—Hecht leaned toward the concierge so that their faces were only inches apart—"I'm going to ask you some questions, and I want you to tell me the answers. Every time I think you're lying—if you even hesitate for just one second before answering—Konrad will cut off one of your fingers. When we've run out of fingers, we'll move on to more sensitive organs . . ." He indicated the damp patch between the man's legs. "Do you understand?"

The concierge nodded furiously, trying to blink away his tears.

"Good." Hecht signaled to Konrad, who ripped the masking tape from one side of the concierge's mouth. It hung limply off one cheek, fluttering every time he breathed out, like a ribbon tied to a fan.

"What's your name?"

"Nikolas," came the unsteady reply. "Nikolas Ganz."

"So tell me, Nikolas Ganz. How did those men find us tonight? Did you call them?"

The concierge nodded and began to cry. "I'm sorry."

"It's okay," Hecht said soothingly. "Why did you call them?"

"Two men came into the hotel a few days ago," he gasped between sobs. "They showed me a photo and said they would pay me ten thousand euro to call them if I saw the person they were looking for."

"Who were they? Police, BND, Interpol?"

Ganz shook his head. "I . . . I don't know . . ." he said haltingly. "They . . . they didn't say."

Hecht stood up and nodded at Konrad. At the signal, Konrad slapped the masking tape back down across Ganz's face before grasping his right hand. Shaking his head violently, Ganz tried to clench his fist into a tight ball, but Konrad prized his fingers apart and splayed them against the chair's flat wooden arm. The concierge began to scream, a muffled noise that in the garage's echoing silence sounded only vaguely human.

Konrad placed the blade of his knife against Ganz's index finger, just above the knuckle, and cut in. At the first sign of blood, Ganz fainted, his body slumping forward. Konrad continued anyway, resting the flat of his other hand against the top of the blade and rocking it slowly from side to side while pressing down as hard as he could. Ganz regained consciousness five or ten seconds later, just as the knife finally sliced through the bone and severed the finger with a sickening crunch.

Hecht picked up the bloody mess and held it in front of Ganz's bloodshot eyes. At the sight of it, Ganz began to retch, his shoulders heaving. Hecht pulled the tape from his mouth and he vomited down his front.

"Get him some water," Hecht ordered. A glass appeared and Hecht pressed it to Ganz's lips.

"Are you okay, Nikolas?" asked Hecht. Ganz nodded, his bottom lip trembling, his breathing snatched and shallow. "Good. Breathe deeply, that will help. Now, I'll ask you again. Who were they?"

"They didn't say!" Ganz half shouted, half sobbed his response. "They just showed me a photo and told me to call them. I didn't think to ask. I didn't care. Oh my God, my finger. My finger!"

"And who was on the photo? Me?" The concierge shook his head. "Him?" He indicated Konrad, who was still holding his knife, blood dripping from its shiny blade.

"No."

"Don't lie," Hecht shouted.

"I'm not!" the concierge screamed as Konrad grabbed his wrist again. "It was him—" The bloody stump of his index finger waggled furiously as he tried to point even though he couldn't move his wrists. "It was him—Herr Smith."

Renwick stood up in surprise. "Me?"

"Yes, yes, for God's sake, yes," the concierge moaned.

Hecht walked over to Renwick. "What does this mean?" he asked in a low voice.

"I have my own problems," Renwick said with a shrug. "They are no concern of yours."

"They are when they compromise our security," Hecht countered.

"Somebody got lucky, that's all. It just proves that, from now on, we need to stay out of sight."

"Well, that's one thing we agree on."

"Hey, boss, what shall we do about him?" Konrad called. Ganz had just been sick again.

"Kill him," Renwick said quietly.

"Kill him?" Hecht's tone made it clear he didn't agree. "What for?"

"He has seen me, he has seen you, he has seen this place. Who knows what he's overheard. Kill him."

"We can do without the police sniffing around . . ."

"Pah!" Renwick pushed past him, snatched Konrad's knife, and grabbed a handful of Ganz's hair, yanking his head back. Then, in one swift movement, he sliced Ganz's throat open, the blade biting deep into his windpipe and opening a livid red smile across his exposed neck.

The concierge jerked furiously three or four times, lifting out of the chair as if he were being electrocuted, before collapsing lifelessly, head to one side, blood cascading from his neck.

Renwick handed the knife to Hecht, his eyes blazing. "From now on we do this my way, Johann. No witnesses. No risks. No loose ends."

CHAPTER THIRTY-SIX

PARC MONCEAU, PARIS

January 8—7:46 A.M.

The two men approached the chipped green bench from different directions. The older of the two sat down and took out that day's edition of *L'Équipe*—according to the front page, PSG were on the verge of another big-money signing. The other, younger man walked on for twenty or so yards, stopped, looked around, and then retraced his steps, sliding onto the bench next to him.

They both wore identical gold rings on the little finger of their left hand. Each was engraved with a twelve-box grid, with a small diamond set in one of the boxes. Where they differed was in the position of the diamond, the old man's being located in the bottom left box, the younger man's in the top right.

"Why have you asked me here?" the first man mumbled from behind his paper.

"The situation has deteriorated," the second man said, his lips barely moving as he stared across the small ornamental lake encircled by an unconvincing Roman colonnade. "I judged that you would want to hear this in person."

"You only call me when you have bad news, anyway," the first man complained. "I don't see why—"

"Kirk is making progress."

"*Tsss,*" the older man snorted dismissively. "What sort of progress?"

"Enough for one of his associates to pay a visit to Lammers's niece yesterday."

A pause. In the distance, children's laughter echoed to the accompaniment of a musical carousel, brightly painted horses rising and falling as they chased each other tirelessly.

"She suspects nothing," the older man replied eventually. "Besides, we turned that place upside down before we set fire to it. It was clean. There was nothing there."

"Apart from the stained-glass window in the local church."

"What window?" The man put down his paper, all attempt at dissimulation now forgotten.

"A window that Lammers commissioned."

"Why didn't we know about this?"

"Because you had him killed before he could tell us."

"What does it show?" A hint of concern had crept into the older man's voice.

"A castle. A triangular castle."

"*Merde!*"

"That's not all. She gave him something. We weren't able to see what it was, but he arrived empty-handed and left with a bag."

Silence as the first man considered what he had just been told. "Where is he now, this associate? Where's Kirk, for that matter?"

"In Zurich. He went to see Lasche yesterday."

"Lasche!" the man exclaimed in disgust. "That old fool will never—"

"Sir," the second man interrupted, "if you'll forgive me, I think the time has come for more . . . radical measures. It is no longer enough to trust to providence and people's incompetence."

"What do you mean?"

"Kirk followed the trail from Weissman to Lammers in only forty-eight hours. It took us three years, albeit working in the opposite direction. Kirk discovered the window. A window that we didn't even know existed. He made contact with Lasche, a man who, whatever you may think of him, knows more about that period than anyone else. How long before he starts to make some connections? How long before he gets lucky?"

"And Cassius?" the man asked sullenly. "Did you get him at least?"

"No," replied the other, turning his head away. A dog trotted past them and then relieved itself in the middle of the gravel path. Its owner followed behind, smoking and chatting on his phone, studiously ignoring the polite signs telling him to keep his dog on a leash and to clean up after it. "We had him last night in Munich, but he got away. It seems he isn't acting alone anymore."

"You were right to call me here," the first man said grudgingly. "If Kirk finds out what's really down there, it will only make him more determined. We must take steps. Events are getting out of control. If we don't act now, it may be too late."

"What sort of steps?"

"The window must be destroyed."

"Obviously. And Kirk?"

"They must all be dealt with—Kirk, his colleague, and anyone else they have come into contact with. Find them and kill them. We can't afford to take any more chances."

CHAPTER THIRTY-SEVEN

Tom had slept badly. Although the two sofas that Dhutta had offered them for the night had been comfortable enough, his overactive mind had kept him awake into the small hours and then woken him again shortly after six. Renwick, Weissman, Lammers, Bellak . . . What was it that tied them all together? What did they know of the Order?

Eventually, unable to bear Archie's steady snoring any longer, he had got up, showered, and dressed in his usual jeans and a fresh open-necked shirt.

He waited until nine thirty before waking Archie with a cup of coffee that Archie accepted grudgingly, protesting about the hour. He was not a morning person, Tom knew, rarely struggling into the office before midday but then working into the small hours. For Tom, it had always been the other way around.

"What's the hurry?" Archie said reproachfully, pulling his sheets around him as he nursed the coffee cup in both hands.

"I got through to Turnbull last night and explained what we'd found out. He agreed to send Weissman's arm over by medical courier first thing. It should be here any time now."

"You got me out of bed for a courier!" Archie remonstrated.

"Don't tell me you were actually comfortable on that thing." Tom kicked the sofa and a cloud of dust danced above the seat cushion.

"Fair point," Archie conceded.

A bell rang and a few moments later Dhutta appeared, his mustache freshly waxed, his hair still glistening from the shower. In his hand was a small set of amber beads that he was fingering nervously.

"Good morning, gentlemen," he called cheerily. "I hope you both slept well. If you will excuse me, it seems I have a visitor."

"Actually, I think it's for me," Tom admitted.

"Oh?" Tom sensed a flicker of concern in Dhutta's voice.

"I needed something delivered and gave them the directions to the back door. Don't worry," he added, seeing the look on Dhutta's face. "You can trust them."

"You gave a courier company the directions to this place?" Archie laughed. "What did you tell them, second brick on the right and straight on till morning?"

"Something like that." Tom smiled. He turned back to Dhutta as the bell rang again. "I'm sorry, I should have told you yesterday, but I didn't want to disturb you any more than we already had."

Dhutta waved his apology away, although Tom could tell from the stiffness in his shoulders that he was annoyed. Unfortunate, but, given the circumstances, unavoidable.

"If you say I can trust them, Mr. Tom, then that's good enough for me. I will go and let them in."

Archie got up and yawned. He was wearing blue boxer shorts and a white T-shirt, the material as crumpled and creased as his face where he'd been sleeping on it. Tom realized that it was probably only the second time he'd ever seen Archie in anything but a suit. He looked strangely out of place without it.

The sound of voices filtered through the open doorway, one Dhutta's, the other female. Archie looked up in surprise as the voices drew nearer.

"This way, please," came Dhutta's muffled instruction.

Moments later, Dominique stepped into the room, her blond hair coiled up on her head like a fine silk rope and held in place with a silver grip. Archie snatched up his bedclothes and held them in front of him.

"Dom?" he said in surprise.

"Morning, boys!" She grinned. "Here you go, Archie—got you a little present." She tossed a carton of duty-free cigarettes to him. He instinctively reached out to catch it, letting go of the bedclothes, which fell to the floor. "Gottcha!" she laughed.

"Very funny," Archie muttered as he stooped to gather his sheets up around him again.

"The look on your face!" Tom laughed.

"You're like a bloody pair of kids, you two," Archie said, shaking his head disapprovingly. Grabbing his suit from its hanger, he stumbled to the bathroom, struggling to keep the bedclothes around him.

"I've just made some coffee," Tom said as Archie disappeared with a final, accusing glare in their direction. "You want some?"

"Sure," she said, stripping off her thick ski jacket and tossing it over the back of one of the sofas.

"I'm guessing you don't want any, Raj?"

"No." Dhutta pulled a disapproving face before disappearing into his workshop.

"You weren't followed?"

"No," Dominique confirmed. "I doubled back a few times, just to be certain, but there was no one there."

"And Turnbull met you at the airport this morning, as agreed?"

"Yeah, although I think he was a bit surprised that I was a woman."

"That's because he doesn't know what sort of woman you really are." Tom grinned. "No problems with Customs or anything?"

"None." She smiled her thanks as he handed her a mug. "I never thought it would be so easy to transport a human body part across Europe."

"Oh yeah." Tom sat down next to her. "It's great cover. Archie and I used to do it all the time. As long as the paper-work checks out, they don't touch the box. Last thing they want is some poor kid in need of an organ transplant dying because they contaminated his new heart or kidney. What about the medals?"

"He gave me those too. Archie was right. Weissman did have a Knight's Cross."

She pulled an envelope from her pocket and handed it to Tom. He opened it and slid the medal it contained into the palm of his hand, flipping it over so he could see the reverse, before giving her a satisfied nod.

"It has the same markings as the one we got from Lam-mers's niece," Tom confirmed. "Raj," he called. "Come and have a look at this."

Dhutta reemerged from his workshop and took the medal from Tom with interest, studying it closely.

"I brought the Bellak painting, as well," Dominique added. "Thought it might be useful."

"Good thinking."

"By the way, did you notice the holes in it?"

"In the painting? Yes. What about them?"

"They struck me as odd, that's all. They're very neat. All exactly the same size. They don't look accidental."

"Why would someone have made them deliberately?" Tom frowned. "Unless they wanted to deface it."

Archie reappeared from the bathroom, his composure seemingly restored now that he had his suit on.

"I meant to ask, Mr. Tom—what is this?" Dhutta pointed at the design on the lid of the walnut box that the key had been hidden in.

"A Nazi symbol," Tom explained. "A type of swastika with twelve arms instead of four, one for each of twelve men. It's known as the Black Sun. Have you seen it before?"

"No . . ." Dhutta shook his head, his finger stroking the veneer. "Although the swastika has been a Hindu religious symbol for thousands of years. It can be found in architec-ture all over the world, from the ruins of ancient Troy to the floor of Amiens Cathedral. Rudyard Kipling even used to decorate the dust jackets of all his books with it, to bring him good luck."

"How did the Nazis come to use it?" asked Archie.

"From what I understand, Hitler considered the early Aryans of India to be the prototypical white invaders. He saw the swastika as an inviolable link to the Aryan descent of the German people," Dhutta explained. "Under the Nazis, the swastika became the *Hakenkreuz* or hooked cross, the symbol of the Aryan master race."

"Does the word *swastika* mean something?" asked Tom.

"The word is derived from Sanskrit. The literal translation is 'good to be.' In holy texts it can mean Brahma, which is luck, or Samsara, which is rebirth." He looked up, his voice suddenly thoughtful. "I wonder, which will it be for you, Mr. Tom?"

CHAPTER THIRTY-EIGHT

Banque Völz et Cie occupied a corner lot in one of Zurich's most expensive districts. It was a neoclassical affair, probably mid-1800s, although inconsistently executed, with the huge stone columns supporting the entrance portico comprising an architecturally jarring combination of Ionic and Corinthian styles.

More telling perhaps, was that while the soaring cost of real estate had compelled the owners of neighboring lots to rebuild higher and higher to maximize the yield of their land, the Völz building remained only two stories high, dwarfed by the towering structures around it. This said more about the bank's wealth and power than the tallest skyscraper ever could.

A smartly dressed man wearing a lightweight blue flannel suit greeted Tom and Archie in the small marbled entrance vestibule. It was more reminiscent of a private house than a bank—two side tables, travertine marble resting on ebony legs engraved with gold leaf, flanked a large bronze door that Tom assumed led into the main hall. Each table supported a large iron urn.

"Guten Morgen, meine Herren."

"Guten Morgen," Tom answered, before switching to English. "We're here to see Herr Völz."

The man frowned and looked them skeptically up and down, Tom especially in his faded jeans and sneakers.

"Do you have an appointment?"

"No."

The corner of the man's mouth twitched, as if he had just been told a mildly funny joke. "I'm sorry, but Herr Völz is a very busy man. If you leave your name and number, I will ask someone to call you." He jerked his head toward the door to indicate that they should leave.

"We have a safety-deposit box here. We wish to inspect it immediately."

Now the man laughed outright. "There are no boxes here. We are a bank, not a left-luggage office."

"Tell Herr Völz that we have the key," Tom insisted, dangling it in front of him. "And that we're not leaving until he sees us."

There was a pause as the man stared at the key uncertainly.

"Wait here," he snapped eventually, walking over to the side table on the left and retrieving a black phone from behind the urn. His eyes never left them as he dialed a three-digit number.

"Herr Völz?" He turned away from them so that they couldn't hear him, at one stage glancing at the key Tom was still holding outstretched, while talking rapidly into the phone. He nodded silently as he listened to what was being said in reply, his shoulders visibly stiffening. Replacing the handset in its cradle, he paused, and then turned to face them, an apology flickering around his lips but left unsaid.

"Herr Völz will see you immediately. This way, please."

He threw open the bronze door and ushered them through. As Tom had suspected, this gave onto the main entrance hall, where a series of somber portraits lined the walls. Their footsteps echoing on the checkerboard marble floor, they followed the man into a small office where two secretaries were furiously typing away, their computers' flat screens housed in mahogany and brass boxes, as if the naked display of plastic might tarnish the bank's patrician image.

"Your coats, please." The man's voice had dropped to an ecclesiastical whisper. He took their coats, hanging them carefully on a cast-iron hat stand. He gestured to take Tom's briefcase, but a firm shake of Tom's head and an unblinking glare seemed to convince him otherwise. Then he knocked gently at the massive wooden door that loomed between the secretaries' desks. A brass plaque indicated in swirling copperplate similar to the design on the key that this was the office of RUDOLF VÖLZ, DIREKTOR.

There was no response from within, and Tom followed the man's eyes to a miniature set of traffic lights positioned to the left of the door. It was on red, so they stood there patiently, the chattering of the secretaries' nails on their keyboards echoing like gunfire until finally the light flashed to green. The man opened the door, indicated with a flip of his hand that they should go in, and then shut it behind them.

Völz's office followed the same traditional lines as the rest of the building—soft red carpet underfoot, books lining one of the walls, an indifferent full-length portrait over the elaborate fireplace. The low winter sun streaming through the left-hand window had cut the room diagonally in two, leaving half swathed in shadow while flooding the other with a blinding light.

"What do you want?"

The voice was clipped and immediately hostile. Tom, squinting, had difficulty in making out where it was coming from. Eventually, as his eyes adjusted, he saw a dark shape hunched over the desk on the far side of the room.

"Herr Völz?" Tom walked toward the desk, while Archie hung back.

"What are you? A journalist? Some hack trying to make a career for yourself on the back of my family's good name?" The shape stood up and ignored Tom's outstretched hand. "Or another ambulance-chaser trying to make a living from our hard work."

"I can assure you that I am none of those things."

"The boxes are all gone. An ill-advised diversification strategy by my grandfather during the war that my father wisely dismantled in the 1960s with the full cooperation of the Swiss Banking Commission—as you would know, if you had done your research. You have no business here."

The man leaned forward as if to emphasize his point. This time Tom was able to see the face. Still quite young, perhaps in his early forties, Rudolf Völz had the same un-flinching gaze and proud demeanor as the portraits Tom had seen out in the hall. His dark brown hair was neatly cut, with just a hint of gray. A closely cropped beard covered the line of his jaw like a strap, extending up around his mouth to frame his pinched lips. The underside of his chin and the flat of his sunken, hungry-looking cheeks were clean shaven. His glasses were frameless with clear plastic arms.

"The sixties?" Tom asked, throwing the key they'd dis-covered in the walnut box onto the desk. "In case you don't recognize it, that's your crest on the key. And, unless I'm very much mistaken, the lock that it opens is state-of-the-art."

Völz sat back into his chair, staring at the key as it lay on the desk. "Do you have an account number?"

Tom nodded.

"Give it to me."

Tom recited the numbers Turnbull had given him the pre-vious night: 1256093574.

Squinting, Völz removed his glasses and typed the digits into his computer, then hit Return. After a pause, he looked up with a smile.

"Welcome to Banque Völz, gentlemen."

CHAPTER THIRTY-NINE

1:10 P.M.

"My apologies. Please forgive the little misunderstanding earlier."

Völz's frosty welcome had given way to candied smiles and a warm stream of apologies.

"Don't worry about it," said Tom, sipping the coffee that Völz had insisted on ordering for them.

"It's just that we get so many people trying their luck that we have to be cautious."

"What are they looking for?" Archie asked.

"What is everyone looking for in Switzerland? Money. In our case, either accounts abandoned by Holocaust victims or something else to sue us for. My father was wise enough to shut down the safety-deposit business and contribute all unclaimed assets to the Holocaust survivors' fund to avoid any future . . . complications."

"But not all the boxes were shut?" Archie again.

"Of course not." Völz smiled proudly. "We are a bank, after all. Our first duty is to our customers, not to the Jewish lobby." Tom bit his lip. "Here at Banque Völz, we never forget that."

"I'm glad to hear it. And our account . . . ?"

"Is exactly as was initially instructed. Nothing has been touched."

"Excellent."

"Not since it was last accessed, at least."

"Which was when, exactly?" Archie asked.

Völz removed his glasses and consulted his screen. "May 1958."

Tom glanced at Archie. The same year Lammers had posted the photos of the three Bellak paintings to Weissman, according to the postmark.

"A long time," said Tom. "All the more reason—if you don't mind, Herr Völz—not to delay any longer."

"Of course, of course." Völz leaped to his feet. "Follow me, gentlemen."

He led them past the secretaries into the hall and then through another doorway into a large square-shaped stairwell. Here, three shallow flights of stone steps, each connected by a broad landing, marched their way up to the first and then to the second floor. Above, a slate sky glowered through a glass cupola.

A door was set into the wall under the staircase, and it was to this that Völz went. Taking a key from his pocket, he unlocked the door, reached in, and flicked a light switch, illuminating a narrow flight of dirty steps.

"The wine cellar," Völz explained.

The stairs led down into a low room, perhaps twenty feet long and fifteen feet wide, that smelled old and musty. The only light came from a couple of weak lightbulbs that hung forlornly from the unfinished ceiling. The room was lined with wine racks cradling row upon row of dusty bottles, their labels worn and stained.

"Nice little collection you've got down here," Archie observed appreciatively, pulling a bottle of Château Lafleur '61 from the rack.

Völz went to a rack at the rear of the cellar and pulled it toward him. It swung forward to reveal a large steel door. Reaching into his pocket, he took out another key and unlocked it.

As the door opened, the lights inside blinked on, revealing a room of almost antiseptic whiteness, from the tiled rubber floor to the whitewashed walls and ceiling. It was quite empty apart from a stainless-steel table that took up the middle of the room, a flat-panel computer monitor set at chest height on the far wall, and, to the right of it, what looked like a steel drawer. Strangely, there were no sharp edges: every corner and angle was subtly rounded, as if shaped and smoothed by thousands of years of glacial meltwater.

"How many accounts do you have here?" Tom asked, careful to keep his tone casual.

Völz rubbed his chin in thought. "Accounts like yours? We have about two hundred dating from the war that are still active."

"How do you define 'active'?"

"Ones for which we have contact addresses—post-office boxes mainly—for the designated account holders. That's where we send essential information, such as the new key that was sent out when we upgraded the security system about three years ago. If it doesn't get returned, we deem the account active."

"And if they are returned?"

"It usually means that the original owners or trustees have died, and with them all knowledge of the box's existence. But we hold the box for them all the same, just in case someone makes contact. You see, most of these boxes were taken out on ninety-nine-year leases, payable up front, so we have a duty to hold them until the end of the period. By the time the leases expire . . . Well, let's just say that it probably won't be my problem."

He laughed and turned to the computer panel, tapping it lightly with his finger. Immediately the screen pulsed into life, displaying ten white question marks across its dark surface. He paused, then turned back to face them.

"The account number again, please."

Tom typed in the code recovered from Weissman's arm, selecting each number from a list at the bottom of the screen. The screen went blank, then flashed a greeting:

Wilkommen
Konto: 1256093574
Kontoname: Werfen
Bitte Schlüssel einführen

Account name Werfen, Tom mused. What or who was that? Völz interrupted his thoughts.

"Please insert your key," he translated, pointing at the small square hole beneath the screen.

Tom slipped the key into the hole and a few seconds later a small graphic of a padlock opening confirmed that it had been successfully read by the lasers.

"Now the infrared," Völz prompted.

Tom pressed the button on the key's rubberized handle until another graphic of a door opening confirmed that the algorithms had matched. So far, so good.

"Well gentlemen, your key matches your account. So all that is left is the palm scan."

"Herr Völz," Tom said, turning to face him. "I wonder whether you could give my colleague and me a little privacy?"

"Of course," said Völz. He was nothing if not the professional Swiss banker. "Just place your hand against this panel . . ." He indicated a glass plate on the left of the computer screen that Tom had not noticed before. "The system will retrieve your box and place it in here." He pointed at the drawer front. "When you are finished, replace the box in the tray and the system will reset. I will come down and close the room up myself after you have gone."

"Thank you for your help," Tom said, shaking his hand.

As soon as the sound of the banker's footsteps had receded up the stairs, Tom slid his briefcase onto the table and opened it. Weissman's arm had been packed with ice and then sealed inside a clear plastic bag that had itself been covered with further ice packs. Even so, outside of a properly refrigerated environment it had begun to smell, and the flesh had turned a funny shade of yellow.

"Christ!" muttered Archie, peering over Tom's shoulder. "That is rank."

Breathing through his mouth, Tom reached into the bag and extracted the arm from under the ice, holding it just above the wrist. It felt hard and slippery, like a dead fish.

Tom approached the glass panel and placed the lifeless hand against it. A crosshatch of red beams lit up from deep within the glass and scanned the hand's surface. The screen flashed a warning.

"Scan failure," Tom translated grimly.

"How many tries do we get?"

"Two more. Then it locks us out."

"I hope we've got this right."

"Turnbull told me that Weissman only traveled abroad once and that was three years ago to some conference in Geneva. The same time, according to what Völz just told us, that they upgraded the security system here. I doubt it's a coincidence. Weissman could easily have got the train here, had his palm scanned into the system, and then got back to Geneva in time for dinner. No one would have suspected a thing."

"Maybe the fingers need to be pressed harder against the glass," Archie suggested.

Tom pressed his own hand to the back of Weissman's, forcing it flat. The red grid flared into life once more, then extinguished itself.

"Scan failure," Tom said with a rueful shrug. "I think the reader's picking up the edge of my fingers where they overlap. Maybe you should try. Your hands are a bit smaller than mine."

"Okay," said Archie, taking the arm and pressing his hand against Weissman's so that the fingers were splayed across the glass. Again the laser grid scanned the hand. The screen went blank, then flashed up another message.

"Scan successful." Tom breathed with relief.

Holding the arm between his fingertips and as far away from his body as he could, Archie dropped it back into the plastic bag, sealed it, and shut the briefcase with relief.

There was a whirring noise from behind the wall. Tom glanced at Archie. They both knew what was happening, having studied the workings of these types of systems many times. Somewhere deep below where they were now standing, a robotic arm was matching their access details to one of the hundreds of bar-coded boxes that were stacked on shallow trays in a fireproof vault. Once located, the box slid from its housing into a tray that carried it to the drawer. On cue, the drawer front buzzed and jumped forward a few centimeters.

Archie pulled the drawer toward him. It contained a battered-looking metal box that he lifted out and placed on the table. The box was about three feet long, a foot wide, and six inches deep.

"Ready?" Tom asked with an anxious smile.

He slowly lifted the lid and they both peered inside.

CHAPTER FORTY

CIA SUBSTATION, ZURICH

January 8—2:20 P.M.

"Mobile One, this is Central. Come in, please."

"Go ahead, Central," came the crackled response.

"Are you in place, Roberts?" Agent Ben Cody leaned over the female operator's chair and spoke into her microphone.

"Affirmative. Stand by to receive transmission."

A few seconds later one of the three flat-screen monitors in front of the operator flickered into life. On the large overhead screen a live satellite feed showed the agent's location as a blinking red dot. Five other dots pulsed around it, showing that the rest of the team were also in place.

"Are you sure about this?" Cody asked.

"Sure about what?" Bailey couldn't help but sound defensive in the face of Cody's skeptical tone.

"I mean I've pulled people off three other teams to cover this thing." Cody indicated the frantic activity that was consuming the CIA's secure operations room—four operators were monitoring the ongoing transmissions with the six field agents, while behind them two more of his staff were fielding calls, accompanied all the while by the constant buzz of computers and the high-pitched shriek of encrypted fax machines. An armed sentry stood by the swipe-card-activated door. "I wouldn't have done it for anyone other than Carter. He's a good man. One of the best. But, I gotta tell you, I've had enough bureau wild-goose chases to last me this life and the next."

"I can't promise anything," said Bailey. "Let's be clear, we're following a hunch here. But Carter wouldn't have sent me if he didn't think it was worth running with."

"Well, I guess we'll soon find out whether you're right." Cody sighed. "Either way, we'll get a fix on whoever goes in or out of that hotel. If your guy shows up, we'll nail him."

CHAPTER FORTY-ONE

"That's it?"

Tom understood the disappointment in Dominique's voice. The lengths to which Weissman and Lammers had gone to guarantee the safety-deposit box's safekeeping had had them all speculating feverishly about what exactly lay inside it.

They had all been wrong.

No gold. No diamonds. No long-lost Vermeer. In the end, all it had contained was the thin brown leather pouch, cracking along the seams, that Tom had just placed on the tea chest in front of them.

"Someone's having a laugh" was Archie's typically forthright analysis. "It's a practical joke. Must be."

"What is inside, please?" Dhutta inquired, his mustache twitching.

"A map," Tom answered, flipping the pouch open and drawing out a yellowing document that had been folded several times to fit inside. "Where we can pin it up?"

"I have the very place." Dhutta's tongue flicked against the corners of his mouth with anticipation. "This way, please." He darted through to the computer area and pointed at the expanse of bare wall above the printers and scanners. "It will fit there, I believe."

Standing on a chair, Tom tacked the four corners to the wall, then jumped down again.

"Deutsche Reichsbahn—German National Railways," Dominique translated. "It's a map of the Nazi rail network."

"That's right," said Archie. "The various countries of the Reich are shaded the same color as Germany: Austria, Luxembourg, Czechoslovakia, Poland—"

"Given that the Nazis didn't absorb that much of Poland until 1942 or '43," Tom butted in, "this was probably printed toward the end of the war. Before then, central Poland was governed from Krakow as a German colony."

"June 1943," Dominique confirmed, pointing at the date in the bottom right corner.

Tom moved in for a closer look. "It shows all the major towns and cities. The thick black lines are the actual railways. The thinner lines must be sidings or branch lines or something."

"And the dots are stations," Archie added.

"So why keep it?" Dominique frowned.

"Good question," Archie agreed. "They must have produced tens of thousands of these maps."

Tom pinched the end of his nose in thought. "This one must be different in some way . . . Raj?" Dhutta sprang forward at the sound of his name. "Have you got a projector here?"

"Of course."

"Great. Dom, see if you can find a 1943 map of the German railway network on the Web. We'll blow it up to the same size as this one and overlay the images. That way, if there are any differences, we should be able to see them."

Dominique busied herself at the computer while Tom readied the projector, raising it to the same height as the map so as not to create a distorted picture. A few minutes later, Dominique turned around with a smile.

"Got it?" Archie asked.

She nodded. "You were right: the 1943 printing was

standard issue. I found a copy on a university Web site. We may need to play with the sizing a bit, but it should work."

The image flashed up on the wall, and Tom adjusted the focus and the proximity of the projector until he was satisfied that he had got as close a fit as he could. Then all four of them approached the overlaid maps and studied them carefully.

It was almost ten minutes before anyone spoke. Predictably, it was Archie.

"Well, if they are different, I can't see where."

"Me neither." Tom rubbed his eyes wearily.

"Same here," Dominique chimed.

"What about ultraviolet light?" Dhutta suggested brightly. "It might show something. I have a black light here."

"UV?" Archie exclaimed. "Did they know about that back then?"

"It was discovered in the early eighteen hundreds by Johann Ritter, a Polish scientist," Dominique confirmed.

Archie shrugged, experience clearly having taught him not to challenge Dominique on factual matters such as this.

"Have you got something we can use, Raj?" Tom asked.

Dhutta dived into his workshop, emerging a few moments later with a handheld fluorescent tube trailing a long black cord. Dominique killed the lights. Tom, taking the black light from Dhutta, approached the wall and began to move the tube across the map's surface, his face lit with an unnatural purple glow. Almost immediately, black marks began to appear—small circles around place-names, and next to them, numbers.

"You guys seeing this?" Tom asked excitedly.

Archie nodded.

"I'll read them out to you."

A few minutes later, Dominique had compiled a list from the names Tom had called out. "There's a funny mark here too," he said, pointing at a large L shape that had been drawn in the bottom left-hand quadrant of the map. He marked it with a pencil.

Dhutta turned the lights back on.

"Read them back," Archie suggested.

"I've arranged them alphabetically," she said. "Brennberg—30/3, Brixlegg—21/4, Budapest—15/12, Györ—4/2, Hopfgarten—15/4, Linz—9/4, Salzburg—13/4, Vienna—3/4, Werfen—16/5."

"Werfen?" Archie turned to Tom. "Wasn't that the name of the safety-deposit account?"

"That's right," said Tom.

"So what do you think this is?"

"Maybe those numbers are dates," Tom suggested. "You know, the day followed by the month. What do you get if you order them that way?"

Dominique quickly reordered the place-names and then read them back.

"Budapest—15/12, Györ—4/2, Brennberg—30/3, Vienna—3/4, Linz—9/4, Salzburg—13/4, Hopfgarten—15/4, Brixlegg—21/4, Werfen—16/5."

"Look"—Tom had placed a small pin in each place as it had been read out—"the place-names move east to west as if this is some sort of itinerary. A journey that was made or planned from Budapest, across Europe, to . . . well, look where it was headed until it got to Brixlegg." Tom pointed to the border just a hundred miles from the small village.

"Switzerland." Archie this time.

"And by the looks of things it almost made it, but then turned back to Werfen." Tom tapped the map with his neatly clipped right index finger. "We should go and see Lasche again, find out whether he knows anything about this."

"What about that?" asked Archie, pointing at the L shape that Tom had faintly penciled on the map.

"We'll ask him about that too."

"Whatever Lasche knows, I doubt it'll explain why this map was hidden behind armor-plated security with a couple of town names circled in invisible ink," observed Dominique.

"Not invisible ink," Dhutta said, his voice suddenly serious. "Although the tint has faded over time, in my experience there is only one substance that you would expect to fluoresce less than its surroundings and yet show up under black light in this way."

"Which is . . . ?" asked Archie.

"Blood."

CHAPTER FORTY-TWO

HOTEL DREI KÖNIGE, ZURICH

January 8—4:04 P.M.

I t was, as Tom had remembered, an awe-inspiring sight—
battle flags shimmering from the rafters, petals of Napoleonic swords winking from the walls, polished pistols
reclining in display cases like fine jewelery. To Archie, though,
it was all new, and he had leaped from piece to piece like an
eager child.

"Where did he get all this stuff?"

Tom knew that Archie was attempting a whisper. It wasn't
working. His increasingly excited voice whistled noisily in
the room's stillness. But Tom understood why he was trying,
at least. On his previous visit Tom had been struck by the
polished martial grandeur of his surroundings; this time it
was the dark, soulless intensity that overwhelmed him.

The room, he could see now, nurtured a leaden heaviness
that reminded him of an El Greco painting. It had a strange,
haunting quality that hinted at death, without ever fully ex-
pressing it. Tom felt that his presence was somehow inappropriate, that he had stumbled into the forbidden annex to
some secret library and was having to balance the desire to
find his way out with a terrifying hunger to study the exhibits for as long as he could before he got caught. Under the

circumstances, a whisper seemed the very least the room required.

"Have you seen this?" The suit of armor Archie had paused in front of was an intriguing piece that seemed to be seated rather than standing. The black lacquer that had originally covered it had long since cracked and crumbled, although the faded remains of intricately painted gold characters could still be seen on the wide, fearsome helmet and the chest plate. The arms and the neck were also made from metal, wide flat links tied together with colored string. The remainder, however, seemed to be made of bamboo and patterned cloth.

"It's samurai," Archie explained breathlessly, although Tom had already worked that much out for himself. "From the helmet design, I'd say Muromacho Period. Fifteenth, maybe fourteenth century. Must be worth a small fortune."

"Rather a large fortune, in fact, Mr. Connolly."

Lasche had entered the room unseen and was now advancing rapidly toward them in his electric wheelchair. Archie spun around, clearly surprised that Lasche had known who he was.

"Yes, I know who you are." Lasche gave a rasping laugh. "When you pay as much as I do to supplement my collection, it's essential to know all the key players. You, I was given to understand, are one of the best."

"Was. I've retired now. We both have, haven't we, Tom?"

Tom didn't answer. He had noticed that Lasche's voice was surprisingly strong, compared to their last meeting. And his breathing, while still strained and wheezy, seemed much improved; almost normal.

"It's good of you to see me again, Herr Lasche. You seem . . . much better."

"Full blood transfusion." Lasche gave a red-gummed smile. "I have one every four weeks. For a few days I almost feel human again." He stroked the front of his jacket, and Tom noticed that he had swapped his pajamas and dressing gown for a suit and tie, although the top button had been left undone to allow the shirt's starched fabric to accommodate the fleshy folds of his neck.

"Why is he back here?" Lasche's nurse growled from the doorway.

"Forgive Heinrich"—Lasche gave a small shake of his head—"he is very protective. His question, however, is an appropriate one. Why *have* you returned, Mr. Kirk? I hope it is not regarding the Order, for you will have made a wasted journey. You have already quite exhausted the little I know."

"Only indirectly, I can assure you. It is regarding a map. Or perhaps, more accurately, a journey. A train journey."

"A train journey?" Lasche wet his white lips with a flick of his tongue. "You certainly have the gift of the mysterious. I suppose I will have to hear you out, one final time."

Lasche steered his chair back over to the other side of the room and parked himself behind his desk, indicating with a wave that they should sit opposite, his gruesome lamp still casting its sickly glow.

"Now, tell me about your train journey."

"We came across a map. A railway map. It seemed to indicate a train journey that was made in the war."

"And no doubt you think it leads to some fantastic hidden treasure," Lasche said dismissively. "Some long-lost masterpiece."

"Why do you say that?" Tom couldn't mask his surprise. Did Lasche know more than he was letting on?

"Because why else would you, of all people, be here, Mr. Kirk? You know your history. You know that Hitler understood the cultural significance of art—its emotional pull on people's imaginations and their sense of identity. War offered him an opportunity to reshape the world's perception of great art."

"You're talking about Sonderauftrag Linz, aren't you?" said Tom. "The unit dedicated to building an art collection that exemplified everything that was best about Aryan art."

"Sonderauftrag Linz yes, but also Einsatzstab Reichsleiter Rosenberg and the SS-Ahnenerbe. They all played their part in the most sophisticated, well planned, and thoroughly executed theft in history. The plunder of Europe and the genocide of its Jews walked hand in hand. Millions of items were taken. Tens of thousands remain lost to this day. Hundreds still surface every year, never having been returned to their rightful owners. And now I expect you think you may have found some small crumb that has fallen from their table."

"All we think we've found at the moment is a train journey," Tom said firmly. "A journey that we hoped you might know something about. Perhaps if we read you the names of the places the train passed through . . ."

Lasche scratched his head, the pink skin flaking in several places under his touch and dropping to his collar.

"I very much doubt it. Of all the millions of journeys that were made during that period, why should one mean more to me than another?"

"Because we think this one might have been special," Tom said confidently, although he realized with a sinking heart that Lasche was probably right, and that this was even more of a long shot than he'd first feared.

"Then by all means, read away." Lasche shrugged. "But I wouldn't hold out too much hope."

Tom began to read from the list Dominique had prepared. "Budapest, Györ, Brennberg, Vienna, Linz . . ." Lasche's face remained impassive, just a little shake of his head with the mention of each successive name to indicate that they meant nothing to him. ". . . Salzburg, Hopfgarten," Tom continued. "Brixlegg, Werfen."

Lasche's eyes narrowed. "Werfen? Did you say Werfen?"

"Yes." Tom nodded eagerly.

"You want to know about a train that started in Budapest and ended up in Werfen?"

"Why, does that mean something to you?"

"You are forcing an old man to operate at the limits of his memory." He turned to his nurse, who had remained standing at the rear of the room. "Heinrich, please go and fetch me file number fifteen. Oh, and sixteen too. It's in one of them, I'm sure of it."

CHAPTER FORTY-THREE

4:30 P.M.

Tom and Archie swapped questioning glances, but Lasche was not to be drawn out, staring pensively up at the ceiling until the nurse returned a few moments later clutching two large red files bound with string. Lasche opened the first one, leafed through it, then turned his attention to the second. Eventually, he seemed to find what he was looking for.

"Read me those place-names again," he demanded, his nose buried in the file.

"Budapest, Györ, Brennberg, Vienna . . ." Tom began.

"Linz, Salzburg, Hopfgarten, Brixlegg, Werfen." Lasche completed the list in a perfunctory manner and looked up. When he spoke next his tone was curious. "Well, it seems I may know your train after all. What you have just described is the exact itinerary of the Hungarian Gold Train."

"Gold train?" Archie turned to Tom, his staring eyes underlining the excitement in his voice.

"How familiar are you with what was happening in Hungary during the closing days of the war?"

"Not very," Tom admitted.

"Well, then, let me set the scene for you," Lasche said,

pouring himself a glass of water and helping himself to a mouthful.

"By December 1944, overwhelming Russian forces had almost totally encircled Budapest. The Germans were in disarray, their thousand-year Reich collapsing around their ears. So, by express order of Adolf Eichmann, a train was prepared."

"Adolf Eichmann?" Archie frowned. "Wasn't he the bloke the Israelis kidnapped from Argentina and executed?"

"The same," Lasche confirmed. "He is notorious now as the architect of the Final Solution, but at that time, Eichmann was in charge of the Office for Jewish Emigration in Vienna. The train he had commandeered was to take vast quantities of treasure plundered from some of the half-million or so Hungarian Jews he had sent to their deaths, and carry it far beyond the reach of the advancing Russian troops."

"What sort of treasure?" Tom this time.

"Gold, obviously. More than five tons of it, ranging from ingots seized from national banks to teeth broken out of their owners' mouths. They say that the wedding bands alone, stripped from the fingers of their victims, filled three crates. Beyond that . . ." Lasche consulted his file and read: "Nearly seven hundred pounds of diamonds and pearls, one thousand two hundred and fifty paintings, five thousand Persian and Oriental rugs, over eight hundred and fifty cases of silverware, fine porcelain, rare stamps, coin collections, furs, watches, alarm clocks, cameras, topcoats, typewriters, even silk underwear. The list goes on and on." He looked up. "The spoils of war. The fruits of murder."

"It must have been worth millions."

"Two hundred and six million dollars in 1945 money, to be exact. Several billion dollars today."

"And all this on one train?"

"One train of fifty-two carriages, of which"—Lasche consulted his file again—". . . twenty-nine were freight cars. Heavy-duty and, in some cases, specially reinforced freight cars, the best that the Nazis could lay their hands on at the time."

"So it got away safely?" Archie asked. "The Russians didn't capture it?"

"It left Budapest on the fifteenth of December." Tom checked his list as Lasche spoke. The train's departure date tallied with the date marked on the map. "Then it stopped in Györ, where its load was increased by a hundred old masters from the local municipal museum. Over the next three months it traveled barely a hundred miles, its journey hampered by the battles raging around it and ten unsuccessful robbery attempts—nine of them by rogue elements of the SS—which the Hungarian soldiers detailed to protect the train's special cargo successfully fought off."

"Where was it headed?" Archie again.

"In all probability Switzerland. But by the time it reached the outskirts of Salzburg, the war was almost over. And although it had successfully outrun the Russians, the Allies were making rapid progress into Austria. On the twenty-first of April, the 405th Bombardment Group of the Fifteenth Air Force destroyed the railway bridge at Brixlegg, and a few days later the Seventh Army joined up with the Fifth Army at the Bremner Pass. Austria was effectively split in two and the train's route to Switzerland blocked."

"So it was captured?"

Lasche smiled. "I think *found* would be a more accurate description. The 3rd Infantry Division of the 15th Regiment discovered it in the Tauern tunnel, only a few miles from Brixlegg, where the Germans had abandoned it, still crammed with its precious cargo. The Americans moved it to Werfen and then on to Camp Truscott on the outskirts of Salzburg, where all twenty-seven freight cars were unloaded into secure warehouses."

"And what happened to it then?" Tom asked.

Lasche shook his head ruefully, his voice suddenly hard. "Although it was known that the assets on the Gold Train were Hungarian Jewish in origin, they were designated 'enemy property,' making it possible for high-ranking U.S. officials to requisition the entire load."

"Requisition?" said Archie.

"A euphemism for legalized theft. Rather than return the remaining goods to the Hungarian State for restitution to the survivors and relatives of those who had been robbed and killed, a few greedy and unscrupulous American officers simply helped themselves to what they wanted, decking out their field offices with all the trappings of a conquering army and then shipping most of the remainder home to the United States." Lasche sounded almost angry now. "The Americans handed over a thousand works of art to the Austrian rather than the Hungarian government and then auctioned the remainder in New York."

Tom shook his head, his tone suspicious. "Forgive me for asking, Herr Lasche, but you seem remarkably well informed about this one train."

"You forget, Mr. Kirk, before I was reduced to pissing into a bag"—Lasche patted the side of his leg disconsolately—"I used to pursue foreign companies and governments on behalf of Holocaust victims. It was my job to know about incidents such as these." He tapped his finger on his file. "Rumors about the Gold Train have been floating around for years, but it was only after I'd retired that the Presidential Advisory Commission on Holocaust Assets finally admitted to what I have just told you. A class-action suit was mounted by survivors. Predictably, the U.S. Department of Justice opposed all attempts at compensation, at first denying the charges, then saying that the events were too long ago for a contemporary court to consider. But the courts ruled in the survivors' favor, and they received a payout of close to twenty-five million dollars. A tiny fraction of what they were owed."

"Hang on a minute—" Archie had been frowning in concentration for the past few seconds. "You just said that the Yanks unloaded twenty-seven freight cars? But earlier you said there were twenty-nine."

"Indeed I did." Lasche turned to Archie, seemingly impressed at his alertness. "Because it appears, Mr. Connolly, that somewhere between Budapest and Werfen, two carriages disappeared."

"Disappeared?" Archie frowned. "Two railway carriages can't just vanish into thin air!"

"That would indeed be the logical assumption," Lasche agreed. "And yet the fact remains they were gone. And what was in them, and where they are now, is something I fear we will never know."

CHAPTER FORTY-FOUR

CIA SUBSTATION, ZURICH

January 8—4:51 P.M.

It's him!" Bailey exclaimed, tapping the screen excitedly with his finger. "It must be."

"Are you sure?" Cody urged. "We only get one shot at this. If we tail him and someone else shows up, we'll miss them."

"Sure as I can be. Stocky, cropped blond hair, early forties, smoker. He matches the description we were given. And, according to your guy on the inside, he's just come down from Lasche's floor."

"Fine. Get a still off to the lab and have them run it through the system," Cody instructed the girl standing next to him. "See if they come up with a match."

"What about his buddy?" Bailey asked, angling his head slightly for a better view of the jittery picture being beamed in from the agent stationed opposite the hotel entrance. "We should check him out too."

"Good idea," said Cody. "Chances are, he's not acting alone."

The girl nodded and then disappeared into the adjacent room.

"What do you want to do, sir?" asked one of the operatives, looking over her shoulder at Cody.

"Our FBI friend says he's a match"—he winked at Bailey—"so tell Roberts to roll."

She turned back to face her screen. "Mobile One, this is Central. Be advised that the subject has been confirmed as our primary mark. Track and hold your distance."

The image on the monitor jerked unsteadily as the agent wearing the concealed camera set off, the shifting red dot on the plasma screen above confirming that he was on the move.

"All agents," the operator continued, "primary mark is leaving the hotel and heading north toward the river. Move to intercept at grid point—"

"Correction, Central," the speaker hissed. "Primary mark has turned east. I repeat, primary mark has turned east toward Bahnhofstrasse."

"Bahnhofstrasse? Shit," Cody muttered, approaching the back of the operator's chair. "Who else have we got down there?"

"Mobile Two and Three are—"

"Their names, Jesus, give me their names," Cody snapped. "We haven't got time for all this code-word bullshit."

"Marquez and Henry can be there in sixty seconds. Jones, Wilton, and Gregan will take about two minutes to get in position."

"Get them all down there, ASAP. I need as many pairs of eyes on this guy as we've got."

"What's the problem?" asked Bailey.

"The problem is that Bahnhofstrasse at this time is like Fifth Avenue on the first day of the winter sales," Cody replied with an anxious shake of his head. "If he gets down there and we're not sticking to him like a hot date on prom night, we'll lose him in the crowds."

Bailey glanced up at the plasma screen. Six red dots were rapidly converging on Bahnhofstrasse.

"Okay, here we go," Cody said with a rueful sigh, as the image on the camera showed the backs of the two men as they filtered into the thick stream of rush-hour shoppers and commuters. "Stay with him, Roberts," he muttered. "Don't lose him."

The man identified by Cody as Roberts stayed close, the image he was beaming back suggesting that he was only twenty feet behind the two men. That was much closer than was typically safe or advisable, but under the circumstances it was an unavoidable risk. Two more agents closed in on the targets, one from each side, so that they now had three camera feeds of the same scene, each showing a slightly different angle, on the small monitors in front of them.

The targets paused in front of one of the innumerable jewelers, paused, shook hands, and then separated, heading briskly off in different directions.

"What do you want to do?" Cody spun to face Bailey.

"Shit!" Bailey anxiously rubbed the bridge of his nose. "I don't know. I need to ask Carter."

"Carter isn't here. This is your call now."

Bailey was silent as he considered what to do. Carter had told him that he was there to observe, not to make decisions. But if he didn't make one now, both men would get away.

"Seconds count, Bailey," Cody urged.

"Blondi. Follow Blondi."

"You sure?"

"That's who we came here for," said Bailey, hoping his gut instinct was the right one. "We can't lose him now."

"You got it. Roberts, Marquez, Henry—stay on the primary mark," the operator intoned. "Jones, Wilton, Gregan—take up your positions and be prepared to relieve the others as they come past. I don't want him seeing the same face more than once."

"Roger," came the crackled response.

The man known as Blondi moved on, casually surveying the shop windows, pausing momentarily in front of one particularly gaudy display. And then, without warning, just as a tram came past, he broke into a run.

"Shit, he's made us," Cody exclaimed. "Okay, all units move in. Repeat, move in. Let's take him down."

"What do you mean, he's made us?" Bailey took a worried step toward the screen. "How did he make us?"

"Because he's good."

"He's getting on the tram," the speaker crackled.

"Well, get on it with him. Don't lose him."

The images being beamed back bounced wildly as the three agents broke into a run, the sound of their breathing echoing through the room. No one was talking, their eyes and attention totally focused on the screens.

Rapidly closing the gap on the tram, the two agents leaped aboard, one closely followed by the other, just as the doors shut behind them.

"Where is he?" Bailey whispered.

"Find him and get him off," Cody ordered.

The images showed the tram's interior and close-ups of other passengers' surprised faces. But there was no sign of the man they had followed.

"There!" Cody exclaimed, thumping his finger against the screen.

On one of the monitors they could see, through the tram window, a man standing on the pavement, waving them good-bye.

"How did he do that?" Bailey asked, his voice a disbelieving whisper.

"Because he's a pro." Cody banged the table in front of him with the palm of his hand. "Jesus, it's like he knew we'd be waiting for him."

"Maybe he did, sir." Returning from the room next door, the young operator handed Cody a piece of paper.

"What's that?" asked Bailey.

"Austrian police have just put out an APB on a man they are looking for in connection with the murder of a woman, Maria Lammers, and the fire-bombing of a church in Kitz-bühel in the Austrian Alps early this morning," Cody replied, reading from the sheet.

"What's that got to do with this case?"

"Several witnesses have reported seeing a stranger with the victim the previous day. They were able to give a description."

Cody held up the composite sketch faxed through by the Austrian police and next to it the still photo just taken of Blondi leaving the Hotel Drei Könige.

It was unmistakably the same man.

CHAPTER FORTY-FIVE

W hat's wrong?" Dominique's eyes were wide with concern.

"Is Archie back?" Tom was breathing heavily, his voice strained.

"Why, what's happened? Are you okay? You're not hurt, are you?"

"No, I'm fine. It's Archie I'm worried about. A man followed us when we came out of the hotel." Tom took off his overcoat and threw it over the arm of one of the worn sofas. "He was waiting for us." He turned to Dhutta. "Have you told anyone we're here?"

"No, Mr. Tom, I can assure you that—"

"I hope for your sake you haven't," Tom said coldly. "I can think of several people who would be very interested in your current whereabouts. If you've breathed so much as a word about us to anyone . . ."

"We have made a deal," Dhutta pleaded, furiously rolling something invisible between his right thumb and forefinger. "I would never betray that trust. It's all people like us have left."

There was a long, uncomfortable silence until the shrill sound of the bell broke the spell.

"Maybe that's him," Dominique said with a hopeful smile. Dhutta slipped gratefully out of the room, then reappeared moments later with Archie only a few steps behind him.

"Sorry I'm late." Archie sat down heavily on one of the sofas. "Spot of bother. I'm sure Tom filled you in."

Dhutta made straight for his medicine shelf, ran his fingers along the line of brown bottles, selected one, opened it, took a swig, and replaced it. Whatever it was, it seemed to calm his nerves.

"Any idea who it was?" Dominique asked.

"I didn't exactly hang around to find out."

"What the hell did he want with us?" Tom asked.

"They, you mean," Archie observed drily. "I counted at least three. And in case you hadn't noticed, it was me they were after, not you."

"You been up to anything I should know about?" Tom eyed Archie suspiciously. "You've never had heat like that before."

"'Course not." Archie sounded almost offended.

"Your recent American trip, for example. You never did say what that was about."

"Oh, come on," Archie protested. "I'm out of play, and you know it."

"What were you doing there, then?"

"Nothing that's got anything to do with this. That should be enough for you."

"You're right, I'm sorry," Tom conceded. "Guess I'm a bit jumpy. Anyway, I'd say it's about time we moved on. I don't know about you, but I don't want to hang around to find out who they were and what they wanted. Besides, we got what we came here for."

"Did we?" said Archie. "Fine, so we found out that Weissman and Lammers were both members of some secret order of SS knights. We know that they spent a small fortune protecting a map that concealed the final journey of a train loaded with stolen Jewish treasure—"

"Lasche told you that?" Dominique asked excitedly.

Tom quickly recounted the story of the Hungarian Gold

Train. Dhutta's eyes widened with each new revelation, the feverish twirling of a pen through his fingers increasing, until it was a blur of black plastic.

"The point is, two carriages were taken from that train and we haven't got a bloody clue what was on them or where they are," Archie said resignedly. "So I'm not sure we did get what we came for."

"Oh, I wouldn't say that," Dominique said, a smile playing around the corners of her mouth.

Tom looked around, recognizing the tone in her voice. "You've found something, haven't you?"

"The map wasn't the only thing they were protecting in that safety-deposit box," she said.

"Wasn't it?" Archie frowned.

"This was kept in there too." She picked up the frayed leather satchel that the map had been kept in.

"It's just a regular satchel," said Tom. "German made, late forties. Probably one of millions."

"Come on, Dom," Archie said impatiently. "What are you getting at?"

"Well, after an hour of turning it up and down and shaking it, nothing. But then I noticed this." She pointed at the front flap.

"The stitching?" Archie eyed it carefully, then looked up with interest. "It's a different color."

"It's newer than the rest. So I unpicked it. And I found something inside."

"Another map?" Dhutta suggested eagerly, moving in for a closer view.

"No. Not even close." She slipped her hand between the two pieces of leather that made up the satchel's front flap and withdrew a small flat shard of what initially looked to be orange-brown plastic. She handed it to Tom, who examined it, then passed it silently to Archie.

"It's lined with gold leaf," Dominique said.

"No." Archie shook his head, turning the shard over in his hands. "It isn't. It can't be."

"Why not?" Tom said quietly. "It makes sense. It makes

perfect sense. Why else would the Order have been involved with that train? That must have been what was on those missing carriages."

"Christ!" Archie looked up, his voice caught somewhere between fear and reverence. "You realize what this means?"

"No, Mr. Archie, I'm afraid I don't," said a confused-looking Dhutta. "What is this, please?"

"It's amber," Dominique said slowly. "Jewelry-grade amber."

Tom nodded. "Renwick is after the Amber Room."

CHAPTER FORTY-SIX

5:26 P.M.

The room was quiet, the only sound the muted commentary from an unseen cricket match being screened on one of the plasmas in the other room. All eyes were on the small shard of amber that lay cradled on Archie's rough palm. It was Dhutta who broke the silence first.

"Please forgive my ignorance, but what is this Amber Room?"

Tom paused. How to describe the indescribable? How to frame in base words the jeweled essence of an object of such ethereal beauty that it seemed to have been created by sheer force of imagination rather than by human hands?

"Imagine a room so beautiful that it was called the eighth wonder of the world. A room commissioned by Frederick the Great of Prussia, gifted to Peter the Great of Russia, and completed by Catherine the Great. A room created from tons of Baltic amber resin, which at the time was twelve times more valuable than gold, infused with honey, linseed, and cognac, and then molded into a hundred thousand panels backed with gold and silver—nine hundred and twenty-six square feet of it, accented with diamonds, emeralds, jade, onyx, and rubies. Then imagine that it disappeared."

"Disappeared?" Dhutta asked, his eyebrows raised quizzically.

"When they were laying siege to St. Petersburg in 1941, the Nazis removed the room from the Catherine Palace and reinstalled it at Königsberg Castle before dismantling it again in 1945 because they feared a British bombing raid."

"Then it vanished," Archie continued. "Not a whisper. Until now, maybe."

"You really think that's what was on the train?" Dominique said excitedly. "The actual Amber Room?"

"Why not?" said Tom. "It was one of the greatest works of art ever made. It must be worth hundreds of millions of dollars. What else would have warranted Himmler assigning his most elite troops to guard duty? What else would they have gone to such lengths to conceal?"

"Remember how fascinated your father was with the story of the Amber Room," Dominique reminded Tom.

"He'd been looking for it for as long as I can remember." Tom nodded. "Hoping to pick up some whisper of its fate, however tenuous. Dreaming of bringing it back from the dead."

"That's what this is all about," said Dominique. "The Bellak portrait must contain some clue to where the Amber Room is hidden."

"But what would Renwick—or Kristall Blade, for that matter—do with the Amber Room? It's not as if they can sell it," Archie pointed out.

"Not whole, no. But they could break it up. Sell it piecemeal—a panel here, a panel there. Maybe even enough to line a small room. There's no shortage of people who'd pay hundreds of thousands for a fragment of the Amber Room and not ask too many questions about where it came from. They could clear fifty, maybe even sixty million easy."

"Enough for Renwick to get back on his feet and for Kristall Blade to fight their war," said Archie.

"Which is why we've got to stop them." Tom's eyes blazed with determination. "Now more than ever. This isn't just about Renwick anymore. This is about protecting one of the world's greatest treasures from being broken up and lost for ever."

"If Renwick's got the portrait, we'll never catch up with him now," Archie said ruefully.

"But he doesn't have it," Tom observed. "If he did, he wouldn't have left Weissman's arm and the other Bellak painting for me to find. It's lost in some private collection somewhere and he's trying to use us to connect the dots."

"What did you say?" Dominique's eyes narrowed, her forehead creasing into a quizzical frown.

"I said, why else would he have left Weissman's arm and—"

"No. About the dots?"

"What dots?"

"Connecting the dots. Isn't that what you said?"

"What the hell are you talking about, Dom?" Archie said impatiently.

She didn't answer. Instead, clicking her tongue with frustration, she hurried through to the far room and unpinned the railway map from the wall. The others followed, swapping confused glances.

"Here, lay it out on the floor," she said, handing it down to Tom. "I wondered what those holes were for," she continued, shaking her head ruefully.

"What holes?" asked Archie.

"The holes in the painting." She snapped her fingers impatiently, indicating that Archie should hand her the rolled Bellak painting that lay on the desk. "They'd been made too carefully to be accidental." She unscrolled the canvas and laid it flat on the map, aligning the bottom left corner with the L shape that had revealed itself under the black light. "Give me a pencil." Dhutta pulled one from the neat row of pens he kept clipped in his shirt pocket and handed it to her.

Gripping the pencil tightly, she pushed its end into the first hole and swiveled it around so as to mark the surface of the map underneath. She then did the same in each of the nine other holes until, satisfied that she had covered them all, she peeled the map away and let it spring shut, revealing the pencil marks she had just made.

Archie whistled slowly.

"They show the same route we revealed before," Dhutta exclaimed.

"It's like you said"—Dominique was beaming proudly—"connect the dots."

Tom stared silently at the map, hardly believing what he was seeing. Dhutta was right, the pencil marks had fallen precisely on the towns revealed by the black light earlier and confirmed by Lasche as the route of the Gold Train.

All the dots apart from one. A small village in northern Germany whose name he had to squint to read because the pencil mark had gone right through it. Above it was a small symbol which the key told him denoted a castle.

Wewelsburg Castle.

CHAPTER FORTY-SEVEN

CIA SUBSTATION, ZURICH

January 8—6:01 P.M.

So you lost him?" Even the several thousand miles between them could not hide the disappointment in Carter's voice.

"Yes, sir." Bailey winced, picturing Carter's face. "And he doesn't show up on any of the systems."

"I'm sorry, Chris." Cody sighed, leaning in toward the speakerphone. "I put my best guys on this. I guess we didn't figure he'd read us so fast."

"I know you did what you could," Carter reassured him. "And I really appreciate all your help on this. All of it."

"I guess at least next time you'll know what he's capable of," Cody added. "I'd suggest taking him down as soon as you see him."

"If there is a next time," Carter said with a hollow laugh, his voice booming around the room. "He was our one and only lead."

"Not quite," said Bailey thoughtfully. "We've still got Lasche to follow up on. And there's the guy we saw with Blondi as well. He did show up on the system."

"It's about time we caught a break," Carter said with relief.

"It turns out he's got form. Some sort of high-end art thief. His name is Tom Kirk, also known as Felix."

"A thief!" Carter exclaimed. "That makes sense. He must be in on this whole thing too."

"Except that it turns out he cooperated with one of our agents on a case last year and got his slate wiped clean by way of a thank you. Now the general view is that he's gone straight."

"Which agent?"

"Jennifer Browne. You know her?"

"Name rings a bell," Carter said slowly. "She was mixed up in some shooting a couple of years back. I'll check into it."

"Meanwhile, we could get his name and description out to all airports, railway stations and border police," Bailey suggested. "That way, if he tries to leave the country, we'll know about it. With luck, his friend Blondi may not be far behind."

"Make it happen," Carter agreed. "And next time, let's make sure we bring at least one of them in."

CHAPTER FORTY-EIGHT

WEWELSBURG, WESTPHALIA, GERMANY

January 9—2:23 A.M.

It was clear from their journey up the hill that Wewelsburg Castle occupied a commanding position over the neighboring countryside.

More surprising, perhaps, was its design. Wewelsburg was the only triangular castle in Europe, with one large round tower in the north corner and two smaller ones south of it, each linked by heavily fortified walls. But then, as Dominique had told them during the seven-hour drive from Zurich, so far as she had been able to establish from the research she had been able to do whenever her laptop was able to get a good phone signal, its design was just one of the ways the castle broke with convention.

In 1934, a hundred-year lease had been taken out on the castle and its grounds. The signatory? A certain Heinrich Himmler. His plan, which was rapidly put into effect, was to establish the castle not just as an Aryan research and learning center but as the spiritual home of the SS, a place as sacred to the Aryan race as Marienburg had been to the medieval Teutonic Knights.

To that end, each room commemorated a legendary Nordic

hero or a pivotal moment in Aryan history. One room had even been set aside to house the Holy Grail, on the assumption that Himmler's men would eventually succeed in their quest to find it.

Himmler's own quarters had been dedicated to King Heinrich I, founder of the first German Reich. Apparently not only had Himmler believed himself to be the earthly reincarnation of Heinrich's spirit, he had also believed he would be endowed with supernatural powers once he was able to locate the legendary island of Thule—a supposedly lost civilization that he spent vast sums trying to locate—and make contact with the "Ancients."

To Tom, it all sounded horribly familiar, echoing Lasche's account of the hate-filled ideology with which Himmler had shaped and inspired the SS to new heights of inhumanity. But there was an even darker edge to the story. A concentration camp, brutal even by Nazi standards, had been established close by in order to provide slave labor for the alterations needed to bring the castle in line with Himmler's aspirations. And even though the castle was never fully operational, or indeed finished, it was rumored that pagan, even satanic rituals had been conducted within its dark walls.

As if to emphasize Tom's thoughts, the castle chose that moment to loom out from behind the skeletal vault of interlocking branches that had previously masked it, its mullioned windows glinting like animals' eyes in the yellow sweep of their headlights before slinking back into the cold embrace of the surrounding forest.

A small church stood silhouetted against the night sky as they rounded the final corner, its steeple casting a long shadow on the ground. Tom killed the lights and put the car into neutral, and they silently coasted the final hundred yards in the moonlight, a fox slinking lazily back into the undergrowth as they approached. Archie broke the silence as the car came to rest in front of what Dominique identified as the old SS guardhouse, now a museum.

"Well, we're definitely in the right place," he said. Tom nodded. The castle was unquestionably the one in the photo of the Bellak painting recovered from Weissman's secret room and the stained-glass window commissioned by Lammers.

"I thought you said Himmler had had it destroyed?" Tom asked.

"He did," Dominique replied. "Or at least, he tried to. Following his orders, it was blown up in March 1945, but the ceremonial hall and the crypt in the north tower survived pretty much intact. The rest of the castle was rebuilt after the war."

Tom turned to face Archie and Dom's expectant faces. "You're sure it's empty?"

"It's a youth hostel and a museum these days, but it's pretty quiet this time of year. There won't be anyone around until morning."

They got out of the car. It was drizzling, a thick, icy rain. Tom opened the trunk and took out two large packs; he handed one to Archie and strapped the other to his back. Then he turned to survey the castle walls.

The wide moat, no doubt once a formidable obstacle, had long since been drained, its formerly treacherous banks now sheltering a manicured garden. A narrow stone bridge supported by two arches led across the void to the castle's main entrance, an arched doorway surmounted by an ornately carved bay window. This was presumably a later addition, given its frivolous variance from the building's stern aspect.

They crossed the bridge to the imposing main gate, a solid wall of oak inset with six large roundels. Unsurprisingly, it was bolted shut, so Tom set to work on the narrow door set into it. Within a few seconds the rudimentary lock sprang open.

They stepped into a short vaulted passageway that in turn gave onto the castle's triangular courtyard, the yellow glow from a few lanterns vanishing into the shadows. Apart from the muted drumming of the rain, it was eerily quiet and still, the wind seemingly unable or unwilling to penetrate this cobbled sanctuary.

Dominique gestured toward a doorway in the base of the North Tower, a wide, squat circle of stone that loomed portentously above them, blocking out the night sky. By comparison, the two other, more delicate, towers that they could just about make out above the roof's steep slope seemed as if they might flex in a strong wind.

They approached the door, the walls closing in on them as the sides of the triangle met, an ancient inscription indicating that this had once been the entrance to a chapel. The door was unlocked and they stepped inside, only to find an iron grille blocking their way.

Tom reached for his flashlight and pointed it through the bars, revealing a large chamber. Twelve stone pillars encircled the room and supported a succession of low arches that gracefully framed the slender windows set into the tower walls. But his eyes settled almost immediately on the floor. At the center of the floor, black marble had been laid in the now familiar shape of a disc surrounded by two further circles, with twelve runic lightning bolts radiating from its center. The Black Sun.

"This was the Hall of the Supreme Leaders," Dominique whispered. "A place where the SS staged ritual ceremonies."

"You make them sound almost religious," observed Archie.

"In many ways, they were," Dominique agreed. "Himmler's doctrine of unquestioning obedience was inspired by the Jesuits. The SS was more like a fanatical religious sect than a military organization, with Himmler as Pope and Hitler as God."

"Is all this original?" Tom asked, surprised at the room's condition.

"It's been restored."

"Well, in that case, whatever we're looking for won't be here, or they'd have found it," Tom said. "Where's the crypt you mentioned?"

"As far as I recall, directly underneath us. But we need to go back outside to get to it."

She led them back through the main gate, which they shut

behind them, and across the bridge, the wind whistling through the two arches below. To their left, a flight of steps led down to the floor of the moat, where two doors had been set into the base of the east wall.

"That one," she whispered, pointing at the right-hand door.

It was locked, although again it was only a matter of seconds before Tom had it creaking open. They stepped into a vaulted passage, and Dominique indicated with a wave of her flashlight the narrow staircase that led off to their right. The staircase ended at another iron grille, which Tom had to pick open. Dominique located the light switch on the wall outside before following Tom and Archie inside.

The circular crypt was about twenty or thirty feet across and looked to be of solid construction, the walls built from carved stone blocks, the floor of polished limestone. A vaulted ceiling climbed perhaps fifteen feet above their heads. In the middle of the room was a round stone pit with two steps leading down to a shallow depression at its center.

It was to this smaller circle that Tom went, stopping in the middle, directly beneath the apex of the ceiling.

"Look." Archie pointed his flashlight up above Tom's head. The outline of a swastika, made from a different-colored stone, was clearly visible above.

"What was this place?" Tom asked.

"A sort of SS burial ground, apparently," said Dominique. "Presumably a final resting place at the center of the universe for the spirits of the Order when they passed away." Her voice had a strange deadened timbre, no echoes despite the confined space, as if every sound was being absorbed into the walls.

Tom looked curiously around him. Four light wells were set high into the thick walls, narrow shafts that angled steeply toward the night.

"According to Himmler, the center of the world lay not in Jerusalem or Rome or Mecca but here, in the hills of Westphalia," she explained. "He planned to build a massive SS complex composed of a series of concentric fortifications, barracks, and houses that radiated out for miles from where you're standing."

Tom looked down at his feet and shifted uncomfortably.

"At that precise spot an eternal flame was to be lit," she continued. "And although the guidebooks don't mention the Order by name, the theory is that the ashes of senior SS leaders were to be placed on one of these . . ." She crossed to the wall and indicated a low stone pedestal that Tom had not noticed before. He looked around him and saw that there was a total of twelve identical pedestals spaced around the chamber's walls. "Clearly, the Order were to remain united in death as they had been in life."

"Then this is where we'll start," said Tom, stamping on the stone floor. "Where the flame was to have burned. Right under the swastika. At the center of their world."

CHAPTER FORTY-NINE

Crouching in the pit, Tom and Archie set to work chiseling away at the mortar surrounding the large stone set into the center of the floor. It was slow, painful work, the hammer handles slippery in their grasp, the vibrations through the steel chisel stinging their fingers despite the strips of rubber used to muffle the blows. After five or ten minutes, however, the sound of metal striking stone gave way to another, unexpected sound.

"There's something under here," said Archie excitedly.

They levered the first stone out, then set to work on the ones surrounding it, eventually clearing a wide area and revealing the outline of a three-foot-square metal plate, about half an inch thick.

"Use this." Dominique handed Tom a long metal spike from one of the packs. Tom banged it under one side of the plate, then used it to pry the heavy metal slab away from the ground until there was a big enough gap for Archie to slip his fingers into. Archie hauled the plate upright until it was standing on edge, then pushed it away, sending it toppling to the floor with a crash. As the cloud of dust cleared, a thick, fetid stench rose slowly from the dark hole.

Dropping to their hands and knees, they crawled to the

hole's edge and peered into it, their hands covering their mouths in an unsuccessful attempt to filter out the smell. A dark, impenetrable nothingness stared back at them, and for a few moments they were all silent.

"I'll go down first," Tom volunteered. He grabbed a rope and secured one end to the gate, then threw the other end down the hole. Gripping his flashlight between his teeth, he lowered himself into the inky void, allowing the rope to slide slowly through his hands, controlling the speed of his descent with his legs.

The floor appeared to be made from some sort of white stone, although he could also make out a dark disc at its center, directly beneath where he was coming down. It was only when his feet unexpectedly landed on the disc that he realized it was, in fact, a large table. He let go of the rope and took the light from his mouth.

The table was made of wood and was surrounded by twelve high-backed oak chairs, each adorned with a tarnished silver plaque engraved with a different coat of arms and a family name. But Tom's eye was drawn less to the chairs than their motionless, grinning occupants.

For assembled around the table, like macabre guests at some apocalyptic dinner party, were twelve gleaming skeletons in full SS dress uniform.

Hardly daring to breathe, he let his flashlight beam play across chests gleaming with medals and ribbons, down to the lower left arm where he found their embroidered cuffbands.

The gold lettering glowed against the black material, revealing their owners' regimental title: Totenkopfsorden. The Order of the Death's Head.

CHAPTER FIFTY

"There you go." Lasche pointed to the typewriter-sized wooden box on his desk. "I've only sold one Enigma before. A few years ago now. He was a Russian collector, if I remember rightly."

"And the other components?" The voice was soft and lilting, hinting at lazy, humid evenings on a porch somewhere in South Carolina or Louisiana.

"Already in the machine. Of course, the final settings are up to you, Mr. . . . I'm sorry, I've forgotten your name." The beneficial effects of the blood transfusion were already beginning to wear off, and Lasche was feeling tired and a little more unfocused than he would have liked for this meeting. It was unavoidable, given the hour. He'd had little warning, merely a phone call informing him that someone would be coming to make the exchange and to ensure that he was alone.

"Foster. Kyle Foster." He was a large, rugged-looking man, his thick beard melting into wild, unkempt light brown hair, his steel gray eyes still and watchful. A dangerous man, thought Lasche. "Any problems getting hold of this?"

"Not really. I have my contacts. People I trust for this sort of job. They're reliable and discreet and keep themselves to themselves. Besides, they're the last people on earth anyone would imagine I was involved with."

"You mean the Sons of American Liberty?" Foster asked with a smile.

"How do you know that?" Lasche was at once amazed and angry. Amazed that they knew, angry because it meant that they'd been watching him. That they hadn't trusted him.

"Cassius does not take chances. Just because he asked you to get him an Enigma machine, doesn't mean he didn't care how you did it. As soon as he was certain that your man Blondi—was that his name?" Lasche nodded dumbly. "As soon as he was certain that your man Blondi had taken delivery of this"—Foster patted the wooden box protectively—"and was on his way home, he asked me to go and . . . meet with your people."

The hesitation, the slight edge that Lasche detected in Foster's voice, hinted at some sinister implication to this seemingly innocent remark. Though he feared he already knew the answer, Lasche couldn't resist putting the question: "*Meet* with them? What do you mean?"

"I mean that I locked them all in a booby-trapped room and tipped off the Feds so that they'd be the ones to set it off." Foster seemed to smile at the memory. "They'll be too busy blaming each other to ever figure out what really happened."

"All of them?" Lasche gasped, feeling his chest tightening, his breathing becoming ragged. "Why?"

"Loose ends." Foster reached into his pocket and pulled out a silenced 9mm pistol. "Cassius won't stand for loose ends. Which brings us to you . . ."

Lasche locked eyes with Foster, saw his cold and unblinking gaze, the gun pointed at his chest.

"I assume there's no possibility of a reprieve?" His voice remained calm and businesslike. He had been around long enough to know that neither tears nor tantrums would have any effect. "No amount of money that would convince you to put down your gun and walk out of here?"

Foster gave a half smile. "Then I'd be the dead man and not you."

"I see."

A pause.

"But my employer did have one offer to make you."

"Which is?" Lasche's voice was fired by a faint glimmer of hope.

"You get to choose."

"Choose?" He frowned in confusion. "Choose what?"

Foster jerked his head at the room full of weapons behind him. "How you die."

Lasche gave a rueful shake of his head. He had been foolish to expect anything else from Cassius. Even so, it was a concession. A concession that Lasche valued because it gave him some element of control in his passing. Ridiculous as it may have seemed, he really did appreciate the gesture.

"Tell him . . . tell him thank you."

Lasche reversed his wheelchair out from behind his desk and slowly rolled past the display cabinets along the left-hand wall, appraising their contents. Foster followed him, his gun still drawn, the sound of his footsteps like the steady, inexorable beat of the drum as the tumbrel rolled toward the steps of the guillotine.

Lasche's eyes skipped from item to item, weighing the merits of each against the other. A Kukri knife presented itself as the first possible candidate. It had belonged to a Gurkha in the British Army who had died in the Indian Mutiny of 1857. The hooked slash of its blade was covered, for legend has it that a Kukri can never be unsheathed without drawing blood.

Then there was the polished elegance of the pistol used by Alexander Pushkin in a duel fought on the banks of the Black River in 1837. The poet had entered into the duel to defend his wife's honor against the unwanted advances of a dashing officer. Mortally wounded, he died a few days later, plunging the whole of Russia into mourning.

Another possibility was the Winchester M1873—the rifle that "won the West" with its fearsome accuracy and reliability. Lasche's two examples were especially rare, modern ballistics having confirmed them as two of the eight 73s used by Native Americans at the Battle of the Little Bighorn in 1876.

But he kept going, past these and many more like them, until his wheelchair hummed to a halt in front of the suit of samurai armor. At its feet, carefully mounted on their stand, were two swords. In the end, he knew now, these had been the only possible choice.

"A samurai wore two swords," Lasche said softly. He could sense that Foster was standing behind him, although he did not look around. "The *katana* and the *wakizashi*." He pointed first at the long sword, then the shorter one mounted above it. "They were a symbol of prestige and pride, and along with the Sacred Mirror and the Comma-Shaped Beads, are said to be one of three sacred treasures of Japan."

"They're old?" Foster sounded uninterested.

"Edo period—about 1795. So old, yes, but not as old as the armor."

"And that's what you want?" Foster had stepped forward so that he was alongside Lasche, his voice skeptical.

Lasche nodded.

"Okay." Foster bent toward the display, then looked up to see which of the swords Lasche wanted.

"Have you heard of Bushido?" asked Lasche.

"No." There was irritation in Foster's voice now, as if he wanted to get it over with. Lasche took no notice.

"Bushido is the way of the warrior, the code by which the samurai ruled their lives. It teaches that, to save face, a samurai may commit seppuku, a form of ritualized suicide."

"You want to do it to yourself?" Foster looked worried, as if this fell outside the remit that he had been given. "You sure?"

"Absolutely. You will be *kaishakunin*, my officer of death. You'll need both swords."

Shrugging, Foster took both swords from their ebony stand and followed Lasche back over to the other side of the room where he had stopped, just in front of the large cannon.

"Traditionally, I would be wearing a white kimono and in

front of me would be a tray bearing a piece of *washi* paper, ink, a cup of sake, and a *tanto* knife, although the *wakizashi* will suffice. I would drink the sake in two gulps—any more or less would not show the correct balance of contemplation and determination—and then compose a fitting poem in the *waka* style. Finally, I would take the sword"—he took the shorter sword from Foster and unsheathed it, throwing its black lacquered scabbard to the floor—"and place it against my belly, here." He pulled his shirt out of his trousers and exposed his soft, sagging stomach on the left-hand side, pressing the tip of the blade against it. "Then, when I was ready, I would push it in and slice across from left to right."

Foster had already discarded the scabbard from the longer sword and was feeling its weight in his hand, tapping his foot impatiently as he stood behind him.

"Then you," Lasche continued, "as my *kaishakunin*, would step in and take off my head. This was intended to—"

Lasche never finished his sentence. With a flash of steel Foster decapitated him, the impact knocking his body out of the wheelchair so that he slumped forward onto the cannon, his head rolling across the floor.

"You talk too much, old man," Foster muttered.

CHAPTER FIFTY-ONE

WEWELSBURG CASTLE, WESTPHALIA, GERMANY

January 9—3:23 A.M.

"They're here," Tom shouted as he jumped down from the table between two of the skeletons and walked around the table behind them, flicking his light from one corpse to the next. The heads of a few had rolled onto the floor, but most were remarkably intact, peaked hats perched on white skulls, empty eye sockets seeming to follow Tom's every movement like some grotesque Mardi Gras carnival float. "They're all here," he whispered to himself, not sure whether he should feel exhilarated or horrified by the discovery.

"Who?" Archie shouted from the floor above.

"The Order." He noticed a small hole in the right temple of one of the skulls, saw the same wound in the others, then a gun on the floor next to one of the chairs. "Looks like they killed themselves in some sort of suicide pact."

"I'm coming down," Archie announced. A few seconds later, his large frame momentarily eclipsed the small circle of light from the crypt above before sliding down the rope and landing in the center of the table.

"Christ!" he exclaimed as his flashlight picked out the Nazi skeletons, the silver plaques behind their heads winking as the light caught them. "You weren't joking." He sounded genuinely shocked. "I wouldn't have thought it possible, but they're an even creepier bunch dead than when they were alive. Gathered together for a last supper like the twelve apostles."

"They must have lowered themselves in here, got someone else to replace the stones upstairs, then pulled the trigger."

"And assured themselves of a much more pleasant death than they had ever allowed anyone else," Archie said with feeling as he jumped down to the floor, shaking his head in disgust. "See anything else?"

"Not yet. Let's take a look around, see what was so important about this place."

"Wait for me—" Dominique had noiselessly lowered herself down the rope onto the table behind them, clutching a lantern.

"I thought you were meant to be watching our backs?" Tom admonished her.

"And let you two have all the fun?" She grinned, holding up her lantern so she could get a good look at the corpses. "Look at them. It's almost like they're waiting for us."

"For us or someone else," Tom agreed, realizing that he should have known better than to assume Dominique wouldn't want to get stuck in alongside them. "Come on, let's see what else is down here."

She hopped off the table, and all three of them turned their attention to examining the chamber itself. It was about thirty feet across, and the walls were rounded as if they were in a large stone barrel. A brief survey confirmed that the only way in or out seemed to be the hole above them, for the walls were uninterrupted by any kind of opening. They reassembled near the middle of the room.

"Well, if there's something down here, I can't see it." Archie shone his flashlight disconsolately around him.

"Agreed," said Tom. "But there's one place we haven't looked."

"The bodies," Dominique whispered. "You mean the bodies, don't you?"

Without waiting for an answer, she turned toward the

table and walked slowly around it, her forehead creased with concentration. The flickering light from the lantern threw rippling shadows across the skeletons' faces, until they seemed almost alive, the occasional glint of a tooth or a shadow dancing across a vacant eye socket suggesting that they might be on the point of waking from their long slumber. Finally she came to a halt behind one of the chairs. "Let's try this one first."

"Why that one?" Tom asked. The skeleton looked no different from the others, although arguably slightly more grotesque, the lower jaw having fallen into its lap, with one eye socket covered by a frayed silk patch.

"Look at the table."

Tom directed his light where she was pointing and saw that the table's surface had been divided into twelve equal slices, one opposite each knight. And each slice had been inlaid with a different type of wood.

"Oak, walnut, birch . . ." She pointed each one out in turn, her lantern moving around the table like a spotlight. "Elm, cherry, teak, mahogany . . ." She paused when she came to the segment of table facing the chair she had stopped behind. "Amber."

"It's worth a try," Archie agreed.

Her jaw set firm, Dominique gingerly unbuttoned the skeleton's jacket, two of the silver buttons coming away in her hand where the thread had dissolved. Then, pulling the jacket to one side, she began checking the pockets, inside and out. There was nothing in any of them.

"What about around his neck?" Tom suggested. "He might have hung something there."

Keeping her face as far away from the skeleton as possible, Dominique unbuttoned its shirt, the material clinging to the desiccated rib cage underneath where the flesh had rotted and then dried. But again, there was nothing. Just the empty void of the chest cavity and the remains of his heart where it had fallen through to the chair and dried like a large prune.

"No, nothing," she said, sounding disappointed. "I must have got it wrong."

"I'm not so sure," said Archie, peering down at the glittering array of medals pinned to the jacket Dominique had just unbuttoned. "He's wearing a Knight's Cross."

He pulled on the remains of the red, white, and black striped ribbon and drew the medal out from under the uniform's collar.

"Does it have any markings on the back?" asked Tom.

Archie flipped the medal over. "Just like the others," he confirmed with a nod.

"Dom, have you got the other two?"

She nodded and removed them from her coat pocket, placing them facedown on the table so that the markings were visible. Archie laid the one they'd just found alongside the other two.

"They must mean or do something," Tom said. "They must go together somehow."

"Maybe it's a picture," Dominique suggested. "Maybe the lines meet up to show you something that you can't see when they're apart . . ."

She grabbed the medals and began to slide them around, placing them against each other in a variety of positions to see if any of the lines matched up.

It was a fruitless exercise. And after ten minutes exhausting every positional combination they could think of, Tom was on the verge of suggesting they try something else when Dominique suddenly clicked her fingers.

"Of course! It must be three-dimensional."

"What?"

"The medals. They don't go next to each other, like a normal flat puzzle. They go on top of each other."

She grabbed one medal and placed it on top of another, sliding it this way and that to see if a pattern emerged. Then she tried changing one of the medals, and then changing the other to make a third combination, until finally she looked up with a smile. "Here you go."

By sliding the second medal over to the left and up from the center of the bottom one, she'd managed to align several of the marks. Then she took the final medal, placed it on top of the others, slid it to the right and then up from the second medal. As she moved it into place, the lines suddenly came together to form an image that could only be seen by looking down from above. Two elaborate crossed keys.

"The keys of Saint Peter," Tom said in a hushed voice.

"Saint Peter? As in Rome?" asked Archie. "Well, it can't be there."

"It's unlikely, I agree," Tom said pensively. "Crossed keys. What else could that mean?"

"Your father said the portrait was the key. Maybe this relates to that particular painting," suggested Dominique.

"Or maybe it refers to the key on a map? Like our railway map?" Tom ventured.

"Well, while you two think that one through," Archie said, stooping to pick up the lantern where he had placed it on the ground, "I'll see whether our friends here have got anything else interesting on them. You never know—hang on," he interrupted himself as he raised his head level with the table. "What's that?"

He pointed at the side of the table where a small shape had been cut into the wood. A very distinctive shape.

"I wonder . . . Here, give me one of those . . ."

Dominique handed him one of the medals and he lined it up with the hole. It was a perfect fit. He slipped the medal inside.

"I'll bet you any money you like there are two more holes just like this one," Archie said excitedly.

"Here's one!" said Dominique, pointing at a section of the table's edge to Archie's right.

"And here," Tom confirmed, having moved around to the other side of the table so that they were now standing at three points of a large triangle.

"Put them in," Archie said, sliding the remaining two medals across the table.

Both Tom and Dominique did as he suggested and then straightened up, waiting for something to happen. Nothing did.

"Well, they must do something," Archie insisted.

"What about if we press them in?" said Dominique. "They might release something."

They duly pressed, but still nothing happened.

"Let's try pressing at the same time," said Tom. "On three. One, two, three—"

Again they all pressed on the medals, and a firm click echoed around the chamber.

"Where did that come from?" asked Archie.

"The table," said Tom. "Look at the middle of the table."

He shone his light at a roundel in the center of the table that had popped a few millimeters higher than the surrounding surface. Kneeling on the table, Tom pulled out his knife and levered the roundel free, revealing a small but deep recess. He reached inside with the tips of his fingers and removed a dagger that the table had apparently been designed to house. From the way the blade had been elaborately engraved with a series of runic symbols, Tom guessed that it must once have fulfilled some long-forgotten ceremonial function. A piece of paper had been carefully wrapped around its ivory hilt. The others crowded around him as he hopped to the floor.

"What does it say?" demanded Archie.

Tom unscrolled it gently, not wanting to rip it.

"It's a telegram," he said. "Here, Dom, you read it. Your German's better than mine."

He handed the piece of paper to her and shone his flashlight on it so she could read.

"'All is lost. Stop. Prinz-Albrecht-Strasse overrun. Stop. Gudrun kidnapped. Stop.'" She looked up questioningly. "Gudrun? Wasn't that Himmler's daughter's name? The one in the portrait?"

"Yes," Tom confirmed with a nod. "And Prinz-Albrecht-Strasse was Himmler's HQ. What else does it say?"

"'Hermitage most likely destination. Stop. Heil Hitler.'" She looked up. "It's dated April 1945. It's addressed to Himmler."

"The Hermitage," Tom said, shaking his head in frustration. "That's what the keys of Saint Peter meant. It's got

nothing to do with maps or Rome—we're meant to be looking in St. Petersburg." He looked up excitedly and locked
eyes with first Archie and then Dominique. "My father was
wrong. The missing Bellak isn't in a private collection. It's
in the Hermitage Museum."

PART III

*I cannot forecast to you the action of Russia.
It is a riddle wrapped in a mystery
inside an enigma.*

Winston Churchill,
1 October 1939

CHAPTER FIFTY-TWO

NEVSKY PROSPEKT, ST. PETERSBURG, RUSSIA

January 9—3:21 P.M.

Tom and Dominique made their way down the Nevsky Prospekt toward the Admiralty's honeyed bulk, occasional dark veins forming along the pavement where it had emerged from under the snow's white marble. They passed two drunks lying slumped over each other in a doorway, each with one hand lovingly wrapped around a half-empty bottle of vodka. As they watched, a stray dog ambled up to the two men and sniffed gingerly around their feet until a flailing kick sent it yelping down the street. A veil of gray clouds clung stubbornly to the sky, torn by icicles of dirty yellow light.

"So when do you think Archie will get here?" Dominique asked, her eyes focused on where she was treading.

"You missing him already?" Tom laughed, his voice muffled by a thick scarf. Although allegedly a mild winter by Russian standards, it still felt dangerously cold. "Don't worry, he should be here by this evening."

"I'm not sure it was worth him traveling separately. I mean, if someone *is* looking for him, they're just as likely to spot him on his own as with us, aren't they?"

"True," said Tom. "But he seemed to think he'd have a better chance with only himself to worry about."

"And Turnbull? Did you get through in the end?"

"I updated him on everything we've found so far. Well, everything he needed to know, at least. He's due here tomorrow. I'll have to break it to Archie gently."

Reaching the end of the Nevsky Prospekt, they turned right into Dvortsovaya Ploshchad, or Palace Square. The Admiralty's gilded spike sat atop a white marble colonnaded cube that resembled the top layer of a gaudy wedding cake. To their right was the Alexander Column, while behind them, the curved sweep of the General Staff Building hugged them into its shadow. Here and there, through gaps in the buildings or over their rooftops came the unforgiving glint of concrete; ugly Soviet-era scars that the city was still trying unsuccessfully to heal over.

Dominique slipped her arm through Tom's, feeling strangely warm and content, despite the icy wind whipping against her cheeks. The events of the past few days, while exhausting, had also been exhilarating. She had always been a bit jealous of Tom and Archie, with their crazy stories of places they'd been or jobs they'd pulled. Now, far from sitting on the sidelines, she felt that she was finally part of the team. It gave her a sense of belonging that she had not had for a while. Not since Tom's father died.

"You've been here before, right?" she asked.

"No."

"No? Why not?"

"I guess I just never got round to it."

Something in his tone told her not to probe further. Not now, at least. She decided to change the subject. "That must be it—the Hermitage."

"That's it," Tom confirmed.

"So that one's the Winter Palace." She pointed at the extravagant Baroque building on the left, its white-and-pistachio-colored façade adorned with gleaming sculptures and covered with an intricate pattern of decorative motifs that flickered with the golden sparkle of a thousand tiny candles.

"I think so."

"It's huge." She shook her head in disbelief.

"I read that if you spent eight hours a day here, it would take seventy years just to glance at every single one of its exhibits."

"That long?"

"Thirteen miles of galleries, three million items . . . Actually, that sounds pretty quick."

"And you really think the missing Bellak painting is in there?" she asked skeptically. Even now, she wasn't sure that their combined logic had led them to the right place.

They had reached the riverbank and were standing on the Palace Bridge, looking out toward the Peter and Paul Fortress. Tom leaned against the parapet, deep in thought, before answering.

"Have you ever heard of Schliemann's Gold?"

Dominique nodded. From what she could remember, back in the 1870s, Schliemann had been a pioneering archaeologist. Obsessed with *The Iliad*, he had set about finding the site of Troy, using Homer's text as his map. In 1873 he had finally hit pay dirt, uncovering the remains of the city and a hoard of bronze, silver, and gold objects that he christened Priam's Treasure, after the ancient King of Troy.

"Just before he died," Tom explained, "he gave the treasure he had found in Troy to the National Museum in Berlin, where it stayed until 1945."

"*Until* 1945? You mean the Russians took it?" Dominique guessed.

"Exactly. The Soviets were almost as obsessed with securing valuables and art as the Nazis. When Berlin fell, Stalin sent in his 'Trophy Squad,' a team specially trained to search out and confiscate as much Nazi loot as possible. They found Priam's Treasure in a bunker beneath the Berlin Zoo, along with thousands of other artifacts. Of course, no one knew all this until recently. The treasure was thought to have been lost or destroyed in the war. Only in 1993 did the Russians finally admit that they had it, only to claim ownership in lieu of reparations. It's on display now in the Pushkin Museum in Moscow."

"And you think something similar must have happened to the painting?"

"That's certainly what the telegram was saying," Tom confirmed with a nod. "It makes sense. Himmler's headquarters would have been one of the Russians' key strategic targets. If Himmler really couldn't bring himself to destroy Bellak's painting of his daughter, I think there's every chance the Russians found it there and carried it back here as a trophy. The problem is going to be finding it."

"Why's that?"

"You know I said there are three million items in there?" She nodded. "Well, only one hundred and fifty thousand are actually on display. The other two million eight hundred and fifty thousand are housed in vast attic storerooms and underground depositories. What's more, most of what they've got down there is so poorly catalogued that they probably don't even know they've got it themselves."

"I still don't understand why Bellak would have cooperated with the Order by hiding messages in his paintings?"

Tom shook his head. "As far as I know, Bellak was already dead by the time the Gold Train set out, so he can't have been involved. Besides, the clue you found wasn't hidden in the painting itself but had been added later by making those holes. I imagine they chose his paintings precisely because of who he was and their subject matter. After all, who would have suspected that a painting of a synagogue by a Jewish artist would have led us to a hidden SS crypt?"

There was a long silence. As she stared pensively out over the water, Dominique was suddenly struck by how, apart from the isolated perpendicular thrust of the Admiralty spires, the Peter and Paul Fortress, and the Mikhailovsky Castle, the city seemed to be dominated by horizontal rather than vertical lines, like layers of rock strata. Partly this was due to the matching rooflines that had largely been kept strictly to that of the Winter Palace or below, but principally it was due to the incredible abundance of water. Everywhere that the flat surfaces of St. Petersburg's forty rivers and twenty canals touched the shore, it created the illusion of a perfectly straight line.

She was about to point this out to Tom when she caught the distant look in his eye and thought better of it.

"Tom, what's really kept you from coming here before?"

He didn't answer right away, his eyes firmly fixed on the far shore. "When I was eight, my father bought me a book about St. Petersburg. We used to read it together—well, look at the pictures, mainly. He told me that he'd bring me here one day. That we'd organize a trip, just the two of us. That he'd show me all its secrets. I guess I was waiting for him to ask me. I never thought I'd come here without him."

Dominique was silent. Then, surprising herself more than anyone, she reached up and gave him a kiss on the cheek.

CHAPTER FIFTY-THREE

DECEMBRIST'S SQUARE, ST. PETERSBURG

January 9—4:03 P.M.

Boris Kristenko felt guilty. It wasn't just that he had slipped out of the office and that if his boss found out there would be questions. He was more worried about letting his colleagues down. With only three weeks to go till the grand opening of the new Rembrandt exhibition, they were working flat out. He should have been back at the museum, coordinating the hanging. But he'd made a promise and he liked to keep his promises—especially when they were to his mother.

So he hurried along, head bowed, trying not to make eye contact for fear someone from work might recognize him, although he could just as well have asked them what they were doing out themselves. That realization emboldened him somewhat, and he allowed himself to look up, although he quickened his step to compensate for his bravery as he crossed the Neva and headed along the Leytenanta Schmidta embankment.

His mother wanted three Russian dolls. Apparently she couldn't get such nice pieces out in the suburbs, although Kristenko doubted she'd even looked. He knew his mother;

this was her way of getting him to both pay for the items and deliver them.

Not that they were for her, of course. The *matryoshka* were intended as gifts for her nephews and nieces over in America, her brother having swapped the cold Russian winters for humid Miami summers about fifteen years ago. God, how Kristenko envied him.

It was a small shop, catering mainly for tourists, with a fine selection of Russian souvenirs. He purchased the dolls and emerged back onto the street, checking his watch. He'd been away twenty minutes. Maybe if he ran he'd be back before anyone had noticed he'd even gone.

The first punch, to the side of the head, caught him completely unawares. The second, he saw coming, although it still winded him as it slammed into his stomach. He dropped to the ground, gasping for air, his head ringing.

"Get him over there." He registered a voice, then felt himself being dragged by his arms and hair into an alleyway. He didn't have the strength or the will to fight them. He knew who they were and he knew he couldn't win.

They threw him to the filthy cobblestones, smeared with rotting food and dog excrement. His head bounced off a wall, and he felt a tooth break as his chin connected with the bricks.

"Where's our money, Boris Ivanovich?" came the voice. He looked up and saw three of them, looming over him like upended coffins.

"It's coming," he mumbled, finding it difficult to move his jaw.

"It had better be. Two weeks. You've got two weeks. And next time, just so you know, it won't be you we come for. It'll be your mother."

One of the men kicked him hard in the head, the boot catching his nose. He felt the warm trickle of blood down his face as the shadows faded, their cruel laughter rising through the air like steam.

Lying there, his head supported by the cold brick wall, he looked down at his bruised knees, his ripped and soiled coat, his scuffed shoes covered in shit. The blood dripped from his nose through his fingers and onto his front with the steady rhythm of an old clock marking time.

Alone, he began to cry.

CHAPTER FIFTY-FOUR

CATHERINE PALACE, PUSHKIN

January 9—4:37 P.M.

Dusk fell with a crimson mantle, lengthening shadows slipping furtively between the naked trees. As Tom stepped through the weaving gilt-and-black filigree of the entrance gates to the Catherine Palace, the first streetlights blinked on.

In a way, he was glad that Dominique had not made the trip out to the suburbs with him. He needed some time on his own to recharge his batteries and take stock. Although he knew she'd been trying to help by making him talk about his father, the conversation had left him feeling uneasy. The problem was that since her confession about her past, and the part his father had played in it, Tom had found himself wrestling with a gnawing feeling of jealousy. This was not an emotion he'd had to contend with before, and he was still having difficulty coming to terms with it.

What was clear was that, in the five years leading up to his father's death, Dominique had had the sort of relationship with his father that Tom had only ever dreamed about. And even if she was right about his father taking her in to compensate for the way he'd failed his own son, it still felt like a betrayal. He wondered whether she suspected as much, and if that had motivated the kiss she'd given him. She wasn't usually one for such open displays of emotion or affection.

Being in St. Petersburg certainly wasn't helping matters. Tom remembered the nights his father would tuck him into bed while telling him about this dazzling city, his eyes growing distant and dreamy as he described the glittering prize it had once contained; its star-struck history; its mysterious fate. Tom would listen, awestruck, scarcely daring to breathe in case he broke the spell.

The palace surged out of the gloom, the arched windows of its three stories encrusted with ornate stucco ornamentation, each separated from its neighbors by columns and sculptures that repeated along its one-thousand-foot length with monumental symmetry. Bands of turquoise scrolled down the white and gold façade like thick ribbons, as if the building had been gift-wrapped especially for him.

Tom ascended the main staircase, passed through the main door into the entrance hall, and turned left. He knew the way, having memorized it long ago from a plan in the book his father had given him. His pace quickened as he drew nearer, the White, Crimson, and Green Dining Rooms—sights he would normally have lingered over, absorbing their unrestrained opulence—warranting no more than a cursory glance. Even the masterpieces on display in the Picture Hall couldn't hold his attention for any longer than it took to traverse the polished parquet floor. Instead he was drawn, as if by magic, to the far doorway, his path lit by the enchanting glow emanating from the room beyond. The Amber Room.

It wasn't the original room, of course, consisting instead of a modern replica, crafted to celebrate the city's three hundredth anniversary. Even so, the result was no less stunning. The glittering walls spanned a spectrum of yellow, from smoky topaz to the palest lemon. And while most panels were undecorated, some were adorned with delicately crafted figurines, floral garlands, tulips, roses, and seashells that looked as if they might have been plucked from a distant beach or some exotic garden and then dipped in gold.

Only one other visitor was present, examining one of the

panels on the far wall. A stern-faced attendant occupied a creaking velvet and giltwood chair near the entrance.

As he stood there, the Amber Room's warmth washing over him, an unexpected thought crept into Tom's mind. Despite its magnificence, he couldn't help but feel that he was somehow glad his father had never stood where he was standing now. After a lifetime of anticipation, to actually see it, as Tom was, might have come as something of an anticlimax to him. By foundering on the rocks of war, leaving only its whispered memory and a few faded photographs behind, the Amber Room had given birth to a myth. A myth that had immediately transcended the limitations of human observation and scrutiny, entering instead the world of the imagination, where its magnificence could never disappoint or be questioned. For that reason, if nothing else, this reproduction, while exquisite, could never hope to equal the sublime image people might conjure up in their own minds.

"It took twenty-four years . . ."

The other visitor had crossed the room to join him. Tom said nothing, assuming the man had taken him for a fellow tourist. "Twenty-four years to rebuild it. Amazing, is it not? See how it glows, how the surface both reflects the light and yet at the same time seems so deep you could plunge your hand in it up to the elbow?"

Tom turned to look at the man properly. From the side, he could barely make out the profile of his face, obscured as it was by a black bearskin hat pulled down low so that it skimmed his upturned collar. And yet there was something in the man's voice that he recognized, a spark of familiarity that danced around the edges of Tom's memory without his quite being able to place it.

"Hello, Thomas."

Slowly, the man turned to fix him with a pair of unblinking steely green eyes. Eyes that were at once familiar and yet totally foreign. Eyes that aroused feelings of hatred and of fear. And loneliness.

Harry Renwick's eyes.

"Harry?" Tom gasped as the spark exploded into a sudden blaze of understanding. "Is that you?"

Renwick, perhaps mistaking Tom's tone, held his gloved hands out, palms upturned, in welcome. "My dear boy!"

But Tom's surprise instantly evaporated, a cold, biting rage taking its place. His next words left no doubt as to his true feelings. "You fucking—" Tom took a step forward, his fist clenching at his side.

"Careful, Thomas," Renwick said softly, edging away. "Do not try anything rash. I would not want you to get hurt."

There was a scrape of wood, and Tom turned in time to see the frightened-looking attendant being bundled from the room by two shaven-headed thugs. Two more marched in after them, their coats open to display the guns casually tucked into their waistbands. The taller of the two made his way to Renwick's side. Tom recognized his massive shape as the man filmed leaving the hospital after Weissman's murder. The other, meanwhile, approached Tom and rapidly patted him down, before relieving Renwick of his bearskin hat and retreating across the room.

"I believe you have not yet had the pleasure of meeting Colonel Hecht?" said Renwick. "He is a . . . colleague of mine."

"What do you want?" Tom asked sullenly. Given the odds, he knew had no choice but to hear Renwick out.

"Ah, Thomas." Renwick sighed heavily. He remained the only person to call Tom by his full name, but then he had always eschewed abbreviation, acronym, or any other form of linguistic shorthand. "It is sad, is it not? After everything that has passed between us, the time we have spent together, that we should not be able to meet and talk as friends."

"Save it," Tom spoke through gritted teeth. "Our friendship was built on your lies. The day you betrayed me, we lost anything we ever had. You mean nothing to me now. So if you've come to kill me, let's just get it over with."

"Kill you?" Renwick laughed and strolled across to the left-hand wall, leaving Hecht staring stonily at Tom. "My dear boy, if I had wanted you dead, you would not be here. Outside the Hotel Drei Könige; at that café in the Hauptbahnhof; as you were walking down the Nevsky Prospekt this very morning . . . God knows there have been any number of opportunities over the past few days. No, Thomas, your death, while satisfying the need to avenge the loss of my hand"—he brought up his gloved prosthetic hand and regarded it dispassionately, as if it wasn't really his—"would not serve my purposes."

"Your purposes?" Tom gave a hollow laugh. "You think I'd help you?"

"Oh, but you have done so much already, Thomas. The key you recovered from Lammers, the safety-deposit box, the identification of a possible location for the contents of the missing carriages—"

"How the hell . . . ?" Tom started, before realizing what this meant. "Raj! What have you done to him?"

"Ah, yes." Renwick sighed. "Mr. Dhutta." He removed the glove from his left hand and gently placed it against one of the panels. "A very loyal friend, if I may say. Right until the end."

"You bastard," Tom swore, his voice cracking at this latest example of Renwick's mindless cruelty. Raj was a good man. Tom blamed himself for getting him involved.

Renwick gave a brief smile but said nothing, gently stroking one of the floral motifs with his ungloved hand.

"So, now you know what I have known for some time," he said eventually. "The Order was sent to protect a train. When they realized it was not going to get through to Switzerland, they took it upon themselves to remove the most precious part of its cargo and hide it, committing the secret of its location to a painting that now lies in some private collection."

Tom said nothing, his thoughts alternating between fear, anger, and revulsion at the sight of Renwick lovingly stroking the amber and the thought of Raj's twisted corpse lying discarded in some alley or hidden room.

"Think about it, Thomas—the original Amber Room." Renwick's eyes flashed. "Finally recovered after all these years. Think of the money. It must be worth two, three hundred million dollars."

"You think I care about the money?" Tom seethed.

"Your father spent half his life on its trail. Imagine what he would say if he could be where we are now—so close."

"Don't bring my father into this," Tom said icily as he stepped forward, ignoring Hecht's menacing gaze. "He wanted to find it so he could protect it. All you want to do is destroy it."

"Your father is already involved, Thomas." Renwick was smiling now. "How else do you think I found out about this in the first place? He told me. He told me everything."

"That's a lie."

"Is it?"

"If he did, it's because he had no idea who you were. That all you wanted to do was break it up."

"You are so certain of that, aren't you?" Renwick shook his head, suddenly angry. "So sure that he was in the dark?"

Tom's heart jumped. "What do you mean?"

"Do not play games with me, Thomas." Renwick gave a cruel laugh. "It does not suit you. You cannot deny that you have thought it, at least. Asked yourself the question."

"Thought what?" Tom's mouth was dry, his voice a whisper.

"How it was that, even though we were colleagues for twenty years, friends for longer, he never knew about me. How there must have been a chance, however slight, that he not only knew but helped me. Worked for me."

"Don't say that. You don't know—"

"You have no idea what I know," Renwick said, cutting him off. "And even if you did, you would never believe it. Just as I know that you will fail to believe this . . ."

He pulled out his pocket watch and dangled it in front of Tom, the gold case winking as it caught the light. Tom recognized it instantly—a rare gold 1922 Patek Philippe chronometer. He even knew its case number: 409792. It was his father's watch.

"Where did you get that?" Tom asked in a whisper. "You have no right—"

"Where do you think? He gave it to me. Do you not see, Thomas? We were partners. Right until the end."

CHAPTER FIFTY-FIVE

PULKOVO 2 AIRPORT, ST. PETERSBURG

January 9—6:47 P.M.

Bailey was waiting under a red neon sign advertising a local strip club, politely fending off a succession of porters eager to scoop his bags into one of the waiting taxis. To his relief, a black shape glided to a halt outside, larger and cleaner than any of the vehicles around it. Hitching his bag onto his shoulder, Bailey stepped outside, the wind stinging his eyes. The trunk popped open as he drew close, and he lifted his bags in and then banged it shut before stepping to the passenger door and climbing inside.

"Man, it's colder than a well-digger's ass out there!" The man extending a welcoming hand through the gap between the front seats was Laurel to the driver's Hardy: tall and thin with neatly combed brown hair, while his colleague was stout with a circle of graying blond hair that hugged his shiny pate like a sweatband.

"Hey, sorry we're late," he continued. "I'm Bill Strange and this is Cliff Cunningham. Welcome to Russia."

"Traffic was a bitch," said Cunningham, meeting Bailey's eye in his mirror.

"No problem." Bailey shook Strange's hand. "Special Agent Byron Bailey. You guys Bureau or Agency?"

"Bureau." Strange smiled. "Carter figured you'd want to see a friendly face."

"Carter was right," Bailey said gratefully. Cody had been helpful enough, but he was happy to be back with his own people. "So, any sign of my guy yet?"

"Look familiar?" Strange handed a photo to Bailey.

"That's him, yeah." Bailey's eyes flashed excitedly. "When did he come through?"

"An hour or so ago. Took the flight from Bonn, like you said. He's just checked in at the Labirint."

"That's where Kirk's staying too," Cunningham added. "It's a dump, but the owners never bother registering guest visas, which has its advantages if you don't want to be found. Checked in with a young female. Separate rooms."

"Looks like you made a smart call," said Strange.

"I got lucky," Bailey corrected him, although he said it with a smile. In a way Strange was right. Once they had lost track of Blondi it had been his idea to switch the focus to Kirk instead, in the hope that, wherever he turned up, Blondi wouldn't be far behind. As soon as they realized that Kirk had booked a flight to St. Petersburg, it had been a simple matter of circulating a description of Blondi to all major European airports offering flights to Russia. Confirmation of Blondi's booking had come through from an alert official at Bonn Airport, and Carter had immediately dispatched Bailey after him—albeit on a very tight leash. Not that Bailey was complaining. However tight the rein, it beat carrying Viggiano's bags.

He settled back into the soft leather seat as Cunningham pulled out into the traffic and headed for the city center.

CHAPTER FIFTY-SIX

The shower consisted of a yellowing curtain covered in small black spots of mold suspended from a sagging length of string over a chipped bath. The bath itself was surrounded by mismatched tiles and was slick with the dirt and grease of previous occupants. But the water was hot, and Tom soon forgot where he was as he stood under its powerful pulse, his mind flicking back to the Amber Room.

To Renwick.

To what he had said.

He was right, of course. At least, partly right. Since discovering what Renwick was really like, Tom had indeed questioned the nature of his father's friendship with him, wondered whether he had suspected the truth. But he had never for a moment considered that his father had not merely known about Renwick but had somehow been directly involved in his murderously criminal activities.

Tom would be the first one to admit that he hadn't known his father as well as he would have liked, certainly as well as he should. But the little he did know had shown him to be honest almost to a fault, a man who never would have harbored anything but the deepest contempt for Cassius and all he stood for. They were almost genetic opposites.

He stepped out of the shower, dried himself, and got dressed. The phone rang but Tom ignored it, guessing that it was one of the local prostitutes tipped off by the receptionist whenever a single man checked in. There was a knock at the door.

"Come in."

Archie's head appeared. "Anyone home?"

"You made it!" Tom smiled with relief. "Any problems?"

"Long day," said Archie, collapsing into a severe-looking armchair, yellow foam peeking through the jagged slash in its brown vinyl seat covering. "Where's Dom?" He looked around as if half expecting her to jump out from behind the curtain.

"Getting changed. She'll be down in ten."

Archie stretched out his legs, visibly unwinding. "So, what have you been up to?"

"Oh, you know. Nothing much . . ." Tom shrugged. "Took a stroll down Nevsky Prospekt; went for a look at the new Amber Room; bumped into Renwick."

Archie nearly choked on his drink. "Cassius? He's here?"

"Oh, he's here all right. In fact, he's been with us ever since London. Watching and waiting."

"For what?"

"For us to do his legwork for him and locate the last Bellak painting."

"So he knows?"

"He knows everything he managed to beat out of Raj."

"What?"

Archie jumped up, concern etched into his face, but Tom held out a reassuring hand. "I tracked him down. Apparently they fished him out of the river last night. Shot twice but still alive. Just about."

"Wait till I get my hands on that bastard." Archie glowered. "I'll fucking kill him."

"You'll have to get past his newfound friends first. He's got Hecht with him. Remember? The Kristall Blade guy Turnbull fingered as having murdered Weissman."

Archie slumped back into his chair and drained his glass. "So what did dear old Uncle Harry want exactly?"

Tom paused as if gathering his thoughts. For the moment, he preferred to keep what Renwick had said about his father to himself. Although he knew it was not in the spirit of openness and trust that he and Archie had tried so hard to bring to their new partnership, he needed time to digest Renwick's insinuations before sharing them. Besides, it had nothing to do with the Gold Train or the Order.

"He wanted to find out what we know."

"Meaning he's no closer to finding the room than we are."

"I'd say he's further." Tom smiled. "He still thinks the Bellak's in a private collection somewhere."

"Won't take him long to figure out why we're here, though, will it?"

"No," Tom conceded. "So I hope you've got a plan."

"Don't worry. It's sorted."

Archie went to light a cigarette, but Tom warned him off. "Do you mind? I've got to sleep in here."

"Oh," said Archie, regretfully replacing the cigarette in its packet.

"So what exactly have you 'sorted'?"

"Well, it's not exactly sorted yet. But it will be. There's this client, or rather ex-client of mine. Of ours, really. This is his turf."

"Which ex-client?" Tom asked skeptically.

Archie held his hands out, palms upturned. "Viktor, of course. Who else?"

"Viktor?" Tom arched his eyebrows. "Wasn't that who you got me to steal those Fabergé eggs for last year? Only it turned out they were really for Cassius. I seem to remember that's what nearly got us both killed."

"Yeah, well, let's not go digging up the past," Archie said sheepishly. "That's all ancient history, water under the bridge and all that. I'd never do that to you now. This time it really is Viktor. And no one is going to get killed."

CHAPTER FIFTY-SEVEN

UNDISCLOSED LOCATION, GERMANY

January 9—9 P.M.

There were twelve men in all. Each wore a gold ring engraved with a twelve-box grid, with a single diamond in one of the boxes.

They had dispensed with names. It was safer that way. Nor were they given numbers, for that would have hinted at some hierarchy among them, some sense of numerical precedence that was at odds with their original conception as a brotherhood of equals. Instead, they were known by the names of cities. That way, at least, there could be no confusion.

"There is no cause for panic." Paris, an elderly man sitting at the head of the table, raised his hand to calm the concerned babble that had followed the latest revelation. "This means nothing."

"Nothing? Nothing?" Vienna, sitting opposite him, spluttered incredulously. "Did you not hear what I just told you? A crypt's been found at Wewelsburg Castle. A secret crypt with twelve SS generals in it. Twelve! It's all over the news. The caretaker went in and there the entrance was, all neatly dug out for him, right in the middle of the floor. A crypt we never even knew existed. It's Kirk. He's following the trail. If that's not a cause for panic, what is?"

A murmur of agreement bubbled up, the candles along the table flickering slightly in their agitated breath.

"He has been far cleverer than we gave him credit for, I'll give you that. But we shouldn't lose sight of the fact that—"

"What if he found something down there?" Berlin interrupted. "How much closer do you want him to get before you start taking this seriously? What if he finds the Bellak?"

At this, Paris went a deathly white and the room around him exploded into argument as the other eleven tried to shout each other down.

"Brothers, brothers!" Vienna stood up, the room subsiding grudgingly into silence once more. "The time for talking has passed. I say it is time to act."

"Hear, hear," Krakow intoned.

"What are you suggesting?" asked Berlin.

"Two things. First, that we eliminate Tom Kirk without further delay. We lost him in Zurich, but I've just heard from one of our sources that he took a flight to St. Petersburg. If we can get a fix on him there, we must act."

"I can take care of that," said Berlin. "Just let me know where he is."

"Second, that we move it."

"Move it?" Paris spluttered. "Is that some sort of a joke?"

"The current location has served its purpose well. But dangerous times call for extreme measures. I say that we break the link. Eliminate all possibility that someone might stumble upon the painting and follow it back. Relocate it in a place where no one will ever find it. A place only we know."

"But this is preposterous!" Paris pleaded. "We have a code—an oath we all swore to uphold. Our duty is to protect it but *never* to move it. To do so would risk alerting the whole world to its existence."

"That code was for a different time," Vienna insisted. "It is no longer appropriate. Just as your being the only person who knows its precise location is no longer appropriate. We need to adapt to survive."

"This is madness," said Paris.

"Is it? Or is it madness to ignore what is happening? To

entrust ourselves to the whims of an old man? We must change before it is too late."

"There's only one person here who has consistently warned us against the danger that we are now facing, and that is Vienna," Krakow urged. "He is the man to hold the secret and take whatever steps are necessary to protect it."

"Only one man is ever to be entrusted with that secret," Paris said firmly. "It is a burden that is to last the course of his natural life. Your predecessors decided that that man should be me, and it is not a duty that I am about to step away from."

"Then I demand a ballot." Berlin slammed his fist down on the table. "Either we vote for Paris and his ineffectual ways, or for Vienna and action."

"This is not a democracy—" Paris began, but his protests were drowned out by the clamor in favor of Berlin's plan.

"I am honored that you deem me worthy of consideration," said Vienna, getting to his feet. "But the choice must be yours."

The room echoed to the sound of chair legs screeching across flagstones as the table emptied. One by one, they lined up behind Vienna's chair. Only three men hesitated, looking at Paris despairingly and then at the eight men on the other side of the table. Paris nodded slowly, and they reluctantly joined the others.

"It is a burden to last for life," Paris said softly. "It is my burden."

"No longer," Vienna replied. "It is the unanimous decision of this group that it is time for another to carry the flame. Alone."

Paris's eyes widened in sudden realization.

At a signal from Vienna, Berlin reached into his pocket and drew out a small pad and a white pill. Walking around to Paris, he laid the pad on the table's polished oak surface and then set the pill next to it, sliding a glass of water within easy reach. This done, he stepped back.

Paris looked down at the items in front of him. When he lifted his gaze to the men across the table, there were tears in his eyes.

"This is wrong. All wrong."

"You have served the cause well," Vienna said gently. "Your time here is over."

Fighting back the tears, Paris took out his pen and wrote on the pad. He then tore out the page, folded it in two, and handed it to Berlin, who walked it around to Vienna. Solemnly Vienna unfolded the note, read the contents, then touched the paper to a candle flame. The paper flared into life, then died almost as quickly.

Eleven pairs of eyes returned to focus on Paris. Shoulders shaking, he removed his ring and placed it on the table in front of him. Then he reached for the white pill, placed it on his tongue, and washed it down with a mouthful of water.

Two minutes later he was dead.

CHAPTER FIFTY-EIGHT

TUNNEL NIGHTCLUB, PETROGRAD ISLAND,
ST. PETERSBURG
January 10—1:13 A.M.

Their driver, Igor, confessed to being a schoolteacher by day. At night, however, he moonlighted as a *chastnik*, cruising through the city's tattered streets offering unlicensed taxi rides to anyone who didn't care about insurance, heating, or the windows going up all the way.

Licensed or not, he had not required any directions to the place where Archie had arranged to meet Viktor. Instead he had taken the opportunity to practice his English by complaining about the cold, the soccer results, and the corruption of local government officials as they had crossed the Neva to the Petrograd side.

From the outside, the Tunnel nightclub was an unprepossessing sight, a concrete shed set into a narrow, muddy plot between two cancerous apartment blocks. The entrance was patrolled by three hulking security guards in black berets and paramilitary uniforms, with a wolflike German shepherd in tow. The door, a solid piece of steel almost eight inches thick, had been wedged open with a decommissioned AK–47. Through the gap they could see a steep concrete staircase lit by red emergency lighting.

"It's an old nuclear bunker," Archie explained as Tom and Dominique looked questioningly at the entrance. "Viktor owns it. Don't worry, we'll be looked after."

The security guards checked their names against the guest list and waved them past a queue of miserable-looking people shivering in the cold.

A blast of warm air, stale with the smell of aftershave and alcohol, hit them as soon as they began to descend the rough stairs, the rhythmic thump-thumping of the music growing stronger with every step, like the muffled beat of a massive heart. At the bottom was another thick steel door, and as it swung open a wall of bass slapped them in the chest like a heavy wave, the noise pressing against their eyes and ears.

Two more guards in paramilitary gear and long-out-of-fashion sunglasses, with batons and CS gas canisters dangling from their belts, waved them to an opening in the wall. A beautiful dark-haired woman wearing little more than her underwear took their money and their coats, then tapped the sign behind her with a varnished nail, chewing gum indifferently. It was printed in Russian, but underneath was a handwritten translation:

No guns or knives. Please to leave at entrance.

Pistols and knives of all shapes and sizes filled the metal basket below the sign. Each weapon had been labeled with a bright pink coatroom number.

"How well do you know this Viktor?" Tom asked Archie.

"We've done business for years. Big collector. Eclectic, though—Picassos and military memorabilia, mostly."

"Yeah, well, nice place he's got here," he said sarcastically.

"I'd rather they made people leave the weapons out here than let them carry the damn things inside," Archie retorted.

His voice was drowned out by a loud beeping. Someone had triggered the walk-through metal detector positioned at the threshold. One of the guards approached the culprit, who casually opened his jacket to reveal a shiny silver Magnum in his underarm holster. The guard turned uncertainly to the hostess, who looked the man up and down and then gave a nod. The man was ushered in, his gun untouched.

"So much for that theory," Dominique said with a grin.

They stepped through the metal detector and entered the club. The bunker extended some fifty feet under a barreled roof that amplified the music and the shouted conversations around them into a deafening roar. At the far end was a cage with a DJ installed at its center and two curvaceous women writhing around brass poles at either side.

Flashing lights and lasers illuminated the dance floor, where bodies writhed to the music's dull pulse. A few nests of tables and chairs hugged the walls, but most people were loitering near the bar, their faces wreathed in a thick haze of cigarette smoke.

"I'll get us a drink," Tom shouted over the noise. He fought his way through the crowd, brushing up against a beautiful woman in a red dress, a huge ruby nestling in her bronzed cleavage. She smiled and seemed about to say something, when she was ushered away by her fearsome-looking escort. A prostitute, Tom assumed; there seemed to be a lot of them pouting invitingly at him as he made his way to the bar.

The bar consisted of two trestle tables staffed by three girls wearing tube tops and miniskirts of camouflage material. One table was stacked with shot glasses and bottles of Stolichnaya, the other with champagne flutes and bottles of Cristal. Payment was strictly in U.S. dollars only.

Tom ordered champagne, secured three glasses, and fought his way back to the others.

"Didn't they have a beer or something?" Archie complained when he saw the bottle.

"It was this or vodka. I've just paid three hundred bucks, so you'd better enjoy it."

"Three hundred!" Archie exclaimed. "Jesus, they might as well mug you on the way in."

"That's loose change to these people," said Dominique.

Tom had to agree. The women were dripping with gold and expensive jewelery. Most wore high stilettos and tight-fitting clothes that exposed their tanned, toned midriffs. They were almost all blond, some more improbably so than others.

The men wore suits, probably Italian, definitely designer; gold jewelery glinted on their fingers and wrists. Every so often, Tom caught sight of a gun handle tucked into a waistband or holster.

"Table, sir?" A waiter had appeared at his elbow and was pointing to a small table in the corner of the room.

"How much is it?" Archie eyed the man with suspicion. The waiter frowned, as if he had misheard the question.

"How much? Nothing. You are Viktor's guests."

"Oh, right." Archie turned to Tom with a smile. "You see, I told you we'd be looked after."

"What about that one?" Tom pointed to an empty table farther away from the stage.

"Oh, no"—the waiter looked momentarily panicked—"Viktor says that table. Please to sit."

Tom shrugged. With a look of relief, the waiter showed them over and refreshed their ice bucket as they sat down.

Dominique took a sip from her glass. "So what now?" she asked.

"I guess we wait," said Archie.

CHAPTER FIFTY-NINE

1:51 A.M.

Tom was getting restless. Thirty minutes had gone by, and there was still no sign of Viktor. Even the pole dancers in the cage, who had started out with seemingly limitless energy and the ability to bend their bodies into the most unlikely positions, appeared to be flagging.

He was about to ask one of the waiters where Viktor had got to when a man, no older than twenty, flanked by a blonde who looked even younger, approached their table and shouted something in Russian.

"What?" said Tom.

"He says this is his table," the blonde translated in a thick accent.

"Like hell it is," Archie countered.

"He wants to sit here," she insisted.

"Well, that's going to be difficult because, as you can see, we're sitting here. But he's welcome to try the floor."

The girl translated and the man's face broke into an un-smiling grin. He said something and the girl translated again.

"He says he's happy to sit on floor, if he can rest his feet on your head."

Archie leaped to his feet and the man stepped back. In a

flash a bodyguard jumped between them, his right hand already reaching inside his jacket, his left hand braced against Archie's chest.

"Okay, okay . . ." Tom stood up with a conciliatory smile, his palms raised in defeat. "Our mistake. Here—it's all yours. Leave it, Archie."

Muttering angrily, Archie followed Tom and Dominique to the other side of the room.

"It's the fucking Wild West out here," he complained, flicking his cigarette butt to the floor.

"You need to stay out of trouble," Tom reminded him. "It's not worth getting shot over a table."

"Okay, okay," Archie conceded, throwing an angry glance back at their former table. The man and his blond companion were laughing at something as the bodyguard busied himself by pouring champagne.

Tom took a sip of his drink and scanned the room, wishing this Viktor would show up soon. Tom hated waiting at the best of times, and right now the traveling, the cold, and the afternoon's confrontation with Renwick were catching up with him.

Two men near the entrance suddenly caught Tom's eye. For a moment, he couldn't put his finger on exactly why they stood out. Then it struck him: despite the heat, they were both still wearing their thick outdoor coats.

The crowd seemed to part in front of them as they strode to the table where the man and the blonde, closely monitored by their bodyguard, were clinking glasses. Then, without warning, they opened their coats and each swung an Uzi from under his arm in one fluid movement. Before any of the table's occupants could react, they started firing in precise, controlled bursts at point-blank range.

At the first sound of gunfire, people dived to the floor screaming. Those nearest the door scrambled toward it, falling over each other in their desperate struggle to escape.

The music stopped, the palpitation of the bass replaced by the mechanical thud of gunshots echoing off the ceiling like a succession of thunderclaps, the spent cartridges plinking off the floor as if someone had dropped a handful of change.

Incongruously, the strobe lights continued to flash, the killers' movements intermittently registering on Tom's retina as if caught in slow-motion replay.

His clip empty, one of the men drew a handgun and calmly fired a bullet into the temple of each of his victims' heads. Satisfied with their handiwork, they retreated across the room, nonchalantly stepping over the people cowering there, and disappeared up the staircase.

As soon as they had gone, real panic set in. Women screamed hysterically, men began shouting. There was a stampede for the exit, shards of glass flying across the room as the bar was upended.

"We've got to get out of here," Tom shouted above the noise, hauling Archie and Dominique to their feet, "before they realize they got the wrong people and come back."

"You think—?" Disbelief and shock spread across Dominique's face.

"Yeah," said Tom. "I think that waiter was a bit too insistent we sit at that particular table. Three minutes earlier, we'd have been there instead of them."

CHAPTER SIXTY

1:56 A.M.

People surged toward the stairs, only to be swept back into the club as flashing blue lights heralded the arrival of the police. Women screamed, men shouted, and guns clattered to the floor. Small white envelopes fizzed through the air as people tried to rid themselves of incriminating evidence, some bursting open midflight so that the white powder they contained danced through the still-pulsing disco lights and settled on the floor like a dusting of fresh snow.

"That way," yelled Tom, pointing at a group of people who were heading through a door by the cage. "There must be another exit."

They found themselves in a narrow corridor; a door on the left led to the men's toilets and a door on the right to the women's. At the end was a small janitor's closet with mops, brooms, and industrial-sized bottles of detergent propped up against the concrete walls. Set into the far wall was a ladder formed of narrow iron hoops that led up to ground level. A chaotic, writhing stream of bodies was scrambling up the ladder's rungs.

"Come on," Tom shouted, fighting his way through to the base of the ladder and holding people off so that Dominique and Archie could climb up ahead of him, before clambering up himself. A woman's shoe, presumably dropped by someone above, flashed past his face, and he felt the sickening crunch of someone's fingers underfoot as he stepped on their hand.

After about twenty feet, the ladder emerged through a submarine-type hatch onto a narrow strip of wasteland. People streamed up the ladder behind them, the women flinching as the cold night air bit into their bare flesh. Tom slipped his jacket around Dominique's shoulders.

"Let's go," he called, the growing cacophony of sirens telling him that it would be only a matter of minutes before the police located the rear exit and rounded up everyone in the immediate vicinity.

They set off, Dominique running in long, effortless strides, Archie huffing after only a few hundred yards. A couple of stray dogs ran alongside, barking with curiosity, until a particularly interesting lamppost brought them skidding to a standstill, their tails wagging furiously.

"I thought Viktor was a friend of yours," Tom observed as they ran. "You must have done something to really piss him off."

"I didn't do anything," Archie wheezed. "It's some sort of mistake. It must be."

They reached a junction and Tom slowed down, trying to get his bearings amid the identical rows of decaying Communist-era concrete apartment blocks whose doorways smelled of stale urine. Before he could orient himself, however, three black Cadillac Escalades roared up the street behind them, rounded the corner, and screeched to a halt, surrounding them in a crude semicircle.

The rear passenger door of the middle car flew open, and the waiter who had shown them to their table leaned out, his face pale, eyes wide, body turned so that they couldn't see into the car beyond him.

"What the hell do you want?" Archie challenged him.

There was a loud crack and the front of the waiter's face flew off in a fine red spray, his body crumpling back into his seat. Dominique gasped.

A red stiletto tipped the waiter's body out onto the street with a shove to the small of his back. Then a bronzed leg emerged, followed by a hand clutching the still-smoking gun, long diamanté-studded nails wrapped around the handle. Finally, an oval face with wild blue eyes framed by long dark hair appeared, and a tanned, full bosom adorned by a flaming red ruby. Tom recognized her immediately as the woman who had winked at him when he brushed against her on his way to the bar.

"*Zdrástvuti*, Archie," she said with a smile.

Tom flashed Archie a questioning look, but he was already climbing into the car.

"*Zdrástvuti*, Viktor."

CHAPTER SIXTY-ONE

2:01 A.M.

As soon as they were all inside, the car accelerated away, its powerful engine growling as the revs climbed. Tom was in the front, Archie and Dominique in the backseat with Viktor, while an unsmiling bearded brute who seemed to respond to the name Max was driving, a Kalashnikov propped against the walnut veneer dash in front of him.

"Stop the car," Tom demanded, as soon as he judged they were far enough from the club. "Enough fucking around—what's going on?"

"Tom!" Archie remonstrated, for once the pacifist. "Easy."

Tom could read from Archie's face what he meant. They were on Viktor's turf now and needed to watch their step. But Tom was in no mood for diplomacy.

"We nearly got killed tonight, Archie. I don't know about you, but I've had enough surprises. First she invites us to her club"—he tilted his head in Viktor's direction but spoke as if she wasn't there—"then she makes sure we sit at a particular table so that two gunmen can use us for target practice." He nailed Viktor with a stare. "By the way, who was the poor shit you just redecorated the sidewalk with?"

"An employee of mine. A traitor." She spoke with a gently

lilting Russian accent, but her face remained impassive as she continued, "I apologize for his betrayal."

"You're telling us you had nothing to do with all that?" Tom snorted disbelievingly.

"Niet." She shook her head, her hair flicking one way, then the other. "I told him to get you a table, that's all. He must have told them which one it was."

"It explains why he insisted we sit at that table," Archie suggested helpfully.

"And probably why they didn't realize that the three people sitting there were not the ones they'd been sent to kill," Dominique added bitterly.

"Who were they?" Tom asked.

"I have never seen them before," said Viktor. "Chechens, most likely. Professionals. They do one job and then disappear. The money buys them weapons for their war."

"But who were they working for?" Archie this time.

"Whoever could afford them. But not me. I have my own people."

"Well, that's comforting," Dominique muttered darkly.

"How did they know where to find us?" Tom demanded. "They even had time to find and bribe that waiter. You were the only person who knew we'd be at the club."

"It was not me," said Viktor. "I put your names on the list, but they were three among a hundred."

"The phone!" Archie snapped his fingers. "The phone must have been tapped." He turned to Viktor. "We discussed all the arrangements then."

"You think it's Renwick?" Dominique quizzed Tom.

"Why would Renwick make a move on me in a crowded nightclub when only a few hours ago he had me on my own?" Tom shook his head. "No, it must be someone else."

"Well, you can't go back to your hotel," said Viktor. "You will stay with me instead. I'll send some people around to collect your luggage."

"No," Tom insisted. "I think we'll be better on our own."

"That wasn't an offer," Viktor replied unsmilingly. "I've got three dead customers and half of the St. Petersburg police crawling over my club. Until I find out what's going on, you're staying with me."

The car began to lose speed as the lead vehicle in their three-car convoy pulled up at a red light. Suddenly there was a blinding flash, followed by a massive boom. The car in front of them lifted seven feet off the ground and smashed down onto its side. The explosion rocked them all in their seats, their car leaping backward in the shock wave.

Through the smoke a figure materialized at the driver's window, slapped something against the glass, then disappeared. Tom recognized the shape at once, despite the distorting effect of the duct tape that secured it to the glass.

"Grenade!" he shouted, sliding into the footwell for shelter.

The grenade detonated with an ugly bang, shards of glass flying like shrapnel across the car's interior despite the windows clearly being armored, fragments embedding themselves in the dashboard and soft leather seats. The figure appeared again, this time opening fire with an automatic weapon. The driver, still dazed from the explosion, didn't stand a chance as the bullets smashed through the now weakened glass, his body jerking in his seat as he was hit in the head and chest.

Grabbing the wheel, Tom leaned across and pressed the driver's lifeless foot to the accelerator. The car sprang forward, careering violently as they clipped the burning wreck of the vehicle in front of them, bullets thumping into the side and rear windows as they accelerated away. As soon as he judged them to be clear, Tom sat up and opened the driver's door, heaving his body out on the street before slipping behind the wheel and stabbing the accelerator down.

"Take this—" He passed the Kalashnikov back over his shoulder. "We're going to need it."

Viktor grabbed it, checked the magazine, then cocked the weapon with familiar ease. Then, kicking her shoes off, she climbed into the passenger seat next to Tom. He saw that she was bleeding from a deep cut on her arm.

"Are you okay?"

"Forget me. What about the others?" she asked. Tom

checked his mirror and saw the second escort car lying in a twisted mangle of burning steel and rubber.

"I don't think they made it. Must have been using a shaped charge or tank mines. We're just lucky we didn't drive over one ourselves."

"When I find out who's done this I will make them pay." Viktor's eyes flashed, her chest heaving. "No one will escape."

"Let's get out of here first," Tom reminded her.

"Head south for the river," she ordered.

Tom nodded, making eye contact in the rearview mirror with a grim-faced Archie, then Dominique, who gave him a nervous smile. She was clutching her jaw as if she'd banged it against something.

Suddenly a car surged out from a street to their left, guns blazing out of both windows.

"Hold my legs," Viktor shouted over the noise of the gunfire.

She pressed her window switch and leaned out, her back resting on the sill so that she was almost lying flat. Steering with his left hand, Tom grabbed her ankles with his right hand to stop her falling as she began to fire three-shot bursts at their pursuers.

"Aim for the tires," Tom shouted. She fired again, and sparks began to fly from the car behind them as the left front tire shredded. As the driver lost control, it veered across the icy road, clipped an oncoming vehicle, and spun into a line of parked cars. Tom watched in the rearview mirror as it flipped spectacularly onto its roof, wheels still spinning.

Viktor snapped off the magazine and looked into it with disgust. "I'm out," she said, tossing it out the window. Dominique grabbed the handgun Viktor had left on the backseat, cocked it, and thrust it toward her. "Use this."

Viktor nodded her thanks, the gun strangely incongruous between her sparkling nails.

"Where to?" asked Tom.

"The bridge," Viktor exclaimed, pointing at the road ahead. "Get to the bridge." She checked her watch, a diamond-studded gold Rolex. "There's still time."

Tom gunned the car in the direction she had indicated, and a minute later they could see the Troitsky Bridge and a long line of traffic leading to it.

"Take the left lane," Viktor instructed.

Tom swung the car into the oncoming traffic, horns blaring and headlights flashing as cars swerved up onto the pavement to avoid them. Ahead, two large barriers had just come down across the road, preventing any more traffic from passing.

"What's happening?" Tom asked.

"They're raising the bridges to let the ships through. They do it every night, except when the river's frozen. Once the bridge is up, it won't go down again until three A.M. If we get across now, they'll be stuck here."

Tom slammed on the brakes as they reached the barrier, the car slewing to a sideways halt.

"We'll have to run for it from here." He hit the ground running and vaulted over the barrier, the others only seconds behind him.

"This way," urged Viktor.

They ran past a gesticulating guard onto the main bridge section. Tom felt it slowly begin to rise under them as they ran.

"We're not going to make it," he panted.

"We have to. Look—" Viktor was pointing at something behind them. Tom turned to see that a second car was accelerating down the road toward them. Two gunmen with semiautomatics were firing at them from the windows, the bullets burrowing into the tarmac around them like pebbles dropping into sand.

He turned and, hauling Archie with him, ran as fast as he could toward the edge, the gradient steepening as the bridge continued its rise. With one final effort they surged toward the edge and jumped the small gap that had opened up between the two halves of the bridge. Only Viktor paused at the top, gripping her gun with both hands and emptying it into the windshield of the pursuing car until it swerved and crashed through the handrail into the river below.

Those few seconds' delay, though, had caused the gap to

become a chasm. Arms outstretched, legs pumping, she launched herself across the void, her fingertips somehow making contact with the rim. She hung there, helpless, the freezing waters of the Neva staring hungrily at her. She felt herself slipping. Suddenly a hand closed around her wrist. Tom's face appeared above her, then his other hand reaching down to haul her to safety. Once over the lip, they tumbled headlong down the raised bridge section, landing in a confused heap at the bottom.

"*Spasibo,*" she said, pulling herself to her feet, her legs and arms raw and bruised where she had fallen.

"Don't mention it," said Tom, smiling. He felt a stab of pain in his left shoulder and winced.

"You've been hit," she exclaimed, kneeling down next to him.

"It's nothing," Tom panted, looking down at his fingers, now scarlet where the blood had run down his arm. He realized with alarm that he couldn't feel them.

CHAPTER SIXTY-TWO

It was more bordello than bedroom. A huge chandelier drooped from the mirrored ceiling, giltwood chairs covered in leopard skin pressing up against the pink walls, and a polar bear rug stretched in front of the massive black marble fireplace.

Tom stared up at his reflection in the mirror over the bed, trying to keep his mind off the searing pain in his shoulder. Viktor, perched on the bed next to him, stopped what she was doing and looked intently into his eyes.

"You don't like it?"

Tom shrugged. "It's not my style."

"Nor mine." She gave a tight smile. "I inherited it. I would have changed things, but in Russia, rooms like this make people respect you. Obey you. Maybe even die for you."

There was no trace of emotion in her voice. Tom knew she was right. He'd seen for himself how the ostentatious display of wealth could both cow enemies and inspire followers.

"This will hurt."

She'd already cleaned the wound with cotton balls and warm water, the dried blood washing away to reveal a small hole in his left shoulder. Tom couldn't remember feeling when he'd been hit. The angle and location of the wound suggested that it had happened early on, when he first grabbed the wheel and accelerated away from the gunman firing through the shattered window.

According to Viktor, who had demonstrated a surprising familiarity with gunshot wounds and how to treat them, the bullet had lodged itself in the muscle around the shoulder blade. A trip to the hospital was clearly out of the question and, although Viktor had access to other, more discreet doctors, she had advised against involving outsiders unless absolutely necessary. The incident with the waiter at the club had proved to them all that, for the right price, even those she trusted could betray her. Tom had agreed, even though he knew it meant allowing Viktor to extract the bullet without anesthetic.

"Ready?" she asked, stainless steel tongs poised over the wound.

"As I'll ever be," said Tom, bracing himself.

She slipped the tongs into the wound, and the burning in Tom's arm burst into a blazing fire. The room seemed to go dark around him as the pain shut out all other senses. His ragged breathing came through clenched teeth in a succession of wet hisses that stuck in his throat.

"I appreciate you helping us," he gasped, hoping that conversation would help take his mind off the pain.

"Until I find out exactly what's going on, you're worth more to me alive than dead." Her voice was hard and unfeeling. "I'm just protecting my interests."

"You've done this before?"

"Many times."

"You're a nurse?"

"No." A smile flickered across her face.

Even in his present state, Tom could see that she was a striking woman, her body slim and firm and imbued with the supple athleticism of a dancer. The events at the bridge had left her red dress torn and dirty, her bronzed skin grazed and bruised, and her sleek ebony hair in disarray. And yet, if anything, this seemed to complement the wild, exotic beauty that burned within her dark eyes. But he saw a hardness there too, an unspoken hurt, almost as if she was resigned to the burden of her own existence.

"I used to work." She shrugged. "You know . . ."

"You were a prostitute?" Tom asked uncertainly. Archie had whispered something about this when they arrived at Viktor's house, an imposing building on the banks of the Fontanka Canal, but Tom had been in too much pain to really take it in.

"Yes."

"So how . . . ?" Tom winced as she twisted the tongs.

"Did I end up here?" She gave a mirthless laugh. "It's a long story."

"I'm not going anywhere."

There was a long silence. As she probed the wound, maneuvering the tongs in an effort to get at the bullet, Tom almost regretted asking the question. It seemed he'd strayed into a no-go area, prying into a part of her life she preferred not to talk about. But then she spoke.

"When I was sixteen my parents sold me to a man called Viktor Chernovsky. He was one of the Mafia bosses here in St. Petersburg. At first I was lucky. He wouldn't let anyone else touch me, just raped me himself."

Tom mumbled something about being sorry, but she didn't seem to hear him.

"Then, when he got bored, he gave me to his friends to use. They were bad men. And when they came back injured from some robbery or shootout, I was the one who had to patch them up. That's how I learned how to do this."

"Where did you learn to speak English so well?"

"One of Viktor's men was American. He taught me. He was the only one who ever really cared. I think I almost loved him."

"Why didn't you just leave?"

"You don't leave this life—either you're in, or you're dead. Besides," she continued tonelessly, "I got pregnant. Viktor found out and made me have an abortion. Got one of his men to do it with a coat hanger. There . . ."

She held the tongs out so Tom could see the bloody lump

of metal, no bigger than a pea, before dropping it onto the steel tray next to her. "Doesn't look as though it hit anything vital."

"Good." The wound had started bleeding again, so she swabbed it with iodine solution that stained Tom's arm purple. Grimacing at the stinging sensation, Tom asked, "Then what?"

"Then . . . ? Then he punished me."

Viktor hesitated for a second, looking into his eyes, then lifted her hair away from the left-hand side of her head. Tom saw with horror that, where her ear should have been, there was just a hole surrounded by angry pink scar tissue.

"So I killed him." She spoke so matter-of-factly that at first Tom wasn't sure he'd heard her correctly. "One night, when he was on top of me, grunting away like the fat sweaty pig he was, I stabbed him in the back of his neck. Then I dumped him in the river. Like Rasputin." She gave a short laugh.

"And all this . . . ?" Tom indicated the room with a sweep of his hand.

"Was his. Like I said: I inherited it."

"Just like that?" Tom's tone was disbelieving.

"There were some who thought a woman shouldn't be head of the family. But in Russia people respect strength. They soon learned to take me seriously. I took on Viktor's name to help ease the blow. A lot of people think he's still around."

She signaled for Tom to sit up so she could bandage the top of his arm and shoulder.

"What's your real name?" he asked.

She paused. "You know, you're the first person to ask me that in almost ten years."

"And?"

Before she could answer, there was a knock at the door. Viktor hurriedly swept her hair back across her ear as Archie and Dominique walked in.

"How are you doing?" said Dominique, concern etched on her face.

"He'll be fine," said Viktor. "In the morning I'll get antibiotics. Right now, he must rest."

"Close one." Archie pulled up a chair and sat down. "Good thing Viktor's used to patching people up."

"So I've been hearing." Tom looked at Viktor, his eyes meeting hers for a moment before she turned away.

"Don't worry, we'll be out of your way in the morning," Archie said to Viktor.

"Make yourself comfortable, Archie," she replied. "No one's going anywhere until you tell me what's going on."

Archie shook his head. "It doesn't involve you. There's nothing to say."

"Doesn't involve me? I lost six of my best men. Believe me, I'm involved."

"Look, I'm sorry about—"

"You came to me, remember? I'm not interested in apologies. Just tell me what you're doing here and why someone wants you dead."

"It's not that simple—"

"This is not a negotiation. Because of you, my club will be shut for weeks. That's money. My money. So now you are in my debt. You understand what that means?"

"It means I owe you," said Archie sullenly.

"No. It means I *own* you. I own you until I say otherwise. So, whatever you're planning, I want a piece of the action."

"Not this action, you don't."

"That's my decision, not yours. Now, I won't ask you again. What's going on?"

Archie looked questioningly at Tom, who gave a reluctant nod.

"We're looking for a painting."

"A painting? I thought you were out of that business."

"I am. We both are."

"Both?" Viktor looked momentarily confused.

"Tom was my partner. The Matisse out there in the hall? He got that for you."

She stared at Tom, clearly reappraising him in the light of this revelation. "I like that painting."

"So did the Fine Arts Museum in Buenos Aires," he replied with a smile.

"So this is just another job?"

"No," said Archie. "Not a normal sort of job, anyway. We think the painting may tell us where something was hidden."

"What is this 'something'?"

"We're not sure yet," Tom intervened, unwilling to share the secret. "But it's valuable."

"And we want to stop anyone else getting to it first," Dominique added.

"'Anyone else' being the people responsible for tonight?"

"Could be," said Archie. "We don't know."

"What *do* you know?" Viktor sounded exasperated.

"We know that someone went to a lot of trouble to hide a series of clues that lead to a painting we think is hidden in the Hermitage storerooms."

"The Hermitage? Forget it!" She rolled her eyes. "You'll never get in there."

"Tom can get in anywhere," Dominique said confidently.

"You think you are the first person to want to rob the Hermitage?" She smiled. "The authorities are many things, but they are not stupid. They may not have the money to invest in cameras and laser trip wires, but guns are cheap and people even cheaper. The Hermitage is heavily patrolled, especially the storerooms. You'd have to be invisible to get past them."

"First things first," said Archie, brushing aside her reservations. "We need to find it. Then we can worry about getting it out. Can you help?"

"Maybe." Viktor shrugged. "It depends."

"On what?"

"On what's in it for me."

Archie glanced at Tom, who gave a small, almost imperceptible shake of his head. He wasn't looking for a partner. Certainly not one like Viktor.

CHAPTER SIXTY-THREE

U.S. CONSULATE, FURSHTADSKAYA STREET,

ST. PETERSBURG

January 10—3:12 A.M.

I t's a fucking war zone down there." Special Agent Strange
entered the small, windowless meeting room, sank wearily into a chair, and put his feet up. Bailey could see that
he wore tan cowboy boots emblazoned with the Stars and
Stripes.

"How many dead?" Bailey asked.

"Three. Two men and a woman."

"Not—"

"Don't worry. They weren't your suspects."

"They were ours," Special Agent Cunningham growled
from the far end of the room. "Local mobster. He was one of
the people the DEA has us keeping tabs on out here. Ran
with a fast crowd shipping drugs and weapons into the U.S.
via the Caribbean."

"What happened?" Bailey asked.

"Some sort of hit." Strange sniffed. "Two guys walked up
to their table, took 'em out, then walked straight out again.
Pretty goddamned cold."

"Local cops let half the people who were in the club get
away. Apparently there was some sort of escape tunnel. The

rest are probably bribing their way out of trouble as we speak," Cunningham growled. "If they're lucky, the cops will get a few descriptions, but that's it."

"What about Blondi and the other two?"

"We saw him and the others go in, but the cops didn't bring them out."

"Then, of course, there's the car bomb." Strange clasped his hands behind his neck and pulled it to one side, then the other, his vertebrae clicking noisily.

"The car bomb?" Bailey exclaimed. This was going from bad to worse.

"Convoy of three Cadillac Escalades got ambushed about two miles from the club."

"That's standard wise-guy issue round these parts," Cunningham interjected. "Makes 'em think they're in the *Sopranos* or something."

"It was a professional job. A remote-detonated Semtex charge on the road to disable the lead vehicle, gunmen standing by with grenades to take out the rest," Strange continued. "But the main vehicle shot its way out. It was found abandoned near the Troitsky Bridge. The occupants managed to get over the bridge just as it went up."

"Any witnesses?"

"From what we've picked up off the police scanner, there were four people at the scene. Two men, two women. Three of the descriptions match Kirk, Blondi, and the girl who's with them."

"And the cars belonged to Viktor," Cunningham added. "So it's short odds that's who the fourth person was."

"Viktor?" Bailey shook his head in confusion. "I thought you said the fourth person was a woman?"

"Viktor's a she. Her real name is Katya Nikolaevna Mostov." Strange slid a file across the meeting-room table. "A hooker from Minsk who made the big time by killing her mafioso boyfriend and taking over his operation and his name. The Tunnel nightclub belongs to her."

"If these guys have joined up with her, then they're mixed up in some serious shit," said Cunningham. "And if they want to disappear, she can make it happen."

"Maybe we should just go in and get them now," Bailey said, "before they have a chance to disappear. Haven't you guys got some sort of arrangement with the local cops?"

"Sure, but they don't apply to her," Strange said with a hollow laugh. "Viktor pretty much runs this town. The police, the judges, the politicians—she's got them all covered. It's like diplomatic fucking immunity."

"Plus, her place is a goddamned fortress," said Cunningham. "She's probably packing more firepower there than the local army barracks. If she is protecting Blondi, trying to go in there and get him would be a suicide mission."

"Our best hope is to sidestep the authorities here, wait till he's out in the open, and send in a snatch team," Strange said slowly. "We can worry about getting him home later. It's not ideal, but we've done it before."

"What about Kirk?" asked Bailey. "We should pick him up too. See what he knows."

"We haven't got the manpower to go after both of them," said Cunningham. "Not unless you want to wait a few days. And you'd need an airtight case before Washington would even pick up the phone to you, let alone sanction sending in reinforcements."

"I'll talk to Carter, see what he says," Bailey said, already knowing what the answer would be. So far, aside from his being an associate of Blondi's, they had nothing on Kirk. Certainly not enough to warrant sending in an extra team. "I guess this is really about Blondi, anyway." He shrugged. "That's who they sent me here for."

"We've got eyeballs on Viktor's place," Strange reassured him. "If any of them leave, we'll know about it."

"That's right," Cunningham said eagerly. "First chance we get, we'll move in. Believe me, Blondi won't see us coming."

CHAPTER SIXTY-FOUR

The throbbing in Tom's shoulder had woken him eventually—a dull, stabbing pain that every movement, every breath, seemed to irritate still further. Checking his watch, he realized that he'd slept through the day, the painkillers and exhaustion finally catching up with him.

He pulled the black satin bedsheets aside and sat up, noticing an untouched tray of food at the foot of the bed. There were no mirrors, no chandeliers, and, thankfully, no leopard skin in this room, although the ceiling had been painted black with the major constellations highlighted in gold leaf. He wondered whether Viktor had taken pity on him and deliberately placed him in a more subdued room. Subdued by her standards, at least.

Giving up on tying his shoelaces, he found his way past several armed guards who were patrolling the wide, parquet-floored corridors as if it were a government facility, and entered the dining room where Archie and Dominique were sitting at a massive ebony dining table.

"Tom!" Dominique exclaimed as she saw him. "How are you feeling?"

"Fine. What about you two?"

"Great, except that Viktor won't let us leave the house," Archie said with a resigned shrug. "We can't even use the phone."

"The good news is, the food's great." Dominique grinned. "Want something?"

"Don't listen to her, she's actually enjoying this," said Archie.

"Well, it makes a change," said Dominique. "Besides—"

Viktor chose that moment to stride into the room wearing beige combat trousers and a tight-fitting black top. A nickel-plated Sig Sauer was tucked into the small of her back.

"You're better." It was a statement rather than a question.

"Much."

"Good. Because we found someone . . ."

There was a scuffle in the doorway as two of her men frog-marched a hooded and handcuffed figure into the room at gunpoint.

"He showed up at your hotel, asking questions. Said he knew you. I just wanted to check before I had him disappear."

She reached up and snatched the hood off the man's head. Turnbull stood blinking at them, disoriented, a piece of tape plastered over his mouth.

Archie got up and walked over to him, his eyes narrowed as if scrutinizing Turnbull's face in minute detail.

"No, never seen him before," he sniffed eventually, sitting back down. "He must be one of them."

"Take him down to the cellar," Viktor ordered.

At this, Turnbull's eyes widened and he began to struggle frantically, the tape muffling his shouts.

"It's okay," Tom said with a smile. "That's Archie's idea of a joke. He's with us."

"Oh." Viktor, looking slightly disappointed, indicated with a wave that her men should remove the gag.

"Very funny," Turnbull said angrily as soon as he could speak. His lank black hair had tumbled down over his flushed and sweating face. He said something in Russian to one of Viktor's men. Viktor nodded her consent, and the handcuffs were whipped off.

"Serves you right for snooping around," Archie shot back.

"I wasn't snooping." Turnbull rubbed his wrists, his skin pink and sore. "Kirk told me you were staying there. He knew I was coming."

"Did you?" Archie asked Tom with surprise. "What for?"

"Presumably because, unlike you, he is mindful of the fact that I'm the one who got you involved in this. We're meant to be working together, remember?"

"Together?" Archie gave a short laugh. "You weren't the one getting shot at last night."

"That was you?" Turnbull gasped. "It's all over the news. What happened?"

"We're not sure," said Tom. "Someone latched on to us in Zurich. Next thing we know . . ."

"You think it's Renwick?"

"No." Tom quickly briefed Turnbull on the events of the previous afternoon, including his encounter with Renwick in the Catherine Palace. "If Renwick wanted me dead, he could have done it there and then."

"So Renwick knows about the Amber Room?"

"The Amber Room?" Viktor stepped forward, her voice eager. "Is that what this is all about?"

"Maybe," Tom said slowly, silently cursing Turnbull's indiscretion.

"But it's just a myth."

"What do you know about it?" Archie challenged her.

"Viktor—the old Viktor—told me all about it."

"Why, what was his interest?"

"He was obsessed with the war. I've got a room downstairs full of his old maps and uniforms and flags. He even had an old Enigma machine restored so that he could use it to send messages to one of his American contacts for fun. But the Amber Room—it's just a legend."

"So what do you call this?"

Archie handed her the fragment of amber they had recovered from the satchel in Völz's vault. She gazed at it suspiciously, but when she next spoke, her voice sounded uncertain for almost the first time since they had met.

"It can't be . . . it's impossible."

"You're probably right. But, to be sure, we need to find that painting."

"And judging from the attention we've been getting, we must be looking in the right place," said Archie.

"Then maybe I can help, after all," Viktor conceded.

"The British government doesn't work with gangsters." Turnbull snorted dimissively.

"The British government, like all governments, works with whoever can get the job done," Tom corrected him. "Unless you just want to call it a day?"

Turnbull was silent, clearly considering his options, before turning to Viktor. "How can you help?" he asked.

"The deputy curator at the Hermitage, Boris Kristenko. He's into me for a bit of money. A gambling debt that he can't seem to shake. He'll play along."

"Are you sure?"

"We just need to squeeze him."

"Nobody gets hurt," Tom warned.

"Do you want the information or not?"

"Not like that."

"I'm just talking about applying a little pressure."

"What sort of pressure?" Tom asked warily.

"The sort which is most effective in getting people to co-operate. Fear and greed."

"The fear being that he has to pay you back or face the consequences?"

"And the greed being that, if he helps us, I'll pay him for his trouble. Fifty thousand should do the trick."

Tom nodded his agreement. "How come you didn't mention this last night?"

"Because last night we'd just met. Now, we're old friends." She smiled. "Besides, last night, you hadn't mentioned the Amber Room."

CHAPTER SIXTY-FIVE

January 10—7:05 P.M.

It was a short drive to Greshniki, or Sinners, a four-story gay club on the Griboyedova Canal. According to Viktor's informants, Kristenko was in the habit of stopping by for a drink here on his way home.

The club opened at six. Though posters at the door promised all-night male striptease, it really got going only after ten. Then the naked dancers would mix with the crowd, handing out paint and brushes, and offering their bodies as a canvas. Telephone numbers were the most commonly drawn items.

The place was still quiet when Tom and Viktor made their way up to the first-floor bar to wait for Kristenko. She ordered a bottle of vodka and two shot glasses, then filled them both to the brim.

"*Nazdorovje*," she said, clinking glasses with him. No sooner had she downed the shot than she poured herself another. Tom did the same.

The room was deserted as they sat together in silence, waiting. Looking around, Tom saw that everything from the carpet to the walls, ceiling, and furniture was black. The only color came from a UV light, hidden behind the shelves where the spirits were displayed, so that it shone purple through the different colored liquids each bottle contained.

Viktor's voice suddenly broke into Tom's thoughts. "Who's Harry?"

"What?" Tom's voice registered his surprise at this unexpected question. Did Viktor know Renwick?

"Harry. When I looked in on you last night, you were talking in your sleep. Something about Harry. You seemed angry."

"He's someone I used to know," Tom said dismissively, not wanting to relive whatever it was he had been dreaming about. "He's no one."

There was a long silence.

"You know, I think maybe we're alike, you and me."

The memory of how she had executed the waiter surfaced in Tom's mind, prompting an immediate and forceful response. "I don't think so."

"I'm not so sure," she said.

A pause.

"Why do you say that?" he asked.

"You're angry, like me. I can see it in your eyes. I heard it in your voice when you were dreaming."

"Am I?" Another pause. "Angry about what?"

She shrugged. "I'd say you've been hurt. A betrayal, perhaps. Someone you thought you could trust. Now you've lost the ability to care about most things, most people— but yourself, especially. You're bitter. Every day is a struggle. You hate yourself without knowing why. You live inside yourself."

"Once maybe," Tom said slowly, surprised at her intuition. "But less so now. Since I stopped."

"You can't suddenly change who you are."

"Are you talking about me or you?"

"I know why I hate myself." She seemed not to have heard him. "I've become like Viktor. Become the very thing that I once despised. The irony is that I'm trapped. I'm even more of a prisoner now than I was when he was alive. At the first sign of weakness, someone will make a move against me and I'll be the one they fish out of the Neva. And nobody will care."

Tom thought back to the leopard skin and the chandeliers and the black ceilings of her house and wondered whether she had thought that, like some sort of primitive headhunting tribe, she would somehow absorb Viktor's strength and ruthlessness if she kept his name and his home. To some degree the totem had clearly worked, protecting her vulnerability. But for the first time he sensed that this second skin was only an imperfect fit for her slender shoulders.

"What did you expect?" Tom ventured. "That you could run this sort of operation and have a normal life?" She smiled ruefully. "The choices that we make have consequences. I should know—I've made some bad decisions, and suffered for them. But you can always get out. I used to think that you couldn't, but you can. It's never too late."

"It's not that easy," she said with a shake of her head. "They'd never let me go."

"Then don't tell them."

"I've saved enough money to live several lives. I could leave tomorrow. But how do you know when it's the right time?"

"You just know," said Tom.

A pause.

"You know, I'm only telling you this because you saved my life yesterday." There was a shift in her tone, as if she felt the need to justify this rare moment of honesty.

"I was saving myself and my friends too."

"In the car, maybe. But up there on the bridge? You could have let me fall. No one would have known."

"I would have known," Tom said. "That's not who I am."

Another pause.

"By the way, it's Katya."

"What is?"

"My name. Katya Nikolaevna. That's who I am."

She held out her hand. Taking it in his, Tom kissed it theatrically. She laughed and snatched it away from his lips.

"You should do that more often," he said.

"What?"

"Laugh."

Her face fell immediately, and Tom sensed that she was even now wishing she hadn't let her guard down quite so far.

CHAPTER SIXTY-SIX

K ristenko walked in a few moments later, a slight, wiry man with steel glasses that magnified his large brown eyes, giving them a look of perpetual surprise. He looked to be in his late thirties, and had clearly tried to disguise the thinning of his fine blond hair by brushing it across his head, although here and there his scalp showed through. He wore a ratty old tweed jacket over a creased polyester shirt, and his shoes looked in need of a polish. Tom guessed that he lived alone.

The curator didn't look the violent type, yet his left eye was yellow and puffy, his top lip split on one side. Tom flashed Viktor a reproachful glance, but she responded with a shrug as if to say she had no idea how he'd received his bruises. Somehow, Tom doubted that.

Kristenko ordered a beer and a vodka, downing the shot immediately and chasing it down with a mouthful of Russian lager. The combination seemed to calm his nerves. He sighed, sat on a bar stool, and nodded slowly to himself before looking along the bar in their direction.

"*Zdravstvuite,*" he greeted Tom.

"*Zdravstvuite,* Boris Ivanovich," Viktor replied coldly, stepping between the two men.

Kristenko's eyes narrowed with confusion as she said his name, trying to place her face.

"You don't know who I am, do you?" she asked. He shook his head dumbly. "They call me Viktor."

At the name, Kristenko's face fell and he glanced desperately around, giving the barman a pleading look. Viktor snapped her fingers and jerked her head toward the door. The barman, who had been slicing lemons, laid down his knife and silently backed out of the room. Kristenko, all color drained from his face, looked as if he was going to be sick.

"Two weeks," he whispered. "You said I had two more weeks."

"And you still do," she said. "Although you and I both know it will make no difference."

"It will," he insisted. "I have an uncle in America. He will send me the money."

"An uncle you haven't spoken to in ten years? I doubt it."

"How do you know . . . ?" Kristenko's mouth flapped open in surprise.

"Because it's my job to know," she said coldly. "You can't pay now, and you won't be able to pay in two weeks' time."

"I'll win it back. I will, I will." He began to sob, his shoulders jerking uncontrollably.

"Your mother, though—she has savings."

"No!" he half screamed. "Please, no. There must be another way. I'll do anything—anything you want. But don't tell her."

Viktor nodded at Tom and then stepped aside.

"We're looking for this . . ." Tom slid the photo of the Bellak portrait across the bar to Kristenko, who wiped his eyes on his sleeve and picked it up. "It was last seen in 1945, in Berlin. We think that it was seized by the Russian Trophy Squad, and that they stored it in the Hermitage. It's by an artist named Karel Bellak."

"I don't understand . . . ?"

"Can you find it?"

"It could be anywhere," Kristenko began uncertainly.

"I'll pay you," Tom offered. "Twenty thousand dollars if you find it. Fifty thousand if you bring it to me."

"Fifty thousand?" Kristenko held the photo with both hands and gazed at it. "Fifty thousand dollars," he repeated, almost whispering it this time.

"Can you find it?" Viktor demanded.

"I'll try," said Kristenko.

"You'll do better than that," Viktor said menacingly.

"Here"—Tom handed him five thousand dollars in cash—"to show I'm serious."

Kristenko's hand curled around the thick wad of notes as he stared at them in disbelief, then his head jerked up and he looked questioningly at Viktor.

"Keep it," she said. "Pay me out of the fifty thousand when you get it."

He slipped the money gratefully into his jacket. "How can I find you?" he asked her.

"You don't. From now on, you deal with him." She nodded at Tom.

"Take these," said Tom, handing Kristenko his digital camera and a mobile phone loaned to him by Viktor. "I'll need proof—photos of the painting—before we line up the cash. When you have it, call me. There's only one number in the memory."

CHAPTER SIXTY-SEVEN

Click. Click. Click.

One by one the shiny brass bullets slipped into the fifteen-round magazine of Renwick's Glock 19. When it was full, he banged it twice on the table, once on its base to ensure that the bullets had settled properly against the spring, then on its side so that they would be flush to the front edge and feed properly.

Renwick picked it up, savoring its weight in his hand, then examined the scratched and worn surface for the telltale outward bulge that comes with extended use. Whereas a new magazine drops freely from the well when released, this one would need to be removed by hand—not an easy task for a one-handed man. But Renwick was untroubled. If he couldn't shoot his way out of trouble with fifteen rounds, it was unlikely he would survive long enough to need any more bullets. He slid it into the frame with a firm slap.

Renwick liked this gun. The short barrel made it easy to conceal, yet the reduced size in no way compromised its performance. The care and ingenuity that had gone into its design appealed to his love of craftsmanship. Hammerless and striker-fired, the Glock's trigger and firing-pin mechanisms, for example, were almost unique. Equally innovative was the hammer-forged hexagonal rifling of the Glock's barrels, which provided a far superior gas seal.

Most important, he liked the way this gun made him feel. In control.

Adjusting his prosthetic hand so that it was more comfortable, he looked up to see Hecht and his men readying themselves and their weapons for the night ahead. He smiled. He was so close now, he could almost reach out and touch it.

Tonight, he'd know.

CHAPTER SIXTY-EIGHT

THE HERMITAGE, ST. PETERSBURG

January 10—8:01 P.M.

On the Hermitage's top floor, lost within the dark labyrinth that makes up the museum's attic storerooms, a dimly lit corridor ends in a rusty door. Very few people are allowed access to this hidden corner of the museum. Even fewer know it exists. Those that do have learned not to ask what lies inside.

Even Kristenko, whose position allowed him to roam freely across most of the Hermitage complex, had rapidly needed to forge a note from the museum director to gain access. Fortunately, the armed escort detailed to accompany him had been happy enough to wait outside, lighting up with typical Russian disregard for the No Smoking signs. Kristenko decided not to press the point—denied this simple pleasure, they might decide to pay heed to the rule that required them to accompany him inside.

The door was stiff from lack of use, and as soon as he was inside he tugged it shut behind him, metal striking metal with a dull, booming crash that echoed off the peeling walls.

Six somber doors led off a corridor lost in shadows, each one opening onto a different *spetskhran*, or special storage area. According to the rough plan he held in his trembling hand, it was *spetskhran* 3 of this, the so-called Trophy Squad Annex, that held the bulk of the paintings seized from Berlin at the end of the war. The other *spetskhran* were similarly arranged into broad categories: sculptures in one, rare books and manuscripts in another, furniture in another, and so on. Beyond that broad classification, records were at best incomplete, at worst utterly unreliable.

Opening the door, his throat dry with anticipation, Kristenko felt for the switch just inside the room. The low-level lighting flickered on. He felt his breathing quicken and, in his excitement, briefly had the sense that the mottled walls and stiflingly low ceiling were closing in on him.

It wasn't just the prospect of finding the Bellak painting and claiming a fifty-thousand-dollar reward that was affecting him. Only once, when he had first been promoted to deputy curator, had he been allowed into this room before. The visit had been supervised, of course, with strict instructions that he wasn't to touch anything. Now, finally, he was free to see and touch these treasures unhindered. The prospect was almost more than he could bear.

The paintings had been loaded on three wooden racks, each two stories high and twenty feet long. Kristenko doubted that they'd been moved since the day they'd been put there. Like the rest of the Hermitage, the room lacked modern temperature monitoring and climate-control equipment, hardly forming an ideal storage environment. But despite that, it was dry and, most important, stable, the museum's thick walls preventing sudden changes in temperature.

Not knowing where to start, Kristenko attacked the rack nearest to him, pulling on a pair of white cotton gloves to protect the paintings from the acids and oils produced by his skin. An added benefit, he recognized, was that he would leave no fingerprints. The canvases were heavy and it wasn't long before he had broken into a sweat, the dust clinging to his face and adding a gray tint to his already pale skin. But his tiredness evaporated when, among the second column of paintings, he discovered a large, badly damaged work.

Still bearing the creases where it had been folded by some

careless previous owner, its surface was cracked and scarred. Most people would not have given the painting a second glance, but Kristenko immediately recognized it as a Rubens. Not just any Rubens, either, but *Tarquin and Lucretia*, regarded by many as one of his greatest early works. It had once been the property of Frederick the Great, who hung it in the gallery of Sanssouci, his palace outside Potsdam, until the Nazis had moved it to a castle in Rheinsberg in 1942. Then nothing—it had simply vanished.

The label on the reverse told the story of those missing years. It had been sequestered by Joseph Goebbels, who had hung it in a bedroom used by one of his lovers—appropriate, perhaps, given that the painting's subject is the rape of Lucretia, a chaste Roman wife. In 1945, when Goebbels's estate in Bogensee was overrun, an officer of the Soviet 61st Army smuggled the painting back to Russia, folded underneath his tunic. It then fell into the hands of the authorities, who had placed it down here along with everything else. Kristenko couldn't stop himself from smiling, as if seeing the painting had somehow initiated him into a secret club.

Reluctantly, he returned the Rubens to the pile and continued his search. But no sooner had his heartbeat returned to its normal rhythm than he found a Raphael. The label identified it as *Portrait of a Young Man*, formerly the property of the Czartoryski Museum in Krakow. Then, ten minutes later he stumbled upon a van Gogh. The label named it as *Flowers in an Earthenware Jug* and recorded that it had been confiscated by the Nazis from a château in the Dordogne in 1944.

By now Kristenko was flying, but his smile collapsed into an angry frown as he was struck by the injustice of such works of genius being consigned to this forgotten place rather than displayed for all to enjoy. For the next hour, as he continued his search, he fumed over the cavalier treatment of these great treasures, despairing at his powerlessness to do anything about it.

It was hardly surprising, therefore, given his mood, that the Bellak portrait almost passed him by. In fact, he had flipped three or four paintings beyond it before the similarity to the photograph registered and he turned back to find it.

Not the most prepossessing of subjects, he thought. A plain, sad-looking girl in a rather severe green dress sat next to an open window with sky and fields beyond. He couldn't imagine why the Englishman should be prepared to pay fifty thousand dollars for this. There was none of van Gogh's inspired use of color or Raphael's mastery of perspective, and the brushwork was clumsy and heavy-handed compared to the genius that had touched Rubens's work. True, most artists would suffer in comparison to those yardsticks, but this was mediocre at best.

On the other hand, if a lost Rubens or a Raphael were suddenly to surface it would create waves in the art world. The museum director or one of the other curators might even remember having seen it in the storeroom. Questions would be asked. Records checked.

This, however, would never be missed.

Kristenko lifted it clear of the rack. Then, holding it carefully in front of him, he flipped off the light, closed the door behind him, and retraced his steps to where he'd left the guards.

"Found what you were looking for, Boris Ivanovich?" one of them asked good-naturedly, stubbing out his cigarette on the metal-tipped heel of his black boot.

"Yes, thank you," said Kristenko. "You can lock up now."

He cautiously navigated his way down the stairs to the Restoration Department on the second floor. The main atelier was dark and empty, as he had known it would be. Here and there, pieces in different stages of repair nestled under protective white sheets. The more valuable items had been locked away for the night in the large walk-in vault at the end of the room.

Kristenko pulled the mobile phone from his pocket and dialed the number stored in the memory. It was answered on the third ring.

"Yes?"

Kristenko recognized the Englishman's voice. "I've found it."

"Excellent." A flicker of surprise in the man's voice suggested that he'd been quicker than they expected.

"What now?" he asked uncertainly. "How do I get my money?"

"You take some photos, as agreed. When we're sure you've got the right painting, you bring it to us and then we make the exchange."

A pause as Kristenko considered this. "How do I know you've got the money?"

"Don't you trust us, Boris?" the voice asked mockingly.

"As much as you trust me."

"Very well." Slight impatience in the man's voice now. "When we come to check the photos, we'll bring the money along so you can see it. We've got it ready. As soon as you give us the painting, the money's yours."

"Good. Let's say ten o'clock in Decembrist's Square. Near the Bronze Horseman."

Kristenko ended the call and placed the phone on the desk in front of him, unable, almost, to let it go. When he finally snatched his hand away, he realized that he was sweating, his palms slick, his mouth dry.

He was really going to do this.

CHAPTER SIXTY-NINE

DECEMBRIST'S SQUARE, ST. PETERSBURG

January 10—9:56 P.M.

Even on a cold January evening, the area around the base of the Bronze Horseman was thronged with tourists and locals taking pictures. Peter the Great and his rearing horse seemed frozen in the glare of the sodium lighting, a gleaming shadow thrown up into the clear night sky.

Tom was talking to Archie on the two-way radio, the microphone clipped to his collar, the clear plastic earpiece invisible against his skin. It felt slightly ridiculous, considering that they were only a few hundred feet apart, but Turnbull had insisted. Kristenko, already jittery, might be spooked completely if he thought that Tom had brought company.

"You feeling any better?" Archie asked.

"Yeah," Tom lied. Although the painkillers and the vodka were helping, just buttoning up his coat had made his shoulder throb and his eyes screw up with pain.

"It's brass monkeys out here, isn't it." Tom could hear Archie's teeth chattering with the cold.

"Well, hopefully he'll be here soon. Where is everyone?"

"I'm on the north side of the square. Turnbull and the others are over on the south side."

Tom glanced around and located him, then looked away.

"I see you. What about Viktor's men?"

"Standing by, in case we need them. Which could be very soon—I've just spotted Kristenko."

"Okay, let's switch to the main frequency." Tom pressed one of the preset buttons on the radio in his pocket. "Viktor, Dom—Kristenko's on his way."

"He's just walking past the Admiralty," Archie confirmed. "Should be coming round the corner soon."

"Any sign of the painting?" Tom asked.

"He's not carrying anything. He must have left it inside, like he said he would."

"Turned into quite the operator, has old Kristenko," Tom observed.

"Maybe I'll offer him a job." Viktor chuckled.

"Okay, you should see him any second now," whispered Archie.

On cue, Kristenko turned the corner of the Admiralty and began to make his way cautiously across the square. Every few steps he threw a furtive glance over his shoulder.

"Christ, he couldn't look more guilty if he tried," Archie muttered, following behind.

Catching sight of Tom, Kristenko gave a half wave, then snatched his arm back to his side as if he'd realized that he shouldn't be drawing attention to himself. Tom gave a barely noticeable nod.

Under the rearing horse's flashing hooves, the two men shook hands.

"Do you have my money?" Kristenko's eyes were wide and scared.

"Show me the painting first," Tom insisted.

Kristenko fumbled in his pocket and brought out the digital camera Tom had lent him. After rapidly scrolling through the images, Tom looked up with a nod.

"And my money?" said Kristenko eagerly.

Tom held out a frayed shoulder bag he'd borrowed from Viktor. Kristenko unzipped the top and peered inside. "I should count it," he said uncertainly.

"It's all there."

Kristenko's face relaxed into an approximation of a grin. "Okay, okay. So now we make the exchange?"

"Where's the painting?"

"Still inside. I'll go back in and get it, then meet you back—"

With a shout, four men who had been taking pictures of each other suddenly ran toward Kristenko, guns materializing in their hands. Terrified, he raised his hands in immediate surrender, the bag tumbling to the ground and almost spilling open.

But rather than grab him, the men ran straight past as if completely unaware of his presence. Instead, they piled into Archie, knocking him to the ground and pinning him there. With a squeal of tires, a white van swerved into the square and screeched to a halt alongside them.

"What the hell's going on?" Tom screamed into the radio.

The side door of the van slid back and the four men bundled Archie inside, then jumped in after him. Before Tom could react, the van accelerated away, the side door slamming shut. The whole operation had lasted less than ten seconds.

Tom turned to Kristenko. The curator stood transfixed, his eyes locked on the retreating van. Finally, with a despairing glance at Tom, he snatched the camera, turned on his heel, and walked briskly away, never once looking back, not even at the bag of money lying on the ground.

CHAPTER SEVENTY

10:34 P.M.

"They looked well trained," Dominique said, still breathless from having run the width of the square to reach him.

"I agree," said Tom. "Military, or some sort of police hostage rescue team."

"Maybe I can help," Turnbull offered. "Use my connections here to make some inquiries."

"No, leave it to me," Viktor said. "If it is the police, we've got some people on the inside. I'll find out what's going on. You two should concentrate on Kristenko."

"You're right," Tom conceded. "We need someone to follow him. See where he's going."

"Already done," said Viktor. "One of my men will call us as soon as he gets to wherever he's headed."

"If he takes the painting back down to wherever he got it from, we're right where we started—worse, even. We've got to get hold of it tonight, before he changes his mind."

There was a crackle of static from Viktor's radio. She turned it up and a disembodied Russian voice rose into the cold night air. "He's arrived back at the museum and gone straight up to the Restoration Department."

"How do you know that?" Turnbull asked.

"Most people end up owing me a favor at some stage. Whether they know it or not."

Tom's phone rang. He checked the caller ID and looked up in surprise. "It's him—Kristenko." He answered the call with a confused look. "Yes?"

"What just happened down there?" Kristenko's voice was a strangled whisper.

"I've no idea," Tom said soothingly.

"I thought . . . I thought for a moment they had come for me."

"Don't be stupid. How could they even know?"

"This was a bad idea, a very bad idea," Kristenko muttered. "I don't know what I was thinking."

"You were thinking about fifty thousand dollars," Tom reminded him gently. "You were thinking about paying Viktor off."

"What's the point, if I'm in prison?"

"Don't you want the money?"

"Yes . . . No . . . I don't know anymore."

"Fine. I'll tell Viktor that you don't want—"

"No, no. But I'm not taking it outside."

"What?"

"I'll leave it for you. Yes, that's what I'll do. I'll leave it for you here in the museum. You can come in and get it yourself."

"That wasn't the deal," said Tom.

"You said fifty thousand if I brought it to you, twenty thousand if I found it. Well, I've found it. Twenty thousand will clear my debts. The rest, well, it's not worth the risk. I'd rather take my chances. I won't survive prison. I'd rather go to the director and tell him—"

"Okay, Boris, calm down. I'll come and get it."

"Good." Kristenko sighed with relief. "I'll leave it in the Restoration Department. There's a vault."

"What's the combination?"

"I'll give you that when you give me the money."

Tom smiled. Kristenko was getting better at this game as time went on. "Fine. I'll call you when I'm in." He punched the Off button and turned to Viktor.

"Kristenko's too scared to bring it out so I'll have to go in. Can you get me some tools and a floor plan?"

"Done," said Viktor.

Tom turned to Turnbull. "How's your Russian?"

"Good enough."

"It'll need to be."

"Why?"

"Because you're coming in with me."

CHAPTER SEVENTY-ONE

Fuck off," Archie snapped.

The short, fat American who'd introduced himself as Cliff Cunningham just smiled. "You'll have to do better than that, Blondi."

"I've nothing to say. Not to you, or any other copper."

Cunningham shook his head. "We're FBI."

"What, am I meant to be impressed?" Archie's voice rang out clear and confident, but he had to admit he was confused. One moment he'd been trailing Kristenko, the next he was in the back of a van, surrounded by Yanks. What the hell did they want? Always sticking their bloody noses in where they weren't wanted.

"We've got the big picture," drawled the other Fed—Bailey, he'd said his name was. "We just need the details."

"Details of what?" snapped Archie.

"Let's start with Lasche . . ."

Archie's heart skipped a beat. "Lasche?"

"Don't play dumb," said Bailey. "We saw you go in there. We know that's who you work for."

"Wolfgang Lasche?"

"So you admit you know him," Cunningham exclaimed triumphantly.

"'Course I know him. Everyone in the business knows him. What's he got to do with anything?"

"Why kill all those people?" asked Bailey, suddenly angry. "What did they know that was so dangerous?"

"What the hell are you on about?"

"We have proof that you were in the States, security footage from the airport—"

"So I went to Vegas—big deal. There was a poker thing on. Ask around. There'll be plenty of witnesses."

"And Lasche?" Bailey didn't seem to be listening. "Why kill him? Covering your tracks again?"

"Lasche is dead?"

"Decapitated with a samurai sword," Cunningham said, eyeing Archie coldly. "But I'd say he was lucky compared to what you did to the Lammers woman. The Austrian police just sent us the crime scene photos."

"Lammers? Maria Lammers? She's dead too?" Now Archie was totally lost. How could all these people be dead? "This is some sort of a joke, right?"

"Why did you steal it?" Bailey spoke up again, his voice calm and measured.

"Steal what?"

"The Enigma machine, of course."

"Okay," said Archie, deciding with this last, fanciful revelation that he'd heard quite enough, "if you're going to charge me with something, do it. It doesn't matter, anyway. My lawyer will have me out of here quicker than you can say extradition treaty."

"Lawyer?" Cunningham gave a hollow laugh. "You think a lawyer's going to help explain the twenty-six people you gassed to death in Idaho? You think a lawyer's going to account for where the Enigma machine is? You think a lawyer's going to stop us flying you back to the States in the diplomatic bag? You're going nowhere, Blondi. Not till you tell us exactly what we want to know."

CHAPTER SEVENTY-TWO

THE HERMITAGE, ST. PETERSBURG

January 10—11:27 P.M.

The queue snaked in front of them, the air thick with cigarette smoke—filterless Russian brands, mainly—and the humid vapor of restless breath. A few consulted their watches; others swapped blue jokes or chatted on their cell phones, final hurried conversations, half an eye on the gate as they waited for their shift to start. At eleven thirty exactly, the guards opened the doors.

Trying to blend in, Tom shuffled forward with the rest, ready to follow Turnbull's cue if anyone spoke to them in Russian. For her part, Viktor had conjured up blue overalls and freshly laminated badges that identified them as working for the company employed to mop the marbled halls and dust the gilded galleries of the Hermitage each night.

The atmosphere was jovial as the guards ushered everyone inside. Somebody made a comment and the line collapsed into fits of giggles, as did the guards. Tom joined in, wondering whether the red-faced youth manning the metal detector had been the butt of their humor.

The first guard gave Tom's badge a cursory glance and waved him in. Turnbull followed. Then Tom walked through the metal detector. It remained silent. Turnbull stepped through after him, the alarm triggering noisily.

"Must be all the iron I've been pumping," Turnbull joked in Russian to the guard who beckoned him over.

"From the size of you, I'd say it's more like all the iron you've been eating," quipped a voice from the crowd. Again, the other cleaners and guards broke into laughter.

"Raise your arms," ordered the guard, a handheld metal detector at his side, the green LED display flickering. He was young, with blond hair shaved close to his head, and a nose that seemed slightly off center, as if it had been broken several times. Turnbull complied, and as the guard moved in with the detector, Tom noticed his thumb slide almost imperceptibly over the On/Off switch. The green LED faded.

"You're clear," said the guard, the LED flashing back on as soon as he had finished.

"Well, that wasn't too bad," Turnbull whispered as they followed the other cleaners along a narrow corridor and down a flight of stairs into the basement.

"Viktor said she could get us in," Tom reminded him, "but from here it's down to us."

The staircase gave onto a large room filled with mismatched chairs and crumbling sofas, the cushions riddled with cigarette burns. Tom and Turnbull took off their coats and hung them on one of the few coat hooks that hadn't snapped off, pictures of topless women smiling down at them from where they'd been ripped out of old calendars and pinned to the walls. A few people had gathered around thermos flasks and were sharing out cups of coffee; others were changing their footwear from heavy boots to more comfortable shoes.

A man entered and, from the way he began calling out names, Tom guessed he was the shift manager. People came up to him in twos, took a piece of paper, disappeared into a small side room, and then reemerged wheeling a small cart bristling with brooms, mops, buckets, bin liners, and bottles of detergent and polish. Thus equipped, they made their way back upstairs via the elevator to wherever their piece of paper had directed them.

Eventually, Turnbull nudged Tom to indicate that their names, or at least the names that corresponded to their badges, had been called.

"You guys new?" the shift manager asked. His name badge identified him as Grigory Mironov.

"That's right," Turnbull replied in perfect Russian.

"No one told me," complained Mironov.

"No one told us until a few hours ago."

He looked at their badges, then at their faces. "You're not on my list."

"That's not our fault."

Mironov sighed. "Don't you talk?" he asked Tom.

"Never shuts up," Turnbull answered for him.

Mironov looked suspiciously at Tom, who returned his stare unblinkingly. Mironov's face broke into a grin. "I can see that," he chuckled. Tom smiled too, still unaware of what was being said.

"Here you go." He handed Turnbull a piece of paper. "You'll find the gear in there. Head for the second floor. You get lost, just ask one of the guards."

They gathered their equipment from the storeroom and rolled the cart to the lift.

"We drew the second floor of the Western Wing," Turnbull said as soon as the door shut. Tom pulled out the floor plan he had brought with him and ran his finger across the page.

"That puts us on the right floor but the wrong side of the building. We need to get to the northeast corner, where the restoration rooms are."

The door rolled open and an armed guard greeted them with an upturned hand.

"What?" Turnbull asked in Russian.

"The work schedule." The guard clicked his fingers impatiently. "What room are you in?"

"Oh"—Turnbull lowered his voice to a conspiratorial whisper—"no schedule tonight." The guard frowned. "The director's expecting an important guest tomorrow, but his office isn't due for a clean until the day after. Well, you know what the Committee are like when it comes to bending the rules, even for him. So he's paid us cash to do it for him tonight. I gave a third to Mironov and here's a third for you. We don't want any schedules screwing things up for us, do we?"

The guard winked and closed his hand around the crisp fold of notes that Turnbull had just slipped him. "Understood." He stepped back from the lift. "Do you know your way?"

"Just down there, isn't it?"

"That's it. Last door on the right before you turn the corner. Anyone wants to know what you're doing over there, just tell them to speak to Sasha. I'll smooth things over."

They headed off in the direction of the administrative offices and workshops. Even though this area was closed to the public, the corridors were no less richly decorated, with their intricate parquet floors and ornate plasterwork, chandeliers drooping to the floor under their own weight like branches loaded with ripe fruit.

Suddenly Tom felt a tug on his sleeve. Turnbull indicated the door beside them and translated the inscription: "Department of the History and Restoration of the Architectural Objects—looks like this is the one."

It was locked.

Turnbull gave a glance over his shoulder to check that there were no guards in sight, then unzipped the front of his overalls and detached the small pouch that had been strapped to his belt. The same pouch that had set off the metal detectors on the way in. Tom was not surprised to see that its removal had not visibly reduced Turnbull's girth.

Tom pulled on his gloves and took his pick and tension wrench from the pouch. Most thieves use the pick to locate the locking pins and, one by one, push them out of the way; the tension wrench is then inserted underneath the pick and turned, like a key, to open the lock. This was too time-consuming for Tom's liking. His preference instead was for a technique known as scrubbing, which requires split-second timing and a level of dexterity that makes it the preserve of only a select few. By moving the pick rapidly back and forth over the pins once, and applying pressure on the tension wrench between each pass to knock the pins off center, Tom had the door open in seconds.

To Turnbull, looking on, it seemed as simple as using a key.

CHAPTER SEVENTY-THREE

BORIS KRISTENKO'S OFFICE, THE HERMITAGE

January 10—11:52 P.M.

Boris Kristenko was sitting in the dark in his office. Having long since exhausted the meager respite that chewing his fingernails could offer, he was now gnawing anxiously on a ballpoint pen. Every so often he would swap it to the other side of his mouth, his saliva filling the pen's clear plastic case with a cloudy liquid.

A pipe gurgled somewhere and he jumped, convinced for a moment that it heralded the arrival of an angry horde of police officers. He fixed the door with a fearful stare, but it remained shut, his heart hammering inside his chest.

Closing his eyes, he leaned back in his chair, the wood creaking under the strain as he balanced on the rear legs. Try as he might, he simply could not make sense of what had just happened on Decembrist's Square.

The moment when those armed police came bearing down on him played over and over again in his mind. Fortunately he hadn't been their target, and some other poor soul was tonight languishing in the depths of a damp jail. But who was to say that tomorrow, or the day after, it wouldn't be his turn? All it would take was for one of the guards who'd escorted him to the storerooms to mention it to someone, or for Viktor to betray him to the authorities rather than hand over the twenty thousand.

He remembered running into an old school friend who'd been locked up for three years after stealing a car. On his first night in jail, the other inmates had taken one look at his soft white hands and gang-raped him. By the time he was released, the diet, the cold, and the guards had broken him; only a desiccated shell remained.

But what could he do? Retrieve the painting from the Restoration Department and return it to the storeroom? Not pay Viktor her money and risk her harming his mother? He screwed his eyes shut, pained at the thought.

The phone rang. All four legs of his chair hit the floor with a thud. This was it. "Hello."

"We're here."

"Where?"

"In the Restoration Department."

"How—?"

"Never mind that. Just get here."

He struggled to his feet. "I'm on my way."

CHAPTER SEVENTY-FOUR

MAIN ATELIER, RESTORATION DEPARTMENT,

THE HERMITAGE

January 10—11:53 P.M.

Moonlight filtered through the overhead skylights, turning the shroud-covered statues and sculptures undergoing restoration into ghostly apparitions that seemed to float above the ground. The worktops were an undulating mass of tins and jars and bottles and brushes, everything covered in a fine coat of dust, the air pungent with the heady musk of cleaning spirits and paint. And in the far corner, black and forbidding, was the vault door.

Tom examined it curiously as they waited for Kristenko.

"Could you get us in?" Turnbull asked.

"If I had to," said Tom. "It must be about sixty years old. Not exactly state-of-the-art."

Turnbull's head snapped toward the door. "Someone's coming—quick."

Not wanting to take any chances, they both ran to the far side of the room and crouched behind one of the workbenches. A few moments later they heard a jangling of metal, followed by the sound of a key being inserted into the lock. The door opened. Tom peeked around the edge of the workbench.

"It's Kristenko," he whispered with relief.

Kristenko jumped in fright as they both stood up.

"Expecting someone else?" Turnbull asked.

"No," said the curator. "You just surprised me, that's all."

"Right," said Tom, "let's get this over with."

"My money?"

"Here—" Tom tossed the shoulder bag over impatiently. "Open the safe."

"I'll stand sentry outside," Turnbull volunteered. "Pretend to mop the floor or something. I'll whistle if I hear someone coming."

"Good idea," said Tom.

Grabbing a mop and bucket, Turnbull let himself out of the room.

Kristenko approached the safe and, shielding the dial from Tom's eyes with his body, fiddled with the combination until, with a heavy clunk, the door eased open. The vault consisted of a steel-lined room, about six feet square. A set of wooden shelves extended down the left-hand wall, sagging under the weight of assorted paintings and other objects.

Kristenko stepped inside and emerged a few seconds later holding a painting.

"Here it is," he said. "Although God knows what you—"

A low whistle came from outside. Tom's eyes snapped toward the door as Turnbull stepped back into the room.

"Who is it?" Tom whispered urgently.

But Turnbull didn't answer. His eyes locked pleadingly with Tom's as he reached toward him, but as his mouth opened to speak he collapsed to the floor. A knife handle jutted awkwardly from the base of his skull.

Kristenko let out a low, terrified moan.

"Good evening, Thomas," Renwick intoned as he swept into the room, Hecht and his two heavies lining up behind him.

"Renwick," Tom said through clenched teeth.

"My thanks for your efforts in locating the missing Bellak. It seems I have been looking in the wrong places." Renwick snapped his fingers at Kristenko, who, with a confused, almost apologetic glance at Tom, stumbled over and handed him the painting. Renwick's eyes narrowed as he studied it. He looked up with a smile.

"Well done. You have what you wanted." Tom's voice was glacial.

"Not quite."

"What's that supposed to mean?"

"Stories like ours rarely have happy endings." Renwick sighed. "It is unfortunately the nature of things."

Hecht stepped forward, a silenced gun clutched in his outstretched hand, and leveled it at Tom's head. Tom's jaw tightened, his mind going blank as he braced himself. Hecht took aim and fired.

The bullet caught Kristenko in the throat and he staggered backward, his hands clutching his neck, blood spurting through his fingers, a strangled coughing echoing through the room. A second shot caught him square in the chest and he collapsed to the floor with a gurgled sigh.

"What was the point of that!" Tom shouted.

"Loose ends, Thomas. You know how I hate loose ends."

The two other men stepped forward, picked Kristenko up under the arms, and dragged him into the safe, smearing blood behind them. They dropped him, his head smacking against the floor with a wet thud, then stepped outside and repeated the procedure with Turnbull, albeit with visibly more effort required this time.

"You too, Thomas," Renwick ordered. "Keep them company. That way the authorities will not have to look too far to find someone to blame."

Tom walked into the vault and then turned to face Renwick. "This isn't over, Harry."

"It is, for you." Renwick smiled. "Believe me, by the time the Russian police have finished their interrogation, you will wish I had just shot you. They have ways of making themselves very persuasive."

The door slowly edged shut, a final sliver of light framing Renwick's face before it too vanished, accompanied only by a dull clang as the restraining bolts slammed home.

CHAPTER SEVENTY-FIVE

January 11—12:07 A.M.

Silence, broken only by the pounding of his heartbeat and the faint whisper of his breathing. Total darkness. A soul-sucking inky nothingness that squeezed and stifled and crushed him like a great weight pressing on his chest.

In a way, Tom knew that Renwick had done him a favor. There wasn't enough oxygen in this airtight space to sustain three people for more than a few hours. By killing Turnbull and Kristenko, Renwick had ensured that Tom, at least, would see through the night. Not that Renwick was acting out of compassion—his only concern had been to provide the Russian police with a convenient fall guy.

Tom pressed a button on his digital watch and a pale neon glow licked around his wrist like a small tongue of gaslight. Squatting next to the two corpses, he ran the cold blue light over their faces. Disgusted at the sight of Renwick's handiwork, he released the button. He was used to working in the dark.

He turned his attention to Kristenko first, patting him down and finding the mobile phone—useless inside the vault—and the digital camera he had given him. He pocketed them both, just in case. Next, he felt his way over to Turnbull, searching the body until he came across his toolkit. He then edged his way gingerly to the door and ran his hands over its smooth, cold surface until he located the square inspection hatch located at about waist height.

Operating solely through touch, Tom located his screwdriver with one hand and the top left-hand screw of the inspection panel with the other. The square blade of the screwdriver slotted into the groove on the screw's head, and he breathed a sigh of relief as it turned easily. He quickly removed the other three screws, then pried away the panel. The gap was just large enough to slide his hand through, his fingers navigating their way between the rods that controlled the locking bolts, to the back plate that concealed the locking mechanism itself.

Again, he had to remove four screws. This time it took him considerably longer, the constrained space making it difficult to maneuver the screwdriver. Eventually the plate came free in his hands and he removed his gloves, probing inside the lock until his fingertips connected with the rear of the combination wheel. The vertical direction of the marker groove indicated that it was set to zero.

Cracking combination locks had been one of the first skills he'd mastered. Although the prevalence of digital security systems had rendered it almost obsolete, Tom put himself through regular training drills to maintain the technique. Less skilled thieves might be content to drill a safe and then use an endoscope to see the mechanism—occasionally a necessary precaution, where an alarmed dial or mercury switch was involved—but Tom preferred to trust his senses. It was just as well, because in this instance, he had no choice.

Tom shut his eyes and began to turn the wheel. His breathing slowed as he concentrated. The noise of the individual tumblers slowly bumping against the wheel's tiny teeth was almost inaudible, but to Tom's highly tuned ear each infinitesimal click was a deafening crash, the minute vibration almost stinging the tips of his trained fingers.

Click, click, click, CLUNK. The change in tone, the slight variation in feel, was minute. But to Tom, it was as clear as if one of the statues in the room outside had just toppled to the floor. He had his first number. He'd counted it as seventeen.

He closed his eyes again and turned the dial the other way. This time the change came quickly. Eight. He moved it back the other way, going past thirty, then forty, then fifty, the lever eventually dropping on fifty-three. Then back again, he assumed for the final time, since this model of safe was usually programmed with four numbers, although it could take up to five. Twenty-seven.

He tugged on the steel rod that controlled the upper set of restraining bolts. Nothing. He frowned and tried it again. Still it wouldn't open. So he placed his finger on the dial, turned it one notch, and smiled as he heard the tumbler fall into place. It was an old trick, placing an additional number just one or two places on from the previous one.

This time when he pulled on the rod it moved down, the upper bolts retracting smoothly. He repeated the procedure on the bottom and side rods, and these too pulled free in his hands. With a firm push, the door swung open.

CHAPTER SEVENTY-SIX

THE HERMITAGE, ST. PETERSBURG

January 11—12:22 A.M.

Grigory Mironov cleared the final flight of stairs and headed for the Western Art gallery. In addition to handing out the night's work rotas, it was his responsibility to check that all the cleaners had followed their instructions and that they were doing a good job. It was a responsibility that he took very seriously.

He entered the Rodin Room and ran a finger along the nearest frame. It came away dusty. Then he made his way to the Gauguin Room, only to discover that it too had yet to be cleaned. They must be in the Monet Room, he muttered to himself, but that too was untouched. He felt the anger building inside him.

The three guards who were supposed to be patrolling that section of the museum were loitering in the Renoir Room, taking a cigarette break. As usual. "You seen the two cleaners for this section?" Mironov demanded. "A big fat guy and his mute friend?"

One of the guards broke away from the other two and hustled Mironov out of the room, draping a protective arm around his shoulder.

"Don't worry. They explained everything. I let them through, no questions asked." He winked.

"What?"

"A third for you, a third for me. The director gets his office cleaned and everyone's happy." The guard patted him warmly on the back. "Good doing business with you." He laughed and went to rejoin his colleagues.

Mironov stood in the middle of the room, seething with rage. So, those two jokers were freelancing, were they? Thought they could get away with cutting him out. Well, he'd have them up in front of the Committee for neglecting their jobs. And he'd report the director, too. He'd never liked him anyway.

Muttering angrily to himself, he set off for the staff offices.

CHAPTER SEVENTY-SEVEN

Tom stepped gratefully into the room. But his elation was short-lived. Someone was approaching. He could hear footsteps that paused suddenly, followed by a rattle, then footsteps again. His eyes shot to the door handle. Would Renwick have bothered to lock it?

Unwilling to take the risk, Tom gently pushed the vault door shut behind him and slipped under the sheet covering a tall statue of Mercury near the door. As the footsteps grew louder, he huddled close to the statue, his nose inches away from a vine leaf that had been strategically positioned to preserve its modesty. The winged god's arms were outstretched in flight, creating a tentlike space under the thin white shroud. Even so, Tom hardly dared breathe in case the rise of his chest could be detected through the fabric.

A sharp rattle on the handle was followed by the groan of the hinges as the door creaked open. A squeak of shoe leather on the marble floor, and then nothing. Tom guessed that whoever it was had stopped for a good look around. There was a slight gap between the sheet and the floor, and he could just make out a pair of old but well-polished shoes.

He heard someone muttering in Russian, and the shoes turned back toward the door.

The shoes were almost out of the room when they stopped again. The man crouched down, Tom able to make out an outstretched index finger being run across the floor's surface. As the finger was lifted, Tom could see the dark stain left by Turnbull's blood.

The man sprang up, the shoes swiveling and following the trail of blood to the vault. Tom leapt from his cover as the man ran past, the sheet coming with him as he shoulder-charged him. The impact sent the guard crashing into one of the workbenches, and he let out a grunt as the wind was knocked out of him.

Tom scrambled to his feet, desperately trying to wrestle his way out of the sheet that was still wrapped around his head and arms in case the guard went for his gun. But in that moment a large bottle on the workbench, unbalanced by the impact of the collision, teetered off the edge and dropped onto the Russian's skull.

Brown glass flew everywhere as the bottle exploded with a crash, and the guard's head slumped to his chest.

CHAPTER SEVENTY-EIGHT

12:25 A.M.

Grigory Mironov turned the corner just in time to hear the sound of breaking glass, followed almost immediately by the sound of the door to the Restoration Department being locked.

"Who's there?" he shouted, beating on the door with his fist. "Open up."

Mironov had done two tours of duty in Afghanistan back in the eighties. His fitness levels might have dropped, but he reckoned he still knew how to handle himself. Certainly, he had no qualms about confronting whoever was inside.

"I'm coming in," he warned. There was no answer, just the sound of more glass being broken.

Reaching for the massive bunch of keys attached to his leather belt, he frantically rattled through them, identified the one he was looking for, tried it, found it didn't work, tried another.

The door opened.

He leaped into the room, his flashlight raised over his head as a makeshift club. But the room was empty. A sharp bite of cold air on the back of his neck made him look up. One of the skylights had been smashed. The intruder had escaped to the roof.

Glass crunched beneath his feet and he looked down. The floor was wet. His eyes followed the stream of dark liquid to the guard's body, slumped against a workbench. Mironov ran to his side and felt for a pulse. Seeing that he was still alive, he laid him down on the floor and radioed for assistance.

Within forty-five seconds, men were pouring through the door, guns drawn.

"What happened?" demanded the senior officer.

"We had two new men start tonight. I sent them up to clean a few of the Western Art galleries, but they never showed up. I think they bribed one of the guards to allow them down here. I came looking for them. All I heard was a shout and then the sound of breaking glass. I think they must have gone up there." He pointed up at the shattered skylight.

"Could you recognize them if you saw them?"

"Absolutely."

"Good. In that case you're coming with us. I want people up on the roof and all exits sealed. Then I want a room-by-room search until we find these bastards. Alexsei?"

"Yes, sir." A young guard who had until now remained by the door stepped forward.

"Stay here with Ivan. I'll get a medical team up here as soon as I can."

"Yes sir."

Mironov and the guards trooped out of the room, their voices excited and determined. Alexsei crouched next to Ivan and loosened his collar, wiping small pieces of broken glass from his hair.

CHAPTER SEVENTY-NINE

12:28 A.M.

As he crouched behind the worktop, Tom's mind was racing. Smashing the skylight had convinced the guards that he must have escaped through it. But it was a trick that would last only as long as it took them to get up there and find the roof deserted. He had to find a way past the guard and out of this room. Fast.

He peeked out from behind the worktop and caught a glimpse of the guard they'd left—Alexsei, the others had called him. Tom's heart leapt. It was the same guard who'd deactivated the metal detector when scanning Turnbull. Clearly, he owed Viktor a favor. Tom hoped the debt would extend to helping him. He was hardly loaded with options.

Tom stood up and the guard's hand shot instinctively to his hip.

"Wait," Tom said urgently.

"You go." The guard looked terrified. His eyes flicked nervously to the door.

"How?" Tom pulled out his map of the museum and pointed at it questioningly. The guard grabbed it and traced a route with a shaking finger. It led down an adjacent stairwell, all the way along the first floor into the Small Hermitage, then into the Great Hermitage until . . . Tom squinted, uncertain that he was seeing it right.

"The canal?" he asked uncertainly.

"*Da*," said the guard, then made some hand and leg movements that seemed to imply Tom should make his escape by climbing down into the canal and swimming away.

Now wasn't the time to explain that, with his shoulder in its current state, he wouldn't be able to climb or swim anywhere. He'd have to figure something out when he got there. With a muttered "*spasibo*" he grabbed the key that the guard was holding out to him.

"Call Viktor. Let her know what's happening," said Tom, acting out making a phone call while thrusting the scrap of paper Viktor had given him with her number written on it into the guard's hand.

The guard nodded dumbly in response, but Tom was already gone, the crunching of feet on the roof overhead as the guards arrived at the shattered skylight echoing in his ears as he sprinted out of the room.

The key the guard had given him unlocked the door at the top of the staircase. Tom flew down it, emerging onto the first floor moments later. The corridor was deserted, the guards having presumably joined the search upstairs and on the roof, and he broke into a run across the polished herringbone parquet floor, his shoulder burning, the pain making him feel faint. He followed the map across the small bridge into the northern pavilion of the Small Hermitage and then used the key to enter the passage gallery that led into the Great Hermitage.

He found himself in the museum's Italian collection, a group of thirty rooms dedicated to the development of Italian art between the thirteenth and nineteenth centuries, and slowed to a cautious walk. The parts of the museum he had just run through were mainly administrative and therefore only sparsely patrolled. The galleries, however, contained two of only twelve paintings in the world known to have been painted by Leonardo da Vinci. Here, security wouldn't be so lax.

His caution was well founded. No sooner had he crossed

into the first room than he made out a man's silhouette in the distance. The rooms here were all interconnected, and it was almost possible to see from one end of the building to the other through the open doorways. Tom estimated that the person he had seen was no more than two rooms away.

He quickly decided against taking him on. Even if his shoulder had been up to it, he couldn't risk the guard getting a shot off. Moreover, he didn't know how many other guards there were on that floor. Any disturbance would bring them all rushing in.

The room offered no natural cover apart from the wood-paneled walls, so Tom crouched by the door, his back flat to the wall, hidden in the shadows. A few moments later, the guard entered the room and walked straight past him.

As soon as the guard had moved on, Tom slipped into the adjacent room, then the one after that. Again, though, he saw the looming shadow of an approaching guard. This time, with light pouring through the window from one of the floodlights outside, there were no shadows to hide him. Tom dropped to his belly and crawled under a red velvet chaise longue. Peering through the golden-tasseled brocade, he saw the guard enter the gallery, pause, look around, then move on.

Tom continued on to the next room and ducked behind the base of a large statue. He was almost at the northeastern corner of the building. Ahead of him, he could see the glazed bridge that led over the Winter Canal to the Hermitage Theatre. But first he would have to evade one final guard, who was loitering in the room, muttering to himself. Finally he gave a sigh, turned on his heel, and retreated south. From his movements, it looked as though he was on some sort of set patrol, which meant that the others would soon be retracing their steps toward Tom. Whatever he was going to do, he had to do it now.

As soon as he was certain that it was safe, he padded over to the far wall and looked expectantly out the window. His heart sank. Not only was the canal's surface frozen, but even if he'd been able to negotiate the thirty-foot drop, his escape route to the river was barred by a thick iron grille that ran between the underside of the bridge's arch and the ice. He was trapped.

He turned, desperately searching for some inspiration, however remote, before the guards returned. Almost unconsciously, he found himself locking eyes with a large white marble bust of Catherine the Great, who leered at him, silently challenging him to escape her palace.

But her unfeeling stare gave him an idea. He examined the windows that gave onto the narrow canal. They were alarmed but, thankfully, not screwed shut. That meant he could open them if he wanted to.

He went back to the bust and, grimacing with the pain, lifted it off its plinth and staggered over to the window, rolling it with relief onto the top of the deep wooden windowsill. He wasn't sure how thick the ice would be, or how heavy the bust was, but he knew that it would fall heavily from that height. If it broke through, he could jump through the hole, swim under the ice and the grille, and come up in the Neva itself, which thankfully had not frozen that year.

Of course, getting out of the river would be another matter. In those temperatures, hypothermia would set in within minutes, so he wouldn't be able to afford to hang around. Whatever the risks, it still beat getting shot in the back by a panicked guard.

He climbed up onto the windowsill, took a deep breath, then lifted the latch and opened the window. Immediately a deafening alarm filled the room and he heard the sound of shouts and running feet.

With a firm kick, he toppled the statue over the edge. Its white bulk sailed gracefully through the air and crashed into the ice, splitting a wide hole in its surface and then sinking out of sight.

The shouts were closer now, the footsteps almost in the same room. Tom stood up and looked over his shoulder. Five guards were bearing down on him, their guns pointing in his general direction. The first shot rang out, the bullet fizzing past his ear and slamming into the plasterwork.

Without hesitating Tom jumped into the dark waters below.

CHAPTER EIGHTY

12:51 A.M.

T he cold water bit savagely into him as he arrowed through the hole in the ice. The shock made him inhale sharply, his lungs only half filling with air as the water closed over his head. His momentum carried him down to the canal floor, and he felt its soft, loamy bed grasp his ankles as he touched down, as if trying to hold him there. Immediately Tom kicked off in what he believed to be the direction of the metal grille and the river, hoping that he could hold his breath long enough to get there.

He tried to open his eyes to see where he was going, but the cold clawed against them like a blunt knife, forcing him to screw them tightly shut. Unable to tell where he was going, or even if he was heading up or down, Tom kicked furiously with his legs, his hands scooping the water ahead of him.

A sharp knock on the back of his head told him that he'd hit the ice, a series of high-pitched pings echoing immediately above him confirming it—bullets drilling into the ice as the guards fired down on him from the rooms above. For a moment he was grateful that the ice was as thick as it was, until he remembered that he was trapped beneath it.

He tried to angle himself down a bit but found that his

legs were becoming strangely unresponsive, as if the cold had wrapped a thick blanket around them that he was trying to kick free. His damaged shoulder had seized up completely.

With his other hand he reached out and felt a wall to his left—the side of the Hermitage. Using it as a guide, he half dragged himself, half swam toward the river, his chest and throat burning as the muscles constricted, his heart pounding, his stomach feeling bruised.

He swam on, each kick of his legs tightening the metal fist that was closing slowly around his lungs. Every muscle, every organ in his body was crying out for air, and Tom was gripped by the strange sensation that he was falling through the water from a great height. He knew then that he was drowning.

With a last, desperate thrust, he propelled himself forward and felt the grille in front of him, cold and hard as the bars on a prison cell. He pulled himself down its face, kicking and kicking until it felt he must have swum almost to the center of the earth, a sharp, stabbing pain in his eyes and ears.

Finally he found a gap between the canal bed and the bottom of the grille. He squeezed through it, his head exploding, small stars and flashes of light strobing across the inside of his eyelids.

He tried one last kick, but his legs barely moved, the riverbed soft and inviting beneath him, the lights of St. Petersburg glimmering soothingly down through the water like stars on the far side of the universe. Everything was quiet and still.

Two hands suddenly surged out of the darkness and grabbed him roughly. He had the sensation of flying, of soaring toward the stars like a rocket, his body screaming, his brain roaring. And then he was free, coughing and gasping, his lungs hungrily sucking in air, his throat uncoiling itself, the knot of his heart slackening off.

"Get him in the boat." He heard Viktor's voice behind him and realized that it was her hand that was wrapped protectively across his chest as she dragged him backward through the water.

Two pairs of arms reached down and hauled him out of the water, immediately wrapping several towels around him. He caught a glimpse of Viktor, fully clothed, climbing up the ladder behind him.

"Let's go," he heard her say. The engine that had been idling roared into life, the speedboat lifting its nose out of the water as it accelerated. The fiberglass hull skipped and slapped across the river's surface as the Hermitage receded into the distance.

Viktor sat down opposite him, handing him a hot drink that he held between his clenched fists, still unable to move his fingers.

"I guess now we're even," she shouted over the engine.

Tom nodded, his whole body shaking with cold.

"Did you get it?" she asked.

He shook his head. "Where's Archie?" he croaked.

"We've found out he's being held at the U.S. Consulate. What happened to Turnbull?"

"He didn't make it."

CHAPTER EIGHTY-ONE

Dominique heard voices and edged her head around the corner. Viktor, her hair still wet, was talking earnestly in a low voice to three of her men. They were listening intently, nodding every so often as if she was giving them instructions. Dominique wondered what Viktor was up to as she watched her handing them several large bags. One of the men then glanced through the open door into the room beyond it and asked something. Viktor's eyes followed his, then looked around with a smile.

"*Da.*"

A board creaked under Dominique's bare feet and she snatched her head back. The voices stopped, then she heard the sound of footsteps fading away.

"You can come out now." Viktor's voice echoed down the corridor.

Dominique stepped sheepishly out of the shadows. "Sorry, I didn't mean to . . . Is he all right?"

"He's fine," Viktor replied. "We got him just in time. He needs to get some sleep, that's all."

"And Turnbull?"

Viktor shook her head.

"How . . . ?" asked Dominique.

"Tom didn't say. But I told him about Archie. He's going to go there in the morning and find out why they're holding him."

"Can I see him?"

"He's asleep," said Viktor, shutting the door gently. "Leave him now."

"Okay."

There was a long, awkward pause as both women stood in silence, neither wanting to be the first to move.

"You and Tom," Viktor said eventually, "you never . . . ?" She let the question hang there suggestively.

"Tom and me?" Dominique laughed. "Is that what you think?"

"I just wondered. I mean, you're very beautiful and he . . . he's very . . ."

"Tom." Dominique finished the sentence for her, smiling to herself at the effect that Tom had on some women, even women like Viktor who appeared to have no soft edges left. His strength seemed to appeal to their need to be protected, his vulnerability to their desire to protect. She had never really felt that way about him herself. There was just too much history there with his father.

"I just wondered . . ." Viktor shrugged, not sounding as casual as she had probably intended.

"The thing about Tom," said Dominique slowly, "is that he's not very good with people. It's not his fault. It's what he's had to do to survive. Everyone who he has ever relied on has ended up leaving him. It's easier for him just to never get close. That way he's never disappointed and he never lets anyone else down."

"And you? What about you—and Archie? He's close to the two of you?"

"Yes. But only because neither of us really needs him. He knows that we are strong enough to survive on our own. In fact, I think that's the one thing in life he's really scared of."

"What?"

"Someone else depending on him."

"Maybe he just hasn't yet found the person he wants to have depending on him," Viktor speculated.

"Maybe," Dom agreed with a smile. Somehow, she wasn't so sure.

CHAPTER EIGHTY-TWO

By the time Tom got to the U.S. Consulate the following morning, a small queue had already formed outside the main door. He patiently took his place in it, mulling over the previous night's events. Images of Turnbull and Kristenko, the lost Bellak, Renwick's sneering face, and his brush with death at the bottom of the Neva kept flashing into his head.

"Yes?" The voice of the suited and spectacled functionary sitting at the front desk interrupted his thoughts.

"I want to see the Consul General," Tom said. The man was waving most people toward the visa section, and he seemed to welcome the change in inquiry, looking up at him with a lazy smile.

"Do you have an appointment, sir?"

"No."

His smile faded. "Then I'm afraid I can't help you. All appointments have to be arranged in advance with his office and cleared by security. Next." He looked past Tom to the person standing behind him.

"It's about a man you're holding in custody here," Tom insisted. "I need to speak to him."

The functionary nodded to two marines, who peeled themselves away from the wall and approached Tom from either side.

"Please step out of the line, sir," one of them droned robotically. Tom ignored him, still fixing the seated man with a firm stare.

"You've arrested a friend of mine. A British citizen. You're holding him here. I demand to be told what he's been charged with and to see him."

"Get him out of here," the functionary instructed the two marines, his nonchalant manner suggesting that he'd handled similar situations many times before. They grabbed Tom, one holding each arm, and marched him toward the door, lifting him clear off the floor so that his feet dangled uselessly beneath him.

"Get your hands off me," Tom shouted, struggling vainly, wincing from the pain in his shoulder.

"Hold it," a voice called out over Tom's shouts and the excited hubbub of the crowd in the reception area. The marines stopped and turned Tom to face the direction the voice had come from. "Are you here about Archie Connolly?"

"Yeah," Tom said with relief. "You know about him?"

"Sure." The man smiled and waved the marines away with an impatient flick of his hand. They released Tom and returned to their posts, their faces never once registering any expression. "I'm Special Agent Cliff Cunningham. Maybe I can help."

"Is he still here?"

"Absolutely. Mr. Connolly is helping us with our inquiries. Voluntarily, of course." Tom didn't comment. The idea of Archie voluntarily helping anyone, especially the Yanks, was ridiculous.

"Look, whatever he's done or you think he's done, it's just a mistake."

"Why don't we talk this over inside," said Cunningham. He turned to the functionary at the desk who had just tried to have Tom thrown out. "It's okay, Roland, he's with me. Sign him in, will you?"

Armed with a visitor's pass, Tom followed Cunningham through a reinforced door that another marine stationed on the other side buzzed open for them, through an anonymous labyrinth of secretarial pens and dingy offices, down a flight of stairs, and then along a narrow corridor that seemed to have six cells along it, three down each side.

"He's in here." Cunningham reached the far left-hand cell and swiped a card through a magnetic reader. The door buzzed open.

"Archie?" Tom stepped inside the cell.

"Tom." Archie's face broke into a smile. "You took your time." He was lying on a narrow bed, thumbing through a two-year-old edition of *GQ*, a cigarette jammed in his mouth.

"You two must have a lot of catching up to do," Cunningham said coldly. He slammed the cell door shut.

Tom stared at the closed door, then turned to Archie and gave a shrug.

"Nice escape plan, mate," Archie grunted, turning back to the magazine. "What did you do? Smuggle a spoon in so we can dig our way out?"

"He's pleasant, isn't he?" Tom sat down heavily on the bed next to him.

"Tell me about it. I've had to put up with his shit all night long."

"What does he think you've done now?"

"Oh, nothing much," said Archie. "Just the odd murder or thirty. Including Lasche, it seems."

"Lasche? But we saw him only a few days ago."

"Exactly. That's when they think I did it."

"But why?"

"For the same reason they think I killed Lammers's niece."

"She's dead too?" Tom gasped.

"Apparently, poor thing." Archie sighed. "This whole business is getting out of control. They think I was trying to cover my tracks."

"Tracks from what?" Tom said dismissively. "This is total bullshit. You haven't done anything."

"I know that. You know that. But as far as they're concerned, I'm not only involved in a theft that Lasche got me to carry out from some museum in the States, but I then gassed a roomful of neo-Nazis I'd recruited to do the job for me. Their kids too." Archie spoke with his eyes still fixed on the magazine.

"You're joking, right?"

"I wish I was."

"Well, what is it you're meant to have stolen, exactly?"

"An Enigma machine."

"An Enigma machine?" Tom's tone switched from outrage to interest.

"Yeah." Archie looked up, his face lifting with sudden understanding. "Why, you don't think . . ."

"Why not?" Tom nodded slowly. "A neo-Nazi group. A wartime decoder. Lasche supposedly involved, then turning up dead. There must be a connection."

"Well, the Enigma's a collectible piece, I guess. But I don't see what use it would be to anyone."

"Unless you needed to decode something."

"The final Bellak painting!" Archie exclaimed. "We need to get in touch with Kristenko again and get it out."

"Unfortunately, it's a bit late for that," Tom said bitterly, briefly recounting the previous night's events for Archie's benefit.

"So Renwick's got the painting and the Enigma." Archie sighed. "We've got nothing."

"Maybe we do," said Tom.

"Maybe we do what?"

"Have something. My camera. The one I loaned to Kristenko. I grabbed it off him when I was in the vault. It'll be ruined, but the memory card should still work."

"I don't see . . ."

"He took photos of the painting, didn't he? To prove that he had it. If we've got that, we might not need the painting at all."

"Then we just need to get out of here," said Archie, motioning toward the steel door.

CHAPTER EIGHTY-THREE

9:27 A.M.

Before Tom could answer, the door flew open and Bailey marched into the room. He didn't bother introducing himself, fixing Tom instead with an excited stare. "Tell me about this painting."

"You've been listening?" Tom shot back, furious with himself for not having been more careful. Bailey indicated a small black hole over the bed that he hadn't noticed before.

"I was on the first shift in case you two got careless. Don't worry, it's turned off now."

"Like hell it is." Tom eyed him with distrust.

"Why don't you tell me what's really going on."

"We're not telling you nothing," Archie snorted.

"Look, you're in deep shit here. Real deep. You want to have a chance of getting out of here, you gotta share. Then maybe I can help."

"Why should you help us?"

"If my boss knew I was in here, he'd kill me," Bailey said earnestly. "But I'm here because, for better or worse, I go with my gut. Always have. And my gut tells me you guys weren't bullshitting just now."

"You first, then," Tom said slowly. "What is it you think we're involved in?"

"Two weeks ago a guard was murdered and an Enigma machine was stolen from the NSA Museum in Maryland. We got a tip-off that a neo-Nazi group in Idaho called the Sons of American Liberty were involved. When we went to check out their HQ, someone had locked them all in a booby-trapped room. Every single person inside died. Gassed."

"But how did that lead you to me?" Archie asked.

"We had an eyewitness. His description was a good match to a man filmed boarding a flight to Zurich. When we checked out the names of Zurich-based major players in the military memorabilia game, Lasche's name came up, so we staked out his hotel. Then you showed up."

"And . . . ?"

"And matched the description."

"That's impossible," Archie said dismissively. "I don't even know where Idaho is. Like I told you, I was in Vegas when this happened."

"Vegas?" said Tom in surprise. "Is that what you were up to?"

"Do we have to go into this now?" Archie said, rolling his eyes, before turning back to Bailey. "Show me the picture."

Bailey reached into his jacket and drew out a sheet of paper. Archie unfolded it, studied the CCTV image, and looked up skeptically. "That's not me," he said with a mixture of relief and indignation.

"That's Lasche's nurse," Tom said grimly, snatching the paper from his hands.

"Lasche's nurse?" Bailey stammered. "Are you sure?"

"I never forget a face. Heinrich, I think he said his name was."

"You're right, now you mention it." Archie nodded his agreement. "He was there when we went to see him the ⟨...⟩r day."

⟨...⟩"What's Lasche's involvement in all this?" Tom asked.

"Well," Bailey began uncertainly, still staring uneasily at the picture, "we guessed that Lasche was the middleman for the Enigma machine. That you'd stolen it and then sold it to him."

"That's about the only thing you've got right so far," Tom

said. "Except that it wasn't Archie he sent to steal it but Heinrich. Lasche must have been betrayed by whoever he sold the machine to. That same person murdered the Sons of American Liberty and, in all probability, Lasche as well, to ensure no one could make the link back to him."

" 'Him' being . . . ?" Bailey quizzed.

"In my opinion Harry Renwick, a.k.a. Cassius—or someone acting on his behalf. Check your records. Last time I looked, he was on your top ten most wanted list. He's the one you should be looking for. He's behind this whole thing, I'm sure of it."

"But what's this got to do with a painting? How did you get mixed up in it?"

Tom paused for a second, debating how much he was willing to reveal. His natural instinct was to say nothing, but there was something about Bailey, an honesty allied with an eagerness that inspired a sense of grudging confidence. He took a snap decision to trust him. But only as far as he had to.

"We were approached by a guy called William Turnbull from MI6's counterterrorist team," Tom began slowly. "They were worried about a terrorist group in Germany who had linked up with Renwick. They wanted our help to find out what they were up to."

"Why you? Did you know him or something?"

"He's an old friend of the family," Tom said with a hollow laugh. "Anyway, it turns out they were looking for something. Something that was hidden at the end of the war. We think the painting is the final clue to revealing its location. I only found out about the Enigma machine just now, but I'm guessing that he needed one in order to unlock some sort of coded message written on the painting."

"And how did that lead you to Lasche?"

"It was just dumb coincidence. The painting was hidden by a secret order of high-ranking SS officers. Lasche is the expert on that period, so we wanted his opinion. We had no idea that Renwick had already involved him in the Enigma theft."

"And the girl—Maria Lammers—what was her involvement?"

"Her uncle was a member of the Order," Archie explained. "We were just following the trail to see whether it led anywhere. But why Renwick should want to kill her, I don't know." He shook his head, mystified. "She knew nothing."

"You're right." Tom frowned. "It's like what happened in the nightclub. There's something else going on here that we're missing."

Bailey blew out his cheeks, leaned back against the wall, his eyes closed. When he opened them again, he stared down at the floor, his voice a monotone. "Okay. You two stay here. I'm going to check some of this out."

Tom jerked his head toward the door. "Somehow, I don't think we'll be going anywhere."

CHAPTER EIGHTY-FOUR

9:35 A.M.

Bailey's eyes widened as the search results flashed up in front of him.

HENRY J. RENWICK, A.K.A. CASSIUS.
RACKETEERING INFLUENCED AND CORRUPT
ORGANIZATIONS (RICO) — MURDER (18 COUNTS),
CONSPIRACY TO COMMIT MURDER,
CONSPIRACY TO COMMIT EXTORTION,
ARMED ROBBERY, HANDLING STOLEN GOODS,
CONSPIRACY TO COMMIT MONEY LAUNDERING,
EXTORTION, MONEY LAUNDERING . . .

He gave a low whistle. Maybe there was more to Kirk's story than he'd thought.

"Find something good?" Cunningham had stepped into the room behind him.

"Not sure yet." Bailey flicked the screen to another program and turned to face Cunningham with a nervous smile.

Carter's instructions had been clear: observe and report. Nothing more. By going into Kirk and Connolly's cell unaccompanied, he had stepped well outside that remit. How could he explain his decision to Cunningham, let alone Carter?

"You come up with anything on Connolly?" Bailey asked casually.

"No. We're still trying to run him down, but it looks like we've never come across him before. I'm going to check with Interpol."

"Makes sense."

"We caught a real break with Kirk, huh?" Cunningham said with a grin.

"How's that?"

"Him just walking in here. We didn't need those extra men to go and take him down after all."

"Yeah, but we've still got nothing on him," Bailey pointed out.

"We got time." Cunningham shrugged. "He ain't going nowhere."

Bailey turned back to his computer, hoping that Cunningham would take the hint and leave, but he hovered near the door, finally breaking the silence with a cough.

"Is everything okay?" Cunningham asked.

"Sure."

"You seem kinda tense."

Bailey took a deep breath, realizing he was going to have to come clean. "There's something you should take a look at." He flicked the screen back to the FBI Ten Most Wanted page.

CHAPTER EIGHTY-FIVE

9:50 A.M.

When Bailey returned about twenty-five minutes later, it was with a pensive expression and Cunningham by his side. The latter took up a position leaning by the door, one leg raised and bent back behind him, so that the sole of his black shoe was flat to the wall.

"Renwick showed up on our system," Bailey began. "He certainly fits the profile."

"No kidding," Tom said drily.

"Lasche's nurse too. Heinrich Henschell. The photo we have on file matches the description. Rough customer. Did time in Spain for murdering a rare book dealer about ten years ago before escaping while being transferred to another prison. The Swiss police think they may have just found him in a ditch twenty miles outside Zurich."

Bailey paused.

"Why do I think there's a *but* coming up?" Archie asked coldly.

"Because there's no William Turnbull."

"The guy's a spook." Tom shrugged. "I'm not surprised he doesn't show up."

"Since 9/11 we have reciprocal information-sharing

agreements with the British on all counterterrorist personnel. Turnbull's not one of them."

"Well maybe he's part—"

"He *was* one of them. Until he got taken out in Moscow six months ago."

"What?" Archie gasped.

"He was shot dead coming out of a bookshop next to Red Square. Whoever approached you wasn't MI6, and certainly wasn't William Turnbull."

"He was a ringer?" Archie's tone was a mixture of surprise and anger. "He can't be. I checked him out."

"You checked that there was an MI6 agent by that name," Tom corrected him, nodding slowly as the past few days rearranged themselves in his mind. "And there was. Only he was dead."

"But the cars, all those men . . . ?"

"Probably hired for the day. Oh, he played it beautifully. He knew that if he mentioned Renwick's name, I'd listen. That if he just pointed us in the right direction and let us off the leash, we'd do all the running." Tom shook his head, furious with himself.

"You think he was working for Renwick?"

"Well, it would certainly explain how Renwick was able to stick so close to us. How he knew exactly where we'd be last night," said Tom.

"And presumably why he topped Turnbull once he'd served his purpose," Archie added.

"So what now?" Bailey interrupted them.

"We're stuck in here, that's what now," Archie snapped. "How can we do anything, unless we get out."

"I can't let you go," said Bailey. "It's a good story, but I need hard evidence to make something like this stick. Besides, I have no jurisdiction here. I'm sorry."

He walked slowly out of the room, nodding at Agent Cunningham on his way out.

"This is crazy," said Tom. "I can't believe you're keeping us in here. We've done nothing wrong."

Cunningham approached them slowly. "Bailey's right. He doesn't have any jurisdiction here," he said. "But I do." His eyes snapped up to meet theirs. "He told me what you guys discussed. He thinks you're telling the truth, that you're not the people we're looking for. Hell, who knows, he may even be right. But that doesn't mean I can just let you go."

"So what are you saying?" Tom asked uncertainly.

"I'm saying that I came in here with Bailey." Cunningham spoke deliberately, his expression leaving them in no doubt that he was serious. "That after he left the room you overpowered me and handcuffed me to the bed." He produced a pair of steel handcuffs from his pocket and dangled them in front of Archie. "That you took my keys . . ." He dangled his key ring with his other hand, the metal chinking noisily. "And found your way up the back stairs to the fire exit on the south side of the building."

"And then what?" Archie asked, cautiously accepting the handcuffs and key ring off Cunningham.

"Then you guys have got about twelve minutes before Bailey comes back and finds me. In fact, make that ten," he said, consulting his watch. "After that, we'll be looking for you. The Russkies too. I'd advise you to get out of town."

"What do you want in return?" Tom asked, snapping the cuffs open and fixing them around the painted metal bed frame.

"A phone call when you catch up with these guys." Cunningham pulled a business card from his top pocket, the corners worn and dog-eared. "We'll take it from there."

CHAPTER EIGHTY-SIX

It had taken fifteen minutes of fielding questions before Tom was finally able to hold up the memory card retrieved from Kristenko's camera and turn to Viktor. "You got something that can read this?"

"Sure."

She led them down a long dark corridor to her office, an understated room lined with books and framed movie posters. Tom sensed that this was probably the only room she had had a hand in decorating herself, although he noticed that here, as everywhere, there were no photos, as if the past was a place she preferred not to be reminded of.

The computer screen flashed into life as the system began to load, an egg timer rolling over onto its back every few seconds. In a few minutes it was done, and the screen filled with Cyrillic characters.

"You'd better let me drive," Viktor said with a smile, slipping into the chair behind the desk. She slipped the card into a slot on the side of the machine and called up the pictures of the painting.

There were six in all. One of the front and rear of the canvas, and one of each of the edges, normally hidden by the frame, but typically included in the photographic record of any major work of art, owing to the difficulty for the would-be forger of replicating something that could not be seen.

Tom soon found himself thanking Kristenko for his thoroughness, for it was on these edges that a series of meticulously inked black capital letters could be seen. A code.

"This must have been what Renwick was after." Tom pointed at the screen.

Dominique grabbed a pen and began to scribble the letters down on a pad.

"A bunch of letters is no use without the decoding machine," Archie pointed out.

"A decoding machine?" Viktor frowned.

"The Enigma," Tom explained. "Renwick had one stolen, remember? It's a German wartime encoding machine, about the size—"

"Of a small briefcase," Viktor finished his sentence for him. "I know. I told you, Viktor had one restored so he could use it."

"Is it still here?" Tom asked hopefully.

"As far as I know, it's in the library with everything else. I'll go and get it."

She left the room and returned a few moments later with two wooden boxes, one much smaller than the other. She placed them both on the desk. "Viktor bought it from some dealer in Switzerland about five years ago for his collection."

"Lasche," said Archie. "It had to be Lasche—he's the only one who would deal with something like this."

"Do you know how it works?" asked Tom.

"Of course. Viktor showed me," she said.

She unclipped the battered and stained case, the wood thick with cracked varnish, and folded it back, revealing a machine that on first inspection looked like an old-fashioned metal typewriter. It sat snugly in its box, the raised black keys large and round, with the letters of the alphabet clearly marked in white.

But a closer look revealed differences. There were no

rollers between which to feed a sheet of paper. Instead, the flat case above the keys was punctured by twenty-six round glass windows with the faint shadow of a letter in each one. And above these were three narrow slots. The front of the box folded down to reveal twenty-six holes, each labeled with the letters of the alphabet, different pairs of which were joined by black cables.

"Viktor, it took a truckload of boffins almost half the war to crack that thing," Archie pointed out. "How the hell are you going to manage on your own?"

"Because she's not trying to crack it, is she?" Dom pointed out. "The hard work's been done. All she's trying to do is operate it."

"Have you ever used one of these?" Tom asked.

"No," said Dominique. "But I know the theory of how they work. Well, some of it at least."

"How . . . ?" asked Archie.

"Codes and puzzles are my thing, remember?" Dominique explained. "I've read some books on it. All she needs to operate it are the settings. After that it's easy."

"What settings?" Tom looked at her blankly.

"The settings for the machine," Viktor confirmed. "What are they?"

"Don't we just plug in the numbers?" Archie frowned in confusion.

"This machine uses substitution encryption," said Viktor.

"When one letter is substituted for another?" Archie guessed. "So *A* becomes *F*, *B* becomes *G*, and so on."

"Exactly. Enigma is just a very complex substitution system."

"Complex in what way?" asked Tom.

"The key to breaking any code is spotting a pattern," Dominique replied, taking over from Viktor. "The beauty of the Enigma was that it changed the pattern after each individual letter."

"Through these?" Tom asked, taking a metal disc with teeth and electrical circuits from the small wooden box that had been brought in with the machine.

"The rotors," Dominique confirmed. "Every time a letter

was encoded, the rotors would change position and so would the pattern. And as a further safeguard each original letter was mapped to a totally different starting letter through the wires on the plug board before it even went through the rotors, and then the entire process was repeated in reverse before the encoded letter would light up." Her fingernail tapped against one of the glass windows. "They say there are one hundred and fifty-nine million million million possible combinations in all."

"So, to decode a message, you would need to know exactly how the original machine had been set up," Tom surmised.

"Exactly." Viktor stepped forward. "They used to issue codebooks so that, on any particular day, everyone would know what setting to use. If we don't have the settings, we're going to have to involve some expert help."

"Which will take time. Something we don't have," Tom said.

"Well, Renwick must know, or he wouldn't have gone to all this bother, would he?" Archie observed. "There must be some way to work it out."

"You're right," said Tom. "Maybe we missed something. Let's have another look at those photos." They turned to the screen once again and examined the painting's edges.

"How many of these wires did you say there were?" Archie asked eventually.

"It varied," Viktor replied. "Between ten and thirteen, depending on the setting. Any unwired letters were passed through the rotors without having been substituted first. It was another way of confusing eavesdroppers. Why?"

"It's just that there are twenty-six letters along the top edge of the painting," said Archie. "And they look like they've been written in pairs."

Viktor nodded. "Thirteen pairs of letters. That could easily be the setting for the plug board—*U* to *A*. *P* to *F* . . ." She quickly reconfigured the wires to match the pairs of letters along the top of the frame. "There."

"Which leaves us with what?" Tom inquired, his voice animated by their apparent progress.

"The choice of rotors and their settings," Viktor replied. "We need to know which three to select and what ring settings to give them." She took the remaining four rotors out of their greaseproof paper and pointed at a small ring that seemed to have been stuck to the side of each rotor. "These rotate and are then locked into a starting position. Without these, we've got nothing."

CHAPTER EIGHTY-SEVEN

6:21 P.M.

They had taken turns in front of the computer, each trying to make sense of the jumbled mass of letters that decorated the painting's edges like elaborate black lace. But no matter how hard they looked at the photos, whatever clever tricks they came up with to count the letters or divide them by the number on the other side, or subtract one from the other, they were no closer to discovering the rotor settings or which rotors they should use.

They had even, in desperation, brought in the items they had recovered—the photos of the Bellak paintings, the Bellak painting of the synagogue itself, the walnut box that had contained Lammers's medal, the medals, the safety-deposit box key, and the leather pouch and map hidden within the box—to see if they could provide some inspiration or reveal some hidden clue or message. But after six hours of fruitless inquiry, the letters had begun to cobweb across their vision.

Archie had long since left the room, complaining of a headache, while Viktor had gone to arrange some food for them. For Dominique, however, solving this puzzle had developed into a personal battle. She knew that Tom and Archie made fun of her for getting like this, often over quite trivial things, but she couldn't help herself, especially when, as in this case, it was almost as if they had been set a formal challenge. It aroused her deepest competitive instincts, which were further fueled by her desire not to let the others down.

She had therefore stayed at the desk, her eyes glued to the screen, pausing every so often only to flex her fingers where they had been gripping the mouse. Tom was sitting behind her, eyes closed, and she couldn't tell if he was sleeping or thinking until he broke the silence with a question.

"Do you think we should call it a day? Maybe we need to take a fresh look in the morning?"

"The morning will be too late," she replied matter-of-factly, without even looking around. She was getting frustrated at herself and was having difficulty masking it.

She sensed Tom was about to say something, but he must have thought better of it because no words came. An awkward silence settled until Dominique looked around with a frown.

"You know, the camera wasn't empty."

"Hmm?" Tom's eyes were shut again in thought.

"Your camera—it had other photos on it when you gave it to Kristenko."

"Oh yeah," said Tom. "I guess I forgot to wipe it. Nothing there that shouldn't have been, was there?"

"Don't think so, no," she said, scrolling through the images on the disk.

First the shots of the synagogue in Prague, the walls scrawled with hate-filled graffiti, the floor carpeted with children's drawings, the painting's empty frame. Then shots of the stained-glass window from the church in Kitzbühel that Lammers had had installed. A castle. A circle of trees. Some birds taking wing through an azure sky. Finally the shots of the Bellak portrait.

Dominique paused, frowning. She scrolled back through to the pictures of the stained-glass window, then picked up the faded black-and-white photo of the same scene that Archie had found in Weissman's secret room. She looked up at the window, then down at the photo.

"Tom?" she called in an uncertain voice.

"Mmmm?" he answered, keeping his eyes shut.

"I think I've found something."

"Really?"

"They're not the same."

"What's not the same?" His eyes snapped open.

"The painting and the window. The photos of each one. They're not the same. Look."

She pointed at the photo of the window on the screen as he sprang to her side, then passed the photo of the painting into his eager hands.

"Let me see." Tom held the photo up to the screen. "Christ, you're right!" He breathed excitedly. "The window's different. He must have changed it."

"It's quite subtle. Here the castle has two turrets, but in the window it has three. Here there are seven trees in the foreground, in the window five."

"And look, four birds in the painting, two in the window. That means we've got two sets of three numbers."

"But which ones should we use?"

"The ones in the window," Tom said confidently. "Don't forget, Bellak didn't know anything about the Order or their plans; he finished that painting years before the Gold Train set out on its journey. But the window was produced after the war and could easily have been designed to include the Enigma settings. The painting is only useful insofar as the discrepancies with the window tell people where to look for the numbers. Reading left to right there are three turrets, five trees, and two birds in the window. That's three, five, two."

"It could be the rotors!" Dominique exclaimed, her earlier frustration evaporating in the excitement of the moment. "There are only five of those. This could be telling us which rotors to use."

"Which means that the rotor settings might be on here too," Tom added. "It would make sense for them to keep everything all in one place."

They analyzed the photos again, looking for further discrepancies that might provide some sort of clue. But, disappointingly after their breakthrough, there were none. In

every other detail the painting had been faithfully repro-
duced, even down to Bellak's signature and the date, just
about visible in the bottom left corner.

"I just don't get it." Tom shook his head in frustration.
"They must have left some way of breaking the code, otherwise why bother going to all this trouble to hide it?"

"Maybe one of the other stolen Bellak paintings had the
last piece of the code?" Dominique suggested.

"Maybe," said Tom. "Hang on, what's that?" He pointed
at a small section of wall below the stained-glass window
that Archie had caught on the edge of one photo. "Can you
enlarge it?"

She clicked a few buttons and zoomed in on the area Tom
was pointing at.

"It's the dedication plaque. 'In loving memory of Eva
Maria Lammers,'" she translated. "'Taken from us on 13
November 1926.'"

"Nineteen twenty-six?" Tom frowned. "That can't be
right. I'm sure Archie told me she'd died in the nineteen fifties."

"What if it's a deliberate mistake?"

"How would that work?"

"Well, the date could be the ring settings—thirteen,
eleven, twenty-six," said Dominique, trying not to allow
herself to get too carried away.

She selected rotors three, five, and two from the tin and
then set the first one to thirteen, the second to eleven, and
the third to twenty-six. Then she lifted the machine's lid,
inserted them, and closed it again so that only the top part of
the rotors poked through the narrow slit. At that moment
Archie and Viktor walked in carrying food and drinks.

"Any progress?" asked Archie in a mournful tone.

"Maybe," said Dominique.

"We're just about to try something," Tom explained.
"Dom noticed that there were differences between the
painting and the window that might suggest the rotor selection."

"And the date on the dedication plaque underneath doesn't
tally with when you said Lammers's wife died." She pointed

at the magnified image of the plaque that was still on the screen. "So we used the dates to set the ring positions."

"Well done," Viktor said, squeezing Dominique's shoulder. "So now all we need is the starting position of the rotors."

"What?" Dominique asked in dismay. "I thought we had everything we needed."

"You see those little windows on the top of the machine?" Viktor indicated three small holes next to the rotors. "The rotors have to be moved until you can see the relevant starting letter through the window."

"How about EML?" Tom suggested.

"EML? Why those?" Archie asked with a frown.

"They were her initials." Tom pointed at the plaque that was still on screen. "Eva Marie Lammers. Or at least, that's the name he put on there. He could have made it up to suit the code."

"Worth a go," Dominique agreed, moving the rotors so that the letters could be seen through the openings.

"So is that it?" asked Archie.

"I guess there's only one way to find out," said Viktor, with a nod at Dominique to continue.

She pressed the first letter—*A*. *Z* flashed up on the light board. Then *L*. *W* appeared. Then *X*: *O* was illuminated.

"ZWOLF." Archie's voice cracked with disappointment once they had deciphered the whole word. "That's not a word. That's not even the beginning of a word. We must have got it wrong."

"It's not a word in English," Tom reminded him. "But this message would have been encoded in German, remember? *Zwolf* is German for twelve."

Soon a second word emerged: *funf*—five. Then *sieben*—seven.

"Twelve, five, seven," Archie murmured, as if saying them again would help reveal the hidden meaning.

Dominique continued, Tom translating each number as it emerged, although with no punctuation it was sometimes difficult to make out where one number ended and the next began. It ended, however, with two familiar words. Archie read Tom's scribbled translation back out loud.

"Twelve, five, seven, three, six, nine . . . Heil Hitler . . ." He paused. "What do you think it means?"

"Aren't map references given with six numbers?" Dominique asked no one in particular.

"It would certainly be the logical way to pinpoint a specific location," Tom agreed.

"And we already have a map," Archie reminded them, pulling the railway map out of the leather pouch and unfolding it on the floor.

Tom followed the grid reference with his finger, first locating the correct horizontal position, then the vertical one. His finger came to rest at a point on the outskirts of a small Austrian village. A village whose name they all recognized as being the final place the Gold Train had passed through before having to turn back.

A village called Brixlegg.

CHAPTER EIGHTY-EIGHT

Tom knew this part of Austria well, although the snow and ice that blanketed the pastures and weighed down tree branches like a heavy blossom made it almost unrecognizable. His previous visits to the Tyrol had been in the spring, climbing holidays with friends, or more often on his own, when bright green mountains had plunged dizzily from snow-capped peaks to the frenzied tumult of rivers half drunk on meltwater.

Brixlegg itself was a fairly ordinary little town just off the A12 motorway that Tom had not been to before. Huddled in the shadow of muscular tree-lined mountains on the banks of the river Inn, it was a hodgepodge of traditional Tyrolean buildings and more modern concrete construction, built to accommodate the ever-growing demand for living space. There was a church, of course, its steeple clawing above the surrounding rooftops like a hand reaching desperately for the sky.

The spot indicated by the coded grid reference on the painting lay a short distance off a distinctive kink in the railway line that snaked along the valley floor, roughly following the path of the river. It was reached by turning into a narrow road before the village itself, and then following it up a shallow incline, past several chalets that appeared to be on the cusp of being swallowed up by the encroaching forest.

The track ended in a gate, the steadily falling snow having already hidden its top edge under what looked like a thick layer of cream. Tom stopped the car and killed the engine. In the rearview mirror he saw Viktor do the same behind him and turn off her headlights.

For a few seconds they sat there in muffled silence, the car suddenly deathly still.

"Are you worried about her?" Dominique asked.

"Should I be?" said Tom.

"I told you what I saw the other night. She was giving instructions to those three men. It looked like they were planning something. Maybe it was a mistake bringing her along."

"It's not like we had much choice, is it?" Archie reminded them. "How else were we going to get out here without being seen?"

Tom nodded. Archie was right. Viktor's offer to smuggle them on her private jet to Salzburg and to provide two cars at the other end had been their only option. The price had been bringing her and her three men with them to, as she put it, protect her investment. And even though they'd flown out on the first takeoff slot Viktor's bribes could secure, they'd still had to delay their departure until that morning.

"I think I trust her," said Tom. "But we should keep our eyes open. Maybe try and split them up."

"Well, we're going to struggle to find anything under that lot anyway." Archie nodded disdainfully at the snow-covered mountains that towered above them. He lit a cigarette and cracked the window open an inch to blow the smoke out.

"That's if Renwick hasn't already beaten us to it," said Tom. "He's had almost two days' head start, minus however long it took him to decode the painting."

"Well, we're here now," Dominique chimed, ever enthusiastic. "I say we go and take a look, at least."

Tom zipped his coat up and opened the door, the snow billowing in through the crack like a fine spray. The air was

crisp and cold, especially compared to the soporific blast of
the car's heating. He stepped out of the car and walked toward Viktor, who was at the back of her car, leaning over
the open trunk with her three men—Grigory, Piotr, and
Yuri—clustered around her.

"Viktor?" Tom called.

She turned, a snub-nosed Beretta pointing straight at him.
Tom froze.

"Here—" She threw it toward him. Tom snatched it out of
the air. "You might need that," she explained.

"I don't like guns. Never have."

"I don't like them either," she said. "But I'd prefer to have
one and not need to use it, than not have one and need it."

As if to emphasize her point, she reached into the trunk
again and took out an AK–47 rifle, its polished wooden
stock and under-barrel grip dark and shiny. She held it with
an immediate familiarity that suggested a long and intimate
relationship, the feel of it seeming to ease the tension in her
shoulders.

Tom knew she was right. From what Turnbull had told
him about Kristall Blade, he knew that Hecht and his men,
assuming they were still with Renwick, would be armed and
would have no qualms about opening fire on whoever got
in their way.

"Argento!" An unfamiliar voice echoed through the air.
Viktor dropped the rifle back into the trunk and slammed it
shut. Tom stuffed the Beretta into his pocket before turning to
see who was there.

An old man, a dog leash looped in one hand like a lasso,
had appeared at the doorway of one of the chalets and was
calling to a large German shepherd who was studiously ignoring him, alternating instead between chasing his tail and
trying to bite the snowflakes as they drifted past his nose,
both activities accompanied by a series of excited barks and
yelps.

"Argento!" the man called again, before shutting the door
behind him and trying to grab the dog's collar as it pranced
around his feet. The dog, however, caught sight of Tom and
the others and broke free, sprinting out onto the track. Tom

knelt, grasped the dog's thick leather collar as it came toward him, and held on as the dog licked his face furiously.

"*Danke,*" the old man said gratefully as he walked up to Tom and clipped the leash to the collar. "Argento always gets very excited when we go for a walk."

"You're welcome," replied Tom in German. "He seems quite a handful."

"Oh, he is. Keeps me young." The man looked down and patted the dog's head lovingly as it lunged at the snow, then peered at Tom quizzically, his eyes almost lost under the brim of his hat. "Are you with the others?"

"The others?" Tom frowned.

"The men who came a couple of days ago. They said some others might come, so I assumed . . ."

"Oh right, yes." Tom nodded. "We're with them. I wonder, can you show us where they've gone? My phone doesn't seem to work out here and I can't get in touch."

He unfolded the map from his pocket and opened it for the man. After a few seconds of trying to find their current location with his gloved index finger, the old man pointed to a spot on the map.

"That's it."

Tom frowned. It wasn't the spot indicated by the coordinates decoded from the painting. "What's there?"

"The old copper mine, of course. I told your colleague that he was wasting his time, but he had the right paperwork so I had to let him through."

"Paperwork?"

"To open the mine up. Diggers too. Big yellow things. He's been at it nonstop. In this weather—can you believe it? But he's wasting his time. There's nothing there."

"How can you be so sure?"

"Because I used to play in it," the man said simply. "Of course that was a long time ago now, before the war, but it had long since dried up, even then. We used to play hide and seek. I remember my mother was always terrified it would collapse and kill us all." He gave a wistful smile.

"And it got blocked up?"

"There was an explosion one night toward the end of the

war. A stray bomb or something. The whole thing just collapsed."

"So what's here?" Tom pointed at the spot indicated by the painting.

The man squinted closely at the map, then looked up with a shrug. "Nothing, as far as I know. Unless . . ." He looked at the map again. "Unless . . . yes, it must be . . ."

"Must be what?"

"The other entrance."

"There are two entrances?"

"Oh yes. You see, there used to be two mines until they were joined up. That one was the smaller of the two, slightly lower down and around the side of the mountain a bit from the main one. It's right next to a ruined cottage. But the entrance has been filled in too."

"Okay, thanks." Tom shook his hand. "By the way," he asked as he turned away, "when did the others get here exactly?"

"Hmmm. Let me see. About three days ago."

"Three days ago?" Tom frowned. "Are you sure?"

"Yes . . . Yes, I'm sure." The man nodded solemnly. "Because it was a Wednesday, and I always take Argento to town on a Wednesday." The dog's ears pricked up at the sound of his name.

"Okay." Tom smiled gratefully. "Thanks for your help. Enjoy your walk."

"We will. Come on, Argento." The man clicked his tongue and they both set off, the leash snapping taut as the dog strained to run ahead.

Tom turned to face Archie, Dominique, and Viktor's expectant eyes.

"There's an old copper mine here," he explained. "Apparently the main entrance was sealed toward the end of the war. Three days ago some men turned up here with mechanical diggers and made their way up there. The painting, though, points to another, smaller entrance to the mine."

"Three days ago?" Dominique frowned. "That's not possible. Renwick only got hold of the painting two days ago. He couldn't have known about this place until then."

"Exactly," said Tom. "Put that together with the hit men in St. Petersburg that we know Renwick didn't send, and the murder of Maria Lammers, and it all starts to add up."

"It does?" Viktor asked.

"What to?" Archie added.

"It tells us Renwick isn't the only one who's been trying to stop us finding this. Whoever these people are, they got here three days ago. And they didn't need the painting to find it."

"Who?" asked Viktor.

"If I had to guess . . ." said Tom, "the same people who hid it here in the first place."

CHAPTER EIGHTY-NINE

4:14 P.M.

Tom was armed with a compass, but it soon proved superfluous. The route up to the mine was easily identifiable even in the fading light, a narrow path that hugged the side of the mountain on a shallow rise, the ground plunging away sharply to their left. Even so, Tom checked their progress every so often, his CIA field training from what seemed like two lifetimes ago filtering back into his memory.

Although not steep, the path was hard going, the snow icy in some places where it had been melted by the sun and then frozen by the moon. Elsewhere it was soft and deep, and their ankles disappeared into the powder that had long since swallowed up any tracks that might have been made by the diggers that had preceded them up the mountain.

They walked on in silence, the only sound the crunch of their feet and the wind whistling past their ears, its pitch growing in intensity as the altitude increased. Occasionally, a particularly vicious gust would spray loose snow up into the air, and then it would ghost around them, spiraling and skipping along the path, until the wind dropped and it would faint gracefully back to the ground.

Eventually the path began to level out. At that moment they heard voices, faint echoes carried to them on the wind, and then the sound of a powerful engine and the dull throb of steel striking stone.

"Quick!" Tom shepherded them off the path, and they half fell, half slid into the trees that lined the steep incline that lay beneath it.

"According to the old man, that's the main entrance up ahead," Tom whispered to the others as they crouched around him in the trees' shadows, their trunks thrusting above them like black marble columns. "From the sound of it, that's where they're trying to get in."

"How are we going to get past them?" Viktor asked.

"You're not," Tom said firmly, sensing that his opportunity to split Viktor from her men had arrived. "Archie and I will go round to the other entrance and see what we can find there. You and Dom stay out of sight and keep an eye on these guys, in case they decide to try the other entrance too."

"Niet." Viktor flashed him an indignant look. "If you're going over there, then so am I."

"Me too," said Dominique, flashing Viktor a supportive glance.

"This is our mess, not yours," Tom insisted. The last thing he needed right now was Dominique being difficult.

"It became my mess when my club got shot up and six of my men killed. We're partners in this, remember? Either we all go or we all stay."

"Look, I'm not trying anything on, okay?" Tom pleaded. "Someone needs to watch our backs. I'd rather it was you two, who I know I can trust."

Viktor and Dominique exchanged a glance.

"Okay," Dominique conceded.

"Fine." Viktor gave a grudging shrug. "But you'll take Grigory and the others with you. That's the deal."

Squatting on their haunches, their eyes expectant and alert, AKs at the ready, Viktor's men exuded a menacing but at the same time reassuring presence.

"Done," said Tom, grateful, in a way, to have them along. "Let's make sure we stay in contact." He patted the radio in his pocket. "First sign of trouble, you let us know."

"The same goes for you." Dominique's voice was stern. "I know what you two are like. No heroics. Go and see what you can find, and then we meet back here to decide what to do."

"Okay. And take this." He handed over a business card. "It's the number for the FBI agent who helped us out in St. Petersburg. If anything happens, call him. He'll be able to get some people up here."

After a final weapons check, Tom, Archie, and Viktor's three men headed off, the sharp hiss of the wind slithering through the trees alongside them and occasionally coiling around their ankles. Above them the slanted curtain of snow ripped itself on the sharp branches overhead, dropping to the ground in narrow ribbons.

About half a mile on, Archie gave a low whistle and pointed ahead of him. As the old man had predicted, the ruins of a cottage lay in a small clearing, its brick foundations grimy with age, poking through the snow like tree stumps blackened by fire. And next to them, disappearing into the side of the mountain, was an opening just large enough to stand up in. An opening that, judging from the large pile of earth and rubble below it, staining the snow like a pool of spilled black ink, had only recently been excavated.

"Someone's already here," Archie whispered, scanning the trees that encircled them.

Tom edged warily across the clearing and knelt to examine the footprints leading to the entrance.

"I'd say there's six or seven of them. No more." With Archie at his side, he padded silently to the side of the entrance and peered in. "It's Renwick, it must be. He's the only other person who could have got this location from the painting. But if he's had to dig out this lot by hand, I doubt he's been inside very long."

"We should radio the others," said Archie. "Tell them what we've found."

"I suppose so." Tom didn't sound convinced.

"Or . . . ?"

"Or what?"

"Or, we could have a quick look inside ourselves. See if he's still down there."

"If we told them, they'd only want to come in with us," said Tom, nodding. "You know what Dom's like. I don't want anyone getting hurt."

"Besides, if it is Renwick down there, I'd rather we had the bastard to ourselves."

"I agree." Tom clenched his jaw. "There's five of us, seven of them. That's not bad odds."

"Plus, they won't be expecting us," Archie added.

"You're right. Let's end this now."

CHAPTER NINETY

"Where are you going?" Dominique asked Viktor, the expression on her face mirroring her surprise.

"To take a look at what is happening up there."

"But Tom said to wait here."

"Do you always do what Tom tells you?" asked Viktor with a smile.

"It depends."

"You don't trust me, do you?"

"I don't know you."

There was a pause. Viktor appeared to be considering what to say. "Here," she said eventually, reaching into the leather holster strapped under her arm, "know how to use one of these?" She held out a .38.

"Yeah." Back when she'd been living rough, a boyfriend had taught her how to handle a gun. Luckily it was a skill she'd never had to use. Until now, at least.

"It's loaded," Viktor said as she handed it to her. "Maybe that'll help you trust me a bit more."

Dominique snapped the gun open, checked the barrels, then flipped it shut again. It was loaded as Viktor had promised.

"It takes more than a loaded gun to make me trust someone," Dominique observed wryly.

"Not in Russia." Viktor smiled. "Now, if we stay out of sight down here in the trees and follow the side of the path, we might be able to find a place where we can take a look over the edge."

Despite Dominique's reservations, there was something about Viktor's reckless energy that Dominique could not help but like. Perhaps she recognized similar traits in herself.

"Okay." She slipped the gun into her jacket. "Let's take a look."

They set off, the snow thick where it had drifted, the steep embankment that led up to the path above them marked by occasional animal tracks.

The sounds of machinery grew ever louder, accompanied now by the throaty roar of at least one engine, maybe two, and the occasional shout or burst of laughter from the crew excavating the mine entrance.

"Get back," Dominique hissed, pulling Viktor farther back into the trees as she heard someone approaching.

A man appeared above them. Visible only from the knees up, his ghostly silhouette seemed to hover in the air. He was wearing a white alpine-commando-style ski outfit, with a submachine gun slung casually over his shoulder.

Peering up at him through the branches, Dominique could just about make out the glowing ember of a cigarette in his mouth. He took a final draw on it, the tip flaring and momentarily staining his cheeks red, before plucking it from his mouth and flicking it away. The butt sailed through the air and struck the branches above where they were crouched, exploding in a firework of orange sparkles that melted into the air. A name was called and, grumbling, the man turned and floated out of sight.

They continued around the side of the mountain, keeping the edge of the path above them in sight at all times, until, the noise fading slightly, they felt that they had moved a safe distance beyond the main center of activity.

"I'll go first," Viktor volunteered. Digging the points of her boots into the snow and using the branches of the surrounding trees to pull herself up, she quickly scrambled her way to

a position from which she was able to get her head just above
the edge of the path for a clear view of what was happening.

"What can you see?" Dominique called in a low voice.
Viktor reached for her binoculars.

"I count . . . twenty people. About half are armed like
that man we just saw. The others must be operating the machinery, judging from the way they're dressed."

"I'm coming up," Dominique replied.

A few moments later, Dominique pulled herself into position at Viktor's side. Viktor handed her the binoculars.

Some of the men were standing around in small groups,
talking and smoking. Others, dressed in hard hats and thick
blue jackets with reflective strips sewn onto them, seemed
to be overseeing the excavation efforts, as Viktor had suggested. A large digger and a bulldozer were attacking the
side of the mountain. Already they had exposed a wide tunnel, the spoil having been dumped on either side of the entrance in hulking ramparts of soil and rock. Two generators
powered several lights that washed the whole scene in a yel-
lowish sodium hue.

Suddenly a shout went up. A man raced toward the entrance and then signaled to the armed men. Though they
couldn't make out what had been said, from the way the
men began to check their weapons, Viktor and Dominique
had no difficulty in interpreting the signal.

"They're nearly through," Viktor whispered. "Get on the
radio to Tom. Let him know."

"Okay," said Dominique, reaching into her pocket. She
depressed the call button and whispered softly, "Tom, are
you there? Come in, Tom."

There was nothing but the muffled hiss of static.

"Come in, Tom," she called again.

Still nothing.

"He's not answering," she said.

"They must be out of range."

"Not likely," Dominique said bitterly. "These things go
for miles, and we're still all on the same side of the mountain. No, if I know Tom and Archie, they've probably found
a way inside and used it."

"In that case, we've got to get down there and warn them."

"Agreed," said Dominique. "Hold up. Who's that?"

"Which one?"

"The man on the left. Fur hat. Next to the light. He seems to be in charge."

Viktor took the binoculars from her and adjusted the focus. "I don't know. I don't recognize him."

"What's he doing?" Dominique squinted.

"I'm not sure," said Viktor. The man had removed his coat and was now unfolding a white sheet that he had taken from a bag at his feet. "It looks like he's getting changed or something."

"Changed? Into what?"

The sheet, once unfolded, turned out to be a white cover-all. The man pulled it on over his clothes, boots included, then fixed a mask and respirator over his face. Finally he pulled the hood over his head and tightened the drawstrings to form an airtight seal against his skull.

"They're all putting them on. Look." All the armed men were getting changed into similar outfits.

"It looks like some sort of NBC suit."

"NBC?" Viktor frowned.

"Nuclear, Biological, Chemical—standard military issue to avoid contamination in the field."

"Contamination!" Viktor dropped the binoculars from her face and locked eyes with Dominique. "Contamination from what? I thought we were here for the Amber Room."

CHAPTER NINETY-ONE

5:03 P.M.

From the symmetrical tool marks that inscribed the walls, the mine looked as though it had been dug out the old-fashioned way, with picks and shovels. Large wooden frames had been positioned every fifteen feet or so to buttress the roof, age having buckled and colored them until they seemed almost to have petrified and become part of the mountain itself, gray and heavy.

Tom paused and aimed his flashlight at the ceiling where blast marks had scorched the stone. "Do you see that?"

Archie nodded. "Looks like some sort of explosive was sunk in there—dynamite, probably—to collapse the roof."

"Yeah," Tom agreed. "They certainly didn't want anyone wandering in here by mistake."

They carried on, the mine shaft rising at a slight angle, Tom and Archie leading, Piotr and Grigory bringing up the rear; Yuri had been posted at the tunnel entrance as a precaution. Their flashlights sliced the air jaggedly as they walked, the beams fading as they disappeared into the distance until eventually the darkness swallowed them whole. Occasionally the light would catch their breath as they exhaled, and the air would momentarily flare like car headlights burning through mist.

Their breathing, even the rustle of their clothes, was amplified and bounced back at them off the tunnel walls, as if they were walking down the nave of some huge, silent church. Every so often their feet would crunch on frozen animal droppings or the occasional rabbit or bird carcass, presumably brought in there by a fox or some other enterprising creature.

Then, unexpectedly, a thin strip of light appeared in front of them. A strip of light that grew taller and taller as the shaft leveled out, until they could see what looked like a large rectangular yellow window set against the blackness of the tunnel.

"That must be it," Tom whispered excitedly, flicking his light off.

They edged carefully toward the light, covering the remaining fifty or so feet silently until they could see that the tunnel emerged into a large, naturally formed chamber. Tom heard Archie gasp behind him as he stepped gingerly inside.

The chamber had been lit with four battery-powered spotlights. A massive Nazi flag hung down from the roof, perhaps thirty feet long and twenty feet across. A Nazi flag with one crucial difference: the usual swastika had been replaced with the now familiar symbol of the Black Sun, its twelve jagged rays extending into the room like skeletal fingers clawing their way out of a grave.

"Christ," Archie whispered as his eyes settled on the two objects positioned directly beneath the flag. "They're here. They're still bloody here."

Tom shook his head, hardly believing what he was seeing. It was an incredible sight. Two missing freight cars from a mysterious train, hauled up an Austrian mountain and hidden deep inside it. Two hulking shapes, squat and solid and functional, like silent extras from a wartime newsreel—except this time rendered in color, rather than black and white.

"They don't look like they've been opened yet," whispered Tom, pointing excitedly at the thick iron bars that had been rammed through the hasp of each door.

"Renwick must be down here somewhere," Archie warned. "Let's deal with him first."

They slowly made their way around the two cars, pausing

on the other side where another, much bigger tunnel—the one the cars had presumably come down—disappeared off into the darkness.

"That must lead to the main entrance," Tom said. The muffled drone of an engine confirmed his suspicion.

"Look." Archie's gaze had settled on a tight bundle of slender tree trunks positioned against the wall by the tunnel entrance. He walked up to them and kicked the nearest one. It made a dull clang.

"Railway tracks," Tom said, kneeling for a closer look. "And sleepers. See, they're piled all the way down the tunnel."

"Presumably, when the mine was active, there was some sort of spur off the main line that ran beside that path we've just walked up," Archie said.

"They must have moved the cars up here, lifted the track behind them, and then collapsed the roof."

"We should check out that tunnel," Archie suggested. "See how long we've got before they break through. Make sure Renwick isn't hiding from us down there."

They set off down the tunnel, treading warily, guns leveled at the darkness ahead of them, the glow of the chamber receding behind them until it was a tiny window of light in the distance. But as the light receded, so the noise of the digging at the main entrance grew, until they could feel the earth shaking beneath their feet to the muffled beat of the machinery on the other side of the sheer wall of stone and earth that confronted them once they reached the end of the tunnel.

"They'll be through any time now," Tom called over the noise.

"Maybe that's what scared Renwick off," said Archie.

"Possibly," Tom said skeptically. "Doesn't seem like him, though—to come so close and then give up. Maybe he's gone to get reinforcements."

"Well, he's not here now. And I don't know about you, but I'd like to take a look inside those carriages."

Tom smiled. "We both would. But I'm not sure there's much point if we can't get it out."

"I thought you said you were going to call that FBI guy, Bailey, once we knew what was going on?"

"That was the deal, but—"

"Before you call in the cavalry, don't you want to check there's something here?"

"What about the people on the other side of that?" Tom nodded toward the collapsed mine entrance. "We don't want to get caught in here when they break through."

"Why don't we leave Piotr down this end? As soon as they look like coming in, he can run back and tell us. We can send Grigory up the other end to keep Yuri company and make sure Renwick doesn't sneak in behind us."

"That should work," Tom agreed. "But we'd better be quick."

After some rapid instructions, mainly communicated through hand signals, Piotr and Grigory left to take up their sentry positions. As soon as both men were out of sight, Tom and Archie turned their attention to the two freight cars.

They were of standard construction, wooden panels slatted horizontally into a rectangular frame, with angled crosspieces at regular intervals for extra reinforcement. Apart from the obvious effects of age, both cars looked remarkably intact, although the left-hand one seemed to be on the losing end of a long fight against rot and woodworm, and a thick beard of rust coated both undercarriages. Against the flaking orange-red paint on the sides, two sets of faded white letters and serial numbers were just about legible.

They both stepped forward to the side door of the first car, a large panel almost a third of the length, that slid back along a set of metal runners.

But just as he was about to pull back on the door, Tom noticed that the holes in the woodwork that he had previously assumed to have been caused by woodworm and rot were far too symmetrical to be the product of any natural process.

They were bullet holes.

CHAPTER NINETY-TWO

5:20 P.M.

A sudden chill ran through the pit of Tom's stomach and he knew it wasn't the cold. Archie, too, from the look he flashed him, had registered the locked door and the bullet holes and was asking himself the same question. Were the carriages empty when those holes had been made, or had the doors been locked for a more sinister reason than simply to ensure they didn't fly open in transit?

Tom grasped the top of the iron bar that had been jammed into the hasp but, corroded by years of disuse, it wouldn't budge. He tugged it from side to side, slowly gaining a bit of play, until it eventually slid free with a shriek that set his teeth on edge. He threw the bar to the ground with a clang and then folded the clasp back, the hinge stiff and cold. It required the combined efforts of both of them to tug the door open. Finally, with Tom pulling and Archie pushing on the massive iron handle, the door scraped back one foot, then two, protesting furiously all the way.

"That'll do," said Tom, panting. "You should be able to fit through there."

"You mean *you* should be able to fit through there," Archie said, smiling. "Here, I'll give you a leg up."

He clasped his hands together to form a cradle, and Tom

stepped onto it and pulled himself through the gap. Crouching in the doorway, he reached for his flashlight but realized that it was very nearly redundant. The lights outside were being funneled through the bullet holes to form hundreds of narrow splinters of light, all of different heights and angles, criss-crossing the interior of the wagon like swords thrust through the sides of a wooden box. It was strangely beautiful.

"You all right?" Archie called.

"Yeah." Tom looked back over his shoulder and gave him a nod. He turned back and this time switched the flashlight on, running it over the ceiling and the walls.

Nothing.

He stood up and took a couple of steps, then stepped on something hard that snapped under his feet. He flicked the light down to see what he had trodden on. Recoiling, he saw that it was a leg bone. A human leg bone.

"Archie, you'd better get up here," Tom called out.

"Why, what's up?" Archie jumped up to the open door, his legs dangling free and his shoulders only just inside the car. Tom hauled him inside.

"Look . . ."

Tom let his flashlight play across the floor. There must have been, he estimated, about thirty bodies there, all lying across each other, awkward and sunken, as if they were slowly being sucked into the floor. Only their skeletons were left, the bones, where they emerged from frayed sleeves and trouser legs or peered out from under rotting caps, glowing white.

"Who were they?" Archie breathed. "POWs? Civilians?"

"I don't think so . . ." Tom stepped forward, picking his way carefully through the twisted remains and picked up a cap that had rolled free. He pointed at its badge, a swastika, each of its arms ending in an arrow point. "The Arrow Cross—it was worn by Nazi troops from Hungary."

"Which is where Lasche said the Gold Train originally set out from."

"Yeah," said Tom. "From what I remember, he said it was guarded by Hungarian troops. This must be what's left of them."

A quick search revealed nothing apart from the bodies they could already see. Nothing, that is, except, frozen in the beam of Tom's light, a single name scratched on one wall, close to the floor. *Josef Kohl*. Someone who, Tom surmised, had survived the slaughter only to die of starvation, surrounded by the rank stench of his decaying comrades.

The discovery silenced them both.

"How do you suppose this played out?" Archie asked eventually.

Tom shrugged. "We know that the train was on its way to Switzerland. When the bridge at Brixlegg was bombed, it must have turned back and hid in a tunnel in the hope that the bridge would be repaired. That's where the Americans found it. Clearly, somewhere between Brixlegg and the tunnel, a decision was taken to uncouple these two carriages and haul them up here with the help of some of the Hungarian guards. Once they'd got it in here, the guards were disarmed, locked inside the carriage, and executed. Finally the tracks leading up here were lifted and the mine entrance was collapsed to ensure that the secret was kept safe."

"So whatever they were protecting must be in the other carriage?"

"There's only one way to find out," Tom said with a tight smile.

But as they turned, the door rolled shut and they heard the unmistakable rasp of the metal pin being slid back into the hasp.

CHAPTER NINETY-THREE

5:20 P.M.

W hat do you think we should do?" Dominique threw a questioning glance at Viktor who, grim-faced, was studying the armed men as they checked each other to make sure the suits were correctly fitted.

"Get down there and tell them."

"We'll never make it in time," Dominique pointed out. "We haven't got the map, and I've no idea where the entrance is. By the time we find it, it'll be too late."

Viktor was silent as she tried to think of a way of getting word to Tom. How could they warn him, not only that he was about to have company, but that the newcomers' expectation of what lay at the bottom of this mine was clearly very different from anything they had envisaged. Her thoughts were interrupted by a sharp tug on her arm.

"Someone's coming," Dominique hissed.

One of the machine operators had detached himself from the crew and was hurrying in their direction. Viktor ducked down out of sight, but the steady crunch of the snow indicated that the man was still approaching. In fact, he seemed to be heading straight for them.

Pressing herself into the face of the slope, her right leg

wedged in the cleft of a low branch, Viktor swung her AK–47 out from behind her back and gently cocked it.

Still the footsteps came. She readied herself to fire, determined to take out whoever had seen them rather than let him raise the alarm.

The footsteps stopped just above her head. Barely daring to breathe, she looked up and could just about make out the man's shape. Standing on the edge of the path, legs slightly parted, he loomed above them like some huge colossus, his face framed against the clear evening sky. Looking back nervously over his shoulder, the man reached down.

A pale gold stream of urine sliced through the darkness and arced gracefully over their heads, melting a jagged yellow zigzag in the snow below, the ground hissing and steaming.

Viktor looked up at Dominique with a grin and saw her stifle a laugh. But then a thought occurred to her. A way of getting word to Tom and Archie. The only problem was, it would require her to act fast.

To act now.

CHAPTER NINETY-FOUR

5:26 P.M.

Tom pressed his face against the wall and peered through one of the bullet holes.

"Renwick," he whispered when he saw the figure standing in the middle of the chamber, a triumphant smile carved across his face. Next to him was Johann Hecht. Five other thuggish-looking men, presumably other members of Kristall Blade, were making their way across the chamber to join them.

"How did they get past Viktor's men?" Archie said in a choked voice, selecting another bullet hole and looking for himself. "I thought they were meant to be guarding the entrance?"

"They were," Tom said grimly, recognizing the two bloody and lifeless bodies lying in a crumpled heap at Renwick's feet.

"As soon as I heard that you were coming through the forest, I knew you would not be able to resist going into the mine, Thomas," Renwick bellowed. "It was very kind of you to climb inside one of the carriages, though. It certainly made the job of rounding you up a lot easier."

"Save it, Harry," Tom shouted. "The gloating doesn't suit you."

"Surely you would not deny me my small moment of

triumph?" Tom didn't answer, but then Renwick didn't seem to be expecting a reply. "In any case, I have to applaud you, Thomas, for finding this place so quickly." Renwick raised his eyebrows in what Tom took to be some form of grudging admiration. "Johann, however, is rather irked by your persistence." Standing next to him, Hecht menacingly fingered the trigger of his Heckler & Koch MP5, his jaw sliding gently from side to side as he chewed a piece of gum.

"I'm sorry if I've disappointed him," Tom said in mock contrition, turning his attention as he spoke to examining the inside of the car again in the hope of identifying an escape route.

"Getting out of the vault was one thing," Renwick continued. "Escaping the museum—well, if anyone could have achieved that, it had to be you. But decoding a painting you did not even have? That was impressive. Especially when I had gone to the trouble of making sure there was no chance of Turnbull giving anything away."

"When did you get here?" Tom asked, trying to buy time as he tested the strength of the walls and the floorboards, trying to detect any that were loose.

"Late last night. It has taken us quite some time to dig out the entrance. As a matter of fact, we had been inside only a few minutes when you appeared. By the way, Thomas, if you are thinking of trying to get out of there, you are wasting your time," Renwick boomed. "Those carriages are quite secure. The Nazis had them reinforced to the highest specifications in order to ensure the security of their most precious cargo."

"Like a platoon of murdered Hungarian soldiers?" Tom called back, giving up on his search with an angry shrug.

"Like whatever is in the second carriage. In fact, we were just about to open it when we got word you were on your way. Now you can have ringside seats for the grand unveiling— the first glimpse of the Amber Room in over fifty years!"

Two men armed with bolt cutters advanced toward the rusting padlock that secured the door. A few moments later, there was the sound of a door being rolled back.

"I can't see anything," Archie whispered. "Can you?"

Tom shook his head. His field of vision was restricted, the bullet holes allowing him only to see to the front and rear of the car. The side where the door was located was hidden from view. But then the two men emerged, stumbling under the weight of a large crate, which they half placed, half dropped on the floor.

"Careful, you idiots," Tom heard Renwick shout.

Soon, five or six crates had been carried out to the center of the room.

"How the hell do you expect to get them out of here?" Tom called. "You know who's digging out the main entrance, don't you? They can't be far off now."

"No more than a few feet, I would say. Would you not agree, Johann?" Renwick turned toward Hecht, who gave a curt nod. "As to who they are, I can only assume—as I am sure you have—that it is some last remnant of the Order. Who else could have located this site without the aid of the code on the portrait? They have been at it for quite a few days now, but then, they had a hundred and fifty feet of solid rock to get through. Our entrance, thankfully, was a somewhat easier one to excavate."

"They've been protecting this place for fifty years," yelled Tom. "You think they're just going to let you walk away?"

"I doubt they will have much choice." Renwick smiled. "You see, among his many talents, Johann is an expert in explosives. He has mined both tunnels. One of his men has replaced the unfortunate chap you left near the entrance, and he will alert us the instant they break through. As soon as they do, we will let them into the tunnel a little way and then set off the charges."

"You'll kill them all," Tom exclaimed.

"That is the general idea, yes."

A sudden roar echoed up the larger tunnel, then the sound of an engine changing gear. Renwick flicked his head toward where the noise had come from, his smile vanishing.

"They're inside," Hecht shouted. "They're inside."

"How can they be?" Renwick seemed shaken. "We have received no word." He grabbed his radio. "This is Renwick, come in," he barked. "Are you there? We heard an engine, it sounds as if it is inside the mine. Come in, damn you!"

He spun to face Hecht, his eyes wide, agitation turning to alarm. "Your sentry must be dead. Set off the charges."

"But we don't know how far into the mine they've come."

"It does not matter. Either we will kill them or block their way. One is as good as the other. We cannot afford to take risks. Not now we are so close."

Hecht gave a nod and picked up a small black box, about the size of a cigarette packet, with four red buttons set into it. Gripping the end of the silver aerial between his teeth, he tugged until it was fully extended, then turned to face the tunnel. The noise was growing ever louder, and in the distance two faint yellow specks glowed like cat's eyes. Eyes that seemed to be growing.

"Do it, Johann," Renwick urged, a hint of desperation in his voice. "Now."

Hecht depressed the top button.

Nothing happened.

"What the devil is going on?" Renwick spluttered. "Do it now or it will be too late."

"I'm sorry, Cassius," Hecht said, exchanging the remote detonator for a gun that he leveled squarely at Renwick's chest. "For you, it already is too late."

"What's going on?" Archie whispered.

"Renwick's being turned over," Tom said excitedly. "Hecht's betrayed him."

CHAPTER NINETY-FIVE

5:46 P.M.

The bulldozer juddered to a halt at the entrance to the chamber, its headlights forcing everyone except Tom and Archie, who could barely see it, to hold their hands in front of their faces, shielding their eyes from the glare. Abruptly, first the engine, then the lights were killed.

Ten heavily armed men emerged from behind the bulldozer, like infantrymen following a tank. To Tom's surprise, they were all wearing white chemical-warfare suits. They looked strangely robotic as they fanned out through the chamber, their faces masked and inscrutable.

Two of them approached Renwick and frisked him. Hecht, meanwhile, jerked his head in the direction of the car that Tom and Archie were in. Immediately, two of the armed men ran to the door and opened it, indicating with a wave of their guns that Tom and Archie should jump down. Once outside, they were frisked at gunpoint, then shoved toward Renwick, who stood silently glaring at Hecht, his eyes brimming with rage.

One of the men in white now made his way to the middle of the chamber. He was carrying a briefcase, which he placed flat on the ground. Flicking the catches open, he removed what looked like a large microphone and held it in the air above his head while consulting the screen of a small computer inside the case.

Moments later, he called out in German and, with a relieved sigh, the men pulled off their hoods and discarded their respirators.

One man, however, remained hooded, his face still concealed by a mask. Unarmed, he walked slowly up to Hecht. Suddenly, the two men threw their arms around each other and embraced warmly, patting each other on the back. Tom could just about make out the hooded man's muffled words and Hecht's reply.

"Well done, Colonel."

"Thank you, sir."

The two men broke off and saluted each other smartly.

"What the bloody hell is going on?" Archie exploded. "Who are you people?"

The masked man turned to them and pulled back his hood before sliding his mask off his face.

Tom spoke first, his voice strangled and disbelieving. "Völz?"

"Who?" Renwick spoke for the first time, his eyes flicking from Hecht to Völz's stout frame.

"He runs the private bank in Zurich where Weissman and Lammers had hidden the map," Tom explained.

Völz ignored Tom, however, and approached Renwick.

"It's a pleasure to finally meet you, Herr Renwick—or do you prefer Cassius? Colonel Hecht here has spoken very highly of your efforts over the past few months."

"Is this some sort of joke?" Renwick hissed through clenched teeth.

Tom couldn't help but give a rueful smile. Despite their desperate situation, surrounded by armed men in an abandoned mine deep under an Austrian mountain, it was good to see Renwick finally on the receiving end of the sort of duplicity that he so regularly served up to others.

"No joke, Cassius," said Völz.

"Then what is the meaning of this?"

"You don't recognize my voice?"

There was a pause, then Renwick's eyes narrowed. "Dmitri?"

"As I said, it's a pleasure to meet you finally."

"What is this circus?" Renwick snapped. "We had a deal. We agreed, no tricks."

"We agreed to lots of things," Völz replied, with a dismissive wave of his hand. "But that was when you thought you had something to bargain with. The situation has, I'm sure you'll agree, changed somewhat."

"Why are you dressed up in that gear?" Tom interrupted their exchange. "What exactly were you expecting to find down here?"

"At last, an intelligent question," Völz said with a clap. "And one that you can help me answer. Would you be so kind as to open that crate." He pointed at one of the crates Hecht's men had unloaded earlier.

"What?" Tom's voice was uncertain.

"You heard me. Open the crate," Völz insisted, grabbing a crowbar off one of his men and tossing it to Tom. "Open it now."

Tom approached the crate indicated by Völz. Like all the others, it had some sort of identification code and a swastika stamped on one side. He slipped the crowbar under the lid and levered it up. It rose a few inches, the nails shrieking as they were pulled free. Tom repeated the procedure on the other side, and the lid came off and flopped to the floor.

The crate was packed with straw, which Tom removed in big handfuls until he was finally able to make out a dark shape. He reached in. It felt soft and silky. He pulled it out.

"A fur coat?" Archie said disbelievingly as Tom held it up. "Is that it?"

He leaped to Tom's side and leaned into the crate, pulling out first one coat, then another and another, flinging them over his shoulder.

"This can't be right," he said when he had reached the bottom of the crate and stood up to survey the mound of black and brown and golden furs. "There must be a mistake."

Renwick was staring at the pile disbelievingly, his eyes bulging.

"Open another one," Völz said gleefully. "Any one. It won't make a difference."

Archie grabbed the crowbar off Tom and opened another crate.

"Alarm clocks," he said, holding one up for everyone to see before dropping it back inside with a crash.

He opened another. "Typewriters."

Then another. "Silk underwear." He held up a bra and camisole before throwing them at Völz. They fell well short.

"Okay, Völz, you made your point," Tom said slowly.

"Surely Lasche told you these were some of the items that were loaded on the train?" Völz asked with a shrug. "I don't see why you're so surprised."

"Don't play dumb. Where is it?" Renwick demanded.

"Where is what?" Völz said, in mock confusion.

"You know damn well what," Renwick snapped. "The Amber Room. Why else do you think we are all here?"

Völz laughed. "Ah yes, the Amber Room. Amazing how that myth refuses to die."

"It's not a myth." Renwick fired back.

"No need to feel foolish. Thousands have fallen for the same deluded fantasy. And I'm certain thousands more will follow."

"You're saying it doesn't exist?" Tom asked.

"I'm saying it was destroyed in the war."

"Rubbish," said Renwick.

"Is it?" Völz sniffed.

"It was moved to Königsberg Castle. Everyone knows that. Then it vanished. It was hidden."

"It didn't vanish and no one hid it. If you must know, it was burned. Burned by the very Russian troops who'd been sent to recover it. They overran Königsberg Castle in April 1945 and, in their haste, set fire to the Knight's Hall. They didn't know that the Amber Room was being stored there. Just as they probably didn't know that, being a resin, amber is highly flammable. By the time they realized what they had done, it was too late."

"If that story were true, it would have come out before now," Renwick said dismissively.

"Really? You think the Soviets would freely admit that their own troops destroyed one of Russia's most precious treasures? I don't think so. Far easier for them to accuse the Nazis of having hidden this irreplaceable gem than face that particular embarrassment. You may not believe me, but I've seen the Kremlin documents in the Central State Archive of Literature and Art that confirm it. Not only did the Russians know that the Amber Room had been destroyed, they used it as a pawn in their negotiations for the return of valuable works of art from Germany."

Völz's eyes shone brightly, and Tom could see that, on this point, at least, he was telling the truth. Or at least he believed he was.

"Then what are you here for?" Tom asked slowly.

"For that," said Völz, pointing at the second car. "Show them, Colonel."

Hecht grabbed the crowbar from Archie and approached the side of the car. He forced the end in between two of the wide wooden planks and levered it sideways. The wood splintered noisily. Then Hecht snapped off more planks, creating a large jagged hole in the side of the car. But instead of being able to see through into the car, as Tom had expected, they were confronted by an expanse of dull gray metal. Something had been built into the walls.

"Is that lead?" Tom asked.

"It is," said Völz. "Merely a protective layer, of course, to reduce the contamination risk.

"Contamination from what?" said Tom, already guessing and dreading the answer.

"U-235," replied Völz. "Four tons of it."

"U-what?" Archie, looking confused, turned to Tom.

"U-235," Tom explained, his voice disbelieving. "An isotope of uranium. It's the basic component of a nuclear bomb."

CHAPTER NINETY-SIX

A nuclear bomb? You intend to build a nuclear bomb?"
Tom couldn't tell whether Renwick was appalled or impressed.

"U-235 has a half-life of seven hundred million years. Even a minute amount, attached to a conventional explosive and detonated in an urban area, will create widespread radioactive fallout, triggering mass panic and economic collapse. Can you imagine the price this material would fetch from armed Middle Eastern groups, or even foreign governments? For years we have been building our organization in the shadows, almost unnoticed. Now, finally, we have the means not just to fight but to win our war. Now we are ready to reveal ourselves."

"But where has this come from?" Tom asked. "How did it get here?"

"Do you know what the markings on the side of this carriage denote?" Völz pointed at the series of flaking letters and numbers on the side of the second.

"Some sort of serial number?"

"Exactly. It identifies the contents as having come from Berlin. From the Kaiser Wilhelm Institute for Physics in

Dahlem, to be precise. The headquarters of the Nazis' effort to produce a nuclear bomb."

"Rubbish!" Renwick said dismissively. "The Nazis never had a nuclear program."

"They all did," Völz snapped. "The Soviets called theirs Operation Borodino, the Americans the Manhattan Project. And Hitler was in the hunt too. In 1940 German troops in Norway seized control of the world's only heavy-water production facility and stepped up production of enriched uranium to supply the German fission program. There were stories after the war that German scientists had deliberately sabotaged Hitler's attempts to build an atomic bomb, but the truth was that they were trying as hard as they could. Some even say they detonated a few devices in Thuringia. But the Americans had thrown a hundred and twenty-five thousand people into their program. In the end, Hitler simply couldn't compete."

"So how far did they get?" Tom asked.

"Far enough to accumulate a considerable amount of fissile material. Material that Stalin was determined to get his hands on before the Americans could grab it. That's why he ordered Marshals Zhukov and Konev to race each other to Berlin: to be certain that the Red Army got there first. They say the effort cost the Russians seventy thousand men. Once there, special NKVD troops were dispatched to secure the institute. They arrived in April 1945 and discovered three tons of uranium oxide, two hundred and fifty kilograms of metallic uranium and twenty liters of heavy water. Enough to kick-start Operation Borodino and allow Stalin to start working on Russia's first atomic bomb."

"So you're saying they didn't find all the uranium?"

"They found what was there. But Himmler, ever resourceful, had already moved several tons by placing it in lead boxes built into the walls of a specially modified carriage. The Order personally supervised the shipment, meeting up with the Gold Train in Budapest in December 1944 and attaching their two carriages to it. As soon as they realized they wouldn't make it to Switzerland, they unhitched the carriages and brought them up here, to be recovered at a later date."

"And now the Order of the Death's Head lives on, is that it?" Tom asked. "Only this time armed with a weapon to destroy anyone who doesn't share your lunacy."

"The Order has nothing to do with me or my men," Völz retorted. "We wouldn't have stood idly by playing at knights while Germany was bleeding."

"Then how do you know all this? How did you find this place without access to the painting? Only the Order would have known this location."

Völz hesitated, as if deciding whether to answer. Then he reached inside his coat and produced a large black wallet. Opening it carefully, he withdrew a tattered black-and-white photograph, which he handed to Tom. The same photograph they had found in Weissman's house.

"Weissman and Lammers," Tom said, looking up. Renwick held his hand out for the photo and studied it closely.

"And the third man?" Völz asked. "Do you recognize him?"

Tom glanced at the photo again, then gave Völz a long, searching look. There was a definite family resemblance in the high forehead, straight, almost sculpted nose, and small round eyes that Tom had also noted in the portraits lining the Völz et Cie offices in Zurich.

"Your father?" Tom ventured.

"Uncle. The other two men were called Becker and Allbrecht. *Weissman* and *Lammers* were names they hid behind after the war like the cowards they were."

"So you learned all this from him?" Archie asked.

"Some I know from him; some you have helped me discover. My uncle and his two comrades were plucked from the ranks because of their scientific knowledge and initiated into the Order as retainers."

Tom nodded, remembering that Weissman was a chemist and Lammers a physics professor.

"Three retainers for twelve knights," Tom said slowly. "In the same way that the Black Sun has three circles and twelve runes." He looked up at the huge flag above them.

"Exactly!" Völz smiled at Tom's perceptiveness. "Just as there were three medals and three paintings. My uncle accompanied the Order on the Gold Train's ill-fated escape across Europe while Lammers and Weissman prepared the crypt at Wewelsburg Castle. Then, as ordered, all three of them made their way back to Berlin, hiding what they knew even from each other. Then, just before the end, all three were entrusted with one final instruction."

"Which was?" Renwick asked, a blood vessel pulsing in his neck.

"To protect an encrypted message. A message that could be deciphered only with an Enigma machine configured with the right settings. A message that they hastily scrawled on a painting in a place that couldn't be seen once the frame was on. A painting that they found hanging in Himmler's office because he couldn't bring himself to destroy it."

"A painting that they then lost to the Soviets," Tom guessed.

"The Russians made it to Berlin far faster than anyone expected. Lammers and Weissman risked everything by returning to the SS building to recover the painting but soon realized that the Trophy Squad had beaten them to it. The only two Bellaks they could find were the ones of Wewelsburg Castle and the Pinkas Synagogue in Prague.

"So, Lammers and Weissman knew where the painting was headed, and they had the settings for the Enigma machine to decode the message, but the one thing they didn't know was the actual location of the Gold Train," said Tom.

"Only my uncle knew that," Völz confirmed. "Realizing this, they drew together a series of clues using the two Bellaks they had managed to save, the specially engraved medals, and the map of the railway system so that others might follow—those of pure Aryan blood, true believers, who could use the riches of the Gold Train to found a new Reich."

"But if you knew all this," asked Archie, "why have you waited until now to come here and find the train?"

"Because *I* didn't know where the train was either."

"I thought you said your uncle had helped put it here? Surely he told you?"

Völz gave an exasperated laugh. "Unlike his two comrades, my uncle ended the war disgusted at what he had seen and what he had done. He realized how potent a weapon had been stored in this mountain and was determined that no one should ever be able to exploit it. So he set up his own council of twelve. But unlike the Order, his council's mission was to protect life, not destroy it. They did this by guarding the location of the site, whatever the cost. When he died five years ago, I was asked to take his seat on the council."

"Didn't they tell you the train's location?"

"My uncle, in his wisdom, had decreed that only one man—the leader of the council—should be entrusted with the location of the Gold Train. Only if the train was in imminent danger of being uncovered was the secret to be disclosed."

"So you used me to make them think their precious secret was in danger," Renwick said through gritted teeth.

"Johann and I had been fueling rumors about the Gold Train, the missing Bellaks, and the need for an Enigma machine to decode a secret message for years in the hope that it might help bring the portrait to light. When we discovered that you had taken the bait, I suggested that we flush you out by putting a price on your head through ads in the *Herald Tribune*. The council agreed, of course."

"So the raid in Munich . . ."

". . . Was not real. Those were my men in the lobby. You were never in any danger. We wanted to make you think you were getting close, and to show the council that their methods were failing. That they needed a change of leader."

"Is that why you involved me?" Tom asked. "To make them sweat?"

"I didn't involve you," Völz said. "Turnbull was working for Cassius." Tom shot Renwick a look, but it went unseen. Renwick's hate-filled eyes were locked on Völz. "I took my inspiration from Stalin's strategy of pitting Zhukov and Konev against each other, and kept you both in the hunt. The irony, of course, was that the key to all this had been lying in my vault all the time. Until you showed up, I had no

idea who that safety-deposit box belonged to. Had I known,
all this might have been avoided."

"But you knew that Weissman and Lammers had left a
map."

"The council tracked Lammers down a few years ago and
made him talk. Unfortunately, his heart gave out before he
could disclose the location of the crypt or the final painting.
But he did reveal the settings for the Enigma machine, and
the fact that Weissman was living in the UK. And of course
we found the number tattooed on his arm, though we didn't
know its significance at the time."

"Why did you excavate the main entrance when you could
have come in the back like us in half the time?" asked Archie.

"Apart from the fact I need to get trucks down here if I am
to move everything out? Simple. Three days ago, when we
first got here, I didn't know about the smaller entrance. My
uncle had passed on only the location of the larger entrance,
through which he'd helped bring the carriages. It was the
painting that divulged the existence of the smaller entrance.
Perhaps the Order felt that route would be easier to access—
who knows? When Johann told me how you'd got here and
what you'd found, I decided to leave you to it. It was a way of
keeping you busy and out of our way."

"The council will never let you get away with this," said
Tom. "When they find out what you're up to, they'll do everything in their power to stop you."

"Which council? This one?" Völz reached into his pocket
and pulled out a handful of identical gold rings with a single
diamond set into an engraved twelve-box grid, which he
threw disdainfully to the floor. "It's a shame, really. I would
have liked to see their faces when they realized that, indirectly, they had provided us with the means to shatter everything they have fought against all these years."

CHAPTER NINETY-SEVEN

Hecht marched them up the smaller tunnel at gunpoint, roughly cuffed them with plastic tags, and then pushed them to the ground. Renwick resisted and got a rifle butt jabbed in his stomach for his trouble.

"I will not forget your betrayal, Hecht," Renwick said through gritted teeth. "I will make you pay."

"I doubt it, Cassius." Hecht sneered. "The next time I press this button, the explosives *will* work." He held up the remote detonator and waved it tauntingly in front of Renwick's face, before aiming a punch at the side of his head, his ring leaving a deep gouge mark just above Renwick's ear.

"How does it feel, Renwick?" Archie grinned as Hecht tramped off down the tunnel, leaving two men to stand guard over them. "Outwitted. Betrayed. Imprisoned."

"Rather than gloat, Connolly, try to think of a way to get us out of here," Renwick snapped, blood running down his face and dripping onto his shoulder.

"Getting *us* out of here." Archie gave a laugh. "Believe me, if I can find a way out, you won't be taking it."

They fell silent and the two guards lit up. The sounds of men working echoed up the tunnel from the chamber.

Hammering, drilling, sawing. Tom guessed that Völz's men were even now dismantling the carriage and preparing to transport its lethal cargo to . . . where? Wherever they wanted—that was the terrifying thing. Once unleashed, Völz would be unstoppable. Archie seemed to be reading his thoughts.

"Can he really make an atomic bomb out of that lot?"

"I doubt it," said Tom. "At least not without buying a lot of extra equipment and expertise. But he doesn't have to. He could make enough money auctioning the uranium off to finance a small army. Besides, there's always the prospect of the dirty bomb he described. Can you imagine the chaos if one of those went off in Berlin or London or New York?"

"So much for the Amber Room," Archie noted gloomily.

"I can't believe that, for all these years, everyone's been looking for something that didn't even exist," Tom remarked.

"Your father thought it existed," Renwick said. "Do you think he was wrong too?"

"Don't even mention his name," Tom snapped.

"You are forgetting that it was to me he turned, not you, when he heard rumors linking the Amber Room to a Nazi Gold Train and an Enigma-encoded message." Renwick gave a faint smile. "I thought nothing more of it until a few years ago when I came across an original Bellak in an auction in Vienna. I knew then that, if one had survived Himmler's cull, perhaps others had too, including the portrait—and with them the chance of finding this place."

"Except you couldn't find any other Bellaks, could you?"

"Unfortunately, your father was in the mistaken belief that the painting had ended up in a private collection, which is where I focused my efforts. Fruitlessly, as it transpired. I enlisted your help because I thought a fresh pair of eyes might be of use. I was right."

"Yeah, well, it didn't do you much good, did it?" Archie pointed out tartly. "In case you hadn't noticed, you're about to get buried under a mountain, same as us."

"There's one thing I want to know." Tom locked eyes with Renwick. "Back in St. Petersburg, you said my father had known all along who you were. That he had worked with you. Was that another one of your lies?"

Renwick returned Tom's stare, but just as he seemed about to speak, Hecht returned from the end of the tunnel. At the sight of him, the two guards threw their cigarettes aside and stood up straight, one of them giving Archie a kick in the ribs for good measure, as if to show Hecht what a good job they were doing. He gave them an approving grunt.

"One of you go and fetch me a drink. Oh, and if you see Dmitri, tell him the charges are armed."

The guard nodded and trotted obediently off toward the chamber, passing a man in hard hat and reflective jacket who was heading toward them.

"What are you doing up here?" Hecht growled as the man approached. "You're meant to be in the chamber with the others helping unload that train."

The man shrugged and then, noticing that one of his laces was undone, stooped to tie it. As he did so, he raised his eyes toward Tom's and winked.

It was Viktor.

CHAPTER NINETY-EIGHT

Tom glanced at Archie, who gave a slight nod. He had seen who it was too.

"I asked you a question," Hecht challenged the still crouching Viktor. "Get back to your work."

"You bastard," Tom shouted, rolling onto Archie and kneeing him in the stomach. "This is your fault. Your greed's going to get us both killed."

Archie kicked out as he tried to roll out from under him, flexing his back like a wrestler trying to break a hold. "If it's anyone's fault, it's yours," he shouted back. "I told you to drop it."

Hecht stepped forward and placed a firm hand on Tom's shoulder to yank him free. Tom, however, reached around and sank his teeth into the flesh between forefinger and thumb. Hecht cried out in pain.

Viktor, meanwhile, stood up behind the other guard, whose attention had been drawn to the fight. Taking careful aim, she landed a heavy blow on the back of his head, dashing his skull. He fell to the floor, unconscious.

Hecht spun around, his bleeding hand clasped to his chest, the other reaching for his gun. Lying beneath him, Archie kicked out and caught his arm, sending his gun clattering to the ground. With a furious roar, Hecht launched himself at Viktor, his huge frame covering the distance between them in no time and sending her sprawling with a punch to the side of the head.

Viktor lashed out from where she had fallen, catching Hecht in the groin with her knee and bringing him down to the ground crying in pain. He immediately spotted his gun lying on the mine floor, and scrambled toward it on his hands and knees.

Seeing this, Tom struggled to his feet, using the mine wall to help push himself upright. He threw himself at Hecht, stars exploding in front of his eyes as he landed heavily on his injured shoulder. Hecht shrugged him off, but the delay was just long enough for Viktor to struggle to her feet and scoop the gun up as Hecht's massive hands were about to close on it.

She stepped toward him, his eyes still flashing with defiance, the muzzle hovering only inches from his nose. Then, in one swift movement, she brought the butt of the gun down hard on Hecht's temple. His face slammed into the dirt floor.

"God, am I glad to see you!" Tom wheezed between pained breaths.

"We told you not to go in there," she smiled as she pulled a knife from her boot and sliced Tom's hands free.

"Where did you get the outfit?" Archie asked as she crouched down next to him and cut his cuffs off too.

"One of Völz's men decided to take a leak a little too close for comfort." She grinned. "Luckily, he fitted."

"How did you know we were in here?" asked Tom.

"I didn't, but Dominique guessed you would be. Said you wouldn't be able to help yourselves. Good thing for you she knows you both so well."

"Where is she?" Tom looked around in concern, as if half expecting her to leap out from the shadows. "She's okay, isn't she?"

"She's gone back down to phone that FBI number you gave her. She seemed to remember seeing a phone line running into that old man's house. Come on, let's get out of here."

"Hold on," said Tom. "We can't just leave them to it. Once Völz makes it out of here with that uranium, no one will ever hear from him again until it's too late."

"You're right," said Archie. "But there's only three of us and over twenty of them. What do you have in mind?"

"Four if you untie me," Renwick observed.

Tom ignored him, considering his options. In the end, it was the sight of Hecht's sprawled bulk that gave him an idea.

"The detonator," Tom exclaimed. "We can use Hecht's charges to collapse the mine and trap them until the police arrive. Search him. He must still have it on him."

Archie turned Hecht over and patted him down, recovering the detonator in one pocket and a folded piece of paper in the other. He smoothed the piece of paper out on the floor and held his flashlight over it.

"It's a schematic of where the charges are. They're numbered one to four. There seem to be two sets in each tunnel, one at the entrance and one near the chamber."

"So if we let off charges two and three, we'll seal off the chamber at both ends."

"I'm not an explosives expert," Archie said with a frown, "but that's what it seems to be saying."

"Well, that's good enough for me," said Tom. "Let's get clear and then we'll set them off. We can't let Völz unload that train."

"You know, there may well be some people in the tunnel when you let those charges off," Archie pointed out. "They probably won't make it."

"I know." Tom compressed his lips. "But a lot more people may not make it if we don't stop Völz now."

They turned to leave, but Renwick, called out and stopped them in their tracks. "Thomas, dear boy. Surely you are not just going to leave me here?"

"Aren't I?" said Tom drily. "Just watch me."

"They will shoot me, you know that."

"Good. Then it will save me the trouble," Archie said.

Renwick ignored him, his eyes boring instead into Tom's. "You cannot do this, Thomas. Think about the times we had together. Think about the way things used to be between us. Unless you help me now, it will be as if you pulled the trigger."

"Don't listen to him, Tom," Archie warned.

"Answer my question." Tom walked over to where Renwick was still propped up against the mine wall. "Did my father know who you were? Did he work with you?"

"Let me go, then I will tell you."

Tom shook his head. "No. I'm fed up with negotiating with your lies." He reached into Renwick's jacket pocket and pulled out the gold Patek Philippe pocket watch that had once belonged to his father. "I'll take this," he said, taking a quick look at it and then slipping it into his coat. "You won't be needing it anymore."

CHAPTER NINETY-NINE

They sprinted down the tunnel until the rectangle of blackness and the luminescent glow of the snow in the pale moonlight told them they were near the exit. Seconds later they spilled out into the fresh air, the relief of emerging from under the mountain's oppressive weight making them momentarily dizzy.

"Are you ready?" Tom asked when he had located a suitably broad tree to shelter behind, grasping the remote detonator in his right hand. They nodded, the mood suddenly somber. He flicked the unit on and extended the aerial. Four small lights glowed red, one next to each button.

"Two and three," Archie reminded him. "That'll seal either side of the chamber. Just two and three."

"Okay." Tom pressed the button marked 2. Far below them they heard a deep boom and then felt the ground shake. The snow that had accumulated on the upper branches of the fir trees above them fell to the ground with a thump. A stiff breeze blew up the mine shaft toward them, strong enough to ruffle Viktor's dark hair.

"Now three," she prompted him gently.

Tom pressed button number 3. This time the sound was much closer, a throaty roar that seemed to grow louder and louder until it was chased out of the mine entrance in a cloud of smoke and dust that cloaked everything it came into contact with in a white shroud. Eventually, the smoke settled and they stepped toward the mine entrance, the air thick with dust.

"You still got your radio, Viktor?" Tom asked. "Let's call Dom and see whether she's managed to get down to that chalet yet."

Viktor located her radio and swapped it for the detonator. He turned it on and entered the encryption code that would allow him to tune it to the agreed frequency. But before he could speak into it, Viktor's voice rang out.

"Tom, look out."

She threw herself across him, shoving him to the ground as the crack of a gunshot split the night. He landed heavily on his back, Viktor on top of him, her body suddenly limp and heavy. She'd been hit.

Tom scrambled backward, dragging Viktor with him, until he reached a large snow-covered boulder, instinctively guessing which direction the shot had come from. A few moments later, Archie slid next to him as two further shots landed harmlessly in the snow.

"How is she?" Archie asked.

"Not good," Tom said grimly, cradling her head in his lap, her face pale. A bullet slammed into the rock above Tom's head, and he pulled back just in time to avoid a second shot, a firework of snow exploding overhead. "Who the hell is it? Where did they come from?"

Archie snatched a quick look around the other side of the rock. "It's Hecht."

"Hecht! Shit." Tom kicked himself for not having tied him up. He rolled Viktor over onto her side and saw the snow sticky and dark where the bullet had penetrated her lower back. "She needs help fast. We've got to do something before he works out that we don't have a gun. We're sitting ducks out here."

"Any ideas?"

"What about the fourth charge?"

"What?"

"The fourth explosive charge. Didn't you say it was near the entrance? If we set that off, we'll bury him."

"Where's the detonator?"

"Viktor had it," Tom said, feeling inside her pockets. "She took it off me when she gave me the radio. Shit, it's not here. She must have dropped it."

He peeked around the side of the rock and saw the detonator's sleek black shape lying in the snow.

"Can you see it?" asked Archie.

"Yeah," said Tom. "About ten feet away."

"Then this is the plan. I'll draw his fire while you run and get the detonator."

"No way." Tom shook his head. "It's too dangerous."

"It's not much more dangerous than waiting here for Hecht to come and find us, is it? And meanwhile, Viktor's bleeding to death."

"Okay," Tom conceded. "But keep your head down."

"Don't worry, I will." Archie grinned. "See you back here in five."

Archie jumped up and burst over to the right, heading for the nearest tree. A barrage of gunfire immediately erupted from the mine entrance, bullets fizzing through the air and embedding themselves in the trees with a thud or landing in the snow with a hiss. At the same time, Tom rolled out from the other side of the boulder and sprinted toward the detonator. The few seconds it took him to reach it seemed to last forever.

He grabbed it and turned to make his way back. The shooting stopped. Tom looked up fearfully and saw Hecht standing in the mine entrance, staring straight at him, a vicious leer etched across his scarred face, the gun raised and poised to fire. Tom froze, momentarily transfixed by Hecht's glittering eyes. But then he noticed a shadow peel away from the mine wall behind Hecht. A shadow with a knife glinting in its hand. A shadow with one hand.

Renwick.

With a frenzied cry, Renwick jumped on Hecht, plunging the knife into the small of his back. Hecht roared in pain, the gun dropping from his grasp as he reached around and clutched his wound, before bringing his blood-soaked hands back to his face. With an angry shout he spun to face Renwick, advancing slowly upon him like a bear walking on its hind legs. Renwick lunged at him again, catching him first across his forearm, then at the top of his thigh, but Hecht didn't seem to notice, advancing irresistibly until he fell on Renwick with a series of heavy punches. Both men tumbled to the ground and rolled out of sight down into the mine.

Tom ran back behind the boulder. Viktor had regained consciousness, and she smiled at him weakly.

"Hang in there," he said with a worried look. "Dom will have some people up here in no time. We'll soon have you back home."

"I'm not going back home," she said simply.

"Of course you are," Tom protested. "We'll patch you up. You'll be fine."

"I'm never going back. I've got it all planned. That's why I came here with you. So they couldn't stop me."

"What do you mean?"

"I've got money saved. I'm getting out. While I still can. Like you."

"Good for you," Tom said, tears filling his eyes as he saw the bloodstain swelling underneath her.

"Like you said, it's never too late," she said with a smile.

Tom said nothing, his throat swollen as he felt the life ebb out of her until, with a final burst of energy, Viktor suddenly reached up and pulled Tom's lips down to hers.

"Thank you." She exhaled, her hand slipping down Tom's neck, along his arm, to where his hand was holding the detonator. Her eyes flickering shut, she pressed the fourth button.

This time the explosion was ferocious and immediate as the mine entrance collapsed, bits of stone and debris flying through the air. Tom threw himself to the ground, his body arched over Viktor's to shield her. The heat of the blast seared into his cheeks, the ground twisting and groaning and moaning beneath him, the trees creaking and whining dangerously.

As the echo faded, a thick cloud of dust and smoke remained, hanging in the air like a heavy fog, making him cough and his eyes stream. He heard a shout and saw Dominique emerging into the clearing, accompanied by about ten armed Austrian policemen.

Tom looked down at Viktor's pale face. A smile was frozen on her lips. He carefully rearranged her hair to cover her scarred ear.

In the moonlight, the large pool of blood that had soaked into the snow around her looked quite black, like a dark mirror.

EPILOGUE

A few people laughed, a few people cried. Most people were silent. I remembered the line from Hindu Scripture, the Bhagavad Gita—"I am become Death, the destroyer of worlds."

J. ROBERT OPPENHEIMER AFTER WITNESSING THE FIRST NUCLEAR EXPLOSION, 16 JULY 1945

T he freshly turned earth lay in a smooth mound, a narrow black finger against the whiteness of the surrounding ground covered in snow. In the distance, smoke rose
from a small mountain range of factory chimneys. Gray and
dirty, it drifted aimlessly upward until, touching the sun, it
suddenly blossomed into a glorious pink cloud that soared
toward the empty heavens.

Tom knelt down and grasped a handful of earth. He rubbed
it through his fingers, the cold already freezing the moisture
so that it crumbled like small grains of ice to the ground.

"What do you think we should put on her gravestone?"
asked Archie.

"Katya. Her name was Katya," Tom said firmly. "Katya
Nikolaevna Mostov."

"To me, she'll always be Viktor," Archie said with a
shrug. "Katya just doesn't seem to fit somehow."

"It fits who she once was and who she hoped to be again,
one day," Tom said. "She never really wanted her life as
Viktor. She just sort of fell into it and found she couldn't
escape."

"I think that's what she liked in you," Archie said, drawing on a freshly lit cigarette. "The fact that you'd also ended up in a place you realized you didn't want to be and had somehow walked away."

There was a pause, and Tom shifted his weight to his other foot as he stared silently at the ground.

"Any news on Dmitri?" he asked eventually.

"Bailey called me last night. There's no sign of him yet. Lucky bastard must have been outside when we set off the charges."

"Any survivors?"

"Sixteen in all. Four dead. They must have been caught in the tunnel."

"What about the uranium? What's going to happen to that?"

"It's safe, although apparently the Germans and Austrians can't agree who it belongs to."

"No surprises there," Tom said with a shrug. "What about Bailey? Is he in the clear?"

"As far as I know. He mentioned something about transferring to New York."

"Good for him."

"You know, he mentioned to me that Jennifer Browne had called him. Asking after you. Apparently she got wind you'd been involved."

"And?" Tom said stonily, his eyes still fixed to the ground.

"And maybe you should call her. Look, I know I gave you a hard time about her before, what with her being a Fed and everything, but you two were good together. All this stuff with your father and Renwick and Viktor . . . it's messing with your head. I mean, what have you got to lose?"

"You see all this, Archie?" Tom gestured at the gravestones around them. "This is what I've got to lose. I've spent too much of my life in cemeteries. Buried too many people I've cared about over the years. It's easier this way. You can't mourn something you've never had."

"Tom? Archie?" Dominique's voice rang out, breaking into their conversation. "Over here. I've found him."

They picked their way over to where she was standing and found her at the foot of an open grave. A pile of frozen earth lay to her left, a shovel handle emerging from it like the mast of a half-buried ship.

"There." She pointed.

Tom could just about make out the brass plaque screwed into the coffin's lid and the name engraved onto its already dull and faded surface.

HENRY JULIUS RENWICK

"It's over, Tom," Dominique said gently.

Tom nodded. He knew he should feel glad that Renwick was gone; some sense of relief, elation even, that this man who had betrayed him, lied to him, and tried to kill him, was finally dead.

But instead he felt sad. Sad as the memories of the good times he had spent with Renwick as a boy came flooding back. Sad that he had lost someone who, for a long time, he had considered to be a friend and a mentor. Sad that yet another link to his father had been severed, never to be recovered.

"You all right?" asked Archie.

"Yeah," said Tom, gently taking out his father's gold pocket watch and twirling it by its chain between the fingers of his left hand, the case winking lazily as it turned and caught the sun.

"You don't really think your father . . . ?" Archie began, catching sight of the watch.

"No, of course not," Tom said with a firm shake of his head. He allowed the watch to spin for a few seconds longer, barely blinking as his eyes followed it. Then in one firm movement he grabbed it and flung it into the grave, smashing it against the coffin lid.

For a few moments the three of them stood there, staring at the watch's white face, hands frozen, the shattered glass scattered around it like small drops of ice, springs and screws strewn like shrapnel.

"Let's go and get a drink," said Dominique eventually.

"Yeah," said Tom, a sad smile on his face. "Let's go and get several."

Archie threw his cigarette to the ground, where it flared for a few seconds, then flickered, then went out.

NOTE FROM THE AUTHOR

In 1999 the Presidential Advisory Commission on Holocaust Assets finally admitted not only that the U.S. Army had been guilty of wrongly identifying the contents of the Hungarian Gold Train as enemy property after recovering it in 1945, but that several of its men had actively conspired in plundering it. Although the U.S. Department of Justice opposed all attempts at compensation, in 2005 the courts ruled in favor of a class-action suit brought by Holocaust survivors. A total of $25 million was ordered to be distributed to Hungarian survivors. A large number of paintings and other works of art taken from the Gold Train remain lost to this day.

Wewelsburg Castle, near Paderborn in northern Westphalia, Germany, was intended by Himmler to be the epicenter of the Aryan world. He had envisioned a vast complex radiating out from the castle's north tower, and over 1,250 concentration camp inmates died bringing the first phases of his plan to fruition. Today the castle operates as a museum and youth hostel. The crypt and the ceremonial chamber where twelve of his generals would meet around a round table, complete with the symbol of the Black Sun inlaid into the floor, are open to visitors.

The Nazis' nuclear research effort was centered at the Kaiser Wilhelm Institute under the physicist Werner Heisenberg, although a military team under the scientific leadership of Professor Kurt Diebner was also in the chase. It is a matter of historical debate as to whether Heisenberg's team deliberately sabotaged their work or were simply lagging behind the Allies. Historians believe that Stalin deliberately ordered Marshals Zukhov and Konev to race each other to Berlin so as to secure the Kaiser Wilhelm Institute ahead of the Americans, sacrificing close to 70,000 men in the process. The special NKVD troops dispatched to the institute recovered over three tons of uranium oxide, a material the Russians were short of at the time, allowing them to kick-start Operation Borodino, their own nuclear program. The first Soviet nuclear test took place in August 1949, over four years after the first American explosion at the Trinity site in New Mexico in July 1945.

The Amber Room was commissioned by Frederick I of Prussia in 1701, and later presented to the Russian czar Peter the Great. It decorated the Catherine Palace, on the outskirts of St. Petersburg, from 1770 until September 1941, when invading German troops carried it off to Königsberg in East Prussia (now the Russian city of Kaliningrad). Fearing Allied bomb attacks, the room was again packed up in 1944 but then vanished. Opinions differ as to what happened to the room. Some believe that it was moved to an abandoned silver mine in Thuringia, others that it was buried in a lagoon in Lithuania. The latest theory suggests that the room was in fact burned by mistake by Soviet troops, with the Kremlin subsequently disguising their actions and propagating the myth of the Amber Room's survival as a negotiating ploy.

In 1997, the son of one of the German officers who had accompanied the wartime convoy from St. Petersburg to Königsberg was arrested for trying to sell a small section of the room. Although it is not known how the officer got it, this fragment remains, along with an intricately inlaid chest, the only part of the original Amber Room known to have survived the war.